A LETHAL INVOLVEMENT

A LETHAL INVOLVEMENT

Clive Egleton

St. Martin's Press ⚎ New York

Library of Congress Cataloging-in-Publication Data

Egleton, Clive.
A lethal involvement / Clive Egleton.
p.   cm.
ISBN 0-312-14313-3
I. Title.
PR6055.G55L48   1996
823'.914—dc20   96-3506   CIP

First published in Great Britain by Hodder and Stoughton,
a division of Hodder Headline PLC

First U.S. Edition: August 1996

10 9 8 7 6 5 4 3 2 1

This book is for Charles.

A LETHAL INVOLVEMENT

CHAPTER 1

Baring looked at the notes he had made so far. All subject interviews followed more or less the same pattern, and this one was no exception. Although details of his career were already on file, he had encouraged Simon Oakham to talk about himself in order to establish a rapport with the younger man.

Simon Oakham would be thirty-seven on 6 July and had joined the Junior Tradesmen's Regiment in the summer of 1973 at the age of sixteen. Eighteen months later he had been posted to the RAPC Depot at Worthy Down where he had completed his training as a unit pay clerk. Thereafter, Oakham had served with a variety of units which included the 1st Battalion The Royal Greenjackets in Rhine Army, the Regimental Pay Office, Leicester, and Headquarters British Forces Falkland Islands. Promotion had come rapidly; private to warrant officer class two in twelve years' man's service before being granted a Special Regular Commission in 1987. A captain with four years' seniority, he was currently the unit paymaster of the 24th Royal Dragoons (Princess Beatrice's Own) stationed at Tilshead Camp on Salisbury Plain.

Where his personal life was concerned, Oakham had told him he was very much a family man, a claim that had been supported by the written reports Baring had received from two of his former superior officers. As for leisure pursuits, he was a keen amateur photographer, something of an opera buff, and enjoyed the occasional game of tennis. He had also written *A Child's Guide to Computer Programming* and was a regular contributor to *New Scientist* and *Information Technology Today.*

Thus far, the proceedings had been easy, but now came the difficult part when it was necessary to probe a lot deeper, and that involved asking the kind of questions some people found deeply offensive; Baring could recall interviewing a certain major general who'd announced that how he managed his financial affairs was none of Baring's damned business and had then ordered him to leave the headquarters.

'What does your wife think of living out here on Salisbury Plain?' he asked, looking up from his notes.

'Louise is only too thankful she doesn't have to,' Oakham told him with a smile. 'We've got our own place in Guildford which we are buying on a mortgage. I live a bachelor existence from Monday to Friday.'

'Do you find that a strain?'

'What, financially?' Oakham removed a sheet of paper from the folder he had been nursing on his lap and passed it across the desk. 'I'm not saying we don't have to budget fairly carefully,' he said, 'but as you can see from those figures, we're not exactly committed to the hilt either.'

It was apparent to Baring that the younger man had gone to a great deal of trouble in order to present his finances in a readily understandable format. Under 'Income' on the left side of the page, he had shown his net monthly pay together with the family allowances his wife received from Social Security in respect of their three children. Mortgage repayments and basic housekeeping, which included the quarterly gas, electricity and phone bills, accounted for over sixty per cent of his income. Children's clothing, the premiums on two life insurance policies and the cost of running a 1988 Volvo estate ate up another twenty-five per cent, leaving seventy-four pounds for entertainment, holidays and incidental expenses.

'Your mess bill seems a bit on the low side, Simon. I mean, fifty pounds a month appears very modest to me.'

'Well, I only have the occasional drink and I don't smoke. The Regiment is also very good to me; as one of the attached officers I don't have to contribute to the Band Fund or the Saddle Club and my share of mess guests equates to that paid by a junior subaltern.'

'Do the officers make you feel part of the 24th Royal Dragoons, that you are one of the family, or do they treat you as an outsider?'

'Absolutely not,' Oakham said indignantly. 'They couldn't be nicer to me.'

'Good.' All the same, Baring couldn't help wondering what the cavalrymen said about the Pay Corps officer behind his back. Simon Oakham might be the working-class boy who'd made good but apart from the army they would have nothing in common with him.

'I haven't omitted any household expenses, have I, sir?'

Oakham was anxious to please, almost too much so. 'You don't have to call me sir,' Baring told the younger man. 'I'm no longer a serving brigadier. I retired in 1980, and no, you haven't left anything out as far as I can see. Matter of fact, yours is one of the most comprehensive financial statements I've ever received.'

'Well, I copied the layout I'd used the last time.'

'You've been vetted before?'

Oakham nodded. 'Eleven years ago when I was a staff sergeant and working on the master order of battle at the Ministry of Defence. My security clearance had lapsed when I was posted to the RPO Leicester on the grounds that I would no longer require constant access to Top Secret material.' Oakham laughed. 'They were right too. I don't think we had anything graded higher than Confidential at Leicester.'

Baring made a note on his millboard to take the matter up with vetting headquarters at Woolwich. They should have told him that Oakham had held a PV clearance in the past when they had posted the appropriate papers to his home address in Winchester.

'Have you made any friends in the regiment, Simon?' he asked after placing the financial statement to one side.

'Not really, Brigadier. All the officers of my age are married and live out so I only get to meet them during working hours. And at lunchtime in the mess of course.'

'Quite.'

Oakham was up for an Enhanced Positive Vetting clearance which meant that in addition to the referees he had nominated, Baring had to find someone who had known him for a long time but wasn't a boon companion. It was essential to get an unbiased opinion of Oakham's character and none of his referees was likely to point out any warts he might be concealing. Finding such a witness would entail a great deal of research and that was best left to the clerical assistants at Woolwich who could access the necessary documents. Meantime, there were other avenues that needed to be explored.

'How do you feel about drug abuse?' Baring asked him.

'I think the people who indulge in it are essentially weak. I don't understand their attitude.'

'You've never experimented with them?'

'Absolutely not. There are easier ways of committing suicide.'

'What about cannabis?'

'Same thing applies. Once you start on soft drugs one thing leads to another and before you know it, you're a junkie. At least, that's my opinion.'

'Have you ever had a homosexual relationship?' Baring smiled wryly. 'I don't mean to offend you but it has to be asked. Purely routine.'

'Of course,' Oakham said, tight-lipped. 'And I'd like you to know that I find the idea of going to bed with another man utterly repulsive.'

Baring believed him; if it wasn't genuine, only a supremely gifted actor could have projected such a note of disgust into his voice.

'I detest them, Brigadier. They don't have the guts to come out and say they're homosexual. No, they use words like gay to describe their perverted sexual tastes and bastardise the English language in the process.'

On the other hand, he couldn't help wondering if Oakham's deep-rooted hatred was the result of a bad experience in his formative years.

'I believe you went to a comprehensive?'

'Yes, the William Wilberforce in Canterbury.'

'Good school, was it?'

'The staff didn't stand for any old buck from the pupils. And it wasn't a single-sex establishment. As I recall, Brigadier, the girls outnumbered the boys.'

'So you didn't get little cliques of fourteen- and fifteen-year-olds indulging in mutual masturbation?'

There was a significant pause before Oakham told him that he'd once seen a couple of youths at it in the school urinals and thereafter had avoided them like the plague. He looked pale and sounded on edge as if Baring had touched a raw nerve. Was it anger or fear? Oakham was slender and small-boned. According to the unit medical officer who had examined him, he weighed a hundred and thirty-eight pounds, was five feet seven and a quarter and was free from infection, or FFI as the army liked to put it. That Oakham looked as if he had only just left his teens behind, had deep blue eyes and the longest black eyelashes Baring had ever seen on a man did not appear under physical characteristics on his medical sheet. If he inadvertently walked into a bar patronised by gays, Baring reckoned they would be all over him.

'I learned all about sex from a girl called Eileen Watts.' Oakham frowned. 'Or was it Watkins? No matter, she was a rapacious little scrubber, initiated damn nearly every boy in the class.'

Baring decided he had pushed this particular line of questioning far enough. Nothing he had heard gave him cause to believe that Oakham was not a suitable candidate for Positive Vetting. The man was a paragon of virtue: his financial affairs were well organised, he didn't smoke, he liked a drink but never over indulged, he'd never experimented with drugs or had an extra marital affair. He also made a point of attending church at least once a month with his family.

'Well, I think that's it, Simon,' he said cheerfully, picking up the financial statement Oakham had prepared for him and clipping it to his millboard. 'Everything appears to be very satisfactory.'

'That's a relief.' Oakham leaned forward. 'I don't know whether you have noticed it, Brigadier, but I haven't included the occasional payments I receive from *Information Technology Today* and *New Scientist*. In an average year I earn approximately three hundred pounds.'

He did not regard this as a regular source of income for budgetary purposes and the money was usually spent on small luxuries they couldn't otherwise have afforded. Naturally he declared any literary earnings to the Inland Revenue.

Bored by the long-winded explanation, Baring fixed his gaze on the window and counted the number of Scorpion light reconnaissance tanks he could see in the unit workshop on the far side of the snow-covered barrack square.

'Of course I only show the net income after deducting expenses which have always been agreed by the Inspector of Taxes at Cardiff.'

'I'm glad to hear it, Simon. Is there anything else you want to tell me in strict confidence before we go our separate ways?'

It was the stock question Baring always asked at the end of an interview and ninety-nine times out of a hundred the candidate had nothing further to add. But not this time. Oakham clasped both kneecaps and looked down at the floor seemingly unable to look him in the eye.

'Well, there was this murder I witnessed,' he said in a low voice.

'Murder?' Baring echoed. 'When was this?'

'1975, the first Saturday in February. I was serving in Admin Company of Headquarters 1 (BR) corps at Bielefeld, my first posting after completing trade training. Anyway, me and another guy from the unit were spending the weekend up at Winterberg in the Rothaargebirge. We'd both attended a course at the winter warfare school and had caught the skiing bug. We'd been taught *langlaufing* and thought it would be fun to try our hands at downhill. We left Bielefeld early on the Saturday morning, got to Winterberg in time for lunch and spent the afternoon on the nursery slopes. I don't know how much *Glühwein* we put away that evening but I was blind drunk when I fell into bed.'

Oakham had woken up in the middle of the night feeling as sick as a dog and had just made it to the lavatory before throwing up. A triphammer still pounding away inside his skull, he had staggered back to the bedroom, tripped over the rucked-up carpet and measured his length on the floor.

CLIVE EGLETON

'I don't know how long I lay there, Brigadier, but when I opened my eyes again the room was revolving. Somehow I managed to get to my feet but I'd no idea where the bed was and I blundered into the window.'

He had wrestled with the curtains thinking they were the bedclothes and had eventually succeeded in bringing the rail and pelmet down. Exhausted by his efforts, Oakham had fallen asleep standing up with his forehead resting against the windowpane. The chilly atmosphere had eventually roused him and he'd woken up shivering, his feet like blocks of ice.

'The stove had gone out, it was the only form of heating we had in the attic room of the *Gasthof.*' Seemingly unaware of what he was doing, Oakham pulled the index finger of his left hand until the knuckle cracked. 'There was a full moon,' he continued nervously, 'and it had stopped snowing. About three hundred yards from our *Gasthof* I could see two men fooling around on the nursery slope . . .'

'Fooling around?' Baring queried. 'You mean they were skiing?'

'No, they appeared to be wrestling. Then the taller man made a diagonal run down the slope towards the village and I assumed he was going to fetch help.'

'Why do you say that?'

'Well, there was nobody else around and he obviously wasn't physically able to pull his companion out of the snowdrift. He had gone into it head first and was buried up to the waist. The guy was almost vertical, legs sticking straight up in the air, the skis still attached to his boots.'

'My God, what did you do?'

Oakham had tried to wake his friend but his fellow skiing enthusiast had been in such a drunken stupor that not even a major earthquake would have disturbed him. Admitting defeat, he'd simply crawled into bed and gone to sleep. When next he had opened his eyes, it had been broad daylight and the travelling clock on the bedside locker was showing twenty minutes to eleven.

'By that time there were a fair number of people on the nursery slopes and there was no sign of the guy who'd dived into the snowdrift. Naturally I told my mate what I had seen and he—'

'His name?' Baring asked, interrupting him.

'Steve something or other.' Oakham tugged at the lobe of his right ear in a desperate attempt to recall the name, then smiled apologetically. 'I'm sorry, I can't remember. It was a long time ago and we were never that close. Matter of fact, I believe Steve left the army later that same year after completing six years with the colours. Anyway, he said that I must

6

have dreamed it, but then we went to this *Konditorei* to have coffee and a Danish in lieu of the breakfast we'd missed and Steve overheard these two civilians talking about a fatal accident. Although his German wasn't perfect by any means, he knew enough to understand what they were saying. According to them, the victim had stunk of liquor and the police were convinced he'd been paralytic. Why else would a man go skiing in the middle of the night if he hadn't had a skinful?'

'What about the victim's companion? Was he drunk?'

'That's something we'll never know, Brigadier. The man I saw never came forward, never even reported the accident anonymously.'

'And the police didn't suspect foul play?'

'They'd no reason to; there had been another snowfall before dawn and all the tracks in the immediate area had been obliterated.'

'Did you report the incident to anyone when you returned to barracks?'

'I told the sergeant in charge of the pay section.'

'And what was his reaction?'

'He said he would pass it on to the officer commanding Admin Company.'

It seemed to Baring that Oakham had chiefly been concerned to cover himself, but then wondered what he himself might have done as an eighteen-year-old soldier.

'I thought no more about it until the OC sent for me some weeks later. He told me the victim was a Long Service List warrant officer from Soest Garrison who had been on a three-month warning at the time of his death. Apparently he was a heavy drinker and if he didn't mend his ways, the army was going to discharge him. The appropriate military authority had convened a Board of Inquiry and on the evidence supplied by the German civil police, the members had recorded a finding of death by misadventure which had been accepted. I was pretty relieved at the outcome I can tell you.'

'Can you remember the name of this warrant officer?'

'I'm afraid not. Oh, I was told who he was but it didn't really register.'

'Who was commanding the Admin Company at Headquarters 1 (BR) Corps in those days?'

'Major Richard Cosgrove,' Oakham said.

No hesitation, no time out for thought, the name instantly recalled. Baring thought the younger man had a convenient memory.

'Did you mention this incident when you were being interviewed for PV clearance eleven years ago?'

'No.'

'So what made you bring it up at this juncture?'

'The army's a small world, Brigadier. Four years ago while on detached duty in the Falkland Islands I was socialising in the sergeant's mess with the regimental sergeant major of Force Headquarters. We were comparing notes about the various postings we'd had and it transpired that he had been stationed in Soest and vaguely remembered the accident. He couldn't put a name to the Long Service List NCO either but he thought the warrant officer had been about my height and weight.'

'And that chance remark set you thinking again?'

Oakham leaned back in his chair looking inordinately pleased with himself. 'Precisely. The second man on the nursery slope that night had been at least six feet tall and well-built. If I had gone head first into a snowdrift, he could have pulled me out with ease, drunk or sober.'

Baring was sixty-four. Except for three unhappy years as a personnel manager from 1980 to 1983, he had spent his entire adult life dealing with soldiers and the man had yet to be born who could pull the wool over his eyes. Oakham however had tried to do just that with his sanitised version of the incident at Winterberg. He couldn't think why the RAPC captain had brought the subject up after all these years or why, having done so, he should then have consistently lied to him.

'Thank you for being so frank with me, Simon,' he said, concealing his reservations about the younger man.

'Not at all. May I ask a question, Brigadier?'

'By all means.'

'How long does it take to clear a person for PV?'

'About four months.'

In Oakham's case it was likely to take a damned sight longer but he was not about to tell him that. Driving back to his house in Winchester, Baring was haunted by the vision of a small man who had been rammed head first into a bank of snow and held there until he suffocated.

CHAPTER 2

Peter Ashton left the Northern Line at Hampstead and walked towards the Heath, hands thrust deep into the pockets of his overcoat, head lowered against a biting east wind. A quarter of a mile down the road from the Underground station he turned right into Willow Walk and made his way to the large Edwardian residence that had been subdivided into three properties. He had lost count of the number of times Victor Hazelwood had summoned him to the maisonette called Willow Dene but he had never before been invited to breakfast. He pushed open the wrought-iron gate set in the hedge and followed the footsteps the milkman had left in the snow round to the front entrance on the left side of the house.

'A lousy morning, Peter,' Hazelwood said, looking up at the leaden sky after opening the door to him.

'Been a lousy winter.' Ashton kicked the snow from his shoes, then stepped into the hall and removed his overcoat.

'I thought we would eat in the study, it's more convenient.'

Ashton smiled; it was also the only room in the house where smoking was permitted. The curtains, the furniture and the books on the shelves were all impregnated with the aroma of the Burma cheroots which Hazelwood favoured. Although one of the least domesticated men Ashton had ever met, he had covered the desk with a linen tablecloth and fetched the best china from the dining room across the hall.

'Grapefruit, orange juice, fresh rolls, coffee, marmalade, black cherry jam; I'm impressed, Victor.'

'Well, get stuck in, let's not waste time admiring the feast.'

Ashton pulled up a chair and sat down. The grapefruit was nearly all skin and Hazelwood had forgotten to divide the segments with a fruit knife so that Ashton was obliged to dig each piece out with a spoon, but when all was said and done, it was the thought that counted.

'How's Harriet?'

9

'Very large,' Ashton told him. 'She'll have to give up her job early next month?'

'When is the baby due?'

'The beginning of May.'

'And how is she in herself?' Hazelwood asked, continuing to show what he thought was a proper concern for a former officer.

'I think you could say Harriet is almost as good as new.'

Almost was the operative word. Harriet would never be quite the same again; the stone that had fractured her skull during a race riot on the streets of Berlin back in July '93 had knocked a lot of the stuffing out of her.

'And how are things with you?' Hazelwood asked between mouthfuls. 'Getting enough work?'

'Not as much as I would like,' Ashton said, 'but it's early days yet.'

Four months ago he had been a grade one officer in the Secret Intelligence Service on 32K a year plus Inner London Weighting Allowance. He had resigned because Harriet had retreated to her parents' home in Lincoln and he had been convinced he would lose her if he stayed in London. In truth, the SIS had been happy to let him go; his face had become too well known in Moscow and the Director General had felt that in view of the cuts demanded by the Treasury, it was difficult to justify his retention. So he had left with a tax-free golden handshake equivalent to eighteen months' salary. He had planned to make use of his language qualifications, but German-speaking linguists were two a penny and not too many manufacturers were keen to sell into Russia. The irony was that he was still living in London for business reasons and he suspected that what little work had come his way was largely due to Hazelwood.

'What have you got on at the moment, Peter?'

'I'm checking the proofs of a catalogue I translated into Russian for Adler Beauty Products. It's no big deal.'

'Could you find the time to do a small job for us?' Hazelwood asked casually.

'Depends what it is. I won't be a courier and I won't go to any country that used to be a member of the Warsaw Pact. Anyway, why are you going outside The Firm?'

'It's very simple. Our establishment has been cut to the bone and we don't have anyone to spare. What we do have is a contingency fund to hire someone like you for a specific job. And it so happens that you are well qualified for this one because you've been a soldier.'

A member of the University Officers Training Corps while reading

German and Russian at Nottingham, Ashton has joined 23 Special Air Service Regiment in the Territorial Army after he had been taken on by British Aerospace as a technical author and translator. Disenchanted with the work he was doing, he had volunteered for a nine-month tour of duty with the regular army's Special Patrol Unit in Northern Ireland, a move that had rapidly cost him his job.

Back in civilian life again, he had found temporary employment teaching Russian to mature students at a night school funded by the London Borough of Camden. Still a part-time soldier with 23 SAS when the Argentinians had invaded and captured the Falklands, Ashton had volunteered for active duty again and had travelled south with the Task Force, taking part in the raid on Pebble Island which had resulted in eleven Pucarà ground attack aircraft being destroyed at their base.

'There's nothing like gilding the lily, Victor.'

'You also know your way around the Ministry of Defence,' Hazelwood continued blithely.

Ashton had been in charge of the SIS cell in Military Operations (Special Projects) from July to October last year and had been out of the country on duty for most of the time. What he knew about the inner workings of the MoD was next to nothing, but he let it pass.

'We will pay you two and a half thousand a month for however long it takes and you won't be going anywhere near Moscow because you will be working hand in glove with the army. Now, are you interested or not?'

'It beats proofreading.'

'Good.' Hazelwood leaned across the desk, opened an ornately carved wooden cigar box and helped himself to a Burma cheroot. 'I take it you've finished eating,' he said and promptly lit it.

'I have now,' Ashton told him drily.

Hazelwood raised the tablecloth, opened the top right drawer and took out a thin, buff-coloured folder. 'We have a proprietary interest in this man,' he said and passed the folder to Ashton. 'Captain Simon Oakham of the Royal Army Pay Corps, a leading authority on information technology. We wanted him to design a programme for us which would simplify the control of and access to Top Secret and codeword material. To do that, he required an EPV clearance. The subject interview was done a week ago yesterday by Frank Baring, a retired brigadier. You'll find his biographical details on page two.'

Ashton opened the folder and found the appropriate enclosure. Baring had had a distinguished career. At age twenty-two he had won a Military

Cross in Korea and had subsequently seen active service in Kenya, Borneo and Northern Ireland. Along the way he had also been made a Commander of the Order of the British Empire.

'Anyway, the interview proceeded smoothly and was almost over when Oakham started talking about a murder he may or may not have witnessed in February 1975.'

Oakham had claimed that he was unable to remember the name of the victim or the *Gasthof* in Winterberg where he had spent the weekend with a soldier from his unit called Steve but whose surname he had also forgotten. There had been other inconsistencies in his account which Baring felt should be investigated.

'On Friday afternoon, Oakham left his unit at Tilshead Camp to spend the weekend with his family who live in Guildford. He didn't return. Before posting him absent without leave, the adjutant of the 24th Royal Dragoons rang Mrs Oakham to ask if he had been taken ill at home. She told him she hadn't seen her husband all weekend and was under the impression that he was on duty.'

For an officer to go absent was almost unheard of but Ashton couldn't think why the SIS should be interested. 'Oakham hasn't been allowed to have access in advance of the requisite security clearance, has he?'

'Of course not.'

'Then why is his absence any concern of yours, Victor? He's the army's problem.'

'Simon Oakham knew he was coming to us long before he was interviewed. If he hadn't wanted the job he could have said so and we would have looked elsewhere for a computer whizz kid. But no, he waits until the Enhanced Positive Vetting process is nearing completion and then virtually goes out of his way to torpedo the clearance. Four days later, having led his wife to believe he is on duty over the weekend, he goes AWOL.'

'Maybe he's run off with another woman,' Ashton suggested.

'That's for you to find out,' Hazelwood told him. 'I want you to make your number with Brigadier Norman Wells, the Provost Marshal, and ask him what progress his military police are making.'

'He's going to love that.'

'Well, I know I can rely on you to be tactful.'

Wells was not the only senior officer he was required to handle with kid gloves. There was a list of them, together with their office and home telephone numbers on the last enclosure in the folder.

'You want me to call on all of these people?'

'Only if you think it's necessary, Peter.'

Ashton removed the enclosures from the file cover, folded the pages in four and tucked them into the inside pocket of his jacket. 'Is the Provost Marshal's Department still located at Empress State?' he asked.

'For the time being.'

'Is Wells expecting me?'

'He will be by the time you get there.'

'Let's hope I can persuade the MoD policeman to let me enter the building.'

'He won't give you any trouble.'

Hazelwood opened the top right-hand drawer again and took out a piece of plastic slightly larger than a credit card. It was, Ashton saw, his old MoD ID, complete with laminated head and shoulders photograph and his signature. According to security regulations, it should have been destroyed the day he left the SIS but then Hazelwood had always been a law unto himself.

The Empress State in West Brompton towered above all the other buildings in the neighbourhood. In striving to design an office block of some originality which, at the same time, would be pleasing to the eye, the architects had gone for a sickle or crescent shape like a waning moon. Translated into steel, concrete and glass, the effect was quite startling in more ways than one. It took only a Force 3 to 4 breeze for the building to become a magnet for any litter in the surrounding area. Sucked into the swirling maelstrom, empty cigarette packets, wrappers and tissues were borne aloft and held there bobbing up and down supported by a fluctuating jet of air. But the views from the upper floors were spectacular and none more so than from the office of the Provost Marshal on the eleventh floor which looked out over the Earl's Court Exhibition Centre to Holland Park in the distance.

Brigadier Norman Wells in no way resembled the conventional image of a military policeman. Attired in a charcoal-grey suit that clearly had not been bought off the peg, double-cuffed shirt with gold links and knitted tie, he could have been a merchant banker, a senior civil servant or an up-market public relations consultant. He was slim, was almost three inches shorter and twenty-odd pounds lighter than Ashton, who tipped the scales at a hundred and seventy pounds and was half an inch under six feet. The years had been kind to the Provost Marshal and Ashton found it hard to believe that at forty-six, the brigadier was nine years older than himself. But if Wells didn't look the part, he certainly had all the natural inquisitiveness of a police officer. From the moment Ashton shook hands with him, he did his best to discover why the Intelligence Service should be interested in Oakham.

'He is after all only the unit paymaster of the 24th Royal Dragoons.'

'Quite.'

'Is it something to do with an incident that happened in the past?' Wells asked, still fishing.

'Search me, Brigadier.'

'I'd heard the army's Directorate of Security had called for the Board of Inquiry proceedings.'

'What Board is this?' Ashton asked, contriving to appear mystified.

'The one that was convened to inquire into the circumstances in which WO2 Leonard Jackson, Long Service List, was fatally injured at Winterberg on Saturday, 1 February 1975.' Wells waited for Ashton to comment and when he didn't, said, 'Ring a bell with you?'

'No. Should it?'

'Oakham claimed to have witnessed the incident and cast doubt on the Board's finding of Death by Misadventure. Oakham didn't come forward until after the Inquiry had been completed and his evidence was highly suspect. At that stage of his career, he was a very young and immature soldier and he subsequently withdrew the statement he had made to his company commander, a Major Richard Cosgrove of the Queen's Westminster Rifles.'

'How odd.' Ashton frowned. 'Perhaps I'd better have a quick look at your copy of the Board of Inquiry proceedings in case there is a connection.' He smiled. 'I assume you have one to hand,' he said disarmingly, 'the details being so fresh . . .'

'Of course.'

Ashton could tell from his tight-lipped expression that the Provost Marshal was not best pleased. He had tried to pump him for information and was irritated that he had been outmanoeuvred. It showed in his tone of voice when he spoke to the staff captain on the intercom and instructed him to look out the Jackson Inquiry and have it ready for Mr Ashton when he left.

'Is there anything else we can do for you?' Wells asked with brittle politeness.

'It might be helpful to know what action is being taken to apprehend Oakham and who is in charge of the case.'

'All enquiries are being handled by the Assistant Provost Marshal Headquarters United Kingdom Land Forces at Wilton. Tilshead Camp is practically on his doorstep and he has a military police company at his disposal. Naturally, he answers to me.'

The coded message was immediately apparent to Ashton. Wells was determined to keep a tight grip on the investigation and no outsider would be allowed to bypass the chain of command and talk directly to his officers and NCOs on the ground. If Ashton wanted to know how the case was progressing, he had only to ask him.

'Oakham's description has been sent to the Chief Constables of Wiltshire, Dorset, Hampshire, Kent, Surrey and Sussex with a request that it is circulated throughout their respective forces. Same applies to his dark blue 760 Volvo estate, registration number D147 AZX.'

The military police had also checked the personal effects which Oakham had left behind in his room at Tilshead Camp but had found nothing unusual. Yesterday evening they had talked to Mrs Oakham.

'A very pleasant woman by all accounts,' Wells continued. 'She lost her first husband in a traffic accident in 1987.'

'I didn't know she had been previously married,' Ashton said quietly.

'Oh yes; only the youngest girl aged five is Oakham's child. However, they give every sign of being a close-knit family and the two older girls are said to be extremely fond of their stepfather. Of course they are all very shocked by Oakham's disappearance.'

Louise Oakham had become even more distressed after one of the military policemen had asked hear if she and her husband had a joint bank account. But that was nothing compared with how she had felt when he'd then advised her to put a stop on it in order to freeze the funds.

'We didn't find Oakham's chequebook in his room at Tilshead and there is every reason to believe he has both his credit and cashpoint cards on him.'

'Does he have a passport, Brigadier?'

'Yes. It was supposed to be in a deed box he kept at home.'

Ashton wasn't surprised to hear there was no sign of it when Louise Oakham had used her own key to open it. However, the Provost Marshal did not feel justified in asking the Home Office to alert the Immigration Service.

'Officially, Oakham has only been absent since the first parade yesterday morning. Before we go overboard, I want to be sure he hasn't been injured in a traffic accident and is lying unconscious in a hospital somewhere.'

'And when will you know the answer to that?'

'Oh, I would expect to hear something later on today.' But even then, Wells was not prepared to involve Immigration without some corroborating evidence to show that he might have left the country.

'Are we talking about his car?' Ashton asked.

'Yes. I would certainly get on to the Home Office if his Volvo estate was found in a long-term car park near Heathrow or any other airport.'

'Suppose the Volvo is no longer in this country?'

'You mean, what if he's nipped over to the Continent with it to look up some old girlfriend?' Wells said irritably. 'The fact is we've no reason to believe that Oakham is having an affair, and even if he is, that's hardly grounds for initiating a nationwide manhunt for him. So far as the civilian authorities are concerned, absence without leave is not a major crime and neither is adultery. Frankly, without more information to go on, there is a limit to what we can do and I am satisfied we haven't overlooked anything.'

Ashton wasn't so sure but didn't think it politic to say so to Wells, especially when it was evident the Provost Marshal thought he had already outstayed his welcome. Furthermore, no one liked being told how to do his job and he therefore waited until he was closeted with the Staff Captain in the outer office before tactfully suggesting that it might be a good idea if Mrs Oakham rang Access and asked for a read-out.

'With what object in mind, Mr Ashton?'

'To see if her husband used his credit card to book the Volvo on to a ferry. If he did, that statement will show the date of the transaction, the name of the ferry company and its address which, as it happens, will also be the port of embarkation. Better advise her to get a bank statement too while she's at it. He might either have drawn a large amount in cash recently or written a cheque for the ferry. Whatever option he may have chosen, the sum involved is bound to stand out from the other entries in the account.'

'That's a thought.'

'Do yourself some good,' Ashton told him. 'When you see the brigadier, let him think you thought of it. The suggestion will carry more weight with him coming from one of the staff than it will from me.'

His motive owed more to self-interest than to altruism. Should he ever need a favour, he would be able to remind the staff captain that he owed him.

Meantime, there was the copy of the Jackson Inquiry which the Provost Marshal had obtained from the Public Record Office where it had reposed since 1980. The recorded evidence however didn't add to what Hazelwood had already told him about the incident. The one thing he did learn was that the victim had been a Regimental Sergeant Major in the Royal Military Police when he had completed his twenty-two-year engagement and had dropped down to Warrant Officer Class Two when he'd joined the Long Service List.

'It's standard procedure,' the Staff Captain told him. 'Every Warrant Officer or NCO who wants to extend beyond the twenty-two-year point has to do so.'

'Jackson was an alcoholic, he was on a three-month warning at the time of his death.'

'I can guess what you're thinking, Mr Ashton, but he couldn't have been a lush when he applied to join the Long Service List. The army would never have allowed him to sign on if he had had a reputation for being a heavy drinker. They would have got shot of him before you could say knife.'

'Well, you should know,' Ashton said mildly. 'After all, he was a member of your corps.'

'And I'll tell you something else. Jackson was in the SIB, the Special Investigation Branch of the military police. In other words, he was a plain-clothes detective, one of the élite who investigate major crimes in the army – rape, theft, grievous bodily harm, manslaughter, fraud, embezzlement, armed robbery, murder . . .'

Suddenly, Ashton could see a glimmer of daylight. If Jackson had been murdered, it was possible that the motive might have something to do with one of the cases he'd investigated while in the SIB. It also seemed likely that once the preparatory spadework had been done, he would be reminding the staff captain that he owed him one.

'You don't get to hold down a senior post in the SIB unless you have an unblemished character.'

'Quite.' Ashton pushed his chair back and stood up. 'Thanks for all your help,' he said.

'You've seen everything you want to?'

'For the time being.'

It was sleeting when Ashton left Empress State, the snow underfoot becoming a grimy slush. On the way to West Brompton station on the District Line, he stopped off at a pay phone to make two calls. The first was to the Armed Forces Desk at Vauxhall Cross to request that they obtain the personal documents of Warrant Officer Leonard

Jackson, Long Service List, formerly of the Royal Military Police, from the Records Office at Hayes as soon as possible. The other was to Mrs Frank Baring in Winchester who told Ashton that she expected her husband would be home by 5.30 at the latest and was quite sure he would be delighted to see him.

CHAPTER 3

There was hardly a day went by but that Victor Hazelwood didn't remind himself that luck had played a significant part in his career. In 1991 he had been a senior Intelligence officer in charge of the Russian Desk and had been resigned to the fact that having apparently reached his ceiling, he would never be promoted. Then the Head of the Eastern Bloc Department had suddenly died of a heart attack and he had been moved upstairs and elevated to Assistant Director. Barely eighteen months later, Stuart Dunglass had been appointed to the post of Director General and, much to his surprise, Victor had been informed that he was to be the Deputy DG.

The two men were as different as chalk from cheese. Dunglass hailed from Kilmarnock, didn't smoke, rarely drank anything stronger than a small glass of dry sherry and always looked immaculate. Hazelwood too had his suits made to measure by Gieves and Hawkes but with his burly figure and happy knack of making everything he wore look like an unmade bed, no one would have guessed it. He was addicted to Burma cheroots, enjoyed a drink before, during and after dinner and unlike the DG, was a hugely extrovert character. They complemented one another because Dunglass, who was known as 'Jungle Jim' behind his back, had spent most of his service in the Far East whereas Hazelwood was the acknowledged expert on the Kremlin and the former republics of the USSR.

Unlike the Government and the Foreign Office, who appeared to believe the world was a much safer place following the break-up of the Soviet Union, Dunglass had been one of the few senior civil servants to think it was a sight more dangerous than when Brezhnev had been in control. In those days, both power blocs had known where the line was drawn; with many of the newly independent states possessing their own nuclear arsenals, that degree of certainty no longer existed. If that wasn't bad enough, Dunglass had to contend with a Treasury hellbent on cutting the armed services and the SIS vote to the bone.

The need to make the best use of limited resources had meant that Hazelwood had been the DG in all but name. His advice had been accepted without question, but that was long ago before Dunglass had found his feet. There was nothing to beat on-the-job training and after nearly two years in the chair, the DG was now very much his own man. As a result, Hazelwood had become accustomed to having his recommendations queried at length and he assumed this was why Dunglass asked if he would pop into his office for a few minutes.

'Roy Kelso tells me Ashton is working for us again,' the DG announced tersely before Hazelwood had time to sit down.

Kelso was the Assistant Director in charge of the Administrative Wing which was still located at Benbow House over in Southwark, where it would remain if Hazelwood had anything to do with it.

'Roy didn't waste much time,' he grunted.

'The pay section is part of his fiefdom, Victor, and I assume Ashton will be drawing a salary?'

'Well, he won't be doing it for nothing, but I don't see why Kelso should concern himself. After all, I am the controller of the personnel contingency fund.'

'And I still like to be consulted before we hire anybody.'

There were several ways of making a telling point and despite the faint smile and mild tone of voice, Hazelwood knew he was skating on thin ice and felt threatened.

'This has to do with Simon Oakham,' he said, a touch defensively, 'the Pay Corps officer who was coming to us. We spoke about him last Thursday and came to the conclusion that it was desirable to find out why he should have gone out of his way to shoot himself in the foot.'

'Did we actually come to a decision, Victor?'

They hadn't and that was the trouble. 'Perhaps I was a little hasty,' Hazelwood admitted reluctantly, 'but when I learned he'd gone absent without leave, I thought we ought to look into it. I knew our own Security, Vetting and Technical Services Division had no one to spare and I believed Ashton was the best man for the job, especially as at one time he had been in charge of that department.'

'I'm not sure we are justified in poking our nose into what is the army's business.' Dunglass frowned. 'Or do you know something I don't?' he asked.

'I had wondered if this warrant officer on the Long Service List was the same Leonard Jackson our people in Hong Kong had dealings with back in 1969. Shortly before lunch, Ashton rang the Armed Forces Desk and asked the girl on duty to obtain his file.'

Dunglass got up, walked over to the window and stood there looking down at the river, hands stuffed deep into his pockets. 'I remember hearing of a Warrant Officer Jackson in the SIB when I was serving with the Far East Bureau,' he said quietly.

'He's the man,' Hazelwood said.

'In that case, you were right to hire Ashton, but I want him kept at arm's length. Tell him to submit his reports through the Admin Wing.'

'You want Kelso to run him?' Hazelwood said incredulously.

'Why not?' Dunglass turned about to face him. 'Security, Vetting and Technical Services are also part of his empire.'

Brigadier Frank Baring was not a hunting, shooting or fishing man. He had not aspired to a house of great character deep in the heart of the countryside miles from the nearest town of any consequence. Nor had he and his wife, Nancy, spent every spare weekend haunting auction rooms far and wide in search of antique furniture before he retired from the army. Instead, they had bought a smart, five-bedroom executive house, one of four in Woodside Close off the Winchester to Stockbridge road. The furniture was modern too, a perfect background for a collection of unusual pieces of oriental porcelain and bronze figures.

The house was warm, so was the welcome Ashton received. Before he had time to remove his overcoat, Baring had announced that of course he would be staying to supper which, though she did her best to disguise it, was obviously news to Nancy. Unabashed, he had then ushered Ashton into the sitting room and poured him a very large malt whisky. In the space of a few minutes, Ashton learned that the Barings had two sons and a daughter. The daughter was a teacher married to a teacher while the elder son was a commodity broker. The younger one was a barrister married to a solicitor.

'Very handy,' Baring told him cryptically, 'never have any trouble-some disputes with the neighbours.'

'I can imagine.'

'Still, you didn't come all the way to Winchester to hear me talking about my family.'

Baring made it sound as though forty minutes on the rush hour fast train to Bournemouth out of Waterloo was one of the great epic journeys of the world.

'You want to know if Oakham bolted because of something I said to him.'

'No, I'd sooner hear what you made of him.'

'I thought he was a smarmy little blighter. I don't mean Oakham was the "Yes sir, no sir, three bags full" type – he was a serving captain and I was a retired brigadier so there was no need for him to go the whole hog because there was nothing I could do for him careerwise.'

'Except recommend him for an EPV clearance,' Ashton said quietly.

'And he knew it; perhaps that's why he was so anxious to please me. I've interviewed over twelve hundred commissioned officers, warrant officers, NCOs and men since I started this job and I can't recall anyone who was so well prepared for a subject interview.'

The income and expenditure balance sheet he had produced for Baring had been a model of its kind. Every outgoing had been meticulously recorded and went to show how prudent he was where money was concerned. The figures hadn't been conjured out of the air either; they had been supported by the latest bank statement from Lloyds and his receipted mess bill for January.

'I could believe it when Oakham told me that while he enjoyed the occasional glass of wine, he never overindulged. The proof was there in his mess bill; the man was definitely abstemious. He was also a paragon of virtue; didn't smoke and was scathing about people who used drugs. But that was nothing compared with what he had to say about homosexuals.' Baring sipped his whisky, then put the glass down on the low coffee table between them. 'Oakham made it very clear how much he detested gays. I got the impression that had he been living in Germany fifty years ago, he would have happily sent every last one of them to the gas chamber.'

It was part of Baring's job to ascertain the sexual orientation of the candidates he interviewed, male and female. Of the young women he had positively vetted, the vast majority had had no time at all for lesbians and found their sexual preferences distasteful. The men were, on the whole, much more aggressive and intolerant. A small number professed to be open-minded, while those who prided themselves on being macho were contemptuous. To them, homosexuals were poofs, queens, faggots, queers or fairies, objects of ridicule and derision. Then there were a handful like Oakham who were enraged that society should tolerate people they regarded as perverts, let alone condone their predilections.

'Have you seen a photograph of Oakham?' Baring asked.

Ashton shook his head. 'My boss was unable to provide one.'

'Well, take it from me, with his features he could probably earn a living as a female impersonator.'

'Are you saying that his anger was contrived to disguise the fact that he is that way inclined himself?'

'I'm not sure, but I do believe he genuinely hates them.' Baring reached for his whisky and took another sip. 'I've a feeling he may have had a bad homosexual experience when he was a young soldier.'

'Are you referring to that weekend skiing trip to Winterberg in February '75?'

'Well, think about it. If you had witnessed a murder which had made such a lasting impression, wouldn't you remember the name of the guy you'd shared a room with even though you were only eighteen years old at the time?'

'Chances are he hasn't forgotten,' Ashton said. 'Two private soldiers could share a room in a *Gasthof* without causing any eyebrows to be raised. But it would be a different story if word got out that Oakham's companion that weekend had been a senior NCO or an officer. No doubt his friend would have pointed that out to him quite forcefully.'

'I think you're right,' Baring told him. 'It would explain his reluctance to say anything about the incident other than mentioning it vaguely to the sergeant in charge of the pay section when he returned to barracks.'

'If that's what Oakham told you, he was lying. The fact is, he didn't come forward until after the Board of Inquiry had submitted their findings to the convening officer. I guess his conscience finally got the better of him. Anyway, he made a statement to his company commander, Major Richard Cosgrove, which he subsequently withdrew.'

'Because his boyfriend heard about it and got on to him?' Baring suggested.

Ashton nodded. Had their relationship come to light, the army would have dealt with them harshly. Because of his age, Oakham would probably have been dealt with summarily by his commanding officer and awarded twenty-eight days' detention before being dishonourably discharged. The actual wording was 'services no longer required' but it amounted to the same thing. As for Oakham's boyfriend, had he indeed been an officer or senior NCO, he would have been court-martialled and sentenced to a minimum term of six months' imprisonment and discharged, forfeiting any terminal grant that might have been due to him.

'The thing I don't understand is why, having chanced his arm once and got away with it, Oakham should have risked exposure a second time by drawing your attention to the incident nineteen years later?'

'Don't think I haven't asked myself the same question,' Baring said, draining the rest of his malt whisky.

'Shortly after completing the EPV form listing his former commanding officers and referees, his past somehow caught up with him again and he decided to tell you about the incident at Winterberg. Then, for some reason, the situation deteriorated alarmingly and he did a runner.' Ashton grinned. 'I'm just speculating.'

'No harm in that.'

'So what's your theory?'

'I don't have one,' Baring told him. 'I came to the conclusion that Oakham wasn't a suitable candidate for EPV and returned his papers to Woolwich giving my reasons in writing. Next thing I hear is that you want to have a word with me. Now, drink up and have another malt.'

'Thanks all the same, but I don't think I should.'

'Why not? You're not driving, are you?'

Ashton swallowed the remains of his whisky and handed the empty glass to Baring. 'You just talked me into it,' he said.

From the day he had started work, Wilfred Zachery had always been on nights, his shift invariably ending before 02.00 hours. In the trade, he was known as 'Windowpane Willie' because that was his favourite way of effecting an entry. He was forty-three years old and had only two previous convictions for burglary, the second of which had been in 1967 when he was still a minor. He attributed his success to good information, forethought and meticulous planning; luck also played a major part. In addition, Zachery observed two golden rules: he neither fouled his own doorstep nor outstayed his welcome.

He hadn't been near Poole since 1988 when he had burgled a house out on the Blandford Road and had walked away with twelve thousand in cash. However, as far as the local police were concerned, this would be the first time he'd visited the town because the previous burglary had not been reported. This hadn't been altogether surprising; anyone who kept that amount of bunce in a wall safe behind a David Shepherd print had to be up to no good and was obviously diddling the Inland Revenue.

In 1988 he had targeted three houses, two of which had been left untouched and were therefore in the frame this time round. That morning he had picked out two more likely-looking properties and had then visited the Central Library at the Dolphin Centre where he had looked up the names of the occupants in the electoral roll.

After lunching at The Dolphin in the High Street, Zachery had driven off towards Wimbourne Minster and checked into the Dorset Lodge Motel. As was his usual practice, he had registered under an assumed name and given a false address. He had also indicated on the form that he would pay cash when settling his bill. He told the receptionist that he was a self-employed insurance broker and would be visiting a number of clients that evening.

Before leaving his motel room at 6.30 to drive back to town, he looked up the telephone numbers of his intended victims in the directory and made a note of them on the back of an old envelope. From a pay phone outside the railway station in Poole, he then started to work his way down the list. The first two calls were answered and he quickly apologised for dialling the wrong number. The third connected Zachery to an answer machine and a recorded message from a man with a fruity voice who regretted no one was available at the moment but invited him to leave his name, number and any message after the tone. In Zachery's experience however, this did not necessarily mean the occupant wasn't at home. More in hope than anticipation, he tried the last one on the list and was more than a little relieved when the subscriber failed to answer.

Oak Tree Cottage was two miles out of town on the A35 trunk route to Wareham. It was set back from the main road and was approached by a snow-covered narrow lane. The nearest oak was in the middle of a field approximately fifty yards north of the cottage, which was enclosed by a dense laurel hedge some ten feet high. There were two gaps in the hedge on the west side facing the lane where a U-shaped drive swept up to the house and back.

Zachery made a right turn into the lane, then switched off the main beams and day-running lights on the Saab. He put the wheels in the tracks left by other vehicles for better traction and to blur his own tyre treads. Still in third gear, he turned into the drive and pulled up outside the front door. He switched off the engine, got out of the car and quietly closed the door.

Oak Tree Cottage was the sort of place up-market estate agents were apt to describe as a country gentleman's residence. Built of stone, it was at least a hundred years old, had a slate roof and walls encrusted with Virginia creeper. No lights were showing, the curtains hadn't been drawn upstairs or downstairs, and if the smoke-free chimneys were anything to go by, the owner hadn't bothered to light a fire. On a more downbeat note, there was a burglar alarm above the front porch.

Zachery opened the boot, took our a pair of dark blue overalls and his tool bag. He was wearing a worsted, single-breasted suit and he couldn't return to the Dorset Lodge Motel looking dishevelled. He slipped the dungarees on over the suit, pulled on a pair of cotton gloves, then shoved an aerosol can and a pair of wire cutters into his pocket and shinned up the creeper. He could tell at a glance that the alarm was linked either to the central police station or to a private security company. Neither possibility worried him. With the aerosol spray, he gummed up the works with paint, then cut the wires and climbed down having neutralised the system in under half a minute.

Zachery picked up the tool bag and walked round to the back of the house. Normally the sashcord windows wouldn't have been a problem for him but the cottage was in an isolated position and with the aid of a pencil-thin flashlight he could see the owner had fitted locks top and bottom of each frame. The one exception was a small square window measuring eighteen by eighteen inches which didn't open. Selecting a carpet knife, he hacked out the putty securing the pane, then holding the glass in place with a suction pad, he cut it out as close to the wooden frame as possible. Then he removed the windowpane and leaned it against the outside wall.

Although he was a thin man, squeezing his body through the narrow frame wasn't easy for him and he had to go in sideways, head and left shoulder first. A marble shelf a couple of feet below the window told him he was in the pantry, so did the cold joint on a plate he sent crashing on to the floor. Zachery followed it involuntarily, performing a somersault before landing up on his back, his feet jammed against the door. Had anyone been at home, they couldn't have failed to hear the racket, but nothing happened. There was no latch or handle on the inside; however, there was a certain amount of give in the door and putting his shoulder to it, he forced the hasp.

Zachery left the kitchen and checked out the dining and sitting rooms, looking for small items of silver he could dispose of at car boot sales he attended up and down the country. There was precious little to be had; the two ashtrays incorporating a Maria Theresa silver dollar and the engraved cigarette box were too readily identifiable, and the candlesticks were only plated. Disappointed, he went upstairs hoping to find a few bits and pieces of jewellery and perhaps a wad of banknotes hidden away in one of the drawers. Turning left on the landing, he tried the end bedroom first.

The woman was lying flat on her back, arms and legs spread-eagled and lashed to the old-fashioned brass railings at the head and foot of the bed. Her head was inside a plastic bag that had been loosely tied at the neck. She was wearing a bra, French knickers, suspender belt and stockings. Hand shaking, Zachery trained a pencil-thin flashlight on the body again, starting with the feet, then moving the beam slowly upwards towards the head. This time he noticed that the right leg of the French knickers had been rucked up to expose a flaccid penis around which somebody had tied a pink satin bow.

Unnerved by what he had seen, Zachery dropped the flashlight, ran downstairs and let himself out of the cottage. His one idea was to get the hell out of it in the shortest possible time. Leaping into the Saab, he started the engine, engaged first gear and took off like a rocket. On the way out, he managed to sideswipe a gatepost with the rear end, then got an angry blast from a motorist when he turned on to the A35 without looking to see if the road was clear. A Ford Escort XR3 swept past, the driver shaking his fist at him before cutting in front. For a brief, frightening moment, Zachery thought he intended to force him to stop but then, much to his relief, the driver suddenly accelerated and drew away.

It was only when he reached the outskirts of Poole that Zachery remembered he'd left the tool bag behind. He didn't think there was anything in the bag which could identify him, but it was possible that the driver of the Ford had made a mental note of the registration number of his Saab. Getting done for burglary was one thing, being in the frame for murder was something else. There was, Zachery decided, only one thing he could do; turning off the Old Wareham Road, he drove round and round the Haymoor Bottom estate until he found a pay phone in one of the back streets.

He punched out 999 and told the operator to connect him with the police. A cool voice asked him for his name and address.

'I want to report a murder,' he yelled at the girl, 'at Oak Tree Cottage two miles out of the town on the A35 to Wareham. You got that?' He paused, then said, 'My name's Major Richard Cosgrove,' and slammed the phone down.

CHAPTER 4

Ashton didn't like to think how many times he had walked across Blackfriars Bridge to the south bank of the river and turned left into Southwark Street to make his way to Benbow House. Although it was close on seven months since he had last set foot inside the place, it was anything but a trip down memory lane for him.

He had been transferred to Benbow House from the Russian Desk in 1991 after he had got a shade too close to a GRU half colonel, and some people had felt he had been contaminated as a result. A sideways move to head the Security, Vetting and Technical Services Division had taken him away from the main stream, restricted his access to classified information and placed him under Roy Kelso. The only thing to be said in favour of the move was that he would never have met Harriet Egan had he not been sent to Benbow House.

The MoD policeman on duty in the entrance hall was a new face who didn't recognise Ashton and regarded his old ID card which Hazelwood had returned to him with suspicion. The civilian staff had changed too but in a different sense. Where there had been two ladies on the enquiry desk, there was now only one, visible evidence of the cuts imposed by the Treasury. The downside to her cheerful greeting and warm smile was the news that Kelso wanted to see him in his office.

The Assistant Director in charge of Administration was responsible for just about every routine matter from the provision of stationery, clerical support, claims and expenses to internal audits, control of expenditure and Boards of Inquiry. His empire included the financial branch, the motor transport and general stores section, plus the Security, Vetting and Technical Services Division. To run such a diverse and semi-autonomous organisation required a sense of humour, an attribute which Roy Kelso sadly lacked. Aged fifty-three and eligible for early retirement in 1996, Kelso was a tired, disappointed, small-minded and deeply embittered man.

During his stint at Benbow House, Ashton had learned from experience that the best way to get on with Roy Kelso was to avoid him as much as possible. There had been occasions however when this had been impossible, as was the case this morning. Recognising he had no option, Ashton walked over to the nearest vacant lift, closed the trellis gate behind him and punched the button for the top floor. There was a noticeable interval before the machinery responded; when it did, the car ascended slowly, wheezing like an old gentleman suffering from chronic asthma.

Although Kelso had never been in the navy, he had picked up a lot of the jargon after taking a helmsman's course and sailing a dinghy on the Solent. He was fond of telling people that he ran a tight ship which, amongst other things, meant that the staff on the desk in the entrance hall were required to warn him whenever he had a visitor.

'Come on in, Peter,' he said breezily before Ashton could tap on the open door. 'It's good to see you again. How are you keeping?'

'Fine.'

'And the lovely Harriet?'

'Blooming.' Ashton remained standing. The only spare chair in the office was a wooden upright which for some reason occupied the far left-hand corner of the room by the window. He wondered if Kelso had deliberately put it there in rear of his desk when Reception had informed him he was on the way up.

'So how long do you think you will be with us?' Kelso asked, having got the obligatory social pleasantries out of the way.

'I've no idea.' Ashton shrugged. 'How long is a piece of string?'

'Well, let's not stretch it too far, Peter; the money tree isn't exactly overloaded. Times are hard.'

Ashton eyed the large buff-coloured folder in the pending tray. Although sideways on to him, he could read the serial number, surname and initials printed in blocks along the top of the envelope. 'I see Jackson's documents have arrived,' he said, ignoring Kelso's snide remark.

'Yes. I presume Victor has been in touch to explain the setup?'

Ashton nodded. Hazelwood had phoned on Tuesday night after Ashton had returned from Winchester. The SIS might have returned his old ID card but it looked as though they had declined to restore his security clearance which had automatically lapsed the day he left the Service. At any rate, it was quite clear that the DG was not prepared to let him set so much as a foot inside the portals of Vauxhall Cross.

'I am to submit everything through you,' Ashton told him. 'Reports, requests for documents, the lot.'

'Will you have any difficulty complying with that directive?' Kelso asked, his voice silky smooth.

It had been a bitter pill to swallow when Hazelwood had put it to him and he'd come close to telling Victor to take his money and shove it. Since then, he'd had all day yesterday to think about it and had been in a more amenable frame of mind when Hazelwood had phoned him again to say Jackson's documents had arrived from the Records Office at Hayes.

'I'm sure we can make it work, Roy,' he said enigmatically.

'Good.' Kelso picked up the folder and handed it to him. 'I thought you could have the office that used to be occupied by the staff assistant to Head of Security Vetting before the post was abolished.'

'Sounds fine to me.'

But it wasn't. This was Harriet's old office and he could feel her presence the moment he walked into the room. He remembered their first meeting two years ago as if it was only yesterday. He had just returned from a field trip to Moscow to find that she had been posted in as the exchange officer from MI5, the Security Service. Their relationship had hardly been a case of love at first sight. In fact, they had fought like cat and dog to begin with because Harriet hadn't approved of his ways of doing things which she had believed were highly questionable if not downright illegal. Later, he had learned just how very close she had been to asking her superiors to find someone else to fill the appointment.

Ashton removed his trenchcoat and hung it up from the hook on the back of the door, then tried the phone on the desk and wasn't surprised to discover it was dead. Anger welling inside him like an oil gusher, he stormed off down the corridor in search of the Chief Clerk.

'I'd like the phone in Harriet's office reconnected,' he said before the unfortunate man had a chance to say a word.

'But—'

'No buts, just do it.'

'I'll have to get Mr Kelso's permission first,' the Chief Clerk told him.

'We seem to have a communication problem,' Ashton said in a dangerously quiet yet loud enough voice to remind the two clerical assistants that it was time they visited the ladies room. 'Now, I don't want to offend you,' he continued in the same menacing tone, 'but I don't really give a shit about Mr Kelso's instructions. When I pick up the phone, I expect to hear a dialling tone. I hope you don't think that's unreasonable of me?'

'Absolutely not. I'll see to it right away, Mr Ashton.'

'You do that.'

Ashton returned to Harriet's old office, undid the folder and tipped the contents out on to the desk. Both the company and Regimental Conduct sheets were blank. Had Jackson collected an entry on the latter, he would never have been awarded the Long Service and Good Conduct medal at the eighteen-year point. The medical and dental charts were of little interest to Ashton, neither was Army Form B2066 which recorded the annual assessments received from his superior officers whilst Jackson had been a junior NCO.

The Record of Service was an altogether more informative document. It showed every posting and promotion in Jackson's long army career from the day he had been called up for National Service at the age of eighteen in 1948 to his final appointment as Garrison Warrant Officer, Soest. It also listed every course he had attended together with the gradings he'd obtained. On a more personal note, there were separate boxes for the name and address of the next of kin, marital status, and the names, dates and birth places of his children.

Ashton found a wad of scrap paper in one of the drawers and began to compile a brief history of the man. Jackson had started out in the infantry and had done his basic training with the 1st Battalion of the Cheshire Regiment at Whittington Barracks, Lichfield. He had then served with the 1st North Staffords in the Suez Canal Zone where he had signed on as a regular. Twenty-one months later, having gained some experience as a regimental policeman, he had transferred to the RMP. Apart from a spell in Rhine Army in the late fifties, Jackson had spent the greater part of his overseas service in the Far East, serving in Singapore and Malay from 1953 to 1956 and again from 1962 to 1965, which had included an emergency tour in Borneo during the confrontation with Indonesia. His last posting before joining the Long Service List had been to Hong Kong where he had been in charge of the Special Investigation Branch from 1968 to 1970.

His confidential reports as a senior NCO and warrant officer written on Army Form B2048 were very similar and could have been compiled by the same superior officer. There were ticks in all the high-scoring boxes for initiative, leadership qualities, foresight, intelligence, loyalty, common sense, application and devotion to duty. Almost without exception, the main body of each report was practically a eulogy, which made Ashton wonder why he had not been commissioned from the ranks. The annual confidential report for the period 1 April 1969 to 31 March 1970 was different only in that it looked as though an insert by someone other than Jackson's commanding officer had been neatly removed with a razor-sharp knife.

Ashton placed the 69/70 assessment on one side, extracted the reports for the two years before and after the mutilated report and went through them line by line to see if he could find a link which might explain why the odd one out had apparently been doctored. Halfway through the task, the phone trilled briefly; lifting the receiver, he learned from the Chief Clerk that the line had been reconnected. Shortly thereafter, one of the clerical assistants brought him a cup of coffee and he took time out to read the *Daily Telegraph* he'd bought from the newsagent outside Victoria station and had been physically unable to look at before alighting from the crowded District Line train at Blackfriars.

Major Richard Cosgrove rated a brief paragraph at the foot of page four of the newspaper under the headline, 'Oak Tree Cottage Victim Identified'. The surname was not uncommon and he thought it reasonable to assume there had been more than one Major Cosgrove in the army. What clinched it for him was the fact that the dead man had been a regular officer in the Queen's Westminster Rifles. Borrowing the MoD telephone directory from the clerks, he looked up the number of the staff captain to the Provost Marshal at Empress State and then rang him to find out what the military police made of it.

'We're looking for an absentee,' the staff captain told him. 'The civil police are involved in a murder investigation.'

'And Cosgrove was Oakham's company commander when he was an eighteen-year-old soldier.'

'There is that coincidence.'

'Well, it occurs to me that perhaps the major was more than just his superior officer. Maybe he was the guy who went skiing with Oakham and shared the same hotel room? Maybe they were lovers then and still were? Hell, Poole is no distance from Tilshead Camp.'

'I hear what you are saying, Mr Ashton, and of course I'll make the point to the brigadier.'

'Tactfully, I hope.'

'Don't worry, I'll be suitably diffident.' The staff captain paused, then said, 'We followed your advice and persuaded Mrs Oakham to ring Access and ask for a read-out. As of yesterday, the last entry was a payment in settlement of a debtor balance from the previous month. There have been no large withdrawals from their joint bank account either, but of course any cheque issued over the weekend won't be cleared until close of business today.'

Ashton thanked him and replaced the phone, then picked it up again and rang MI5 in Gower Street. Although Clifford Peachey had worked alongside Harriet, Ashton had met him back in 1991, a good year before she had been seconded to the SIS. Annoyingly, there was no reply from his extension. Breaking the connection, he tried again and this time raised the switchboard operator who pretended she had never heard of Mr Peachey. Undeterred, Ashton said what his extension was on the government private network and told her to call him back. When she did, he learned that Peachey was lecturing at the New Bond Street training centre. It then took a further two attempts before he managed to contact the MI5 officer during the mid-morning coffee break.

'This isn't a social call, is it?' Peachey said after exchanging pleasantries.

'You're right, I need a small favour.'

'I heard you were out on the street.'

'I was,' Ashton told him. 'But now I'm back in – at least for the time being. You can check with Victor.'

'That won't be necessary.'

Ashton smiled to himself. As soon as he hung up, Peachey would be on to Hazelwood. In the event of an adverse reaction from Victor, he wouldn't keep their appointment. It was as simple as that.

'I assume you know where I'm performing today?'

'How else would I have got in touch with you, Clifford?'

'Quite so.' Peachey cleared his throat. 'Let's meet here at 12.30,' he said and put the phone down without waiting for an answer.

Ashton replaced the receiver, collected Jackson's documents together and put them back inside the folder. He then wrote a memo to Kelso giving his reasons why he would like him to obtain the personal file of Major Richard Cosgrove, late Queen's Westminster Rifles. It would have been far quicker to pick up the phone and ask the Armed Forces Desk at Vauxhall Cross to get the papers but he wanted the Assistant Director, Admin, to think he was following his instructions to the letter. He made no mention of meeting Peachey. The trick was to tell Kelso just enough to keep him happy.

The training centre run by MI5 was in fact located in Bruton Place off New Bond Street. It was situated directly above a picture gallery and shared a common entrance with the firm. The Security Service did not advertise its presence and in the absence of any information board in the hallway, the uninitiated frequently blundered into the picture gallery. The attendants had become used to this and cheerfully redirected all such intruders to the spooks department on the floor above. This description wasn't entirely correct; the centre existed purely to train those civil servants from other government ministries who had been designated as branch security officers in addition to their normal jobs. Officers of the Security Service itself were trained elsewhere.

Clifford Peachey had been and still was, for all Ashton knew, one of the leading lights of K1, the section of MI5 commonly referred to as the Kremlin Watchers. At the height of the Cold War, it had been their job to ferret out the KGB and GRU officers in the Soviet Embassy. Despite the popular notion that with Glasnost and Perestroika all was now sweetness and light, they were, at the very least, as busy as ever. Where previously there had been only one embassy, one trade delegation and one consular service to keep an eye on, they now had to contend with a proliferation of independent states, each one happily engaged in the spying game. The Security Service had not been given additional manpower to deal with this situation; on the contrary, K1 had seen its establishment cut under the much-derided Options for Change review. It had also suffered because, in seeking to justify the continued existence of MI5, the top brass had persuaded the government they should be responsible for conducting anti-terrorist operations against the IRA.

The Ferrets had been one of the less complimentary nicknames for the Kremlin Watchers. Recalling the first time they had met, Ashton remembered thinking that Clifford Peachey was typecast for the job. A small man with sharp pointed features, he bore an unfortunate resemblance to a rodent. Once dark, his sleek head of hair cut short back and sides was now a uniform shade of grey. Until a few months ago, he had cultivated a neat toothbrush moustache which was not at all flattering. Since their last meeting, someone had persuaded him to remove it, a most noticeable improvement that had knocked years off his age.

'It's good to see you again,' Peachey said, greeting him at the top of the stairs. 'I thought we'd use the chief instructor's office.'

'Is that your new appointment, Clifford?'

'Only for this week. We take it in turns to run these courses.'

The chief instructor's office wasn't much larger than a boxroom. The solitary window was shoulder high and offered no view whatsoever. With only nine feet by nine to play with, the desk had had to be placed diagonally across the room.

'I'm afraid it's a bit cramped,' Peachey said apologetically.

'It doesn't matter.'

'So how's Harriet?' Peachey asked and waved Ashton to the only other wooden chair.

'Heavily pregnant.'

'And when are you two getting married?'

Had it been anyone else, Ashton would have told him to mind his own business, but Peachey was special; he had been Harriet's guide, mentor, father figure and trusted friend.

'Who can tell, Clifford? It's really up to Harriet and she isn't saying. I think subconsciously she blames me for what happened to her in Berlin.'

'Well, you people should have taken better care of her. Unfortunately, it's guilt by association where you are concerned.'

'Look,' Ashton said with a hard edge to his voice, 'I'm not defending the DG, Victor Hazelwood or anyone else, but Harriet wanted to go to Berlin. And you should know that once she has made up her mind to do something, no one on God's earth can stop her. No one could have foreseen that riot in the Kreuzberg District; it was simply Harriet's bad luck to be in the wrong place at the wrong time. The rock that struck Harriet didn't just fracture her skull; it shattered her confidence and she suddenly came to believe that when faced with extreme danger, she didn't have what it takes.'

'She should have had counselling,' Peachey said.

'Well, we all know the world is stiff with clinical psychologists wanting to do their thing, but you try getting Harriet to put her name down for tea and sympathy and see where it gets you. I've tried, believe me, I have tried.'

'I'm sure you have.' Peachey took out his pipe which was almost a badge of office for him, and methodically filled the bowl with tobacco from a much-used pouch, then lit it. 'Now let's talk about this favour you want from me.'

It was the invitation Ashton had been waiting for and he told the older man what he knew about Simon Oakham, the long-dead Warrant Officer Jackson and the late Major Richard Cosgrove and the slender thread which linked all three men.

'Let's assume Cosgrove was humping young Oakham. He can't afford to let the lad make a statement because the civil police will undoubtedly question him and he might just let the cat out of the bag. In that event, Cosgrove is looking at a custodial sentence and you can bet the major pointed out to Oakham that he would unquestionably end up in a Military Corrective Training centre. In other words, the glasshouse.

That should have persuaded Oakham to keep his mouth shut, but no, he insists on making a statement.'

'It doesn't make sense,' Peachey said, frowning.

'No, it doesn't. I've a hunch the little bastard was blackmailing his company commander. It got to the point where Cosgrove decided he had to call his bluff, so he told Oakham to submit his statement in writing, probably in the knowledge that the Board of Inquiry had already reached their finding. I'm still guessing, of course, but I think Oakham subsequently got cold feet and asked to withdraw his statement. Shortly after that, Cosgrove got him posted out of Headquarters 1 (BR) Corps.'

'It's a plausible theory, Peter, but can you prove it?'

'I've sent for Cosgrove's file; it will be interesting to see exactly when he left the army and why.'

Peachey tapped his pipe over an ashtray until he was satisfied the bowl was empty. 'What about Oakham?' he asked.

'I can't get at his security dossier; it's with the army's vetting unit at Woolwich.' Ashton snapped his fingers, suddenly realising there was another source he could tap. 'But they won't have his personal file; that will be lodged with the Adjutant General's Branch and it will incorporate his previous service in the ranks.'

'Looks as though you don't need my help after all,' Peachey observed.

'Oh, but I do. I want to know if Oakham had taken up with Cosgrove again and stayed with him at Oak Tree Cottage. The Provost Marshal's Branch isn't going to help me there. They're not convinced there is a connection between Oakham going AWOL and Cosgrove's murder and they may not have informed the civil police that the two men had served in the same unit in 1975.'

'You're referring to the Dorset Constabulary?'

'Yes.'

'Okay, I'll see what I can do.'

'I'm sorry?'

'You want to meet the officer in charge of the murder investigation, don't you?'

'Damn right,' Ashton said.

'Then I'll be in touch,' Peachey told him.

The dark blue Volvo 740 estate was on the third floor of the Gunthorpe Centre multistorey car park in Portsmouth's North End District. The attendant wasn't too sure how long the vehicle had been there but recalled first noticing it when he'd clocked on for the afternoon shift on Tuesday. When the Volvo was still there forty-eight hours later, he had informed the day supervisor who in turn had called the police.

The nearest patrol car was directed to the multistorey car park and arrived there some five minutes later. The estate was amongst the list of vehicles the two officers had been told to look out for. The registered owner was Simon Oakham. The car park itself was across the dual carriageway from the Continental Ferry Port.

CHAPTER 5

The Dorset Constabulary was organised into three divisions, covering the west, east and central districts of the county. Since Oak Tree Cottage was situated within the boundaries of the central division based on Poole, the officer in charge of the suspicious death investigation was Detective Chief Inspector Harry Farnesworth. The last thing he needed was yet one more person breathing down his neck when he already had to contend with the Chief Constable, Deputy Chief Constable and the Detective Chief Superintendent in charge of the Criminal Investigation Department at Force Headquarters, never mind the ever-increasing band of newspapermen and TV reporters who dogged his footsteps.

But Ashton had been wished on him by the Head of Special Branch at Winfrith with the concurrence of the Chief Constable who was next in line to God in the scheme of things. That Farnesworth was not best pleased was evident to Ashton when they shook hands and the Chief Inspector told him that he should be out on the ground driving the investigation instead of wasting time in the station.

'I could always tag along if you're that busy,' Ashton said affably.

'Don't take any notice of me,' Farnesworth told him, 'I just got out of bed the wrong side this morning.' He opened a door off the hall marked DCI CID and waved Ashton to go on in. 'Fact is, this investigation is getting nowhere. It could be that all we've got is a death in suspicious circumstances.'

'You surprise me; the press are definite that Cosgrove was murdered. Are you saying they've got it wrong?'

'I don't know. To begin with it certainly looked as if we were dealing with a homicide. There was unmistakable evidence of a break-in and Cosgrove couldn't have put his head inside the plastic bag unaided the way he was tied to the bed.'

'So what made you change your mind?'

'The post mortem. The pathologist reckons the victim had been dead for at least forty-eight hours before Mr Wilfred Zachery made his anonymous phone call on Tuesday night.'

'Is he the man who broke into the cottage?'

'Yes. He left his tools behind. No prints on the jemmy, pliers, glass cutter or spray can but there was a latent one on the bag. Been there a long time by all accounts.' Farnesworth took out a packet of Silk Cut and offered one to Ashton before lighting up. 'Last time Zachery came to notice was back in '68. Anyway, he obviously got the shock of his life when he found Cosgrove, couldn't get out of the house fast enough. I guess he wasn't the only one who panicked.'

'What makes you say that?' Ashton asked.

'There were no signs of a struggle. Cosgrove lay down on the bed and allowed himself to be tied up. I'm told by clinical psychologists that some sexual deviants get a terrific kick from going close to death when they masturbate. Partial suffocation is the most popular and a plastic bag is considered a very effective method of achieving the desired stimulus. I think Cosgrove was asphyxiated because the friend who was obliging him didn't remove the bag in time.'

The cigarette smoke got to Farnesworth and brought on a paroxysm of coughing. He was a big man in his early forties and was a good fifteen to twenty pounds overweight for his height. He had a high colour which could be the sign of a man who spent the great part of his life outdoors in all weathers. In Farnesworth's case however, Ashton was prepared to bet it was due to high blood pressure.

'I wish I could give these things up but it's not easy when you've been a smoker all your life.'

Ashton could sympathise with him. Apart from the fact that smoking was an expensive habit, there were two reasons why people eventually gave it up. Either they were sufficiently worried about their health to realise it was slowly killing them, or else they happened to find themselves in a situation where it was physically impossible to smoke. Ashton had kicked the habit twelve years ago in the Falklands during the latter stages of the campaign. After the raid on Pebble Island, he and two signallers had operated behind enemy lines directing counter battery fire on the artillery supporting the Argentine positions on Mount Longdon. Unless you were tired of life, that had been one place which was strictly a no-smoking area. Having survived three days without a cigarette, he had decided to give it up for good, a challenge that had demanded tremendous willpower. There had been many times when he had been sorely tempted but he had managed to stick it out and within four months, the desire had gone.

'Why is MI5 interested in Cosgrove?' Farnesworth suddenly asked.

'They aren't.'

'That's not what I heard from our own Special Branch. Some old friend called Peachey twisted the Chief Inspector's arm.'

'Well, that's not wholly correct.'

'I see.' Farnesworth squinted at him, elbows propped on the table, the smoke from the cigarette between his fingers drifting into his eyes. 'Could it be that one of your lot was playing footsie with the major?' he asked.

'No, but someone who was almost admitted to the club was certainly acquainted with Cosgrove back in the mid-seventies.'

'Does this guy have a name or is it a state secret?'

'The name isn't, the connection is.'

'I'm still interested in the name,' Farnesworth told him.

'Simon Oakham; he's a thirty-six-year-old captain in the Royal Army Pay Corps. He was posted absent when he failed to appear for first parade on Monday. He might have spent the weekend with Cosgrove. Matter of fact, it wouldn't surprise me if he had visited the cottage more than once.'

Farnesworth stubbed out his cigarette, asked Ashton to excuse him for a moment and left the office. Five minutes later he was back clutching an official-looking brown envelope.

'I knew we had something on Oakham,' he said. 'Seems his Volvo was found in a multistorey car park in Portsmouth yesterday evening. No one is sure how long it had been there, but the car park is very handy for the Continental Ferry Port.'

'Did he catch a boat?'

'If he did, I doubt whether anybody will remember him. Who is going to pay any attention to a foot passenger these days? Passport control hardly exists; Europe is one big, happy family. Besides, the army failed to supply a photograph that might have jogged someone's memory. All we got was a description that could fit nearly anybody.' Farnesworth opened the envelope and tipped the contents out on to the table. 'Oakham wouldn't be among this little lot, would he?'

Ashton sifted through the colour snapshots. Frank Baring had told him that with his features, Oakham could have earned a living as a female impersonator, but neither of the two men whose pictures Cosgrove had presumably taken fitted that description. Both were under the age of thirty, if he was any judge, and looked as if they had taken the same body-building course. Their biceps and pectoral muscles were over-developed and glistened with oil so that they shone like well-polished oak. Both men had blond hair. The taller of the two fancied himself as a boxer and was wearing a tight-fitting pair of satin trunks and shin-high, lace-up boots. His companion wore a peaked cap belonging to an an SS *Obersturmführer*, a gold chain and a pair of jackboots. In one photograph, the would-be stormtrooper was posed with an elderly, scrawny-looking man whose pot belly protruded beneath the hemline of a silk blouse worn under a bolero jacket. The two men were standing shoulder to shoulder, arms encircling each other's hips and smiling into the camera as they played with one another.

'Oakham's photograph isn't amongst this lot.' Ashton passed the snapshot of the amorous couple to Farnesworth. 'Am I right in thinking the elderly man is Cosgrove?' he asked.

'Yes, that's the major.'

'Any idea where the snapshots were taken?'

'Not at the cottage, though we did find the photos there, locked away in a small deed box in the main bedroom. One thing I have learned about Cosgrove is that he was very well thought of; people round here reckon he was a proper gentleman. I'm not saying that he never invited any of his boyfriends to spend the weekend with him, just that he was very discreet and kept them out of sight. He would have been safe enough, providing he didn't go out. The cottage is pretty isolated and his cleaning lady only came in twice a week, on Wednesdays and Fridays, except when he was hosting a luncheon or dinner party.'

Cosgrove had been a staunch member of the local Conservative Party Association, the secretary and treasurer of the Parochial Church Council and had ridden to hounds with the West Dorset Hunt. A member of the Army and Navy Club in St James's Square, he had apparently travelled up to London twice a month, allegedly on business, occasionally staying the night at his club.

'He used to drive into Bournemouth, leave his Range Rover in the car park and catch a fast train to Waterloo. According to the cleaning lady, he was either going to have lunch with his broker, solicitor or accountant.' Farnesworth lit another cigarette, then snapped the spent match in two and dropped both halves into the ashtray. 'We don't know who they are or even if they exist. What we do know is that Cosgrove inherited Oak Tree Cottage from a maiden aunt who also left him approximately eighty thousand pounds in stocks and shares. Both his parents are dead, he never married, has no brothers or sisters, and his nearest relative is a second cousin who lives in Andover. He had two bank accounts, one with Lloyds in Poole, the other with Glyn Mills in Pall Mall.'

Cosgrove was in receipt of an army pension of just under nine thousand a year which was paid into Lloyds. At the time of his death, his current account had been in credit to the tune of seven hundred and ninety-three pounds forty-five. He also had two thousand on deposit and the current account with Glyn Mills was exactly seventy-one pounds in credit.

'There is no sign of the stocks and shares,' Farnesworth continued. 'However, Cosgrove had kept all the quarterly bank statements he'd received from Lloyds for the past four years and if the receipts are anything to go by, it looks as if he gradually realised them.'

'What about the payments? Any regular sizeable amounts?'

'You mean, was he being blackmailed? There are a number of sub-stantial payments, but the sums vary. He was keen on racing – the flat, over the sticks, point to point; he had an account with William Hill, the bookmakers. He must have been one of their favourite punters – loved the horses but the gee-gees didn't like him. He was also part-owner of a racehorse which was helping to eat him out of house and home. By all accounts, the bloody animal was only fit for the knacker's yard. I reckon the man was living beyond his means and had been doing so for a number of years.' Farnesworth stubbed out his cigarette. 'I've told you all we know,' he said. 'Now what are you going to give me in return?'

'All I know about the relationship between Cosgrove and Oakham,' Ashton told him. 'It's not much and a lot of it is guesswork.'

The facts were simple enough to relate and he covered them in a few brief sentences. Explaining why he believed Cosgrove had been more than just the company commander of the eighteen-year-old pay clerk back in 1975 took a great deal longer.

'Of course, I assumed Cosgrove had been the dominant partner but these snapshots suggest otherwise and maybe I've got it wrong.'

'I don't think so; you've only looked at a few of them. Sometimes the major was compliant but more often than not, he was the ram-pant bull. Don't be fooled by the macho-looking stormtrooper; he was the passive one who bent over.'

'I'll take your word for it,' Ashton said and pushed the rest of the photographs across the table. 'They're a damned sight too strong for my stomach.'

'And most other people's.' Farnesworth paused, then said, 'Have you got a photo of this guy Oakham? Doesn't have to be a negative, we can reproduce from a print.'

'I'll get you one.'

'Good. I'd like to show his face around; maybe somebody will remember seeing him or his dark blue Volvo estate. If you're right about his relationship with Cosgrove, it's likely he will have paid more than one visit to Oak Tree Cottage. Right now, we can't find a single person who saw anything, not even the bloody milkman when he delivered to the house on Saturday and called again on the Monday morning. That's when he found a note stuck in one of the empties telling him no milk until Wednesday.'

The day the cleaning lady arrived. Whoever had been there at the cottage with Cosgrove had been familiar with his domestic arrangements. And if his death had been due to a deviant sex game that had got out of hand, the other man had demonstrated considerable presence of mind in taking steps which should have ensured the body wasn't discovered until the Wednesday morning.

'Whose fingerprints were on the note?' Ashton asked.

'We'll never know,' Farnesworth told him. 'The milkman doesn't remember what he did with it.'

'What about the handwriting?'

'Printed – block capitals. And before you ask, the man from Unigate told us he had no reason to suppose the note hadn't been written by Cosgrove.'

Farnesworth sounded a touch irritated, the way any professional would who felt an amateur was telling him how to do his job. Before Ashton could ask any further questions, he gave him a terse but complete rundown on the investigation to date. Parts of the county had still been affected by snow as late as yesterday morning and yes, the police had found a number of different tyre tracks both in the lane and in the driveway which they were still trying to eliminate. And yes, Forensic were in the process of cross-checking the various fingerprints that had been lifted from the furniture in the master bedroom.

'Happy?'

'Absolutely.' Ashton stood up and shook hands with the Chief Inspector. 'It's very good of you to have spared me the time,' he added.

'My pleasure.'

'Would it be okay if I called you now and again to find out how things are going?'

'I don't see why not.' Farnesworth lit yet another cigarette.

'Only I'd like to know if you do get a match from the Volvo.'

'What?'

'Simon Oakham. I imagine his fingerprints must be on the steering wheel and the gearshift, as well as elsewhere inside the car.'

Farnesworth nodded sagely and said the matter was already in hand, which Ashton thought was pretty rich considering the Chief Inspector hadn't been aware of the connection between Oakham and Cosgrove until he had told him that they had known one another.

Leaving the central police station, Ashton collected his Vauxhall Cavalier from the car park near the Dolphin Centre and headed out of town on the A348 to Ringwood. It was a few minutes after one o'clock and with the weekend looming, he decided to make tracks for Lincoln and surprise Harriet by arriving early for once.

A quarter to four on Friday afternoon, the river as grey as the sky above. The view from Hazelwood's office was no different from the one in the DG's though Dunglass appeared to think otherwise. He had drifted in half an hour ago to pass the time of day with his deputy because nothing too violent was going on in the world at that moment, not even around Sarajevo, and his in-tray was empty. However, he had apparently run out of small talk several minutes ago and now stood in the window contemplating the Houses of Parliament across the river, presenting his back to Hazelwood.

'We don't want any publicity,' he announced suddenly.

Hazelwood presumed the DG was referring to the elected representatives of the people and their desire to make the SIS more accountable.

'It might help if the Secretary of State pointed out that we won't be a Secret Intelligence Service if every Tom, Dick and Harry is entitled to know what we are up to.'

Dunglass turned about. 'I think we are talking at cross-purposes, Victor. I was thinking of Ashton. Of course, I don't know him as well as you do but he strikes me as the sort of man who is difficult to rein in once he gets the bit between his teeth. I don't want him raising a hullabaloo over Simon Oakham.'

'He won't.'

'Correct me if I'm wrong,' Dunglass continued, 'but, so far, the newspapers have paid little or no attention to this Pay Corps captain.'

'Tuesday's edition of the *Independent* carried a short paragraph at the bottom of page six. I believe his absence was also reported in the *Daily Telegraph* and *The Times*.'

'But not in the popular press?'

'No, they didn't run the story.'

'They will, however, spread it all over the front page if they have reason to believe that Oakham was about to be seconded to the SIS. You see what I'm getting at, Victor?'

Hazelwood nodded. 'It's a story which could run and run.'

'"Could" is not the appropriate word. The story will run and, in the process, will sell thousands of extra copies which will please Fleet Street no end.'

'Wapping.'

'What?'

'Most of the press have moved out of Fleet Street,' Hazelwood said.

'A figure of speech, Victor. And it doesn't alter the message – you need to keep an eye on Ashton.'

Hazelwood was about to remind him that he had virtually delegated that job to Kelso when the telephone intervened. Normally, the incoming call would have been intercepted by his PA but she had been off sick all week and the line was permanently switched through to his office.

'Do you mind, Director?' he asked.

'No, you go ahead.'

Hazelwood lifted the receiver, heard the familiar voice and wondered why he should be surprised that Ashton had found some reason to call him. One of the quirks in life was the fact that potentially embarrassing situations invariably arose at the most inopportune moments. He also had to contend with a curious background mush which meant he often had to ask Ashton to repeat himself.

'For God's sake, where are you calling from?' he asked irritably.

'A service station on the A46 roughly five miles south of Newark-on-Trent,' Ashton told him. 'I've just stopped to fill up.'

'Sounds as though you're calling from the far side of the moon.'

'That's the passing traffic you can hear. This is an open booth and I'm freezing. It's bloody cold in this part of the world.'

'You'd better make it snappy then,' Hazelwood said.

The words were no sooner out of his mouth than he wished he had told Ashton to call him back later. Dunglass had lost interest in the Houses of Parliament and had gravitated towards his desk where he hovered like a bird of prey.

Aware that it was an open line, Ashton was being suitably guarded but while their conversation might baffle an interloper, it didn't fool the Director even though he could only hear one side of it. The interrogation began as soon as Hazelwood put the phone down with Dunglass demanding to know what Ashton had had to say for himself.

'Not a lot.'

'Then why did he phone you, Victor? He's supposed to channel everything through Roy Kelso.'

Hazelwood opened the ornately carved wooden box on his desk, one of a pair which he had bought on a trip to India, and took out a Burma cheroot. Smoking was now officially banned in the work place and he had no intention of flouting the rule. The whole charade of piercing the end with a matchstick before placing the cold cigar in his mouth was simply a manoeuvre to give himself time to think. Had it been anyone else, he might get away with a sanitised version of what Ashton had told him but Dunglass was nobody's fool and Hazelwood had no desire to get on the wrong side of him.

'Ashton went down to Poole this morning,' he said, choosing his words carefully. 'Reading between the lines, it looks as though he's been talking to the police about Cosgrove.'

'My God . . .'

'That's not all. Oakham's Volvo estate has been found at a multistorey car park in Portsmouth.'

'And?' Dunglass said, grimly prompting him.

'Ashton wants us to obtain Oakham's photograph from the Passport Office.'

'To give to the police?'

Hazelwood nodded. 'That would be my guess. It's reasonable to assume they are now aware that Oakham had been acquainted with the dead man. And that in turn means they will have already put their forensic people on to the Volvo.'

Dunglass closed his eyes briefly as if in pain, then turned about and went over to the window again. 'Do we know who is in charge of the murder investigation?' he asked presently.

'Detective Chief Inspector Farnesworth.'

'Really? Well, I doubt he would have spared Ashton a moment of his time if someone hadn't pressured him into it. So who paved the way for him, Victor? Someone in MI5?'

'Probably.'

'I'd like him to stay away from DCI Farnesworth. Don't get me wrong,

I've nothing against the Chief Inspector *per se*; it's just that in nearly every police station of any size there's always someone with a hot line to the press. You understand why I am concerned?'

'We don't want to be in the limelight?' Hazelwood suggested.

'Ashton's out of control,' Dunglass said forcefully, 'and you've got to hobble him.'

CHAPTER 6

L ast Tuesday, Hazelwood had summoned him to breakfast at Willow Dene; six days later, Ashton was playing host to the Deputy DG at his flat in Churchill Gardens, the only difference being that Victor had invited himself. He had telephoned late on Sunday evening, shortly after Ashton had returned from Lincoln, to say he was coming. The only fresh sustenance in the flat was the loaf of sliced bread, packet of butter and carton of milk he'd bought from a corner shop just after saying goodbye to Harriet. A jar of instant coffee, the leftovers in the jug of fresh orange juice he'd prepared for breakfast on Friday and had subsequently left in the refrigerator completed the repast.

'Toast and coffee is fine,' Hazelwood assured him. 'I'm not a big eater.'

'That's just as well, there's not a lot to eat.'

'How was the weekend?' Hazelwood asked, changing the subject.

'Quiet but enjoyable.'

'Did you talk to Harriet about Oakham?'

'No, why should I?'

'Does she know you're doing some freelance work for The Firm?'

'Strange as it may seem, Victor, your name never entered the conversation.'

'Good.'

Although Hazelwood didn't actually sigh with relief, Ashton thought he came close to it. 'What's on your mind, Victor?'

'The Director isn't happy with the way things are going. He's worried the press may learn that the police are investigating a possible link between the dead man and the Intelligence Service. Right now, Cosgrove isn't exciting much interest. Certain newspapers whose proprietors and editors have got it in for the Government have tried to play on the fact that he was a Conservative, but since he was only a member of the party association, they're beginning to look pretty foolish. But sex and spies . . .' Hazelwood shook his head. 'Well, that's something really juicy they can get their teeth into.'

'Why don't you get to the point instead of going all round the houses?'

'There is to be no further liaison with Detective Chief Inspector Farnesworth, you are not to approach Oakham's family on any pretext whatever and you can forget about the late Major Richard Cosgrove.'

'So where's the cheque, Victor?'

'What cheque?'

'For my expenses; the train fare to Winchester plus motor mileage allowance from London to Poole and back again. I mean, you are sacking me, aren't you?'

'Don't be bloody ridiculous, the DG is merely laying down some additional ground rules.'

'You employed me to find out why Oakham deliberately sabotaged his Enhanced Positive Vetting clearance—'

'That hasn't changed. Even if he hadn't gone over the hill, Oakham wouldn't have given you his reasons. Neither would his wife, even supposing she had the faintest inkling.'

Hazelwood was right. Oakham wouldn't have made a voluntary statement if it had meant incriminating himself in some way. And Cosgrove was now past answering anyone's questions.

'I suppose you could argue that it all begins with Jackson,' Ashton said doubtfully.

'That's my view,' Hazelwood said with conviction. 'In fact, I had the duty officer at Vauxhall Cross do a little research over the weekend. Jackson was married and although his wife divorced him after he transferred to the Long Service List, she has never remarried.'

'Do we have an address for her?'

'Number 19 Thurleston Road, Wembley.' Hazelwood finished the rest of his coffee and wiped his mouth on a paper napkin. 'Shouldn't take you more than forty-five minutes on the Underground.'

'I'd need to make sure Mrs Jackson was in before I traipsed all the way out there.'

Hazelwood searched through his pockets and found a piece of paper torn from a memo pad. There were some figures scrawled on it. 'We looked her up in the telephone directory.'

The royal 'we' being the unfortunate duty officer, it also becoming clear to Ashton that Victor was not going to hand over the scrap of paper and expected him to make a note of the phone number.

'You mind if I smoke?' he asked, producing a Burma cheroot in a Cellophane wrapper from the breast pocket of his jacket.

'Be my guest.' Ashton left the kitchen table, went in search of the pocket diary Harriet's mother had given him as a small plate present on Christmas Day and unable to find it in a hurry, returned with a used envelope. 'What was that number again?' he asked.

Hazelwood gave it to him. 'You're a writer who has been commissioned to do a non-fiction book on the Hong Kong police – *Great Criminal Cases* or some such nonsense.'

'Do you know something I don't, Victor?'

'You've seen Jackson's record of service. He did three separate tours of duty in the Far East and his last overseas posting was to Hong Kong. Mrs Jackson accompanied him—'

'The guy met his death in Germany,' Ashton said, interrupting him, 'five years after returning from the crown colony. All right, the marriage had broken up by then and she presumably stayed at home in England and can't tell us much about those last few years in Soest. But Hong Kong? I mean, come on, Victor, it's not like you to clutch at straws. You've got to have a reason for zeroing in on that period in his life.'

'The Director said Jackson's name sounded familiar, seemed to remember hearing it when he was with the Far East Bureau, but can't recall the circumstances.'

'He's not being coy, is he?'

'I'm quite certain Stuart isn't. Take it from me, Peter, the older you get, the less reliable your memory becomes. And the Director isn't willing to rely on his; he's ordered a complete search of the Far East records covering the period 1953 to 1970. In other words, from the time of Jackson's first posting to Singapore and Malaya to the final tour in Hong Kong.'

It all sounded very thorough, but who did Victor think he was kidding? Ashton knew damned well that the task was hardly something which could be achieved overnight. Successive reorganisations of the SIS had resulted in the Far East papers being split between the Asian Department and the Pacific Basin which, in turn, had subsequently been merged with the Rest of the World Department.

'What other lies am I going to tell Mrs Jackson? For instance, does this very generous publisher of mine have a name?'

'Ayre and Foulks; their offices are in Bedford Square.'

Thanks to Hazelwood, it seemed he had an editor as well in James Ayre, the younger son of the senior partner. Should Mrs Jackson doubt him, she had only to phone Ayre who would confirm that indeed Mr

Ashton had been commissioned to write a book on Hong Kong, one of a series Ayre and Foulks intended to publish before the colony reverted to China in 1997.

'If things get a bit sticky, let her see the colour of your money. Fifty to seventy-five pounds should loosen her tongue and overcome any objections she may have.'

'Right.'

'Your angle is that soldiers commit offences which are punishable under civil law and her former husband, as a senior warrant officer in the army's Special Investigation Branch, must have had dealings with the Hong Kong police. Ask her what it was like to be a service wife out there, then you can steer the conversation round to Malaya and Singapore.'

'I've got the drift,' Ashton told him, 'you don't have to spell it out.'

'Good.' Hazelwood stood the empty coffee cup on his plate, then stubbed out the cheroot in the saucer. 'I'll be interested to hear how you got on with the lady.'

'Are you saying I don't have to go through Kelso?'

'Well, they do say a change is as good as a rest.'

'The trouble is, I asked him to obtain Cosgrove's personal file . . .'

Hazelwood snapped his fingers. 'Oh, didn't I tell you? It arrived on Friday.'

'That was bloody quick.'

'Yes, wasn't it? I expect some desk officer in the army's Directorate of Security wanted to impress us. Anyway, the file arrived from the Records Office at Hayes by Special Delivery.'

'Can I see it?'

''Fraid not, we turned the file straight round, sent it back to the army.' Hazelwood got up from the table and went out into the hall to collect his raincoat. 'You didn't miss much,' he continued breezily, 'very dull reading.'

Cosgrove had left the army in 1976 at the age of forty-two, having been advised by the Adjutant General's Branch that he was extremely unlikely to be promoted to half-colonel. A perusal of his file had revealed that immediately after his written application to retire, there was a demi-official letter from the commanding officer of the 6th Queen's Westminster Rifles, a Territorial Army battalion which Cosgrove had joined as the training major when he had been posted from Headquarters 1 (BR) corps in Germany. When he wasn't wearing a uniform, the commanding officer was a stockbroker; as a Territorial, he was understandably reluctant to complain about the conduct of a regular officer, but in this instance, he hadn't any choice. One of his junior officers had complained that one evening during the annual camp when the battalion was assembled for collective training, Major Cosgrove had been unduly familiar with him.

Hazelwood opened the front door, stepped out on to the landing and turned about to face him. 'You know what I think, Peter?' he asked. 'No, you tell me.'

'If Cosgrove hadn't gone voluntarily, the army would have booted him out on his arse. And I'll tell you something else, I'd bet my pension he and Oakham were lovers.'

'You won't hear me denying that assumption,' Ashton told him.

'Good. Don't bother to come with me to the Rover, it's only a few yards up the street. Besides, I'd much sooner you got on the phone to Mrs Jackson.'

Ashton waited until the Deputy Director turned the corner and started on down the next flight of steps, then went back inside the hall and closed the door. Returning to the kitchen, he picked up the phone and rang the Wembley number on the off chance. The woman who answered and told him she was indeed Mrs Kathy Jackson had a friendly-sounding voice. She became even more friendly after Ashton told her what he wanted and indicated his publishers would expect to pay her a small fee.

Hazelwood was wrong about one thing. With no Underground service to Wembley Central on the Bakerloo Line other than during the morning and evening peak hours, the journey by bus and train took Ashton a damned sight longer than forty-five minutes. Like all the other houses in the street, 19 Thurleston Road was a three-storey semi-detached that had been built six years before the First World War when metroland was beginning to reach out into the countryside along the spokes of the railways. Ninety years later, the neighbourhood was part of the urban sprawl of Greater London and had a large Asian and West Indian community.

Ashton pushed open the front gate to number 19. Subsidence had affected the tiled path so that the rain which had accompanied the recent thaw had collected in large puddles. The house itself had recently been repainted and looked in good condition until, on closer inspection, he could see that the gloss paint had been applied with a heavy hand to disguise the fact that the window frames and sills needed to be replaced. There were other ravages; several panes in the stained-glass windows either side of the door were cracked and clear glass had been used to replace those that had been broken. As a result, the swallow depicted in the left-hand window looked distinctly bald.

The door itself was brand new and fitted with an electronic lock. He pressed the button for the top flat and stepped a little closer to the mike. Presently, a distorted voice wanted to know who was there.

'My name is Ashton,' he said. 'I phoned you earlier this morning, Mrs Jackson.'

'So you did. Come on up.'

A buzzer tripped the lock and he stepped into the hall to be greeted by the all-pervasive smell of a highly spiced curry. Somewhere else in the house a radio was playing none too softly.

Mrs Jackson was waiting for him on the top landing. Her date of birth according to the original entry of Jackson's Record of Service was 11 January 1933 which made her just over sixty-one. If the lady was a grandmother, she was the most unlikely-looking one Ashton had met. Blonde hair framed a heavily made-up face that must have taken her hours to put on. She wore a figure-hugging mini skirt and angora sweater under a suede jacket, four inch heels raised her height to five nine, a bracelet loaded with silver charms on her left wrist and thin silver chain around the opposite ankle made her look even more grotesque.

'You didn't have no trouble finding me then?' she said.

'No, your directions were very clear, Mrs Jackson,' Ashton said as he shook hands with her.

'Kathy,' she told him firmly. 'No need to be all formal with me.'

'Right.'

'You first.' She stepped aside as if to let him go ahead yet somehow managed to partially block the doorway so that he had to squeeze past her. The aroma of the scent she was wearing was overpowering. 'I was about to make myself a cup of coffee. Will you have one?'

'Thank you – white, please, no sugar.'

'Okay. Sit yourself down, I won't be a minute.'

The sitting room was dominated by the old chimney breast which no longer served a useful purpose, for where the coal grate had once been, there was now a large gas fire. Most of the available space was taken up by a three-piece suite angled to face the colour TV and video in the corner nook opposite the door. A nest of tables and a small bookcase filled the other nook. Half a dozen Hummel figures flanked by two photographs in chromium-plated frames gathered dust on the mantelpiece above the original fireplace.

'My son and daughter,' Kathy Jackson told him from the kitchenette off the sitting room.

'They do you credit,' Ashton said, then asked her where they were living.

'Cheryl's in Vancouver, Rod was in Leeds last time I heard from him two years ago. You want to get one of those tables out from the nest?'

Ashton removed the smallest one of the three and placed it between the armchair and sofa so that Kathy Jackson had something to rest the tray on. When he sat down in the armchair, the table also served to keep her at a reasonable distance.

'So you're a writer?' she said and handed him a cup of coffee.

'Yes. You may not earn a fortune but it's not a bad way of making a living.'

'How many books have you written?'

'This will be the first one under my own name,' Ashton told her, implying there had been others written under a pseudonym.

'And it's about the Hong Kong police and the RMPs?'

'And their families.'

'Sounds boring.'

'Fortunately, my publisher doesn't agree with you.' Ashton, digging into his pocket, brought out a recorder about the size of a Sony Walkman and placed it on the tray. 'You don't mind if we use this when I need to take some notes, do you?'

'Can I ask you a question first?'

'By all means.'

'Why do you want to interview me? I mean, I wasn't the only service wife in Hong Kong whose husband was a military policeman.'

'The Provost Marshal's Branch were very co-operative. My publishers wrote to them asking if they could help us and they suggested we should approach you because your husband had been involved in a number of high-profile cases when he was running the SIB detachment in Hong Kong.'

As explanations went, Ashton thought it was one of the least convincing he'd ever been obliged to deliver. It was convoluted and had more holes in it than a colander. He hoped Kathy Jackson wouldn't ask how he had managed to obtain her address because the army certainly hadn't been able to supply it. They had lost interest in her whereabouts after she had divorced her husband. Knowing the lady was in receipt of a basic pension, he was prepared to bet that Hazelwood had twisted a few arms in the Department of Social Security up at Newcastle-upon-Tyne and had persuaded them to extract her address from the data base on their computer. If that was the way the information had been obtained, everyone involved was skating on thin ice and could even be prosecuted under the Data Protection Act if their activities ever came to light.

'You said something about a fee when we spoke on the telephone.'

'That's right, I did.' Ashton took out his wallet with a sense of relief that she had been content to accept his explanation. On the way to Thurleston Road, he had drawn a hundred pounds from the cashpoint outside Lloyds Bank in Wembley High Street. Although Hazelwood had suggested fifty to seventy-five would be a suitable reward, Ashton didn't want to waste his time here and felt this was not the moment for cheese-paring. He therefore gave her the lot and knew he had made the right decision when she took the money without a moment's hesitation and then wondered aloud how and where she should begin.

'There was this nurse at the British Military Hospital who claimed that she had been raped by two Chinese medical orderlies. That was a pretty big case.'

Ashton switched on the tape recorder and relaxed, content to let her ramble on. He did not expect to hear any startling revelations. Had Jackson been involved in some kind of crooked operation that had eventually led to his death, it was unlikely that he would have told his wife what he was up to.

After a long-winded and somewhat incoherent account of the rape case, she changed tack and he found himself listening to a torrent of chit-chat about the parties she had attended at the garrison warrant officers' and sergeants' mess. A hectic social life had included picnics on Lamma Island, Saturday afternoons spent at the Happy Valley and Shatin race courses, dining in one of Aberdeen's floating restaurants or at Jimmy's Kitchen and dancing the night away to a Filipino band at Gripps. From time to time she would remember that he wanted to hear about the work of the SIB but none of the investigations she could recall could be described as sensational. An outbreak of petty thieving in one unit, embezzlement of public funds by a pay clerk and a captain in the Royal Corps of Transport who had been suspected of stealing property belonging to Her Majesty the Queen, namely five hundred gallons of high-octane fuel. There was nothing there to get excited about.

'I think there's a cardboard box up in the loft containing some papers and a lot of old snapshots. You can have them if they are of any interest to you.' She smiled, affecting modesty. 'Of course, you will have to fetch them down, I can't go climbing a ladder in this skirt.'

'Have you got a torch I can borrow?'

'In the kitchen, along with the stepladder,' she told him.

In all probability there was nothing in the cardboard box apart from a load of junk but at least the snapshots would help to substantiate the claim for expenses. Even so, Kelso would quibble about the sum involved and would be extremely reluctant to hand over a hundred pounds.

Collecting the stepladder from the broom cupboard, Ashton carried it out on to the landing and positioned it directly beneath the trap door in the ceiling. Kathy Jackson volunteered to hold the ladder steady while he stood on the top step and levered himself up into the loft and was more of an embarrassing distraction than a help when she hoiked her skirt and stretched out to pass the flashlight to him.

The loft was a glory hole full of the sort of junk people were reluctant to discard even when they had no further use for it. Amongst other naff items, there was an empty golf bag with a good ten-inch rip in the canvas and an unframed discoloured print of a steam train passing a gang of plate-layers entitled *Rest Day Working*. After exploring a dozen cardboard boxes of all shapes and sizes, he discovered the snapshots in a carton for a steam iron.

'Can you grab hold of this?' Ashton said, and passed the box down to her.

'You found it then?'

'Yes, between the rafters near the water tank.' Ashton lowered himself on to the stepladder, replaced the trap door, then descended to the landing and put everything back where he had found it.

The earlier black and white snapshots were taken when the children were young; only those relating to the final tour in Hong Kong were in colour. Kathy Jackson appeared in most of them, in shorts and suntop, a bikini, street clothes or a low-cut slinky evening dress; a popular, youngish-looking woman who was always smiling into the camera while linking arms with and snuggling up to various men.

'I've weathered well, haven't I?' She pressed a hand against her stomach, then turned sideways on and stuck out a hip and looking at him over her shoulder, patted her right buttock. 'Might have put on a few pounds here and there but I'm no balloon.'

Once a flirt, always a flirt, and maybe a bit more, he thought. But there was no denying that she could knock at least ten years off her age and no one would be any the wiser. She had lost none of her libido either, but the fact remained she was drawing an old age pension and Ashton found her provocative antics in bad taste.

'I didn't know we had so many photos.' Kathy Jackson edged round the armchair and leaned over him, one hand resting lightly on his left shoulder. 'Ought to put the best of them in an album sometime.'

The snapshots, he learned, had been languishing in the loft ever since she had returned from Hong Kong in 1970 when her parents and grandmother had still been alive and living in the house.

'Don't know what I would have done if they hadn't provided me and the kids with a roof over our heads after Len and I split up. Of course, the house is all mine now, had it converted into three flats.'

The newspaper cuttings from the *South China Morning Post, Hong Kong Standard* and the *Star* were right at the bottom of the carton. Ashton removed the paper clip which held them together and looked at each clipping in turn. Dated Monday, 11 and Tuesday, 12 May 1970, they were concerned with the accidental death of a twenty-eight-year-old Chinese American girl called Bernice Kwang who had been drowned at sea. The *Star* carried a photograph of her dinghy which had been found drifting off Cheung Chau Island; the *Hong Kong Standard* said she had been a notable beauty and showed a head and shoulders portrait to prove it. There was another picture of Bernice Kwang in the *South China Morning Post*, this time with a group of Chinese, Eurasian and European friends at a barbecue somewhere out in the New Territories. Among the blurred faces, one looked vaguely familiar; sifting through the batch of colour photos which the Jacksons had taken, he came across the same man again.

'Do you know who this is?' he asked.

Kathy Jackson leaned even closer to him. 'Oh, I remember this picture,' she said. 'The SIB detachment hired a junk to go fishing off Lantau and invited all the wives and girlfriends along. It didn't appeal to me, so I didn't bother. Don't know who the bloke is though, don't remember meeting him either.'

'Any idea what your husband intended to do with these clippings?'

'Search me.'

'May I keep them?'

'I don't see why not. After all, you have paid for them.'

'Thanks.'

'You can have all the snapshots too, except the ones of my kids.'

The only person who interested Ashton was the tow-headed man who had also been photographed at the barbecue with Bernice Kwang. But Kathy Jackson had other ideas and insisted he take all the snapshots she didn't want. Then, having spent an age sorting through the pictures, she managed to delay him a further ten minutes looking for an envelope to put them in, so that it was almost noon by the time Ashton eventually left the house.

Richard Cosgrove had managed to asphyxiate himself while seeking to gratify his kinky tastes, Leonard Jackson had suffocated after diving head first into a snowdrift and Bernice Kwang had fallen overboard and drowned during a sudden squall. While Ashton couldn't see the connecting thread, there were just too many accidental deaths for it to be a coincidence.

CHAPTER 7

Proof that the bush telegraph was functioning as well as ever came when the phone started ringing barely a minute after Ashton had walked into the office which had been set aside for him at Benbow House. Answering it, he wasn't surprised to find Kelso on the line. 'My office now,' the Assistant Director told him curtly and hung up before he had a chance to point out that there was such a word as please.

As if to demonstrate his independence, Ashton made no effort to hurry, thereby giving himself time to cool off while driving Kelso a little closer to apoplexy. Instead of calling for one of the lifts, he walked up to the top floor and as a further wind-up, he exchanged a few words with the PA next door before finally breezing into his office.

'Afternoon, Roy,' he said cheerfully, 'and how are you today?'

'What time do you call this?'

Ashton glanced at his wristwatch. 'I make it 1.35 but I may be a few minutes slow. What have you got?'

Kelso held up a finger and wagged it from side to side like a metronome. 'Don't try coming the old soldier with me,' he said. 'The Director's rung several times wanting to know where you were.'

'He should have asked Victor, he could have told him.'

'Are you trying to be funny?'

'No, but I think someone is.' Ashton pulled up a chair and sat down without waiting to be asked. 'Now, I know I'm supposed to submit everything through you, but I'm a simple soul and when the Deputy DG tells me to do something, I assume it's not a matter for debate. Furthermore, it didn't occur to me that I needed to obtain your permission first. However, perhaps we should seek guidance on that point from Victor Hazelwood himself.'

It was the last thing Kelso wanted to do, and they both knew it. Crossing swords with the Deputy DG was a highly dangerous pastime and it wouldn't be the first occasion Victor had cut him down to size.

'We do like to make things difficult for ourselves,' Kelso said with a nervous laugh. 'This would seem to be yet another classic example of the left hand not knowing what the right is doing.'

There was more than a grain of truth in that, Ashton thought. Sometimes, Victor did forget to inform all concerned, but on this occasion, the oversight had probably been deliberate.

'I went to see Mrs Jackson; Victor thought she might be able to throw some light on her former husband's activities in the Far East.'

'And you asked her straight out?'

'Give Victor a little credit for knowing his job. You don't think he sent me in there without a foolproof cover, do you?'

'Of course not.'

'Is there anything else?'

'Yes. Was she able to help you?' Kelso asked in a small voice.

By imposing a dual chain of command, Hazelwood had placed him in an impossible position where he either lied to Kelso or offered a sanitised version of his conversation with Kathy Jackson. Ashton supposed he could always play down Bernice Kwang and concentrate on the rape case.

'I'm not sure,' he said, temporising. 'You and Victor will have to be the judges of that after you've seen my report.'

'Well, at least we can be thankful she's unlikely to give us anything like the aggro we're having from your friend Detective Chief Inspector Farnesworth.'

'Come on, Roy, I've already had my knuckles rapped over him.'

'You're not exactly the flavour of the month with Brigadier Wells either.'

'The police have found Oakham's fingerprints in the cottage?'

'Thanks to you. They wouldn't have gone over his Volvo with such a fine-tooth comb if you hadn't told told them he had served under Cosgrove.'

Ashton stood up, put the chair back where he had found it and started towards the door.

'Where do you think you're going?' Kelso demanded.

'To write my report.'

'That can wait, I haven't finished yet.'

'Have you listened to yourself, Roy?' Ashton turned about to face him. 'Have you? I mean, are you seriously suggesting that I should have sat on the information and deliberately hampered the investigation? I'm damned sure the Provost Marshal doesn't share your opinion.'

'You know very well I meant nothing of the kind.'

Of course he hadn't. Cosgrove had died in circumstances that were a bonanza for the tabloids. Throw in a serving officer who had computerised the Master Order of Battle for the Ministry of Defence, then add the whiff of an SIS connection and the quality Sundays would see it as their duty to expose the shortcomings of the Intelligence community. That was the very real nightmare which had dominated Kelso's thinking. Ashton, however, was not prepared to be the scapegoat. If the DG, Hazelwood and the rest of the high-priced help had wanted to keep their collective noses clean, they should never have sent him in to kick over a few stones.

'Listen to me, Roy,' he said, talking the Assistant Director down. 'We're not in the business of shielding a murderer. At least, I'm not.' He held up a cautionary finger. 'Now, unless you've got something really important to say to me, I propose to go and write my report. Okay?'

He didn't wait for an answer and Kelso didn't call him back. He wondered how long it would be before the older man saw through his assertion. Just because a matching set of fingerprints had been found in Oak Tree Cottage, it didn't follow that Oakham had killed his former company commander or even that he had been there before doubling back to Portsmouth. The only positive thing to have come out of the whole business was the fact that the Pay Corps captain must have renewed his acquaintance with Cosgrove after being posted to the 24th Royal Dragoons at Tilshead Camp.

Ashton went on down to the third floor and, on impulse, decided to look in on Terry Hicks, the electronics specialist, known as Mr Clean in the trade. Hicks had upset a goodly number of diplomats in his time. The more pompous he thought they were, the more pleasure it gave him to order them out of their offices so that he could sweep the room. A wizard at detecting miniature cameras and listening devices, he was equally good at planting them. Not the easiest man in the world to get along with, he was perpetually at daggers drawn with Kelso.

'Hello, Terry,' he said. 'How's life been treating you?'

'Same as ever,' Hicks told him, 'getting crapped on from a great height.' He smiled and held out his hand. 'Nice to see you again, Mr Ashton. I'd heard you were back.'

'I'm using Miss Egan's old office.'

'Yeah? I miss her too, she was a nice lady.'

'Are they keeping you busy?'

'Got a tour of the Mid East coming up the week after next. Bi-annual security inspections of the embassies in Cairo, Amman, Damascus, Khartoum and Tripoli are due.'

Ashton wondered how to put it because there was no easy way of finding out what he wanted to know. He had danced on tiptoe around the subject but Hicks had failed to pick up on the veiled question and had taken his enquiries literally.

'Don't think I'm being paranoiac,' he said, 'but you haven't been told to bug the phone in my office, have you?'

'What the fuck do you take me for?' Hicks turned brick red, looked as if he was about to burst a blood vessel. 'You think I'd do a thing like that and keep shtoom about it? In the first place, I don't take orders from that prick upstairs and secondly, you'd be the first to know if the acting head of Technical Services had told one of my assistants to do it.'

'Look, I'm sorry. No offence meant, Terry. I should have known you would never pull a stunt like that.'

'And I'll tell you something else,' Hicks said, as though he had never spoken. 'Even if Kelso was daft enough to hire some private contractor to do the business during silent hours, I would have heard about it from the night duty watchman first thing the following morning.'

'I'm sure you would.' Although there were only an infinitesimal number of Secret and Top Secret documents lodged in Benbow House, outside contractors were always accompanied by an MoD policeman who stood guard over them while they carried out the works service.

'Listen, if it will set your mind at rest, I'll give the room a good spring clean after normal office hours today. How does that suit you?'

The suggestion made Ashton feel even more neurotic and he wished he'd never raised the subject. As tactfully as he knew how, he declined the offer and then spent a further five minutes mollifying Hicks who was miffed by his refusal.

Back in Harriet's old office again, he lifted the phone and pressed 9 to obtain an outside line. Much to his surprise, the switchboard operator cut in to ask him what number he wanted while he was still punching out the area code.

'I was trying to make a private call,' Ashton told her with a grain of truth. One of the three phones on Hazelwood's desk was a private number known only to Alice and his closest friends. Incoming calls on that line bypassed both the switchboard and his PA. There was, however, no bypassing the operator at Benbow House; unable to fob her off, he said he was trying to get a Lincoln number, and gave her that of Harriet's parents.

He listened to the high-pitched trill of the slimline in the Egans' drawing room which looked out on to the cricket ground behind the cathedral and wondered who would pick up the phone. He didn't have to wait long to find out.

'Hello, Harriet,' he said, 'it's me.'

'Peter?'

She sounded as if she couldn't believe it was him and he could picture her standing there, forehead wrinkled in a puzzled frown. A tall girl, Harriet was half an inch under six feet, a fact of life which at one time she had tried to disguise by wearing low heels and walking with a stoop. She had large hands with long tapering fingers and was still very self-conscious about the size of her feet, which he had always thought was ridiculous because she would have looked over-balanced with anything less than a seven and a half. Seven months into her pregnancy, Harriet weighed a hundred and sixty-four pounds and was talking wildly of shedding at least forty after the baby was born. If she did take off that amount, Harriet would end up looking like a War on Want poster. And he didn't want her cheeks falling in because although she had had a good figure and would undoubtedly get it back again, it was the perfect symmetry of her face that had first captured his attention and had remained firmly imprinted on his mind ever since. Although unaware of it herself, Harriet was, in fact, quite beautiful.

'Are you still there, Peter?'

'Sorry,' he said, 'I was thinking.'

'About what?'

'You,' he said truthfully. 'I just wanted to be sure you were okay.'

'I'm fine, I've been doing my exercises.'

'Good, that's what I like to hear.'

'I'm sorry I was so bitchy to you on Sunday. I didn't mean to be; it's just that I hate the way Victor keeps making use of you. I know you feel indebted to him but as I see it, the scales are pretty evenly balanced.'

They were heading straight for the quicksands. He had phoned Harriet because the operator had intercepted his attempt to obtain an outside line and had asked what number he wanted. He had told Hazelwood that his name hadn't even been mentioned when he'd seen Harriet over the weekend, never mind Oakham's. Neither statement was true; he wasn't prepared to deceive Harriet, and had told her he was freelancing for the SIS.

'I shouldn't have taken my anger out on you—'

'Hey,' Ashton said, chipping in, 'there's no need to apologise to me.'

But she wanted to, and there was no stopping her. After a while, he didn't even bother to try. If the operator was monitoring their conversation, Hazelwood would learn what she regarded were a few home truths about himself. It would have no effect on Victor however; he would only conclude that the injury she had suffered in Berlin had made her somewhat irrational.

'Where are you calling from?' Harriet suddenly asked.

'Your old office.'

'Well, you be careful.'

'And you,' he told her.

'Oh, I will. Having this baby means more to me than anything else in the world.'

Or anyone, Ashton thought as he slowly replaced the phone.

He walked along to the clerk's office, told the Chief Archivist he was just popping out to pick up a sandwich from the local delicatessen, then took the lift down to the ground floor. Before returning to Benbow House with a cheese and onion roll, he rang Alice Hazelwood from the pay phone near the junction of Southwark Street and Blackfriars Road. After living with Victor for more than twenty years, she had long since ceased to be surprised by anything. The fact that one of her husband's former subordinates who had left The Firm should insist on inviting himself to drinks at six that evening was almost par for the course. Nor did she think it odd when Ashton insisted she phone Victor to remind him they had people coming to dinner and not to be late home.

The telex which Detective Chief Inspector Farnesworth had drafted was addressed to Interpol Headquarters, St Cloud. It read:

Request that Red Notice be issued in respect of Simon Oakham. Description: Age – thirty-six; Height – five feet seven and a quarter; Weight – one thirty-eight pounds; Colour of hair – black; Colour of eyes – deep blue. No visible distinguishing marks but is slender and small-boned, has long black eyelashes and could pass as a woman. Wanted for questioning in connection with the murder of Richard Cosgrove at Oak Tree Cottage, Poole, Dorset on night 19/20 February 1994. Subject known to have boarded Brittany Ferry departing Portsmouth for Cherbourg at

20.00 hours Sunday, 20 February. Photograph follows under separate cover. Grateful if Red Notice could be allocated an XD prefix.

A Red Notice was the equivalent of an international arrest warrant, the XD prefix would indicate that it had top priority. The head and shoulders photograph of Oakham had been provided by the army and was the duplicate of the one affixed to his officer's identity card. Before the telex could be dispatched, the draft had to be seen and approved by the Assistant Chief Constable (Operations).

Farnesworth just hoped the great man wouldn't object to the wording and be tempted to amend it. Unfortunately, it was by no means certain Cosgrove had been murdered and in stating that Oakham was wanted for questioning, there was a definite implication that the police believed he had killed him. Furthermore, there was no proof that he had boarded a ferry, merely a not unreasonable supposition. In Farnesworth's opinion, any dilution of these assertions would have serious repercussions. Oakham already had a week's head start and there was a very real risk that the notice would be treated like a request for information if the text was watered down.

Ashton wasn't sure who was the more relieved when Hazelwood finally arrived from the office, himself or Alice. Although Victor was only half an hour late, the minutes ticked by painfully slowly. Alice had an alarming habit of asking the most direct and personal questions, and she had spent the entire time grilling him about Harriet. To say Alice was nosy was an understatement; she had wanted to know when he proposed to marry Harriet and why he hadn't already done so. And no matter how many times he told her, she had refused to accept it was Harriet who had postponed the date indefinitely. The fact was, he wouldn't have been quite so forthcoming nor Alice quite so inquisitive if she had been a little less heavy-handed with the whisky bottle. With the equivalent of two very generous doubles under his belt, Ashton thought it was a good thing he wasn't driving. It was also the reason why he had refused Hazelwood's offer of another one after they'd adjourned to his study and Alice had stomped off to the kitchen.

'So what's all this cloak-and-dagger stuff?' Hazelwood asked and busied himself with the inevitable Burma cheroot.

'I tried to ring your private number at Vauxhall Cross from the office. All I got was the operator at Benbow House.'

'Are you saying you couldn't obtain an outside line?'

'I could last Thursday,' Ashton told him, 'but not today.'

'I'll look into it.' Hazelwood struck a match and held it to the cheroot. 'Now tell me what you've got,' he said between puffs.

Ashton took out the small tape recorder he had used that morning and placed it on the desk, then depressed the play button and adjusted the volume to give Victor the full benefit of Kathy Jackson's tittle-tattle.

'You don't know what I went through to get that,' he said when her rambling account came to an end.

'What was in the cardboard box she mentioned?'

'Mostly dross, except for some newspaper cuttings about a Chinese American girl called Bernice Kwang. Ever heard of her?'

'The name doesn't ring a bell with me.'

'She arrived in Hong Kong in January 1969 and was drowned six-teen months later when her dinghy was caught in a sudden squall off Cheung Chau Island.' Ashton produced the clippings from the *South China Morning Post, Hong Kong Standard* and the *Star* and gave them to Hazelwood. 'In between time, she had become something of a celebrity and had acquired a wide circle of friends.' He placed the snapshot of the fishing party from the SIB detachment beside the photo-graph of a barbecue which had appeared in the *South China Morning Post.* 'Among them was this man.'

'A military policeman?'

'I don't know. Kathy Jackson couldn't put a name to him. Further-more, she was pretty sure they hadn't met one another. I wondered if the DG might recognise his face?'

'Stuart was based in Singapore. What trips he did make to Hong Kong were few and far between. When he did fly into Kowloon, he wasn't in the colony for more than two or three days at a time.' Without looking up from the clippings, Hazelwood reached out in the direction of the ashtray, aimed his cigar at it and missed the intended target by a good couple of inches. 'Did Mrs Jackson know why her husband had kept these clippings?'

'She told me she had no idea what he had intended to do with them.'

'Jackson never did anything without he had a reason,' Hazelwood said, and then looked as if he could have bitten off his tongue.

'You've been holding out on me, Victor,' Ashton said quietly. 'Jackson isn't just a name the Director vaguely remembers hearing somewhere; the guy's on record.'

'One of our officers attached to JSIS crossed swords with him in 1969.'

JSIS was the official abbreviation for the Joint Services Intelligence Section. As the title indicated, the unit was staffed by personnel drawn from the army, navy and air force. Working alongside them was a small SIS cell and a Mandarin-speaking signals intercept detachment from Government Communications Headquarters, Cheltenham.

'You know, 1969 was not a good year,' Hazelwood said after a long reflective silence. 'With over half a million men on active duty in Vietnam, the Americans had accepted they were not going to win the war. The Russians were busily supplying the Viet Cong with enough material to keep four hundred thousand men in the field and in China, the Red Guards were still on the rampage spreading the message of the Great Proletarian Cultural Revolution which had started in 1966. Not surprisingly, the Intelligence community worldwide were burning the midnight oil. At our behest, the army element of JSIS ran a countersubversion operation code-named Cyclops in what is now known as Guangdong Province. Their task was to destroy the cross-border threat posed by the Red Guards.'

To do that, they had first to recruit a network of agents from within Hong Kong which had meant going cap in hand to the police for help. Their Special Branch hadn't been too happy about this because they felt the army was muscling in on their territory. The key to success had lain in establishing good relations with the police, and no one had been better at this than Sergeant Gary Newton of the Intelligence Corps.

'He and his Chinese counterpart were as close as two peas in a pod,' Hazelwood continued. 'Between them they recruited far and away the best team of agents committed to the operation.'

'So how does Jackson enter the picture?'

'You know as well as I do that most individuals who allow themselves to be recruited as covert agents by a foreign power are scarcely admirable characters. A few, and only a very few, sign up because they are politically motivated and there are some who do it for the thrill it gives them. Most, however, get involved because they are greedy and want the money, or else they're crooked and expect us to keep the police off their backs while they go about their business.'

Apart from one or two exceptions, Newton's team had been recruited from the Black Dragon Triad who had dealt in opium for the masses, heroin for the up-market people and girls for every socioeconomic group known to man. In return for a percentage of their turnover, members of the Triad working for British Intelligence had been granted immunity from prosecution by the Drug and Vice Squads. The cut had been used to buy gold, the most potent weapon for bribery, corruption and ultimately destroying the Red Guard leadership in the border region of Guangdong Province. It had been a risky business all round; some of the Triad agents who had been sent across the border had been caught, tried and publicly executed by Chairman Mao's disciples.

'The drug and vice squads detested the setup and never ceased to complain about it. Then the SIB got into the act and went after Newton. He was a member of the garrison warrant officers' and sergeants' mess and had fallen out with Jackson. I don't know the cause but there was certainly a great deal of mutual antagonism. Anyway, Jackson had put him under surveillance; apparently, he persuaded the Assistant Provost Marshal that Newton was trafficking drugs.'

After playing tag with him for roughly a fortnight, the RMP in conjunction with the Kowloon division of the Hong Kong police had raided the Nanking Palace Hotel on Jordan Road. To all intents and purposes, the Nanking had been a brothel and Newton had been caught in a hotel bedroom with two Triad agents, a prostitute, eight thousand pounds worth of gold bullion and six ounces of heroin pills. The bullion had been destined for Canton where it would have ended up in the pockets of a particularly nasty member of the Red Guard which would have done him no good at all. The heroin had been a kickback for the couriers who were to deliver the gold.

'The SIB alleged that Newton was on the take; he claimed that Jackson had offered to keep his mouth shut for a consideration and had only launched the investigation after he had turned him down.'

'Was there any truth in either accusation, Victor?'

'I'm inclined to believe Newton,' Hazelwood said, 'but at the same time, I think he allowed himself to become slightly tainted. Whatever the truth of the matter, Operation Cyclops was terminated after the raid on the Nanking Palace. Now you know why Jackson came to our notice and why the current DG remembers his name.'

'What happened to Sergeant Newton?'

'I understand he bought himself out of the army.'

'I think we should do our best to locate him,' Ashton said.

'Why?'

'Well, let's assume Jackson did try to put the bite on him. Maybe he also thought he had something on the tow-headed man who was at the barbecue with Bernice Kwang? Maybe that's what got him killed five years later.'

'You're hoping Newton can put a name to the mystery man?'

'It's got to be worth a try,' Ashton said.

CHAPTER 8

Brian Lambert was thirty-one years old, came from Brisbane and was the Australian exchange officer at Vauxhall Cross. He had initially been attached to the Pacific Basin Department but was now soldiering on in the Rest of the World, following the merger of the two under one Assistant Director. The reorganisation had prompted him to wonder aloud if the poms weren't trying to convey some subtle message concerning the status of his country. No slouch, he was fluent in both Mandarin and Cantonese. He also had a droll sense of humour which appealed to Ashton who knew Lambert by sight but had never had much to do with him before. Neither had Kelso who found him hard to take although he did his best to disguise it.

'This fella Newton is like an Abo,' Lambert said, exaggerating his Australian accent because he had already discovered it grated on Kelso. 'Gone walkabout long time.'

'Really?' Kelso inclined his head and put on a wise expression.

'Took me two days to find the bugger,' Lambert told him, poker-faced. He bent down and extracted a file from the briefcase on the floor by his right ankle. A pale buff colour with a St Andrew's cross in blue on the front and back covers, it was also stamped Secret in block capitals top and bottom. 'The guy's security clearance was downgraded to Confidential by the Director of Security (Army) on 4 November 1969. I guess that did for him. Right?'

Ashton nodded. The Intelligence Corps was a closed arm, meaning that every soldier needed to be PV cleared in order to have constant access to Top Secret material. Confidential in those days was defined as material being damaging to the nation if disclosed to an unauthorised person.

'The minute sheets on the inside of the front cover make interesting reading,' Lambert said, pushing the file across the table to Ashton. 'The head man of the Int Corps was really pissed off with the Director of Security.'

Newton had been trained as an Operator, Intelligence and Security; he had also attended a photo interpreter's course and obtained an 'Outstanding' grading which was rarely awarded. But without a PV clearance, his qualifications were of no use to anyone. The point-blank refusal to restore Newton's clearance to anything higher than Secret over two years after the restriction had originally been imposed had really sent the Director of the Intelligence Corps into orbit.

'Fascinating though they may be,' Kelso said in an aggrieved tone of voice, 'I don't believe these biographical details are of any relevance.'

They were seated round a twelve-by-six mahogany table in what the Assistant Director, Admin liked to call his conference room, a facility that had come into being when it was decided that a reference library was no longer required. His PA had provided coffee, not your usual instant stuff, but the real McCoy made from ground Colombian beans in a cafetière. She had also tastefully arranged half a dozen shortbread biscuits in a fan on a Crown Derby plate that had not been provided by the Property Services Agency. But instead of according him the deference due to a senior officer, Kelso felt that they had treated him like an interloper.

'What we want to know is the present whereabouts of Newton,' he said, asserting his authority.

'You're quite right.' Ashton put the security file to one side. 'Whenever you're ready, Brian,' he added with a faint smile.

'Well, he's living near Nottingham, has a house in a place called Burton Joyce, and is doing pretty well for himself by all accounts. The police told me Newton's got fifty people working for him.'

'The police?' Kelso echoed.

'He has his own security outfit; the head office is in Friar Lane off Maid Marian Way.' Lambert reached for his briefcase again and this time placed it on the table. He took out two sheets of A4, passed one to Ashton, the other to Kelso. 'I think you'll find I've covered the essentials – home address and private number, precise location of office including phone number of security firm, particulars of family – four children, three girls aged twenty-five, twenty-three and twelve and a boy aged eight. Only the younger two are living at home. Wife's name Roberta, Robbie for short. Incidentally, she's wife number two, that's why there's a big age gap between the second and third child.'

'You have been busy,' Ashton said.

'Well, like the call girl said to the client, we aim to give satisfaction.' He snapped his fingers. 'Almost forgot. A copy of the certificate Newton signed, which reminded him that he would still be subject to the Official

Secrets Acts when he left the army, is pinned on the inside of the back cover of his security file. You may have to wave it under his nose; he can get pretty stroppy at times.'

'You've been in touch with him?'

Lambert scratched an itch under his chin. 'I haven't, your army has. His former Record Office warned him he could expect a visit from an officer in the Security Service. He got the same message from the Commandant of the Int Corps Depot and Training Centre.'

'When is this supposed to happen?' Ashton asked.

'This afternoon or first thing on Friday morning.'

'That doesn't give me much time.'

'It can't be helped. Both the Record Office and the Int Corps Depot had a hard time getting in touch with him. Newton wouldn't return any of their calls. In the end, the Commandant of the Training Centre told his wife that if he didn't ring back, there was every chance the police would come knocking on their door. He was bluffing of course, but she wasn't to know that.' Lambert shook his head, apparently in sorrow. 'I tell you, Newton is one very pissed-off joker. That's why you've been given so little notice; I guess it's his way of getting back at us.'

'Thanks for the tip. Have you had any better luck with Bernice Kwang?'

'No, we're busy getting nowhere with that one. We haven't uncovered anything you haven't already learned from the *South China Morning Post* and the *Hong Kong Standard*. By the way, do you need the press cuttings?'

Ashton shook his head. 'I made photocopies of them.'

'Seems the Deputy DG was right, he told my boss you would. How about the snapshot?'

'I've still got the original.'

Before seeing Victor at his house on Monday night, he had got Hicks to produce several copies of the photo of the barbecue which the tow-headed man had attended with Bernice Kwang. The technicalities of how this was done still escaped him despite a detailed step-by-step explanation from Hicks; what counted with Ashton was the fact that the copies were almost as good as the original.

'Well, I guess that about covers it,' Lambert said, looking at each man in turn. 'Unless you two gentlemen have any points you'd like to raise?'

'I don't believe we have,' Kelso said in his most authoritative manner which only came to the fore in matters of little consequence.

It wasn't the best note to end on and the Australian was looking pretty tight-lipped when he left. Ashton thanked him and said he would be in touch if he needed any further information, but the damage had already been done.

'Congratulations, Roy,' he said drily when they were alone, 'you really put him in his place.'

'I didn't care for his attitude. He was also extremely verbose and we would have been here all day if I hadn't cut him short. And there are things we have to discuss.'

'Such as?'

'Such as the line you are going to take with Newton.'

This, it rapidly transpired, was a matter on which Kelso had very definite views. Ashton wondered what was the more galling, to find he had no real quarrel with the guidelines or the fact that he was taking instructions from a man who had never conducted a hostile interrogation in his life. The truth was that he had no intention of linking Jackson to Cosgrove and Oakham when he questioned the former Intelligence Corps sergeant.

'I think I can handle it,' he said with heavy irony when Kelso finally ran out of breath.

'Good. I'll get my PA to ring British Rail and find out about the trains to Nottingham.'

'That won't be necessary, I'm taking my car. If there's any running around to be done, I don't want to have to rely on public transport.'

'It's quicker by rail and we're on a tight budget.'

'Well, don't let it get you down, Roy. I won't bill you for motor mileage allowance.'

Ashton picked up Newton's security file, told Kelso he needed to study it before going to Nottingham, and returned to his office. He concentrated on the minute sheets beginning with the note from a junior desk officer drawing his superior's attention to the SIB report from the Hong Kong detachment which had just been received by the Directorate. Initially, the army's Director of Security had wanted to deny Newton access to all classified material, but the Commandant of the Intelligence Corps had lobbied hard on his behalf and in the end, it had been agreed that he could have a sight of material graded Confidential.

However, long before this compromise had been agreed, Newton had been removed from post and returned to the Intelligence Corps Depot at Ashford. Two years later, he had bought himself out of the army, convinced in his own mind that no matter what he did, his PV clearance would never be restored. And he had been right; every appeal for a review had been rejected, apparently after consulting other Intelligence agencies. There was nothing on the minute sheet to show whether the objections had been raised by MI5 or the SIS. Furthermore, neither agency had conveyed their views in writing. Turning to the back, Ashton removed the warning certificate under the Official Secrets Act which Newton had signed, then locked the file away in the safe.

He estimated it would take him just over an hour to return to the flat in Churchill Gardens, pack a bag and get to the M1. In the event, a much reduced off-peak service on the Underground and a traffic accident on the Edgeware Road made a nonsense of his calculations.

Ashton had spent three years in Nottingham reading Russian and German at the university and fancied he knew the city like the back of his hand. However, as he rapidly discovered, much had changed since those days. Unfamiliar with the one-way system, he managed to get in the wrong lane and compounding the error, found himself heading out of town on the A52 to Derby. He turned right, then right again at the junction of Milton Boulevard with the Ilkeston Road and made his way back to the centre. Feeding into Upper Parliament Street, he abandoned the notion of leaving the Vauxhall Cavalier in the multi-storey car park off Maid Marian Way and settled for the Victoria Centre instead. From there it was only a five-minute walk to Newton's offices in Friar Lane.

The Vanguard Security Company was on the second floor of a grey, undistinguished building at the top end of Friar Lane. If Newton had deliberately set out to hide the firm from the general public, he could not have done a better job. There was no sign above the street door and only a black arrow on the interior wall of the narrow hallway which pointed to the concrete staircase. Above the directional sign there was a logo depicting a watchful eye and a fierce-looking German shepherd that seemed to conflict with an invitation to 'Please Walk Up'.

There was an open-plan waiting room off the landing which was just big enough to accommodate two fireside chairs and a small round table facing a frosted glass partition with a wooden, sliding panel that resembled a serving hatch. The magic word 'Enquiries' was stencilled above it and there was a buzzer to attract the attention of the clerical staff lurking behind the partition. Ashton pressed the button, identified himself to the frizzy blonde who appeared in the hatchway and told her Mr Newton was expecting him. As if to demonstrate his contempt for Whitehall, the former Intelligence Corps sergeant kept him waiting for a good twenty minutes.

The last subject interview in the security file had been carried out in 1965 when Newton had been aged twenty-one. Nearly thirty years later, he was no longer the slim, compact young man the vetting officer had described. His face had filled out and he had acquired a double chin. Despite the well-cut double-breasted suit, no tailor could disguise the middle-age spread occasioned by a largely sedentary job coupled with a high standard of living. Lambert had said he might be an awkward cuss to deal with and the Australian was plumb right. Before shaking hands with Ashton, he demanded to see his identity card.

'I want to be sure you are who you say you are. One thing I've learned about you people in MI5 and the SIS is that you have a nasty habit of using names which don't belong to you.'

'Mine does,' Ashton told him.

'So it would seem.' Newton returned the ID. 'I had a phone call from the Commandant of the Int Corps Depot and Training Centre. He wouldn't explain how he'd managed to trace me but I guess you did it for him through my national insurance number. You lifted it from my Record of Service and got the Department of Social Security to run it through their computer. Am I right?'

'You could be,' Ashton said and sat down.

'I can be equally vague.'

'About Warrant Officer Jackson?'

'That bastard.' Newton scowled. 'He really fitted me up. Of course, Jackson couldn't have done it without a little help from his cronies in the Drug and Vice Squads.'

Newton's version of the raid on the Nanking Palace Hotel in Jordan Road was at odds with the one he had heard from Hazelwood. The former Intelligence Corps sergeant had been caught in one of the bedrooms with two Triad agents and eight thousand pounds worth of gold bullion but the prostitute and six ounces of heroin had arrived with the Hong Kong police. After smashing the door down with a sledgehammer, they had charged into the room and set about the two Chinese with their truncheons.

'I wasn't actually present when the police beat them up because this British plain-clothes officer had two of his constables frogmarch me into a vacant bedroom down the other end of the corridor. But I could hear them hollering blue murder. When they fetched me back, there were spots of blood all over the place – on the tiled floor, the bedcovers and on the wall abutting the shower – but no sign of the Triad men. They were long gone and I never did see them again. There were, however, a couple of newcomers – a Chinese whore who was blubbing her eyes out and Warrant Officer Jackson. The whore claimed she had grabbed her clothes and run into the shower room when the police started to break the door down. I was supposed to have picked her up on Nathan Road and taken her to the Nanking Palace.'

'Why?'

'Because according to the police, I didn't want the hotel staff to remember my face. Lots of Europeans used to check into the hotel with a Chinese girl; the place was as good as a knocking shop. Anyway, this scrubber claimed she was present when I was haggling with the Triad men over the price of the heroin on offer.'

'Eight thousand pounds worth of gold bullion for six ounces of H,' Ashton said derisively. 'They didn't seriously expect anyone to believe that fairy tale, did they?'

'No, they had a much cleverer scenario. The bullion was simply proof of my ability to buy what they were prepared to sell; likewise, the heroin was just a sample of their wares. If we had agreed a price, the deal would have been concluded at some future date at some other place.'

'And what were you going to do with the heroin?'

'The police reckoned I was planning to sell the stuff to the Yanks. In those days, lots of American servicemen flew into Hong Kong for R and R from Vietnam.'

'Was Jackson present while all this was going on?'

'No. He arrived some time after the police broke into the bedroom and before I was wheeled back inside. The bastard must have been sitting in his unmarked car outside the hotel. He had one of his sergeants with him, I forget his name now but it would be in the SIB report.'

The sergeant had not been a party to the conspiracy. In Newton's opinion, Jackson had brought him along because he had needed an independent witness who could testify on oath that a quantity of heroin had been found in the bedroom.

The rest of Newton's story tallied with Hazelwood's account of the affair; elements of the Hong Kong police had always been bitterly opposed to Cyclops and they had taken what they considered appropriate action to close the operation down. Jackson had put him in the frame for personal reasons.

'He thought some of the money allocated to the operation was going into my pocket because my life style was way above what a sergeant could afford. And, in a way, he was right. But it so happened that my first wife had a well-paid secretarial job with Butterfield and Swire's, one of the largest business corporations in the Far East.' Newton cleared his throat, then looking anywhere but in Ashton's direction. 'Later I discovered she'd received a number of very generous presents from guys she had dated whenever I happened to be on duty. Anyway, it looked pretty bad for me, especially when the police had proof that my Chinese Special Branch officer was on the payroll of the Black Dragon Triad.'

Newton's career in the army had been finished. Although he had soldiered on for almost another two years, there had never been the slightest chance that his security clearance would be fully restored and in the end, this simple fact had finally dawned on him and he had purchased his discharge. Ashton thought he was a lucky man in one sense; with so much damning evidence against him, he could have ended up in prison if his superior officers hadn't stood by him.

'How big a crook was Jackson?' he asked.

'The quick answer has to be pretty small. To be accurate, he was basically dishonest. Jackson would entertain his police cronies in the garrison warrant officers' and sergeants' mess and put them down as official guests, which meant we all had to pay for the booze they consumed. Since he was the mess president, there wasn't much we could do about it. He enjoyed a great reputation with the American consular officials as a fixer. A number of the US servicemen who came to Hong Kong on R and R would go pretty wild – get blind drunk and beat up on some Chink – that kind of thing. Anyway, whenever one of them got into trouble with the police, Jackson would sort it out by greasing a few palms to get the charges dropped. Rumour had it that he would then shake the Yank down for twice the amount he had paid out in bribes.'

'You're saying he was just a petty crook?'

'I don't think he had an opportunity to be more than that. But don't run away with the idea that he didn't have the nerve; he was ruthless enough for anything. The bastard would have left me to rot behind bars and slept easy in his bed at nights.' Newton shot back his cuff, glanced at the Rolex wristwatch and frowned. 'Five thirty,' he said. 'Time I called it a day and went home.'

'Two more questions.'

'No. You arrived late and I've better things to do.'

'You made your point by keeping me waiting for twenty minutes.'

'Come back tomorrow.'

'Don't think I won't,' Ashton told him. 'I'll be waiting outside your house when you come down to breakfast and from then on, where you go, I will follow. Now, I don't know how that will affect your business or what your clients will think . . .'

Newton mulled it over. Outside, the sky grew darker, reflecting his expression, and then the rain which had been around all day, started falling again.

'All right, Mr Ashton,' he said eventually, 'you can have your twenty minutes.'

Ashton reached inside his jacket, took out the press clippings and passed the one from the *Hong Kong Standard* to Newton. 'This is Bernice Kwang, a Chinese American girl,' he said. 'Maybe you know of her?'

Newton looked at the head and shoulders photograph, ran his eye over the column inches describing her accidental death at sea, and then returned the clipping to Ashton. 'After my time,' he said. 'I left Hong Kong in October '69, this girl died in May '70.'

'She arrived sixteen months earlier.'

'Doesn't make any difference, I'd never heard of her until just now.'

'Have a look at this one,' Ashton said and gave him the piece from the *South China Morning Post*.

'What's the matter with you? I've already said I don't know the bloody woman.'

'Look at the man standing next to her at the barbecue.' Ashton slapped the colour snap face up on the desk and pushed it towards Newton. 'Here he is again on a fishing trip with members of the SIB detachment.'

There was a long silence broken only by the sound of the rain slashing against the window as the wind got up. The longer it went on, the more Ashton hoped he hadn't driven damned nearly a hundred and thirty miles in god-awful weather merely to draw a blank.

'I remember this guy,' Newton said, 'or at least someone who looked remarkably like him. What's he done?'

'I haven't the faintest idea.'

'I saw him on a couple of occasions with Mr Reeves.'

Ashton didn't ask him who Reeves was, taking the view that sometimes it was wiser to pretend to know more than was actually the case.

'One time they were having a drink at this topless bar in Wanchai. Second time, I caught a glimpse of them boarding the Star Ferry to Kowloon. Can't remember the guy's name though – Tom something or other.' Newton shook his head. 'One of the bar girls told me he was a rich American with a house up on the Peak above Victoria.'

'That's a good one.'

'It certainly is. You need to be a millionaire several times over to buy a house in that district. He was having her on, but there was nothing unusual about that. I mean, everybody used to take the mickey out of the bar girls, it was practically a national pastime. But this Tom struck me as being a bullshitter through and through. I think his whole life was one big lie. You meet guys like him who get a vicarious thrill from being on the fringe of the Intelligence world. They're going somewhere on their own account and they do the odd errand for you and all of a sudden they're talking the in language and passing themselves off as members of "The Firm", "Box", the SIS or MI5.' Newton returned the snapshot with the clipping from the *South China Morning Post*. 'Sorry I can't be of more help,' he said and even sounded as though he meant it.

'I'm the one who should be apologising,' Ashton told him. 'I've taken up a lot of your time.'

'Forget it.' Newton walked him to the door, locking up as he went. 'Do you know what happened to that toerag Jackson?' he asked.

'He's dead.'

'Really? Well, I can't pretend I'm sorry to hear that. He stitched me up and finished my career in the army. Now I've got a six-bedroom house in a two-acre plot of land, the youngest daughter is at Roedean, the boy's down for Eton and I'm driving around in a '93 top-of-the-range BMW, but even so, I'd sooner be in uniform. Crazy, isn't it?'

'It is from where I'm standing,' Ashton said with a smile.

They parted company outside on the street, Newton hurrying to the underpass which would take him to the multi-storey car park the other side of Maid Marian Way, while Ashton set off in the opposite direction towards 'Slab Square' and the Victoria Centre. He had driven a long way for just a name but the man called Reeves was not untraceable. Ashton believed there was every chance he was an SIS officer detached from the Far East Bureau. If his assumption was correct, then Reeves would certainly be known to the DG.

CHAPTER 9

T he girls called goodbye from the hall, then slammed the front door behind them before they ran off down the path, and suddenly the house on Greenham Avenue was oppressively silent. Long after the school bus had picked them up from the stop at the bottom of the road, Louise Oakham was still hunched over the breakfast table in the kitchen, eyes hooded against the drifting smoke from the cigarette in her left hand. The dreamlike state persisted until the glowing ember reached her fingers and burned the skin.

'Damn.' Louise Oakham shook her left hand to dislodge the cigarette, then shoved both fingers into her mouth and licked them. In the time it took her to pick up the cigarette with her free hand and stub it out on her side plate, the hot ash had made a neat round hole in the tablecloth. 'Damn, damn, damn.'

The outburst was a measure of her pent-up feelings. She just knew it was going to be one of those stressful days when there was one disaster after another, but what was so unusual about that? Life had been one long nightmare ever since the adjutant of the 24th Royal Dragoons had telephoned her that Monday morning to ask her what had happened to Simon. 'You tell me,' she had snapped, 'you put him in charge of the rear details for the past fortnight while the Regiment was away playing soldiers.'

And that had led to shock number one because the toffee-nosed upper-class twit had coldly informed her that the 24th Royal Dragoons were busy preparing for the annual 'Fitness for Role' inspection and had never left Tilshead Camp.

Louise Oakham cleared the breakfast things, stacked the side plates, cups and saucers in the Indesit, then put the tablecloth in the washing machine before going upstairs to change. The phone call from the adjutant had started the ball rolling. Shortly after lunch, the Assistant Provost Marshal from Headquarters United Kingdom Land Forces had

81

turned up on her doorstep accompanied by the major commanding the RMP company stationed at Wilton and a police constable. The two army officers had said they were very concerned about Simon and had wanted to know when she had last seen her husband and whether he had seemed worried or distracted. 'About what?' she had asked.

The APM had wondered if they were finding it hard to make ends meet and had then coyly raised the possibility that perhaps Simon had been seeing another woman and it had all got a bit too much for him. Louise opened the right-hand drawer in the dressing table, took out a clean pair of socks and put them on. Another woman? God, that had been a laugh. Simon's libido was practically non-existent and how they had managed to conceive five-year-old Lucy had to be something of a miracle. But of course she had kept that bit to herself; just how well Simon performed in bed was no business of theirs. As far as the army was concerned, they were not strapped for cash and Simon hadn't got a bit on the side.

The APM had been very sympathetic and understanding, unlike the RMP major who had brutally advised her to put a stop on their joint bank account before Simon cleaned it out. There had been another bad moment when she had unlocked their deed box to produce Simon's passport for their perusal and had discovered it was missing. In the circumstances, the two army officers had had no difficulty in getting her to agree that she would try to persuade her husband to give himself up should he get in touch with her.

What a joke. How long had Simon been on the run now? Three weeks going on four? And still no word from him. Louise shucked off her dressing gown and the cotton nightdress she had purchased from the local branch of Marks and Spencer. Despite central heating, the room was none too warm and she finished dressing as quickly as possible, choosing a roll-neck sweater to go with her slacks. She looked at her reflection in the dressing table mirror and automatically reached for the hairbrush. No one was going to hear from Simon if what Detective Chief Inspector Farnesworth had told her on Friday were true.

Richard Cosgrove: Simon had never mentioned his name, but it would seem that they had known one another rather well. She had gone through her diary for 1993 counting the number of weekends when Simon had allegedly been on duty. None in the first quarter, five between April and late July, then a fortnight off in August when they had gone to

Salcombe on holiday. Home every weekend in September, on duty once in October, twice in November, the same in December and again in January of this year. She wondered how many of those missing weekends Simon had spent with Cosgrove?

In a roundabout way, Farnesworth had asked her the same question when he'd wanted to know if there had ever been any occasion when her husband's behaviour had seemed a little strange to her. At the time, she had been too upset by the discovery that Simon was a practising homosexual to give the question any serious consideration, but that had been on Friday and this was Monday. Thinking about it now, Louise recalled that Simon had seemed on edge and jumpy all over Christmas. When she'd asked him what was the matter, he'd mumbled something about a glitch in a computer programme he was writing which would make them very rich if only he could iron out the bugs. Computers were a closed book to her and she hadn't understood a word he'd said, and still didn't.

Louise put the hairbrush down and chose a coral-pink lipstick from the array on the dressing table. She heard the postman come and go while she was still making up her face and assumed it was either yet another bill or the usual junk mail. She was right in one respect but there was also a postcard from Nice depicting the Promenade des Anglais. Turning it over, she read the message on the back, then lifted the phone and rang the number Detective Chief Inspector Farnesworth had given her.

'I've just heard from my husband,' she told him when he came on the line.

William Henry Reeves, only son of Sir Michael Reeves, Knight Commander of the Order of the Indian Empire (died 1947) and Lady Cecilea née Creech-Phipps (died 1961). Born Lucknow, United Provinces, 17 June 1925. Married 1956 Georgina Parker, youngest daughter of Louis Parker and Mrs Peter Livingstone. Divorced 1960. Education: St Peter's School, York. World War Two: Commissioned 13th Frontier Force Rifles 1944, served India, Burma, Sumatra. Post-War: Hong Kong and Shanghai Bank 1948-1960. Chairman and Managing Director A and P Travel Agency 1961– , CBE 1964. Recreations: Golf, walking, fishing. Clubs: White's, Hong Kong Yacht Club.

Ashton had obtained most of the biographical details from the 1965 edition of *Who's Who* which the Chief Archivist had rescued from the basement of Benbow House, the last resting place of the now defunct library. The rest he had gleaned from the security file which should have been destroyed in June 1991 when Reeves would have reached the age of sixty-six.

Reeves had started doing odd jobs for the SIS in 1953, shortly after the end of the Korean War. In the course of his normal occupation, he had frequently visited Taiwan, South Korea and Japan and while there was nothing specific on his file, a former DG had commented on the valuable information Reeves had brought back each time. Reading between the lines, it was evident that the Hong Kong and Shanghai Bank had finally tired of his extramural activities and had issued an ultimatum. Banking, it seemed, had not been the raison d'être for Reeves and he had been happy to resign after the SIS had indicated they would be glad to find a niche for him. The Far East Bureau of the SIS had in fact provided the financial backing for the Asia and Pacific Travel Agency which he had launched in 1961.

The A and P had been the perfect cover for establishing an Intelligence network stretching from Japan in the north to Thailand in the south. It was also self-financing by 1963 which Ashton thought must have pleased the Treasury no end, and he wondered if the award of the CBE in 1964 was in recognition of the cost effectiveness of his organisation. Whatever the reason, the travel agency had failed on Saturday, 19 September 1970 when Reeves had collapsed and died on the Fanling golf course.

The sudden and fatal coronary had other far-reaching effects, especially with regard to the identity of the agents he had been running. Although the SIS had been able to retrieve the card index which Reeves had kept locked in his office safe, the individuals concerned had been given codenames to preserve their anonymity. For someone who had joined The Firm without attending the induction course at the training school, Reeves had shown more than just a proper concern for security. Only he had known the surname of the man Newton had tentatively identified as 'Tom' and he had taken that secret with him to the grave.

'Well, that's it, you've encountered the proverbial brick wall,' Kelso announced and looked to Hazelwood for confirmation. 'I mean, what other avenues are left?'

'There's always the snapshot of the SIB fishing party,' Ashton said.

'What about it?' Kelso demanded truculently.

'Well, apart from the mysterious "Tom", there are eight other faces in the photograph. Who knows, maybe one of those guys can put a name to him? Anyway, I think we should trace them and find out.'

'After twenty-four years?' Kelso snorted. 'Some hopes you've got.'

'It's not an impossible task, Roy. At least, not according to the man I consulted earlier on this morning.'

'And who have you been talking to, Peter?' Hazelwood asked quietly.

'A grade two staff officer in the Adjutant General's Department.' Ashton grinned. 'That's why you hired me, isn't it, Victor? Because I know my way around the MoD?'

'Let's not make a big production out of the argument I might or might not have advanced at the time. I'd like to know what this man had to say for himself.'

'I learned a few things about the Hong Kong detachment of the SIB and how it is manned.'

The establishment of the Hong Kong detachment consisted of one warrant officer class one, one warrant officer class two, two staff sergeants and four sergeants, all of whom could expect to spend three years with the unit. A system known as trickle posting meant that in the period between January 1969 when Bernice Kwang had arrived in the colony and her subsequent death in a sailing accident seventeen months later in May 1970, upwards of nine warrant officers and NCOs could have served in the SIB detachment.

'RMP units used to be looked after by the Combined Manning and Record Office at Exeter,' Ashton continued. 'Every six months or so, the Hong Kong detachment would have sent them a nominal roll of personnel on strength. The major I spoke to in the Adjutant General's Department reckons these strength returns would have been put on microfilm before they were backloaded to the historical section at Hayes for permanent retention. We could ask them for a sight of the nominal rolls covering those seventeen months and then run the names through the Social Security computer to find their current addresses.'

'But that could take for ever,' Kelso protested. 'And cost a lot of money,' he added, looking at the Deputy DG.

'You let me worry about that,' Hazelwood told him. 'All the same, Peter, surely Mrs Jackson can identify these men in the photograph?'

'Maybe she can, but we need to feed their National Insurance numbers into the computer and we can only get that information from their army documents.'

'I hadn't thought of that.'

'There is one other avenue we might explore,' Ashton said.

'Oh yes?'

'Bernice Kwang. I think there would have been an inquest.'

He had discussed the case with Harriet over the weekend and it was she who had suggested the possibility. Bernice Kwang had been an American citizen and she had died in unusual circumstances. If the Attorney General for the crown colony hadn't directed the coroner to hold an inquest of his own accord, the US consulate would certainly have pressed him to do so.

'A copy of the proceedings would have been sent to the Foreign and Commonwealth Office. If I'm right, the document will now be lodged in one of the Public Record Offices.'

'What do you hope to get from it?'

'It would be interesting to discover who was called to give evidence at the inquest and what they had to say. The newspaper clippings from the *Hong Kong Standard* and the *South China Morning Post* don't tell us very much.'

'It's a pretty tenuous line of enquiry,' Hazelwood said, frowning.

'So is every other lead I've been following. I don't know why Jackson was so interested in Bernice Kwang and it could be that the man who stuffed him head first into a snowdrift did so in the heat of a drunken row. And maybe Oakham went over the hill because the sex game he was playing with Cosgrove went terribly wrong. It's possible that what we have here is a repeat of the Kennedy conspiracy theory. Remember all those witnesses in Dallas who subsequently died violently and how in the end the statisticians showed there was no sinister connection? That the same number of sudden deaths would occur among any other large group of people who had gathered together in the same place at the same time? I was only six years old in 1963 but I've read an awful lot of books on the subject since then.'

'You've just given me a convincing argument for terminating the investigation,' Hazelwood observed drily.

Ashton hoped Victor would do no such thing. He'd finished checking the proofs of the catalogue he had translated into Russian for Adler Beauty Products and there was nothing else in the pipeline. Dipping into the gratuity he'd received from the SIS was the last thing he wanted to do.

'However,' Hazelwood said after a lengthy silence, 'I think we'll keep the investigation going for a little while longer. You'd better get your body round to the Public Record Office in Chancery Lane. If they don't have a copy of the inquest, try the one in Kew. Lambert can get the list of names out of the historical section, he's good at that sort of thing.'

*   *   *

On Thursday evening, the 1988 Ford Escort had been parked in a quiet side street off Coldharbour Lane in the London Borough of Camberwell, south of the river. This afternoon, four days later, it was concealed in a lockup under the railway viaduct in South Harrow, north of the Thames. It had also acquired a different set of number plates that had formerly belonged to a two-year-old Mazda 323 written off in 1993 following a multiple pile-up on the orbital motorway.

The 'vendor' of the stolen Ford lived in East Finchley. The prospective buyer resided in Ealing and had placed his order for a lively but inconspicuous vehicle ten days ago on the recommendation of a mutual acquaintance. The forewarning had given the vendor a breathing space in which to check out the potential client and satisfy himself that everything was kosher. Once it had been established that the man he was dealing with was not a plant, he had arranged for a suitable vehicle to be collected by one of his drivers.

The two men met for the first and only time in the booking hall of the Underground station at Rayners Lane, the next stop down the line from South Harrow. The client had indicated that he was to be known as Stefan. By prior agreement, he wore a pair of black loafers, grey slacks and a check shirt under a V-neck pullover, both garments clearly visible beneath the light blue anorak that had been deliberately left open for ease of recognition.

'I'm Dave,' the vendor said, shaking hands with him. 'My Volks is just round the corner from here.'

'Is good.'

As the vendor had already discovered from their previous telephone conversations, Stefan was a man of few words, but then this was only to be expected of someone whose command of English was somewhat limited. In his early to mid-thirties, Stefan was tall, slim and quite good-looking in a dark, brooding sort of way. He had black curly hair, a sensuous mouth and eyes that were hard and bright. The vendor had him tagged as one of the *Mafiozniki* who preyed on the hundreds of Russian and Ukranian artists and would-be entrepreneurs who'd come to London hoping to make a fortune. By any yardstick, that made him a very dangerous man to cross.

The Vendor wanted to conclude the deal with Stefan and get shot of him in the shortest possible time but the traffic frustrated him and the two-mile journey from Rayners Lane to the lockup in South Harrow seemed to take for ever. Leaving his Volkswagen Passat by the kerbside, the vendor walked across the forecourt fronting the premises under the railway arches, dug a key out of his pocket and unlocked the huge padlock which secured the steel doors. The faded sign above the entrance read, 'Beedle and Hayes, Light Engineering', a firm that had gone out of business in 1990. The Ford Escort was parked inside the barn-like interior surrounded by work benches, rusting machinery and scrap metal.

'Well, there she is,' the vendor said, 'a three-door, one point six fuel-injected XR3. You've got a five-speed gearbox and a top speed of a hundred and fifteen miles an hour. Nought to sixty in under ten seconds . . .'

'You open engine,' Stefan said and produced a pair of cotton gloves from the pockets of his anorak.

'Sure.' The vendor opened the offside door, leaned inside the car and tripped the release catch. 'You've got special alloy wheels,' he said, continuing with the sales patter, 'low-profile tyres, sports suspension. This vehicle belonged to a careful owner who kept it in immaculate condition. No dents, no sign of rust, no scratchmarks – could have come straight from a showroom—'

'You have the ignition key?' Stefan asked, interrupting him.

'You bet your life.' The driver who'd broken into the Ford Escort had had to hot-wire the ignition but once he'd delivered the vehicle to the lockup in South Harrow, the vendor had been able to provide a matching set from the collection he had illegally acquired.

'Please to start the car,' Stefan told him.

'Whatever you say, squire.' He slipped the key into the ignition and cranked the engine. To his relief, it caught first time and ran smoothly. 'Did you ever hear anything so sweet?' he asked.

Stefan didn't reply. Instead, he grabbed hold of the throttle linkage and revved the engine into a deep-throated snarl, then allowed it to fall back. He repeated the process several times, gauging just how quickly the engine responded. Eventually satisfied with its performance, he closed the bonnet.

'A thousand pounds?'

The vendor nodded. 'That's what we agreed,' he said and watched disbelievingly as Stefan took out a thick wad of fifty-pound notes and casually peeled off twenty.

'Is correct?'

'Yeah.'

'Now you don't remember me,' Stefan said.

'How could I?' the vendor asked. 'We've never met.'

Stefan smiled for the first time, then got into the Ford Escort and backing the car out of the lockup, made a U-turn on the forecourt. He engaged first gear, turned left on Roxeth Green Avenue and suddenly put his foot down as if intent on finding out whether the car really was capable of reaching sixty in under ten seconds.

Ruslan Ovakimyan was thirty-four years old and came from Grozny in the Caucasus, nine hundred and fifty miles south-east of Moscow. An industrial town, Grozny was the capital of Chechnya, one of the fifteen autonomous republics of the old Russian Soviet Federal Socialist Republic. Describing himself as Head of Security, Ruslan Ovakimyan had come to London with the newly appointed Prime Minister of the oil-rich republic who intended to place an order for new banknotes, postage stamps and passports, the first step in a determined bid to break away from the Russian Federation.

Although officially responsible for the protection of the Prime Minister, Ovakimyan, together with his younger half-brother, Stefan Afansiev, was also charged with acquiring certain defence-related items of equipment. This task was not something that could be accomplished overnight and with this in mind, the two half-brothers had purchased a large town house near Lancaster Gate Underground station at the cost of eight hundred and seventy-five thousand pounds, having first convinced the Prime Minister that it would make a suitable embassy once their mission had been accomplished. In fact, they had already sold the property to the embryo Foreign Ministry for one and a half million after furnishing it at government expense.

The two men had also used public funds to invest in the UK stock market, opening numbered accounts in Zurich and Geneva, and to buy a penthouse flat in Ealing which they used as a business address. However, today, for only the second time since arriving in London six weeks ago, Ruslan Ovakimyan was obliged to devote all his energies towards resolving a potentially dangerous security problem. To assist him, he had been provided with a 9mm assault pistol manufactured by the Goncz Company, Burbank Boulevard, North Hollywood, and a town plan of Guildford. As he sat there in the drawing room studying the street map, two quick blasts on a horn outside the house told him that Stefan had arrived with the transport.

CHAPTER 10

F arnesworth stubbed out his cigarette in an ashtray already filled to overflowing with old butts. The postcard from Nice which Simon Oakham had sent his wife had been worth the round trip to Guildford even though she had been unable to explain the ambiguous message on the back. The Assistant Chief Constable (Operations) hadn't liked the telex Farnesworth had drafted to Interpol and had downgraded it to a Request for Information which didn't have anything like the same impact. Interpol Headquarters at St Cloud wouldn't have given the request an XD prefix and without that essential top priority notification, it was unlikely to carry much weight with provincial police departments.

But the picture postcard of the Promenade des Anglais put a different complexion on the whole business. It proved Oakham was in the South of France, and he was damned sure he would get his Red Notice this time around. Farnesworth looked at the telex he'd just drafted and was about to compose a covering memo to the Assistant Chief Constable justifying the case for an International Arrest Warrant when the phone rang. Answering it, he heard a voice ask for Detective Chief Inspector Farnesworth.

'That's me,' he said. 'Who's calling?'

'Peachey, Clifford Peachey. I understand you want to have a word with me?'

Farnesworth nodded to himself. On his return from Guildford, he had telephoned the Head of Special Branch at Force Headquarters in Winfrith and asked him to pass a message to Peachey.

'Yes, indeed. I'd like you to tell me how I can get in touch with Mr Ashton.'

'Ashton?'

'Yes, Peter Ashton. He's a friend of yours, a pretty close one judging by the favour you did for him some days ago.'

'I see.' Peachey clucked his tongue. Over the phone, the noise sounded like a couple of pistol shots. 'May one enquire why you want to get in touch with him?' he asked after a short pause.

'I'm looking at a postcard Louise Oakham received from her husband this morning. On the back, he's written, "No need to worry about redundancy now, darling. I've just been offered a well-paid job with the overseas branch of the old firm."' Farnesworth cleared his throat, then said, 'I'd be interested to hear what he makes of that.'

Peachey told him he would ask Ashton to get in contact as soon as possible.

Twenty minutes later, the MI5 man rang back to say that Ashton wasn't answering his phone and appeared to be out. To Farnesworth's suspicious mind, he concluded that the Intelligence Services were giving him the old run-around.

It had taken just one phone call to establish that an inquest had been held on Bernice Kwang and that a copy of proceedings had ultimately been lodged with the Public Record Office ten years after it had been received by the Foreign and Commonwealth Office. A reader's card provided by the Admin Wing had then got Ashton into one of the research rooms at Chancery Lane.

The inquest had been held on Thursday, 28 May 1970, eighteen days after the body of Bernice Kwang had been recovered from the sea off Cheung Chau Island. The coroner had been a Mr Lloyd Ingolby, QC and the principal witnesses had been the pathologist who had performed the autopsy, a Chinese landing dock attendant employed by the Hong Kong Yacht Club, a Mr Li Wah Tung and Ms Lenora Vassman.

Through an interpreter, Yang Bo, the dock attendant, had told the court that he had been present on Friday evening, 8 May when Miss Kwang had arrived a few minutes before five o'clock. She had her own dinghy, a Dragonfly called *Sea Scape Two* and he had assisted her by casting off the mooring line when she'd taken it out. Questioned by a lawyer representing the US Consulate, the witness had stated that he knew Miss Kwang by sight and had gone on to describe the clothes she had been wearing at the time in some detail.

Mr Li Wah Tung had made himself a small fortune out of pearls. Apart from a luxury apartment high up on the Peak above Victoria and a Bentley Continental, he was also the owner of a powerboat. On the afternoon of Sunday, 10 May, he and a party of friends had been returning from a picnic on Lantau by way of Cheung Chau Island when he'd come across a dinghy off Sandy Cove which appeared to have been abandoned. The sails had been struck and the helmsman had dropped anchor. Curious to know what had happened to him, Li Wah Tung had taken his power-boat close inshore and had found the body of a woman floating belly up in the shallows. The lady, subsequently identified as Bernice Kwang, had not been wearing a life jacket which conflicted with the evidence given by the dock attendant. Although the coroner had recalled the witness, he had been unable to resolve the conflicting accounts.

The pathologist had simply handed the coroner a copy of his autopsy report and had then answered a few perfunctory questions for the benefit of the jury. From the contents of the stomach as well as the physical deterioration of the cadaver, he estimated that the body had been in the sea for approximately forty-eight hours when it had been found by Mr Li Wah Tung. As Mr Lloyd Ingolby had then so helpfully pointed out to the jury, this would have coincided with the sudden rain squall that had occurred at 19.30 hours on the Friday evening. Only if he had directed the foreman to make sure his fellow jurors brought in a verdict of accidental death could he have been more obvious.

Ms Lenora Vassman appeared to have had other ideas. She had shared a flat with the deceased and had identified the body. Describing herself as a close friend of Bernice Kwang, she had leaped to her feet before the pathologist had finished giving his evidence to ask him point-blank if he was satisfied that the Chinese American girl had drowned in salt water. The interruption had earned her a mild rebuke from the coroner; Mr Lloyd Ingolby had then become decidedly testy when, after the doctor had stated quite emphatically that he had no doubt on that score, she had asked him what he had made of the abrasions on both wrists of the deceased, assuming he had in fact noticed them.

But her natural antagonism had really come to the fore when she had gone into the witness box. The judge had warned her several times that the jury were only interested to hear the facts, not her opinions. However, this stern warning had evidently cut very little ice with the twenty-five-year-old American girl who had continued to cast doubt on the findings of the Crown's expert witness. In the end, the attorney representing the US Consulate had taken Lenora Vassman aside and told her to cool it. Thereafter, there had been no further interruptions and the jury had obligingly brought in a verdict of accidental death.

At 4.50, one of the lady archivists reminded Ashton that the Record Office was due to close at five o'clock. He therefore spent the last ten minutes checking his notes against the statements made by the key witnesses to make sure he hadn't missed anything. When finally he was obliged to leave, he called Hazelwood from a pay phone and asked to see him. After thinking about it for a moment, Victor suggested they should meet at his club.

'And what club is that?' Ashton asked.

'The Athenaeum,' Hazelwood told him.

'Really? How long have you been a member?'

'Since the beginning of January, and no, the committee haven't taken leave of their senses.'

Ashton wondered aloud what his chances might be, then told Hazelwood not to answer that, and hung up.

The sky had been overcast and threatening all day; as he walked down Chancery Lane towards Fleet Street, the first drops of rain began to fall. By the time he picked up a cab opposite the Law Courts in the Strand, the light shower had become a tropical downpour.

The Athenaeum was on the corner of Pall Mall and Waterloo Place. Ashton had walked past the club a good few times during his brief stint with Military Operations (Special Projects) at the MoD but had never set foot inside the place before. He very nearly didn't on this occasion either. Hazelwood had neglected to inform the club that he had invited Ashton to meet him there and a very security-minded hall porter who had never heard of the Deputy DG had refused to let him enter the club until he'd checked the secretary's list of new members. Hazelwood finally arrived after Ashton had read every notice and every charity appeal displayed on the board tucked away in a corner of the entrance hall, and was about ready to call it a day.

'What you need is a good stiff drink,' Hazelwood announced, and led him into the bar.

Two double whiskies later, Ashton was feeling much more affable and Hazelwood had read and digested his notes on the inquest and was ready to discuss the outcome.

'So what do you make of it, Peter?'

'I think Lloyd Ingolby, QC was highly prejudiced to say the least. He certainly did him damnedest to muzzle Ms Lenora Vassman.'

'Are you inferring he'd been instructed to ensure the jury reached a particular verdict?'

'It's not impossible,' Ashton said. 'It's evident Lenora Vassman had reason to believe that her flatmate had been murdered. Why else would she have asked the pathologist if he was satisfied Bernice Kwang had drowned in salt water? When the answer to that question is an emphatic yes, she asks him what he made of the abrasions on the deceased's wrists and promptly gets slapped down by the coroner.'

But Mr Lloyd Ingolby hadn't wanted members of the jury turning this over in their minds so he had reminded them that Li Wah Tung had stated that *Sea Scape Two* had been trailing an anchor when he'd recovered the dinghy. Then he'd suggested Miss Kwang might have fallen overboard when she had thrown out the anchor and the abrasions had been caused when she had grabbed hold of the nylon rope attached to it and had wrapped the cord around her wrists in a desperate attempt to hang on.'

'And quick as a flash, the pathologist agrees this is the most likely explanation.'

'And isn't it?' Hazelwood asked in a voice which suggested he thought it was.

'Depends on whether you are prepared to ignore what Ms Vassman said when she was in the witness box.'

Ashton fell silent. Until now, they had had the bar to themselves; now it looked as though they were about to be joined by a third party. The newcomer was plump, had thinning grey hair and was in his fifties; he stood in the open doorway and looked round the bar as if hoping to see a familiar face, then suddenly turned about and walked away.

'I didn't have time to flesh out my notes,' Ashton continued in a quieter voice. 'The fact is, those two young women had accepted an invitation to a cocktail party starting at 6.30 that particular Friday evening.'

'So?'

'So why would Bernice Kwang go sailing an hour and a half before the party?'

'There's no accounting for what women will do,' Hazelwood said lugubriously.

'Lenora Vassman was a corporate finance broker with the Bank of America. At twenty minutes to five that Friday afternoon she telephoned Bernice Kwang to say her boss had suddenly decided he wanted her to attend a meeting he'd arranged for five o'clock with a very important client who was flying in from Tokyo.'

Lenora Vassman had had no idea how long the meeting would last but thought it was likely she wouldn't make the party on time. She had asked her flatmate to apologise to their host and hostess and had said she would see her there.

'Maybe Bernice Kwang changed her mind about going to the party?'

Ashton shook his head. 'The coroner wanted the jury to think so but Lenora wasn't having it. The two girls shared an apartment in Belmont

House on Magazine Gap Road near the Peak Tramway and in her opinion, there was no way Bernice could have been seen on the landing dock twenty minutes after she had spoken to her on the telephone. Lenora Vassman was adamant she couldn't had got there in the time.'

'Which means either that it was later than the Chinese attendant thought or else he was lying.'

'Mr Ingolby preferred to think he'd got the time wrong and the jury went along with it.'

'It still doesn't mean there was foul play.' Hazelwood smiled. 'I'm simply looking at it through the eyes of the coroner.'

'Lenora Vassman was trying to say that what her friend was supposed to have done on Friday, 8 May was completely out of character.'

'I don't imagine the landing dock was deserted at 5 p.m.?'

'You're right, it wasn't,' Ashton said. 'The police took statements from a couple of yachtsmen who recalled seeing a girl answering to the description the landing dock attendant had given them. But, if the attorney representing the US Consulate hadn't warned her off, I believe Lenora would have said the young woman they saw was a lookalike. There's something else we should bear in mind; Bernice Kwang couldn't have been a novice sailor. When the storm blew up, she took shelter in Sandy Cove, lowered the sails and anchored. Yet she removes her life jacket. It doesn't make sense.'

'All right, how did the real Bernice Kwang end up in the sea?'

'Ms Vassman never got a chance to explain that.' Ashton shrugged his shoulders. 'Maybe Bernice was lifted from Belmont House, taken some place else and quietly drowned before she was put into the sea? But don't ask me to supply a motive. Bill Reeves, our Head of Station in Hong Kong, crossed swords with Jackson who appeared to have had his eyes on the Chinese American girl. That's all we've got.'

'And the mysterious Tom,' Hazelwood reminded him.

'Yes. Well, he was never mentioned at the inquest.'

'Maybe Lenora Vassman can give us his name.'

'We would have to find her first.'

'Naturally.'

'You can't be serious,' Ashton said.

But he was. Hazelwood didn't care that she was an American citizen who was now approaching fifty and could have had one, two or maybe even three husbands in the last twenty-four years. Lenora Vassman had worked for the Bank of America and came from Chicago. Nothing else was known about her, but Victor appeared to think it was enough to go on.

'It might be helpful if we had a word with the pathologist and Lloyd Ingolby, QC.'

'If they're still alive,' Ashton said. He wasn't being frivolous; both men would now be well into their seventies and no one was immortal.

'And that Chinese businessman,' Hazelwood continued unabashed, 'whatever his name is.'

'Li Wah Tung. You'd better include Yang Bo, the landing dock attendant, while you're at it.'

'Right. I'll get the Assistant Director, Pacific Basin to signal their names to JSIS in Hong Kong.'

Ashton finished the last of his whisky. 'What do you want me to do in the meantime?' he asked.

'Take a breather,' Hazelwood told him. 'I'll be in touch when we have something for you.'

They had left the town house in Lancaster Gate when the rush hour traffic was beginning to thin out. His half-brother had wanted to pick up the M4 at Chiswick and then use the orbital motorway to get on to the A3 to Guildford, but Ruslan Ovakimyan wasn't having that. Too many accidents happened on the orbital for his liking and he certainly didn't want to be involved in a multiple pile-up tonight, not when he was carrying a 9mm Goncz assault pistol complete with noise suppressor and flash eliminator and an eighteen-round magazine in the butt. So they had taken the slower route via Marble Arch, Hyde Park Corner, Knightsbridge and the Brompton Road which had taken them to Putney Bridge and thence to the A3 at the top of Putney Hill.

Thirty miles an hour maximum and they hadn't been able to do that too often, the way the lights had always been against them. The stop-go, stop-go had driven Stefan nearly crazy because he'd wanted to show Ruslan what the Ford Escort XR3 could do when he put his foot down. But what had really angered Stefan Afansiev was Ovakimyan's refusal to let him do more than sixty once they were on the A3 trunk route. Maybe the rain had eased a little but there was still a lot of it around and there was enough water lying on the surface to make aquaplaning on the dual carriageway a real possibility. In this weather, sixty was plenty fast enough.

'This is stupid,' Stefan grumbled. 'I need to know how the car will handle in these conditions. How can I do that without putting my foot down?'

'We do this right and you won't have to put your foot down,' Ovakimyan told him.

'Bad luck or a quirk of fate can upset the best-laid plan.'

Ruslan smiled to himself. Stefan's philosophical turn of phrase was at odds with his character. His half-brother was a mercurial fellow, up one moment, down the next.

'It's too late for speed trials, Stefan, we're almost there.'

Half a mile farther on, they left the bypass to follow the route Ovakimyan had marked on the town plan. It was not the first time he had been to Guildford; he'd visited twice before, using a car he had rented for the day on each occasion. Different agency, different model; a Volkswagen from Hertz, a Nissan from Avis, a routine precaution to ensure no one remembered his face or recalled seeing the same vehicle in the neighbourhood.

After two dry runs, he was familiar with the landmarks and knew the route backwards – in daylight. But things looked different in the dark and the open map on his knees, which he could read with the aid of a pencil-thin flashlight, made him feel less apprehensive. Entering the High Street, he pointed to the pay phone near Lloyds Bank and told Stefan to pull into the kerb. Before you went calling on somebody, it was only sensible to find out if they were at home.

Ovakimyan folded the map away, placed the assault pistol on the floor between his seat and the transmission tunnel and got out of the Ford Escort. Coat collar turned up against the rain, he walked over to the open-ended telephone kiosk, lifted the receiver and fed a ten-pence coin into the meter, then punched out the number. Unlike his half-brother, he was quite fluent in English, which was just as well even though he'd no intention of holding a protracted conversation with the subscriber. The number rang out half a dozen times before a woman with a husky voice answered the phone and said hello.

'Mrs Gaffney?'

'Who?'

'That is 873893, isn't it?' he asked.

'No, I'm afraid it isn't.'

'Oh, I'm sorry,' Ovakimyan said apologetically, 'I must have dialled the wrong number.'

The woman told him not to worry and put the phone down. Ovakimyan followed suit, backed out of the kiosk and returned to the car.

'Is it on?' Stefan asked, as he got into the Ford.

'You can relax, the lady's at home.' Ovakimyan closed the door, buckled the seat belt and reached for the street map he'd left on top of the fascia. 'Whenever you're ready,' he added.

'About time. That bloody policeman is too damned curious for my liking.'

'What policeman?'

'The one I can see in the rear-view mirror. Keeps staring at the car.'

'Then drive away slowly; we don't want to arouse his suspicions.'

Afansiev started up, shifted into gear and, releasing the handbrake, let in the clutch. His mouth dry as dust, he pulled away from the kerb and went on down the High Street. Only when the policeman was no longer in sight did he begin to unwind.

The police constable was twenty-two years old and while lacking experience in some areas, there wasn't much he didn't know about cars. There wasn't a motor magazine on the market that he didn't subscribe to, there wasn't a vehicle on the road he couldn't identify. And not just the make either; he could tell the age of a model by the bits and pieces the manufacturer had added to the original version of the car. With his encyclopaedic knowledge, he knew the H registration plate on the '88 model Ford Escort XR3 had to be false. Although ninety-nine per cent certain of his facts, he nevertheless called the number in. Two minutes later he learned that it had belonged to a Mazda 323 which had been written off in a traffic accident in 1993.

The moment they turned into Greenham Avenue, Ruslan Ovakimyan could see they were going to have problems. Few of the semidetached houses in the road had been built with an integral garage, the implication of which hadn't occurred to him when he had reconoitred the street in daylight after most of the inhabitants had gone to work. Now, all of them were at home and there were cars parked nose to tail on both sides of the road.

'What's the number we're looking for?' Stefan asked.

'It's 104. Don't bother looking for the house, it's on my side.'

They were, in fact, just coming up to the semidetached, but there was no room to park outside the house and they had to go on some thirty yards beyond it before Ovakimyan spotted a vacant space on the opposite side of the road.

'In there,' he said, 'between the Vauxhall and the Toyota.'

It was always going to be a tight squeeze and Afansiev needed several attempts at it before he managed to back into the slot.

'Switch the lights off but keep the motor running. Okay?'

'Sure.'

'And don't rev the engine.'

'Why don't you get on with it and leave me to look after the car?'

Ovakimyan picked up the assault pistol, checked to make sure it was cocked, then got out of the Ford Escort and walked back up the road. He kept to the shadows, giving the street lights a wide berth in case anyone should see him from an upstairs window. If the rain had made driving conditions difficult on the A3 trunk road, it also kept people indoors which meant he had the avenue to himself.

He pushed open the front gate to number 104, walked up the path and tried the bell only to find it didn't work. Swearing under his breath, he banged the door knocker and kept on banging it until a light came on in the hall. Then the letter box rattled and remained half open while the woman with the husky voice asked who was there.

'It's all right, Mrs Oakham,' he said gruffly, 'I'm a police officer.'

The door opened, but only as far as the security chain would allow. Ovakimyan took a pace to his right in order to look into the hall, produced the 9mm assault pistol from behind his back and opened fire. The first round was slightly high and went in just under the left collarbone, the second missed as she staggered back and toppled over, knocked off her feet by the force of the initial impact. She fell sideways and rolled over on to her stomach, her head towards the staircase. Thrusting his arm through the gap between the door and the jamb, he squeezed off another five rounds in rapid succession. He had never heard anyone scream so loudly, a nerve-jangling shriek that surely could be heard above the noise of the television in the back room. He thought it was truly amazing how long the Oakham woman was able to go on screaming even after she had been hit above the left hip and twice in the ribs. In fact, she only stopped when the fourth round bored through the neck and the fifth removed a large part of her skull.

Ovakimyan withdrew his arm, turned about and ran off down the path. He had hoped to make the hit and walk quietly away, but the job hadn't gone according to plan and there was no chance of sneaking away. What mattered now was getting the hell out of Greenham Avenue before the alarm was raised. He raced down the road, feet splashing through the puddles, and thirty yards seemed more like three hundred. Half-brother Stefan saw him coming and revved the engine as if he were a Formula One driver waiting for the chequered flag to drop. But Ruslan wasn't complaining; yanking the door open he tumbled into the car.

'Go, go, go.'

Stefan Afansiev had every intention of doing just that but in the heat of the moment, he forgot to release the handbrake and the Ford Escort leaped forward like a startled kangaroo and stalled. Mouthing obscenities, he cranked the engine into life, let the clutch out and put the wheel hard over. It had been a tight squeeze backing into the kerb but he had even less room for manoeuvre now and he clipped the rear wing of the Vauxhall hard enough to smash the offside headlight on the Escort. Worse still, the sudden jolt triggered the alarm on the car he'd bumped. He reversed the lock, backed up a couple of feet and this time managed to clear the obstruction.

Ovakimyan brushed a hand across his forehead to wipe away the rainwater that was trickling into his eyes and found his fingers came away sticky with blood. He gingerly explored his forehead a second time and discovered there was a gash near the hairline and wondered how it had got there, then recalled he had been fumbling with the seat belt when the car had stalled. Flashing lights, the warble of an alarm and now a man running out into the street to shake a fist at them as they careered down the avenue. Everything had gone to pot and still was.

'Come over to the left,' he screamed at his half-brother. 'You're on the wrong side of the road.'

The make, model, description and registration number of the suspect vehicle which had been called into the Guildford subdivision of the Surrey Constabulary had gone on up the chain to G Division and then outwards and downwards. The two police officers from the Leatherhead subdivision were parked in a side road on the outskirts of Great Bookham when a Ford Escort with a defective offside headlight passed them heading towards Leatherhead at an estimated speed in excess of eighty. Although they only caught a glimpse of the number plate, both officers believed the registration, like that of the suspect vehicle, began with the letter H followed by the figure 9. But above all, it was the reckless way the vehicle was being driven that settled the issue for them. Siren blaring, they went after the Ford Escort, convinced that it had been stolen by joyriders. One minute later, Control informed them that the occupants of the suspect car were believed to have been involved in a shooting incident in Greenham Avenue, Guildford.

Ovakimyan heard the bleee-baa of a siren behind them and looking back over his shoulder, saw the flashing blue lights of a police car.

'We've got company,' he said in a dull voice.

'Then bloody well do something about it.'

'Yes? Like what?'

'Shit, how do I know?' Afansiev screamed at him. 'You're supposed to be the one with the brains in this family. Get in the back and shoot the bastards off the road before they radio for assistance.'

It was the first time in his life that Ruslan had taken orders from his half-brother, it was also going to be the last. The stupid idiot had lost his head and turned right at the bottom of Greenham Avenue instead of left and because of that lunatic error, plus a few others the brainless son of a bitch had made, they were now completely lost. Unclipping his seat belt, he climbed over into the back and looked through the rear window. The police car was about a hundred yards in rear and the chances of hitting it with a handgun were about zero.

'Slow down.'

'Are you out of your tiny mind?'

'Shut your mouth and do it. They have to come within range.'

Afansiev stamped on the brakes, felt the back end begin to fishtail and fought to keep the vehicle under control. He heard the glass shatter as Ovakimyan opened fire on the police car without bothering to knock out the rear window first. Shifting into second, he flattened the accelerator and went up through the gearbox into top. The Ford XR3 was doing seventy-five when the road merged with the Leatherhead bypass.

Traffic coming from the right had priority but it never occurred to Afansiev to slow down and look. Unable to make the tight turn, he drifted across into the outside lane of the dual carriageway, tyres screaming in protest. Ovakimyan was also screaming and suddenly a Volvo juggernaut which had been overtaking a slower vehicle appeared in the wing mirror as the driver of the rig tried to cut back into the nearside lane, his air horn blaring a warning. Thirty-five tons travelling at seventy miles an hour crunched into the Ford Escort and flipped the car over the central reservation into the path of an ICI tanker heading south. There was one long-drawn-out cacophony of tortured metal as the chemical tanker ploughed into the upturned Escort and a dozen other vehicles shunted into one another. Then, somewhere in the tangled wreckage, a petrol tank exploded in a ball of fire.

CHAPTER 11

Ashton printed his name and initials in block capitals on the buff-coloured form, wrote 'Attending conference with Deputy DG' in the box headed 'Purpose of Visit' and added the word 'Self' where he was required to state who or which organisation he was representing. Then he signed and dated the form, handed it to one of the receptionists who stamped it to show the time he had entered the building. On returning the completed document, she gave Ashton a plastic visitor's pass admitting him to Vauxhall Cross which he clipped to the lapel of his jacket.

He also collected one of the elderly messengers whose job it was to escort him to and from Hazelwood's office. Six months ago, there would have been none of this rigmarole; back in September, he could come and go as he pleased on the strength of his ID card, but that kind of unlimited access died the day he left the Intelligence Service. Until this morning, the SIS Headquarters had still been off limits to him even though he was working for The Firm freelance. He was only there now because the Deputy DG had summoned him to Vauxhall Cross.

Clifford Peachey was the last person Ashton expected to find in Victor's office. He sensed his presence had something to do with Detective Chief Inspector Farnesworth before Hazelwood asked him if he'd heard the news.

'Are we talking about the BBC?' he asked.

'Unless you have some other source of information.'

'No, mine's strictly Radio 4 these days. But the fact is I only caught the news headlines this morning.' Ashton smiled lopsidedly. 'There was a domestic crisis in the kitchen; the toaster set fire to the bread instead of ejecting the two slices when they were nicely browned.' He looked from Hazelwood to Clifford Peachey; neither man was smiling. 'This woman in Guildford who was shot and killed last night,' he said quietly. 'Was it Louise Oakham?'

103

'Yes, I'm afraid it was. Officially, her name is being withheld until the next of kin have been informed. Of course, there's no way we can notify the lady's husband; her mother is suffering from Alzheimer's disease and isn't really on this planet, and the brother emigrated to new Zealand in 1969.'

'In other words, the press have been fobbed off?'

'Only for as long as it takes us to get our act together,' Hazelwood said irritably.

Ashton was prepared to bet that time was unlikely to be on their side. The police were the thin blue line holding the media at bay and sooner rather than later, some reporter would discover from the neighbours that the husband was an army officer. Before there was time to blink, Public Relations at the MoD would be fielding an avalanche of questions and it would rapidly emerge that Simon Oakham was absent without leave. The army was fireproof; they had notified the appropriate authorities and hadn't attempted to hide anything. The newspapers, however, hadn't bothered to pick up the MoD press release, probably because an absentee hadn't been considered newsworthy at the time. But now it was a different story and there was a limit to how long the police would be willing to play the next-of-kin card on behalf of the Intelligence community.

'Where do I come in?' Ashton enquired.

'DCI Farnesworth was asking for you yesterday,' Peachey said before Hazelwood had a chance to reply. 'He's become even more insistent since last night.'

'And are we going to accommodate him?'

'We don't have much choice,' Hazelwood growled.

'That sounds ominous. What exactly does he want from me?'

'An explanation,' Peachey said, chipping in again. 'Louise Oakham received a postcard from her husband yesterday morning which had been sent from Nice. On the back he'd written that there was no need to worry about redundancy now because he had been offered a well-paid job with the old firm.'

'We've checked with the army,' Hazelwood said. 'Oakham isn't on the redundancy list, though I dare say they would like to get rid of him now.'

'Is that what you want me to tell Farnesworth?'

'Plus the fact that we certainly haven't offered Oakham a job or even short-listed him for one.'

'You mean I can't even admit we were going to borrow him from the army?' Ashton was surprised how easily the collective pronoun slipped from his lips, as if he were still a fully paid-up member of The Firm.

'I expect you to listen to what Farnesworth has to say and then disclose no more than is strictly relevant. I don't want you to whet his appetite so that he comes back for a second helping with the whole of Grub Street on his heels.'

At the moment, the Surrey Constabulary were in the limelight with the press and TV reporters either camped out on the doorstep of Force Headquarters or dogging the footsteps of the detectives from G Division. So far, nobody was taking any notice of Farnesworth, but that could change very rapidly if it became known that the Detective Chief Inspector had interviewed Louise Oakham only a few hours before she was murdered.

'If he's staying away from Guildford,' Ashton said, 'where am I going to meet him?'

'At Scotland Yard,' Hazelwood said, and nodded in Peachey's direction. 'Clifford arranged it. So far as the Yard's concerned you're with MI5's Anti-Terrorist Section.'

'Will that stand up?' Ashton asked.

'As it happens, the Security Service does have a legitimate interest in the case,' Peachey said quietly.

Louise Oakham hadn't been gunned down by chance. Although the investigation was only a few hours old, the police had already established that the killer had gone straight to her house. He had been armed with a semiautomatic weapon fitted with a noise suppressor and the getaway car had carried false number plates; two additional factors which suggested Louise Oakham had been the victim of a professional hit. The occupants of the same vehicle had also fired on a police car on the outskirts of Great Bookham.

'It's not too unlike a terrorist incident,' Peachey said in conclusion.

'Maybe so,' Ashton said, 'but I think you would have a hard time convincing the press that an active service unit of the IRA was responsible.'

'The Provos aren't the only lot in that line of business.'

'Right. Are you coming to the Yard with me?'

'Someone has to vouch for you.' A thin smile appeared on Peachey's mouth. 'Victor here doesn't want your name appearing on a visitor's pass and I'm the only man who can get you into the building without going through that formality.'

A room next door to the Public Relations Officer had been set aside for Farnesworth, much to the annoyance of his secretary who had had to move in with the clerical staff a long way down the corridor from her boss. With less than good grace, she had made Farnesworth a cup of coffee and had then coolly informed him that they were all non-smokers on her floor and therefore she hadn't the faintest idea where she might find an ashtray. Undeterred by her obvious disapproval, he had used the saucer instead. By the time Ashton arrived, it contained four stubs and a layer of grey ash.

'Glad you could make it,' Farnesworth said acidly.

'So am I,' Ashton told him, completely unperturbed. 'Do you think I could see this postcard Oakham sent to his wife?'

'I'm sure you can. Matter of fact, I'm hoping you can make sense of the message on the back because Louise Oakham said she couldn't.'

'Neither can I.'

'You haven't read it yet.'

'I don't have to. I already know what's on the back, Clifford Peachey told me.' Ashton turned the card over and looked at the date stamp. 'I see it was posted in Nice well over a week ago.'

'Yes. I don't know what the French do with the mail after it's been sorted but postcards to the UK frequently take up to ten days to get here. But you're ducking the question. I may be an outsider but I do know what is meant by The Firm.'

'He hasn't been offered a job by the SIS,' Ashton said calmly, looking him straight in the eye.

'Well, you would say that, wouldn't you?' Farnesworth retorted.

'Oakham is a programmer and there isn't much he doesn't know about computers. If he had been cleared by positive vetting, the Foreign and Commonwealth Office would have borrowed him from the army to write a programme that would enable them to dispose of their dormant files yet retain the basic information in a more compact form. But he wasn't cleared; at the very last moment, he deliberately cast doubt on his suitability for constant access to Top Secret material and the process was suspended.'

'Before or after Oakham absented himself without leave?'

'I've already told you,' Ashton said wearily, 'he said certain things which raised serious doubts in the mind of the vetting officer who was conducting the subject interview.'

'Suppose you tell me why he should want to shoot himself in the foot?'

'Well, my guess is that he was frightened the army would find out that he was having an affair with Cosgrove. If that did come to light, he knew he would be kicked out of the Service on his ear. You can forget all about the 1967 Act and it being okay between consenting adults; it's still an offence in the armed forces, and rightly so. Oakham didn't need to be PV cleared. As a unit paymaster, he could still look forward to a reasonable career in the army if the clearance was denied. So he chose the lesser of the two evils.'

Farnesworth took another cigarette from the packet of Silk Cut he'd left on the desk next to the saucer-cum-ashtray and lit it. Ashton was doing a snow job on him. What he had told him about the Pay Corps officer sounded plausible enough and the story probably contained a few grains of truth, but Ashton was suppressing a hell of a lot more than he had disclosed.

'So why did he do a runner?' Farnesworth asked.

'Opinion was he'd gone to see Cosgrove after the interview to put an end to their association, and the major wouldn't have it. Then things got out of hand and Oakham panicked.' Ashton shrugged his shoulders. 'But after what's happened to Louise Oakham, that theory is no longer tenable.' He looked at the postcard of the Promenade des Anglais again. 'Have you got an International Arrest Warrant out for him?' he asked.

'Of course. Interpol's got it in hand.' Persuading the Assistant Chief Constable (Operations) to okay the Red Notice he'd drafted for dispatch to Interpol Headquarters at St Cloud was the one positive thing Farnesworth had been able to do.

'Let's hope Oakham is still in the South of France.' Ashton smiled. 'Be a hell of a thing if he was back in this country.'

'What are you getting at?'

'Well, like you said, the postal service isn't exactly rapid between France and the UK. Sending your wife a postcard could be a neat way of establishing an alibi. Do we know how much she was worth?'

The sudden and unpredictable change of direction left Farnesworth floundering. Ashton seemed to have the mind of a grasshopper and it was difficult to follow his train of thought. It had to be deliberate; snap judgements were often erroneous but he was damned sure Ashton was no bird brain.

'For God's sake,' he exploded, 'what makes you think Louise Oakham was a wealthy woman? She was living in an anonymous semidetached in an anonymous street.'

'Her first husband was killed in a traffic accident in 1987. It could be she received a tidy old sum from his insurance company. Or maybe she went to court and the judge awarded her several hundred thousand because she had two young children to support.'

'Are you seriously suggesting that Oakham hired someone to kill his wife?' Farnesworth snorted in derision. 'I find that pretty hard to swallow.'

'Well, I don't know of any reason why the IRA should want to target her, or any other terrorist organisation for that matter. Don't you people say that nine out of every ten murders are committed by someone in the family?'

The statistic was broadly correct, the implied assumption wasn't. Unlike Ashton, he had been to 104 Greenham Avenue, had met Louise Oakham, talked to her and seen for himself how she lived. Her life style, like the house she occupied, had been modest and unpretentious. Oakham would gain nothing from having her killed, and there was another, albeit negative factor in his favour. A contract killer would have demanded money up front; these days, the going rate was at least five thousand pounds and Simon Oakham didn't have that kind of money lying around.

'Has Forensic had a look at this postcard yet?' Ashton hastily raised both hands as if in surrender. 'Sorry about that,' he said apologetically, 'but I just wondered if Oakham's thumb or fingerprint was on the stamp.'

'They are on the card.'

'Yes, I assumed they would be since Louise Oakham told you that it had definitely been written by her husband. But if he had actually licked the stamp and put it on, there would be no doubting the fact that he was in France. You see what I'm getting at?'

Farnesworth had had just about enough of Ashton throwing dust in his eyes. It took a lot to make him really lose his temper but the younger man was close to succeeding.

'Oh, for Christ's sake,' he snapped, 'why don't you try out your theories on the detectives of the Surrey Constabulary's G Division? They're running the murder investigation. But I'll tell you this much for nothing: they are likely to get a damned sight more sense out of the survivor if ever he regains consciousness.'

'What survivor?'

'One of the hit men. Their car was involved in that multiple pile-up on the Leatherhead bypass. The guy was catapulted out of the Escort when it jumped the central reservation.'

'What hospital is he in?'

'The Mid Surrey General.'

'Thanks.' Ashton frowned. 'When did you hear this?' he asked.

'A few minutes before you arrived. One of my sergeants is liaising with G Division, giving them all we have on Simon Oakham. He rang me here.'

'Does the Anti-terrorist Squad know about this?'

'I haven't told them.'

'Then I'd better have a quick word with Clifford Peachey.' Ashton walked over to the door and opened it, then turned about. 'I think we've about covered everything, haven't we?' he said.

Farnesworth nodded dumbly, completely taken aback by the assertion. He hadn't got a damned thing out of Ashton and this was the second time the younger man had walked away with more than he'd given.

The signal to Head of Station, Hong Kong and the Joint Services Intelligence Staff had been originated by the duty officer, Pacific Basin at 21.30 hours. It had been classified Secret and accorded an Op Immediate precedence, which meant it had priority over all other transmissions with the exception of those graded either Flash or Emergency. The message was transmitted via the Starlight Satellite network and was received by the addressees at 5.30 the following morning, Hong Kong being eight hours ahead of Greenwich Mean Time.

In addition to the security classification, there was a caveat stating the message was for UK Eyes Only. When decoded, the text read:

Subject is Inquest re Bernice Kwang held at Number One Court Central District on Thursday, 28 May 1970. Request you ascertain soonest present whereabouts of following officials/key witnesses. First – Coroner, Mr Lloyd Ingolby, QC. Second – Mr Ronald Bartholomew, Fellow Royal College of Surgeons, resident pathologist Bowen Road Hospital. Third – Mr Li Wah Tung, owner South China Jade and Pearl Emporiums. Fourth – US national Lenora Vassman, date and place of birth: 23 March 1945, Chicago, Illinois. Fifth – Yang Bo, landing dock attendant employed by Hong Kong Yacht Club 1970.

Head of Station, with the assistance of the JSIS, had no difficulty in tracing the coroner. Lloyd Ingolby had enjoyed a glittering career in the Law which had led to a knighthood two years before retiring from the Supreme Court at the age of sixty-eight. After a lifetime spent in the service of the crown colony, he regarded Hong Kong as his home and in consequence, had purchased the lease of a small villa overlooking Big

Wave Bay on the east side of the Island. Mr Li Wah Tung was also still residing in the colony but for how much longer was open to question. He had been quietly funnelling money into Swiss and US banks ever since the Thatcher Government had reluctantly accepted that the Island, together with the New Territories on the mainland, would revert to Peking when the ninety-nine year lease expired in 1997. Li Wah Tung had moved out of the luxury apartment in the Peak District; when not in San Francisco on business, he now resided in an equally expensive flat in Repulse Bay.

The remaining three witnesses had proved to be far more elusive. From the Department of Health, Head of Station learned that Ronald Bartholomew had returned to England when his contract with the Hong Kong government had expired in 1974. His name had last appeared in the 134th edition of the *Medical Directory* published by J. and A. Churchill Limited in 1978 when his address had then been Greengates, West Heath Road, Minehead, Somerset. Not surprisingly, Ms Lenora Vassman was no longer with the Bank of America.

In drafting his reply to London, Head of Station suggested that in Bartholomew's case, it might be worthwhile checking his personal details with the local Registrar of Births, Marriages and Deaths for the Minehead area. He added that apart from asking the switchboard operator at the Bank of America for Ms Lenora Vassman, he had thought it unwise to initiate further enquiries through the CIA's resident at the US Consulate without detailed guidance.

He also had to confess that the Intelligence staff had been unable to discover the present whereabouts of Yang Bo. Anxious not to give the impression that he was dragging his feet, Head of Station informed London that he had now sought assistance from the Hong Kong police who were confident they could locate the landing dock attendant.

On completion, the message was delivered to the communications centre in Victoria where it was held for the next satellite transmission at 23.15 hours local time. Despite this technical delay, the yeoman of signals assured Head of Station that it would be received by London during normal office hours.

Getting to Leatherhead took longer than Ashton had anticipated. Before leaving Scotland Yard, Peachey had insisted on checking with Gower Street to find out whether they were aware that one of the two men who had killed Louise Oakham was in hospital and were acting on the information. He had then spent a further five minutes discussing whether he or some other officer should get on to it. After that issue had been settled, there had been a problem over transport. Gower Street had been unable to provide a car for them, so had The Firm. Rather than rely on British Rail, they'd taken the Underground to Pimlico and walked the rest of the way to Churchill Gardens where Ashton had left his Vauxhall Cavalier. They had then battled across London and on down to the Mid Surrey General Hospital.

The unidentified gunman was under intensive care in one of the recovery rooms near the operating theatres. There was a nurse in constant attendance at his bedside and an armed policeman on guard in the corridor. The prognosis wasn't good; the assassin had sustained severe head injuries when he had been thrown out of the Escort and both legs had been crushed under the wheels of a minibus which had run over him as he lay unconscious in the road. The minibus had then ploughed into the ICI chemical tanker and burst into flames. Burning fuel from the ruptured tank had spread out in an ever-widening pool of fire until finally it had reached his outstretched left arm, inflicting third degree burns as far as the elbow and frying the fingers to a crisp. His injuries were such that the intern charged with monitoring his condition did not expect him to make it through a second night.

'And he has been in a coma the whole time?' Ashton said in a flat voice.

'Yes. You could say he is brain dead to all intents and purposes.'

'Is there any chance he might regain consciousness, if only for a few minutes.'

'Miracles sometimes happen,' the intern told him.

'What was the victim wearing when he was admitted?' Peachey asked with fine disregard for the fact that the assassin was anything but a victim.

'Jeans, roll-neck sweater, a leather bomber jacket and one black lace-up shoe – the other was missing. We had to cut the clothes off him.'

'Was anything found in the jacket?'

'There was a wallet containing fifty pounds.'

'What else?'

'Nothing.'

'No driver's licence, credit card or anything that could identify him?'

'There was just the money.' The intern frowned. 'The police already know this. I don't understand why you gentlemen are going over the same ground. I mean, who are you?'

'Scotland Yard Anti-Terrorist Squad,' Ashton said, poker-faced. 'We like to build up the picture for ourselves, not get the information second-hand.' He smiled fleetingly. 'You've no objection to answering our questions, have you, Doctor?'

'No.' The intern cleared his throat. 'No, not at all,' he added.

The sister in charge of the surgical ward wasn't in a mood to be quite so co-operative. Ashton could tell she had a bone to pick with them by the way she tossed her blonde head as she advanced down the corridor past the armed guard outside the recovery room. The staff nurse saw her coming and tried to escape before she was asked to explain what these men were doing in her office, but she left it a shade too late.

'This is not a coffee house, Nurse,' she announced from a considerable distance.

Ashton resisted the temptation to tell her that she wasn't God, Jesus Christ or the Holy Ghost, and ignoring her presence, spoke again to the intern. 'What about distinguishing marks?' he asked. 'Does this patient of yours have any?'

'There's a tattoo on his right arm. Well, several to be precise.'

Ashton exchanged glances with Clifford Peachey. 'I think we'd like to see them,' he said, catching an affirmative nod from the MI5 man.

'Out of the question,' the ward sister informed him brusquely. 'The patient isn't to be disturbed.'

'Are those your instructions?' Peachey enquired politely.

'Yes.'

'So whose permission should we seek?'

'You don't understand, those are my instructions. I am responsible for the wellbeing of all the patients on my ward.'

The constable on guard outside the recovery room did his best to look disinterested but was straining his ears to catch every word.

Ashton closed his eyes, counted slowly up to ten, but the short fuse was still burning. 'This man is going to die. Right, Sister?'

'That's not the point.'

'The point is, Sister, your precious patient put five bullets into a young woman who'd never done him a lick of harm before he finally managed to blow most of her head away with the sixth round. Now there are three little girls in Guildford who don't have a mother . . .'

'Naturally, I'm sorry to hear that but—'

'And frankly, I don't give a shit if I end up croaking him in the next five minutes, but I'm going to examine his bloody tattoos and that's all there is to it.'

'We'll see about that. I'm going to summon one of the security guards . . .'

'Better make up a hospital bed for him while you're at it,' Ashton told her.

The ward sister was standing in his way, seemingly intent on preventing him from seeing her patient. She was not a small woman but he picked her up with effortless ease and set her down again to one side. The staff nurse behind him gave a kind of strangled gasp as if trying hard not to burst out laughing. As he approached the recovery room, the police constable got to his feet.

'Don't even think about trying to stop me,' Ashton warned.

'The thought never entered my head,' the constable told him. 'I was only going to open the door for you.'

The dying man looked like a waxworks dummy, the skin drawn tight across his cheekbones and colourless, as if all the blood had been drained from his body. The nurse looked up from the paperback she was reading, then leaped to her feet and tried to push Ashton away from the bed as he threw the sheet aside.

'It's all right,' the intern assured her.

There were three tattoos on the right arm between the elbow and shoulder. The oldest was a hammer and sickle. Above and below it were the more recent additions, the old Imperial Russian Cross of St George and two crossed Kalashnikov assault rifles surmounting a scroll.

'Looks like we've got ourselves a Russian,' Ashton said.

'And one who likes to hedge his bets,' Peachey observed, then pointed to the motto on the scroll. 'What does that mean?' he asked.

'Roughly speaking, it says, "Long Live Chechnya".'

'Chechnya?'

'One of the fifteen autonomous republics of the former Russian Soviet Federal Socialist Republic.' Ashton replaced the sheet. 'Be interesting to know why this man came to England,' he said.

CHAPTER 12

Ashton slowly opened his eyes, peered at the luminous face of the battery-powered travelling clock and eventually came to the conclusion that it wasn't the alarm that had aroused him. It was 2.45 in the morning, a strong wind blowing, the rain slashing against the window and not a vehicle moving anywhere, which was unusual because London was never truly silent. Only this wasn't his flat in Churchill Gardens; this was the Egans' house in Ferris Drive opposite Lincoln Cathedral. And he was sleeping in one of the spare rooms because Harriet had a dozen reasons why she didn't want to share a bed with him, all of them dating from the time she had become noticeably pregnant.

He turned over on to his back and stared blankly up at the ceiling, puzzled to know why he had woken up in the middle of the night. He certainly hadn't been dreaming, nor had he eaten anything which had subsequently disagreed with him. A faint creaking noise supplied the answer and he was instantly alert. Someone had broken into the house and was prowling about downstairs. Throwing the duvet aside, he slipped out of bed, grabbed his dressing gown and put it on, then quietly opened the door. He tiptoed out on to the landing, ears attuned to catch the slightest sound.

The click of a cupboard either being closed or opened told him the intruder was in the kitchen. Carefully testing each step before putting his full weight on it, Ashton went on down the staircase. From the hall he could see a crack of light under the door to the left of the dining room. He moved swiftly towards it and storming into the kitchen, came face to face with Harriet. She had a knife in one hand and a jar of peanut butter in the other. On the table between them was a glass of milk, a butter dish and a loaf of sliced bread.

'I was starving,' Harriet told him before he could ask her what she was doing out of bed. 'Can I make you a sandwich too?'

'No thanks, I'm not hungry.'

'A glass of milk then?'

'I'd sooner have a cup of coffee.'

'You'll find the Nescafé on the second shelf in the cupboard,' she said, dipping the knife into the peanut butter.

He filled the electric kettle under the tap and plugged it in, then measured two heaped spoonfuls of the instant coffee into a mug. 'Since when have you been so fond of peanut butter?' he asked.

'Since I got to be the size of a house.'

Harriet had never been short, but her figure had been perfectly proportioned. Now she was carrying their child high so that her stomach bulged like a small barrel.

'When are you returning to London?' she asked for no apparent reason.

'Tomorrow.' Ashton smiled. 'Well, later this morning to be strictly accurate.'

'Have you checked with Victor Hazelwood? I imagine you need his permission? After all, he was the one who told you to make yourself scarce, wasn't he?'

'I didn't need any urging. If the press had latched on to me, I would have been in all kinds of trouble.'

'I might have guessed you would take that line,' she said bitterly.

Harriet had never been able to understand why he stood up for Victor whenever she attacked the Deputy DG. She was convinced his loyalty was misplaced because, in her book, Hazelwood believed in looking after number one.

'Despite what you may think, Victor wasn't motivated by self-interest.'

There had been two very good reasons why Hazelwood had wanted him to keep his head down. The Russian he'd insisted on seeing had died shortly after he and Clifford Peachey had left the Mid Surrey General Hospital and the sister in charge of the surgical ward had lodged an official complaint about his behaviour. There was no telling how far she would take it; if the hospital management committee failed to dismiss the complaint, it could go on up to the Regional Health Authority and perhaps on across to some politician who felt it was his duty to raise the issue in Parliament. But it had been the inevitable discovery by the press that Louise Oakham's husband was in the army and had absented himself without leave that had prompted Hazelwood to take action.

'No Intelligence service welcomes publicity, least of all the SIS,' Ashton told her. 'Victor was faced with a very tricky situation, but he believed it could be contained provided I was kept out of the limelight. If the media were unaware of my involvement, there was a chance they would limit their enquiries to what the police were doing.'

'I'll say this much for Victor, he can certainly pull the wool over your eyes.'

'He did nothing of the kind. It's the way I would have handled the situation in his shoes. And it worked.'

'Did it?'

'You read the quality Sundays,' Ashton told her.

Ever since the two Russians from Chechnya had been identified, every investigative journalist with any kind of reputation had been piecing together what they had been doing in London. Ruslan Ovakimyan and Stefan Afansiev; the crossed Kalashnikov rifles and the motto within the scroll beneath had pointed Clifford Peachey in the right direction. Even though the KGB was not the force it had once been, the Kremlin watchers of MI5 were busier than ever these days keeping tabs on the diplomatic staffs of the independent states which had emerged following the break-up of the old Soviet Union. Soon after returning from the Mid Surrey General, Peachey must have called on them to see if any representatives from the Chechnya Republic had come to their notice. Ashton could only surmise that this was how it had happened; not long after Peachey had returned to Gower Street, he had been on his way north to Lincoln, but it was the most likely explanation. And once the police had been obliged to release their names along with the other victims of the traffic accident, there had been no holding the press.

'Do you think what the newspapers are saying about Ovakimyan and Afansiev is completely accurate?' Harriet asked between mouthfuls of peanut butter.

'They weren't living in cardboard boxes on the street, that's for sure.' Ashton switched off the electric kettle, unplugged it from the mains and poured the boiling water over the instant coffee in the mug, then sat down facing Harriet across the kitchen table. 'And of course they could afford the most expensive call girls in town,' he continued. 'It wasn't their own money they were using.'

'I was referring to the guided missiles they were hoping to buy,' Harriet said.

According to the *Sunday Times*, the Chechans were looking for two thousand Stinger anti-aircraft guided missiles. It had also been reported that they were hoping to sell on most of the bulk purchase to their fellow Muslims in Azerbaijan.

'Well, that rather puzzled me too,' Ashton told her, 'especially as the Stinger is manufactured by General Dynamics. You would have thought that Ovakimyan and Afansiev would have gone to California to purchase the missiles. I wonder what made them think they could place an order in London for an American weapons system which isn't even in service with the British Army?'

'Maybe they were over here to meet an arms dealer who knew where he could lay his hands on the requisite number?'

'Perhaps.' Ashton had to admit he couldn't think of a more likely explanation.

'Could Simon Oakham have been involved in some way?' Harriet asked.

'Not in a month of Sundays; he was only a unit paymaster.' Ashton paused, then said, 'It's a good thing the press aren't aware yet that the two Russians had gunned down Louise Oakham shortly before they were killed in the traffic accident. We'd have a hard time keeping our head below the parapet if that got out.'

'How long before it does?'

'Your guess is as good as mine.'

The Russian who'd been trapped in the back of the Ford Escort had been reduced to a charred log after the vehicle had been engulfed in the fireball from the chemical tanker. The heat had been so intense that the semiautomatic had been melted down to an anonymous lump of metal. Certainly, the fireman who had retrived it from the twisted chassis had had no idea that it had once been a 9mm handgun.

'Ballistics can't match the weapon; there were a number of rounds in the magazine and they cooked off in the fire, shattering the pistol grip and ripping a bloody great hole in the barrel.'

Harriet raised a quizzical eyebrow. 'And that's lucky?' she asked.

'It leaves the case wide open. The police may rightly believe the two Russians murdered Louise Oakham but without the automatic, they can't prove it. As soon as MI5 and the Anti-Terrorist Squad indicated they had an interest in the case, they were prepared to keep shtoom. In some ways, it makes their lives easier.'

'You seem to be very well informed.' Her eyes narrowed as the reason suddenly occurred to her. 'Have you been talking to Victor Hazelwood by any chance?'

Ashton nodded. 'Yesterday morning after I collected the Sunday papers from the newsagent. I rang him at home from a call box in Bellgate.'

'My God, you really are his lapdog,' Harriet said contemptuously. 'And I suppose it was then he gave you permission to return to London?'

'I am no one's lapdog, but if I want to continue doing freelance work for the SIS, certain ground rules have to be observed.'

'Did I hear you correctly? Are you saying that what you're doing is not a one-off job?'

'Translation work is hard to come by and we need the money . . .'

'Don't lay that on me,' Harriet warned him. 'I didn't ask you to resign from the SIS. I have made no demands on your whatsoever and I don't expect you to support us.'

'But I want to be responsible,' Ashton told her.

But she refused to listen to him and it was like butting his head against a brick wall. When he continued to explain how he felt about their child, Harriet got up from the table and left the kitchen.

'I'm tired and I don't need this,' she told him in a low voice.

Long after she had walked out on him, Ashton was still sitting there. When he finally got around to drinking it, the mug of coffee was stone-cold. Emptying it into the sink, he rinsed out the mug, then returned to the small back bedroom and started packing, ready to make an early start to London.

Monday started just as badly for Hazelwood from the moment he decided to drive into the office rather than use the Underground. During the previous week there had been a number of disruptions on the Northern and Victoria Lines due to signal failures but they were nothing compared with the hiatus he encountered on the road. A flat offside rear tyre in Camden High Street delayed him for a good fifteen minutes while he changed it with the spare wheel. His temper was hardly improved when, less than a mile farther on, he ran into the back of an old Ford Capri whose aggressive driver hadn't bothered to look into the rear-view mirror before pulling out from the kerb. The collision smashed the nearside headlight on the Rover and crunched the wing; the ensuing altercation between the two men would have come to blows but for the timely arrival of a police constable.

The rest of the journey was little better; neighbouring boroughs seemed to be having a competition between themselves to see who could dig the largest number of holes in the road and the traffic lights in High Holborn were on the blink. Things didn't improve when he got to the Embankment, and an octogenarian with a zimmer frame could have beaten him across Westminster Bridge.

He eventually arrived in the office at 10.15, an hour and a quarter after morning prayers had finished. Missing the daily briefing of the

Director by heads of departments was not a mortal sin, but it seemed his absence had caused a certain amount of irritation. From his PA, he learned that Dunglass wished to see him as soon as it was convenient, which was a polite way of saying immediately. It wasn't the kind of summons Hazelwood was used to receiving and consequently he was in no mood to offer either an apology or an explanation. As it happened, neither was required.

'Where's Ashton?' Dunglass asked before he could even say good morning.

'About halfway between Lincoln and his flat in Churchill Gardens I would imagine.' Hazelwood pursed his lips. 'What's he done now?'

'Nothing yet, but I'd rather we didn't take any unnecessary risks now that the cat is out of the bag.'

'I'm sorry,' Hazelwood said, 'I'm not with you. What's happened?'

'You haven't seen the papers this morning?'

'I left home before they were delivered.'

'It's been reported that Ovakimyan and Afansiev fired on a police car shortly before they were killed in the traffic accident. The story only made the stop press in some newspapers, in others it received no more than a small paragraph on the crime page.'

Hazelwood digested the news in silence. It didn't matter when or how the press had learned of the incident; by tomorrow at the latest, the story would be on the front page of every newspaper, and in far greater detail. To believe it wouldn't come to that would be pure wishful thinking.

'Who's in the firing line?' he asked.

'The police,' Dunglass said. 'The unfortunate public relations officer of Surrey Constabulary is handling all enquiries from the media. In consultation with Clifford Peachey,' he added with a wintry smile.

'So what do you want to do about Ashton?'

'I thought we'd send him to Hong Kong. You know the old saying, Victor – out of sight, out of mind. He can make himself useful too; there's no reason why he shouldn't question Lloyd Ingolby about the conduct of the inquest on Bernice Kwang. Ashton probably knows more about the case than our Head of Station. Lambert can accompany him.'

Hazelwood blinked. 'I thought he was otherwise engaged?'

It seemed the advice Ashton had received from his informant in the Adjutant General's Corps had not been entirely accurate, which had made Lambert's task almost impossible. Combined Manning and Records Office was not in a position to supply nominal rolls in respect of the Hong Kong SIB detachment for the period January 1969 to May 1970 or any other date span for that matter. The detachment was not an independent unit, it was in fact part of the Far East Section based on Singapore from which organisation it derived its establishment. The Record Office simply posted individuals to the Far East Section; where they were subsequently deployed was up to the Provost Marshal. All Combined Manning could do was produce a list of warrant officers and sergeants who had served in the Far East during the seventeen months in question.

'In round numbers, we are talking about fifty individuals,' Dunglass continued. 'Some NCOs were just detached for a six-month unaccompanied tour in Hong Kong, others did a full three years on station. Anyway, we shall have to write to all fifty if we want to find out exactly who did serve in the colony.'

By 'we', Dunglass meant that after he had approved a letter drafted by the Pacific Basin Department, the army would then have the pleasure of sending it out under the letterhead and signature of some officer in the Personnel Branch at the MoD. Although not a completely fair division of labour, it did have the undoubted merit of sheltering The Firm. None of the fifty warrant officers and sergeants would ever know the letter they'd received had been sent out at the behest of the SIS.

'Was the Record Office able to produce a list of addresses for these ex-servicemen?' Hazelwood asked.

'Only for those who completed twenty-two years and are in receipt of a pension from the army. The others will have to be located through their National Insurance numbers, which means asking Social Security to extract the data from their computer at Newcastle-upon-Tyne.'

Ashton had said much the same, but it didn't end there. When all the replies were in and the names of those who had served in Hong Kong were known, someone would have to visit the ex-servicemen to see if anyone recognised the mysterious Tom who'd been on the fishing trip organised by the SIB detachment. Hazelwood didn't have to ask how far they had got.

'I understand the army has had one or two replies to the letters they sent out,' Dunglass informed him, as if he knew what was passing through his mind. 'But there's a long way to go yet, which is why we can spare Lambert.'

The decision had obviously been taken at morning prayers. Had he not decided to use the Rover instead of the Underground, he could have put a damper on the idea.

'Ashton doesn't need a nursemaid,' Hazelwood said in a last-ditch attempt to reverse the decision.

'I disagree, and Lambert is exactly the right man for the job. He can speak Cantonese and is also fluent in Mandarin. Ashton isn't.'

Hazelwood knew when he was beaten. 'When do you see them leaving for Hong Kong?' he asked.

The short answer was as soon as possible, and to this end, Kelso was already working on the necessary travel arrangements. Meanwhile, it was his job to contact Ashton and brief him. There was a new purposefulness about Dunglass that was hard to take; less than a year ago the Director General had been only too keen to seek his advice before making an executive decision. Now he felt confident enough to treat his deputy like a bloody errand boy. In a somewhat bitter and twisted frame of mind, Hazelwood returned to his office, picked up the phone and rang Ashton's flat in Churchill Gardens. The number rang out just twice before the answer machine cut in; after the tone, he left a message that was terse and very much to the point.

Ashton let himself into the flat, picked up the mail lying on the mat and, closing the door behind him with his heel, went on through the hall and dumped his bag in the bedroom. Two bills, a statement from Access showing a debtor balance of two hundred and eighty-four pounds, nine pence including interest charges from the previous accounting period, a wad of junk mail urging him to buy things he didn't need and a begging letter from a charity he'd never heard of. It wasn't the most exciting post he'd come home to.

Ashton unpacked his bag, carried the dirty laundry into the bathroom and shoved it into the linen basket ready for the next wash. He then checked the sitting room to see if there were any messages on the Dialatron. The figure 01 in the display window told him there was; depressing the answer button, he listened to Hazelwood urging him to get in touch, which he'd intended to do anyway.

Lifting the receiver, he punched out Victor's phone number at Vauxhall Cross. 'I got your message,' he said when Hazelwood answered.

'Where the hell have you been?'

He had intended to make a quick start from Lincoln, but the Egans weren't exactly early birds and on reflection he had felt it would be damned rude to sneak off without thanking Harriet's parents for having him to stay. But Ashton didn't see why he should offer an explanation; he had been instructed to make himself scarce until further notice and he wouldn't be in London now if he hadn't phoned Hazelwood yesterday morning.

'Is there anything else you want to say to me before I hang up?' he said icily.

'I'd like you to go to Hong Kong with Brian Lambert,' Hazelwood said, immediately contrite. 'I think you know why.'

'I can guess.'

'Will you do it?'

It took Ashton only a few seconds to make up his mind. There was no appeasing Harriet and the yawning gulf between them was becoming an unbridgeable chasm. He could hardly make the situation worse than it was already and, as he'd told Victor once before, what he was being asked to do beat the hell out of proofreading. It was also a fact that there was nothing else in the pipeline for him.

'When do you want me to leave?' he asked.

'There's a British Airways flight departing Heathrow tonight at 21.20 hours. Gets you into Hong Kong at 6.00 p.m. tomorrow . . .'

'Hell's teeth, you're not allowing me much time, Victor.'

'There's a minimum of six hours before you need to check in. How much longer do you want?'

'Well, I doubt if the local branch of Lloyds can supply me with traveller's cheques at the drop of a hat.'

'That's no problem,' Hazelwood said breezily. 'Lambert's drawn enough blanks from the Admin Wing for both of you. Besides, our colleagues out there will make sure you don't go short.'

'Okay, what about a briefing?'

'Lambert will do that. Expect him in an hour.'

'What?'

'He's going to call round to your flat,' Hazelwood said. 'It will save you coming in.'

A more lurid sign above the entrance was the only visible difference between The Golden Horn and all the other topless bars in the Wanchai district of Hong Kong Island. The waitresses were Chinese girls in their early teens who looked pretty much alike with their identical hairstyles, false eyelashes and blood-red fingernails. They wore gold, high-heeled sandals and short, pleated black skirts which only just covered their buttocks. What also distinguished The Golden Horn from other honky-tonks were six live statues posed in the alcoves behind the bar and high enough above it to be out of reach.

The living statues came from Germany, Denmark, Sweden and Finland. All six were tall, slender, blonde and quite naked; their suntanned bodies were the colour of mahogany and glistened as if they had been rubbed down with linseed oil. Looking completely vacuous, they did not move a muscle whether standing, kneeling or sitting cross-legged. Uttley didn't know how they did it, didn't care either; The Golden Horn was not really his scene.

Steven Uttley was forty-four and had spent nineteen years in the Hong Kong police. A former detective constable in the Kent Constabulary, he had become an Inspector the day he'd joined the Hong Kong force. Since that heady moment, he had made exactly one step up the ladder and in 1997 when the colony was absorbed by mainland China, he would be out of a job. The occasional visit to a topless bar like The Golden Horn was his personal equity plan against that rainy day. He was on his second drink and doing his best to out-stare one of the living statues when a pert-looking Chinese girl informed him that he should go sit with Mr Chan.

The Chinese had two girls with him and was sitting in a booth to the left of the entrance. He was two inches shorter and fifteen years younger than Uttley and was never short of money, though he didn't flash it around. He was the original chameleon who blended so well into the background that he could come and go without being noticed. Mr Chan, as he liked to call himself, was the sort of man who looked equally at home dining in the Peninsula Hotel or in a honky-tonk like The Golden Horn whose clientele were merchant seamen, trainee managers from the great trading houses out on a night's razzle-dazzle, servicemen and the odd tourist who'd strayed off the beaten track. Drink in hand, Uttley sauntered over to the booth and sat down.

'Good evening, Mr Steve.' Chan flashed him a bright smile. 'My girl is called Beautiful Jade in English, yours is Heavenly Peace.'

Heavenly Peace was showing all she'd got in a tight-fitting sweater and a short skirt that barely escaped being indecent. The heavy make-up on her face could not disguise the fact that she was well into the wrong side of thirty, and two gold teeth and a suspicion of halitosis killed what little interest Uttley may have had.

'What's that you're drinking, Mr Steve?' Chan asked in a noticeable American accent.

'Brandy Sour,' Uttley told him.

A snap of his fingers commanded the attention of the nearest waitress and in keeping with the kind of service Chan obviously regarded as his due, the Brandy Sour arrived in record time.

'Brandy is good for you,' he observed in all seriousness, 'makes you very strong and virile. Heavenly Peace will like that.'

Uttley glanced sideways at his companion and was rewarded with a brilliant but empty smile. 'Seems she can't wait,' he growled.

'Me neither, so let's get on with it.'

'Are you crazy?'

'It's okay, Mr Steve, Heavenly Peace doesn't understand a word of English, neither does Beautiful Jade. Now, what have you got for us?'

The police officer with his informer, Uttley thought ironically, except that their roles were reversed. 'We've been asked to locate a man called Yang Bo; he used to be a landing dock attendant employed by the Royal Hong Kong Yacht Club. He gave evidence at the inquest on Bernice Kwang, a Chinese American girl.'

'I've never heard of either of them.'

'She died in mysterious circumstances back in 1970.'

'Before my time.'

'And mine,' Uttley said. 'Anyway, London thinks he can shed new light on the case. Could be they will send someone over here to question him.'

'When did you hear this?'

'I only saw the cable today on the float file, but it seems we started looking for Yang Bo a few days ago.'

'Why was that?'

'The Commissioner played this one close to his chest and gave it straight to Special Branch. I've had a word with them but they haven't run Yang Bo to ground yet although they've been given an address for him. If it checks out, they'll let me know.'

'How can you be sure of that?'

'Because I'm the Police Liaison Officer, the link man with the army, navy and air force, but more importantly, with the Joint Services Intelligence Staff. And my nose tells me it's the Intelligence people who are anxious to get their hands on Yang Bo.'

'I'd better tell the elders.'

'Yeah, you do that,' Uttley said, content that a bonus of several thousand US dollars would shortly find its way into his bank account in the Bahamas, courtesy of the Black Dragon Triad.

CHAPTER 13

There was no airport in the world like Kai Tak. A large part of the runway was on land that had been reclaimed from the sea and the final approach was made just above roof top level through the heart of Kowloon. But the first hazard pilots had to contend with was the often shrouded peak of Tai Mo Shan. There were, however, no low-lying clouds that evening and Ashton couldn't see the mountain from his window seat on the 747. The captain had told them to look out for Stonecutters Island which was supposed to be somewhere over to his right but, at the time, he had been too busy adjusting his seat into the upright position to catch a glimpse of it.

What he saw now was a forest of TV aerials and washing lines strung between bamboo poles on the flat roofs of the tenements; then the plane swept in over Prince Edward Road, touched down and started eating up the runway. The sea appeared on both sides of the aircraft and the dour Glaswegian sitting next to Ashton reminded him that a China Airways Airbus had done a belly flop in the water not so very long ago. He seemed almost disappointed when their 747 left the runway and taxied back to the terminal building without mishap.

There was the usual rush to get off the plane before the door was opened which resulted in the inevitable log jam in the aisles. When Ashton eventually left the Boeing, his Glaswegian travelling companion had already passed through Immigration and was nowhere to be seen. He caught up with him again in the baggage claim area where Brian Lambert, the Australian exchange officer, was also still waiting for his suitcase to appear. They might have travelled out on the same plane but they had been seated far apart and wouldn't be staying under the same roof. It was entirely unintentional; the trip had been arranged at the last minute and Kelso had had to accept what was going. That meant that in taking the last two seats on Flight BA 027, one of them had to sit in the smoking section of the Economy Class while the other went Club.

There had been a similar problem with hotel accommodation. All the travel agent could let Kelso have was a single room at the Hong Kong Hotel in Kowloon for three nights only. Head of Station had reluctantly agreed to put one of them up and since Lambert was a serving officer, it had been decided it would be more appropriate if he stayed with the SIS chief in Victoria. At Kelso's insistence, Lambert had also been the one to travel Club Class which had embarrassed him no end.

Lambert made a sudden dart at the carousel, grabbed his suitcase and hefted it on to a cart. Before moving off, he looked enquiringly in Ashton's direction as if seeking some last-minute instruction. Conscious that his fellow traveller from Glasgow had observed the semaphore and was eyeing him, Ashton ignored the younger man. Eventually, Lambert took the hint and walked away towards Customs and the exit.

'Do you know yon fella?' the Glaswegian asked him.

'What fella?'

'The one opposite us who was staring at you.'

'Oh, that guy,' Ashton said as if it had just dawned on him who the Glaswegian was referring to. 'Was he actually looking at me?'

'I thought so.'

'Must be a case of mistaken identity.'

Ashton moved in to snatch his bag from the carousel, then expressing a hope that the baggage handlers at Heathrow hadn't mislaid the Glaswegian's luggage, parted company with him. Passing through Customs, he followed the directional signs for the taxi rank in the concourse and emerged from the terminal building in time to catch a last glimpse of Lambert as he departed in an Audi driven by the Head of Station.

The Hong Kong Hotel adjoined the Ocean Terminal condominium down on the waterfront off Canton Road. The single room which had been reserved for Ashton did not overlook the harbour; instead, he had an unrivalled view of the narrow alleyway between the hotel and Star House. He unpacked, took a shower and then changed into a lightweight suit before dining in the Bauhinia Room. From a table in the window, he could see the Star ferries ploughing to and fro between Kowloon and Victoria over on the Island. An attentive waiter pointed out the Peak tram and other focal points of interest, but after a twelve-and-a-half-hour flight on top of a further eighteen without sleep, Ashton could hardly keep his eyes open, let alone admire the scenery.

He tried to telephone Harriet after dinner to let her know he'd arrived safely but in Lincoln it was only two o'clock in the afternoon and apparently no one was at home. He promised himself that he would try again later but no bed had ever looked so inviting. He stripped off, crawled between the sheets and went out like a light.

The telephone on the bedside table brought him to the surface though it was some moments before Ashton realised it wasn't the wake-up alarm. Still not fully alert, he reached out, lifted the receiver off the cradle and drawing it near, grunted into the mouthpiece.

'It's me,' Lambert told him cheerfully. 'Just thought I'd let you know that the Attorney General had had a word with Lloyd Ingolby and the judge is expecting you for coffee between ten and half-past.'

'This morning?'

'That's what we decided in London. Remember?'

'Yes, of course. I was a little disoriented, that's all.'

'Don't tell me you're still in bed.'

'No, I won't,' Ashton said and hung up.

Lifting the receiver again, he called room service and ordered coffee, fresh orange juice, rolls and butter, then stood under the shower for a good five minutes to liven himself up before shaving. Breakfast arrived shortly after he had finished dressing.

Ingolby had a villa overlooking Big Wave Bay on the Island. For someone who had never been to Hong Kong, taking a cab seemed the simplest way of getting there. Some twenty minutes after leaving the hotel, Ashton was beginning to wonder if it was. The Chinese cab driver, who'd assured the doorman that he knew where the villa was, gave every sign of being less than confident when they emerged from the cross-harbour tunnel in Causeway Bay. Heading east, they passed the Shell oil depot and carried on through one vast housing estate after another, occasionally catching a glimpse of the sea between the high-rise blocks.

North Point, San Wan Ho, Shau Kei Wan; none of the place names meant anything to Ashton, nor did they appear to convey much to the cab driver either. Beyond Chai Wan, they ran out of asphalt and had to double back to the point where they had turned off the main road. A sign at the junction pointed the way to Shek O and sent them on a wide loop in a westerly direction as if they were making a circular tour of the Island. A few more twists and turns and they were heading south, a chain of hills to their left, the sea on the right. Before reaching the tip of the peninsula, the road suddenly turned back on itself and snaked through a gap in the hills. After a couple of miles, the sea came in view again.

'Big Wave Bay,' the taxi driver proudly announced in English and pointed straight ahead 'You see house soon.'

Soon meant a good five minutes beyond the track leading to Shek O village. The villa where Ingolby lived was aptly called Journey's End. The road petered out at the top of his driveway, a narrow strip of concrete which zigzagged down the cliff face to a split-level house which Ashton estimated was some thirty to forty feet above the beach.

'You wait here for me, okay?' Ashton gave the cab driver sixty Hong Kong dollars in part payment and told him to keep the meter running.

'You owe eighty-two dolla.'

'Watch the clock, you'll make a fortune.'

Ashton got out of the Datsun and walked down the drive. Behind him, the cab driver expressed his feelings in Cantonese; even to someone who didn't know a word of the language, it was evident he wasn't best pleased.

Sir Lloyd and Lady Ingolby lived in some style, their every need catered for by a small army of servants. Ashton met three of them before he was shown into a large drawing room with French windows opening on to a promenade deck and a wooden staircase leading to the beach.

For a man of seventy-four, Ingolby was in remarkably good shape. Over six feet tall and without a spare ounce of flesh, he carried himself as straight as a ramrod. No rounded shoulders, no curvature of the spine and certainly no pot belly bulging over the waistband of his cavalry twill slacks. He also had a full head of thick black hair with only the odd streak of grey. There was no sign of Lady Ingolby, but her hand was evident in the Georgian silver coffee pot, sugar bowl, cream jug and porcelain cups and saucers which appeared on an equally magnificent silver tray moments after Ashton had been shown into the drawing room.

'Too cold to sit outside,' Ingolby told him.

There wasn't a cloud in the sky, the temperature was hovering on seventy Fahrenheit, but if you had spent most of your adult life in the Far East, it probably did feel chilly.

'Black or white?' Ingolby asked him.

'White please, no sugar.' A houseboy poured the coffee, then withdrew. 'I believe you know why I'm here, Sir Lloyd,' Ashton said presently.

'I've had a long conversation with the Attorney General. Now what can I tell you about the inquest?'

There was no way of getting to the heart of the matter without the risk of causing offence, but Ashton did his best. 'You were pretty hard on Lenora Vassman,' he began tentatively.

'Maybe I was, but she was a very tiresome young woman. Her constant interruptions would have tried the patience of a saint, which I am not.'

'Reading the transcript, I got the impression she believed there had been foul play.'

'Miss Vassman was blessed with a vivid imagination,' Ingolby said dismissively. 'There was not a shred of proof to support her contention.'

'What about the pathologist? He wasn't exactly on the ball.'

'What do you mean?'

'He didn't appear to notice the abrasions on Bernice Kwang's wrists.'

Ingolby shifted his gaze and stared out to sea while delicately sipping his coffee. 'How well do you know Bartholomew?' he asked after some considerable deliberation.

'I've never met him,' Ashton said.

'Well, Ronald may have had a drink problem, but he didn't miss anything.'

The transcript didn't read like that. If Bartholomew hadn't missed the abrasions on Bernice Kwang, he had deliberately ignored them, and no one would have been any the wiser if Lenora Vassman hadn't spoken up. Furthermore, it had been Ingolby, not the pathologist, who had supplied the explanation for the rope burns on the deceased's wrists.

'I think you are concealing something,' Ashton told him bluntly.

'I'm doing what?'

'You put words into the mouth of the Crown's expert witness, you muzzled the American girl and you made damned sure the jury delivered the verdict you so obviously wanted.'

Ingolby put his cup and saucer on an ornately carved side table that looked as though it had been made in India. 'You want to be very careful what you're saying, young man. If you repeat a word of that scurrilous accusation to anyone outside these four walls, I'll sue you for slander. Do I make myself clear?'

'I know when I'm being given a load of bullshit,' Ashton said coldly. 'I also know the Attorney General has promised you immunity from prosecution in return for your wholehearted co-operation, which I'm not getting. Now, if I leave here empty-handed, the Attorney General will withdraw the offer of immunity, London will order a Judicial Inquiry and you could find yourself in very serious trouble. That's something I imagine you could do without at your age.'

'Yes, it is.'

'So tell me about the fix.'

Ingolby wanted him to know there had been no financial induce-
ment. Two High Court judges and the Colonial First Secretary had
told him it was his patriotic duty to ensure the jury arrived at a
finding of Death by Misadventure.

'An open verdict was the last thing anyone wanted.'

'Why?'

'I was told that Bernice Kwang was suspected of being a double agent
and the CIA had decided to take remedial action, whatever that meant. It
was also alleged that she had betrayed a number of our Chinese agents
who belonged to the Black Dragon Triad. They had been executed
by the People's Liberation Army following a show trial in Peking.
Anyway, a junior British Intelligence officer took it upon himself to
point the Triad in her direction.'

'And they murdered her,' Ashton said flatly.

'There was that possibility.'

Nobody had wanted to find out. When all was said and done, Bernice
Kwang had been an American citizen and it had been felt that there
would be hell to pay it if was suspected that she had been taken out
by the Brits.

'The Americans were just as keen as we were to sweep the mess under
the carpet.'

'You believed that?'

'If you've read the transcript, Mr Ashton, you would know they were. It
was the lawyer representing the US Consulate who really gagged Lenora
Vassman.'

'So you didn't have any qualms about rigging the inquest?'

Ingolby had had quite a few, but he stilled them for two reasons.
Her death could have been accidental because the Triad couldn't have
known there was going to be a sudden and freak rain squall four and
a half hours after Bernice Kwang had taken her dinghy out when the
weather forecasters themselves had been caught napping. But what
had finally anaesthetised a nagging conscience was the personal and
highly confidential briefing he had received from a senior official in the
Foreign and Commonwealth Office.

'At least he said he was from the Foreign Office,' Ingolby contended.

'Can you remember his name?' Ashton asked.

'Reeves. I think his first name was William.'

William Henry Reeves, Head of Station, Hong Kong, Chairman and
Managing Director of the Asia and Pacific Travel Agency funded by
the SIS. Ashton had total recall and could have told him the date and

precise time of the massive coronary that had led to Reeves' dying on the Fanling golf course. Small wonder that Dunglass should want to distance himself from what had happened in 1970 when he had been with the Far East Bureau in Singapore.

'Bernice Kwang was described as a wealthy socialite at the inquest?'

'You can't rent an apartment in the Peak District unless you are well-heeled,' Ingolby told him. 'Her father made all his money out of fruit and vegetables. He also owned a string of Chinese restaurants in San Francisco, Monterey, Santa Barbara and Los Angeles.'

Ashton reached inside his jacket and took out a photocopy of the picture that had appeared in the *South China Morning Post*. 'This was taken at a barbecue in the New Territories,' he said, passing it to Ingolby. 'Can you tell me anything about the man whose head I've ringed in ink?'

'Yes,' Ingolby said without hesitation, 'his name is Gillespie. He used to be a guide with some travel agency here in Hong Kong. Reeves told me he was very close to the American girl. In fact, he suspected Bernice Kwang had used him as a courier on a number of occasions.'

Ingolby could not recall his first name, nor could he remember which travel agency Gillespie had worked for. He fancied Reeves had been a little vague on that score. It could be that the SIS Head of Station had told him no more than he had needed to know; alternatively, Reeves might have had some sly reason for withholding the information. Whatever the explanation, Ashton knew he had got everything there was to be had out of Ingolby.

'You've been very helpful, sir,' he told the former judge.

He also said he regretted taking up so much of his time, which went down well with Ingolby, so much so that when they parted company on the doorstep, a neutral observer might have thought they were close friends.

Ashton removed his jacket, then walked slowly on up the zigzag drive to the road above where the taxi driver should have been waiting for him. Feeling somewhat foolish, Ashton retraced his steps to ask if he could use the phone to ring for a cab. Ingolby said he was welcome to try but doubted if he would get one to come all the way out to Journey's End.

Ashton called Yellow Cabs and was advised by the dispatcher to phone again at noon when the shift changed because right now everything was out on the road.

'I wouldn't put any money on that,' Ingolby told him. 'Chen will run you back in the jeep.'

Ashton didn't protest. To refuse the offer would be churlish and Ingolby might then have felt compelled to ask him to lunch, something neither man wanted.

The jeep was a World War Two left-hand drive Ford Willys that had been lovingly restored and fitted with chrome wheel nuts and plush upholstery. It was also driven with loving care by Chen for whom thirty miles an hour was excessive.

The accident occurred approximately one mile beyond the track leading to Shek O village. There were no wing mirrors on the jeep and they were not aware they had company until the truck driver hit the horn button and pulled out to overtake them. Chen was hugging the nearside of the road and there was sufficient room for two vehicles, but the driver of the Mercedes truck nudged them as he swept past and cut in front. Losing control of the jeep, Chen ran off the road into a dried-out paddy field. They were still doing twenty when both nearside wheels dropped into an irrigation ditch and the vehicle rolled over sideways. As earth and sky changed places, Ashton was flung out of the vehicle. The last thing he remembered was the ground rushing up to meet him.

He was unconscious for no more than a few seconds but it took him considerably longer to comprehend what had happened. Functioning like a robot, he gingerly explored his forehead above the right eye and was surprised when his fingers came away sticky with blood. One of his shoes looked kind of funny too until he realised that the toes of his left foot had burst through the leather upper. He flexed them, half expecting a stab of pain, but miraculously his toes didn't even seem to be bruised.

Ashton scrambled to his feet and turned about looking for Chen. The jeep was upside down and canted over at a slight angle, the right side of the vehicle marginally higher than the other with the front uppermost wheel still rotating. There was no sign of Chen and he feared the Chinese was the other side of the Ford Willys, trapped under the chassis. He stumbled towards the jeep and finding he was impeded by the damaged shoe, kicked it off.

Chen was lying face down in the paddy, the lower half of his body pinned at the waist by the raised ledge of the base-frame. His head was over on one side and he was gasping for breath, his face darkening as the vehicle slowly crushed him. Petrol was dripping from the tank under the driver's seat and the windscreen, which was acting like a car jack, was buckling, thereby increasing the pressure. Somehow Ashton had to raise the vehicle high enough to pull Chen out from under.

There were two major problems: he couldn't lift the vehicle even a fraction of an inch on his own and he couldn't get at the tool kit stored in the locker bin inside the jeep.

The road was deserted, the track leading to Shek O was a mile back and the village itself was probably another mile beyond the junction. If he ran like the wind, Chen would still die before he could summon help. The responsibility was his and his alone.

There were two brackets welded to the rear of the vehicle for jerry cans of petrol and water. Also strapped on the back was a general service shovel. Ashton thanked God that Lloyd Ingolby was evidently a military buff and had equipped the vehicle to World War Two scales. The blade of the GS shovel had been burnished until it gleamed like chrome but the cutting edge was razor sharp which was a piece of good luck because the paddy field was as hard as concrete.

He started digging the first of the two shallow trenches roughly six inches from Chen's waist. Both had to be wider than the length of the shovel so that after he had gone down a foot, he could kneel in the trench and drive a tunnel under the Chinese. Knowing that every minute counted, he went at the task with all the furious energy of a zealot. Thumping the blade into the earth with his right foot, he scooped out a shovelful of dirt in almost the same motion. Bathed in sweat, heart pounding like a steam hammer, he did not let up for a second.

To save time, Ashton decided to dig a hole rather than a second trench on the far side of the Chinese. He didn't like the colour of Chen's face and while it was always going to be a close-run thing, he feared he was going to lose him. Kneeling in the trench, he tunneled a burrow, frequently enlarging it until the earth bridge finally gave way and the full weight of the vehicle was no longer bearing on Chen.

Although Chen did not make an instant recovery, his face began to revert to a more normal colour and he was able to breathe reasonably well. Satisfied with the probability that he would now survive, Ashton retrieved the discarded shoe, slipped it on and then set off at a jog trot to fetch help from Shek O.

There were some useful Chinese phrases in the *Berlitz Travel Guide* which Lambert had given him before they had boarded the plane at Heathrow. Instead of watching the in-flight movie, Ashton had committed some of them to memory. 'Bin gor sik hong ying mun?' he asked the first villager he met and repeated the question to the small crowd that quickly gathered around him. But, from their blank expressions, it seemed that none of the villagers did speak English.

The guide book had also listed some words which it was thought would help a traveller explain his problem to non-English-speaking Chinese. 'Gan meng ah. Yau yi ngoi a,' Ashton said, meaning, 'Help, there's been an accident,' then added, 'Geng tsa yen sang,' hoping they would understand he wanted the police and a doctor. He had no way of knowing if his pronunciation was correct but the headman finally got the message, which was just as well because he had exhausted his small vocabulary. While he went away to telephone for assistance, Ashton returned to the scene of the accident with half a dozen of the villagers.

Together they raised the vehicle and dragged Chen out from under. Shortly after that, Ashton heard the welcome sound of at least one siren in the distance. A few minutes later, a police Land Rover appeared in view, closely followed by an ambulance.

CHAPTER 14

Journey's End; somehow it seemed a more apposite name for the jeep than the split-level house where Lloyd Ingolby lived in retirement.

After Ashton had given the police a preliminary statement and Chen Wan had been carted off to hospital in the ambulance, the villagers had helped him to right the vehicle. The Ford Willys was in a pretty sorry state. One shock absorber had snapped off, oil was leaking from a hairline split in the sump, the windscreen was shattered, the frame crushed, and the nearside headlight was dangling from its umbilical cord. Before driving the vehicle back to its once proud owner, Ashton had dipped the oil to make sure there was enough in the reservoir to prevent the engine seizing up on him.

It hadn't only been the jeep's condition he'd had to explain to Ingolby. There was also the fact that Chen Wan had been taken to hospital with a broken collarbone and a suspected fracture of the pelvis, which meant he was unlikely to see his chauffeur-cum-general handyman for some weeks. Asking Ingolby if he might use his phone to contact Lambert had almost been akin to rubbing salt into an open wound. Consequently, Ashton had thought it best to remove himself from the scene and wait for Lambert up on the road. It was early afternoon before the younger man arrived in a rented Honda and made a flashy three-point turn before stopping to pick up Ashton.

'You look bloody roughed up,' he said bluntly.

It was something of an understatement. Ashton had ruined a perfectly good pair of shoes, his lightweight suit needed the urgent attention of a firm of dry cleaners and the torn and dirt-stained shirt was probably a complete write-off.

'You'll be lucky if the doorman allows you inside the Hong Kong Hotel looking like that.'

'I was hoping to swap clothes with you,' Ashton told him.

'Wrong size, old sport,' Lambert said unsympathetically.

'There is something you can do for me.'

'What's that?' Lambert asked.

'Find my taxi driver. His number is 8469 and he works for the Yellow Cab Company in Kowloon. I asked him to wait for me and he didn't.'

'Perhaps he was keen to pick up another fare.'

'There were eighty-two dollars on the clock, I paid sixty on account and told him to keep the meter running.'

'Maybe—'

'He understood me,' Ashton said, cutting him off. 'His comprehension of English was up to speed.'

'Oh, right.'

'I want you to ask him why he left me high and dry.'

Specifically, Ashton wanted to know if anyone had told him to disappear. At the back of his mind was the thought that maybe the truck driver had deliberately run them off the road.

'Ingolby recognised the guy in the newspaper clipping,' he said, changing the subject. 'Told me his name is Gillespie. According to the judge, Reeves told him he was a courier with some travel agency here in Hong Kong. I think there's a distinct possibility he was on the books of the Asia and Pacific Travel Agency which Reeves set up with funds supplied by the SIS.'

'But where's the connection?'

'Ex-Sergeant Newton. He gave us Reeves and linked him to Gillespie. The A and P Travel Agency went into liquidation when Reeves died in September 1970. So check the Registrar of Companies, the Tax Office, Chamber of Commerce and any other organisation that comes to mind. But get me Gillespie's first name, nationality, date and place of birth. And try to find out where he is now.'

'That's a pretty tall order.'

'Look on it as a challenge. You ran Newton to ground for me and you can do the same with this guy.'

'I'll do my best, but don't hold your breath. I mean, suppose he's dead?'

Gillespie had to be among the living, he was the eye of the storm. Reeves, Jackson, Bernice Kwang and Gillespie; it had started with the interaction between those four, and three of them were now dead – Reeves and the American girl within a few months of each other in 1970, Jackson five years later in Winterberg. If Gillespie hadn't murdered the Long Service List warrant officer, who the hell had?

'If you go looking for difficulties,' Ashton told him, 'it's the quickest way I know to get discouraged.'

'You should spend half an hour in Mr Li Wah Tung's company,' Lambert said plaintively. 'Then you'd really know what it is to be discouraged. The man is disgustingly rich and flaunts it. Two Rolls Royce Corniches labelled his and hers . . .'

'He had a Bentley Convertible when the inquest was held.'

'Did he? Well, he must have traded it in for two Rollers. He's also acquired enough old masters to start his own gallery and a doll-like lady wife dripping with diamonds. And on top of that, he must be the biggest name-dropper in town.'

'Was he trying to intimidate you?'

'I wasn't aware of it,' Lambert said. 'Matter of fact, I thought he went out of his way to impress me because he so obviously has an inferiority complex. He wants to be accepted, even by me, a complete stranger.'

'I bet he was very helpful.'

'You think he was trying to butter me up, don't you?' Lambert shook his head. 'If he was, it didn't work. I put some pretty searching questions to him.'

'Such as?'

'I asked him point-blank why he had chosen to return via Cheung Chau Island after picnicking on Lantau.'

'And?' Ashton was conscious of sounding like a lawyer prompting a client.

'He really couldn't say. He supposed it must have seemed a good idea at the time.'

'Would I be right in thinking Li Wah Tung told you he spotted the dinghy because he was close in shore?'

'That was the gist of his explanation.'

'The other people on the powerboat, those friends he took on a picnic – did you ask him for their names?'

'Yes. Of course, he was a little hazy about where some of them are living now.'

'I bet he was.'

'Hey, come on, sport, be reasonable. This all happened twenty-four years ago and people move on, lose touch with one another. Besides, not everyone who went on that picnic was a close friend. The party included a number of businessmen Li Wah Tung wanted to impress. I'm not saying they can't be traced but it could take a lot of time and effort, and do we really need to interview them?'

Ashton had to admit the Australian had a point. He had originally been hired to find out why Oakham had absented himself without leave after deliberately sabotaging his impending security clearance and from that starting point, the investigation had expanded in ever-widening parameters. It was time to limit the scope of the investigation. They had been sent to Hong Kong to question Lloyd Ingolby about the conduct of the inquest on Bernice Kwang and he had admitted the proceedings had been rigged. They were not required to discover who had killed the Chinese American girl; it was enough to show that in all probability she had been murdered. All they needed was a witness to retract the evidence he'd given at the hearing.

'What about the dock attendant?' Ashton asked.

'Well, as you might guess, Yang Bo is no longer employed by the Royal Hong Kong Yacht Club. But the police are confident they'll find him before today is over.'

'Yeah? Who says so?'

'Chief Inspector Uttley, the Police Liaison Officer. He's also the link man with Special Branch.'

Ashton took out his pocket diary, ripped off the blank end sheet, then discovered he'd lost his Parker ballpoint. 'Have you a pen or pencil on you?'

'Be my guest,' Lambert said, handing him a Biro.

Ashton rested the slip of paper on top of the diary and used his thigh as a platform for both while he composed a signal to London in block capitals. Even so, the constant motion of the car made the finished text look as if it had been written by a man with the shakes.

'I want you to get this off to London,' he told Lambert. 'I hope you can make sense of it.'

'Not while I'm driving. Better tell me what you've written.'

'The signal begins "Personal for Hazelwood" and reads "Ingolby states Bernice Kwang worked for US Intelligence and was believed to be a double agent for Communist China. Recommend allegation is checked with the CIA." Okay?'

'Yes. What's the precedence?'

'Make it Op Immediate, that should shake them up at Vauxhall Cross.'

'And the classification?'

'I hear the terminology has been revised since I left. What does Secret mean these days?'

'Information, which if compromised, would raise international tension, damage seriously relations with friendly governments, threaten life or seriously prejudice . . .'

Ingolby had alleged that a junior British Intelligence officer had pointed the Black Dragon Triad in Bernice Kwang's direction. In the Intelligence world, eavesdropping was conducted against friend and potential foe alike. The possibility that the Brits had taken out an American national was, Ashton thought, unlikely to go down too well in Washington should the signal be intercepted.

'Hold it right there,' he said, interrupting Lambert who was still rattling off the latest definition. 'Secret will do us very nicely.'

'What do you want me to do about the friends of Li Wah Tung?'

'Nothing. You were right, we don't need to question them.'

Before joining the Australian Intelligence Service, Lambert had spent twelve months of his four-year Chinese language course in Hong Kong and although much of the landscape had changed since those days, the roads were still in place and there was nothing wrong with his memory. Unlike the Chinese cab driver, he didn't lose his way and it took him just forty minutes to deliver Ashton to the Hong Kong Hotel in Kowloon.

The doorman looked slightly taken aback when Ashton walked past, so did the clerk on reception when he asked for his room key. And more than one eyebrow was raised as he made his way through the lobby, but no one had the temerity to question what right he had to be there.

Lambert transcribed the signal Ashton had drafted on to the appropriate MoD message pad in triplicate and delivered the flimsies to the communications centre in HMS *Tamar*, the shore-based naval establishment behind City Hall in the Central District of Victoria. He waited for the third copy to be receipted and franked with the time of dispatch by the yeoman of signals, then walked to the police headquarters on Harcourt Road half a mile away. He had returned to the Joint Services Intelligence Staff building to find that Uttley had left a message for him. In the interests of security it had been suitably vague and wouldn't have made sense to an outsider, but Lambert knew straightaway that Special Branch had found Yang Bo, one-time landing dock attendant with the Royal Hong Kong Yacht Club.

Uttley belonged to that rare breed of men who provoked instant dislike. He was unpleasant, snide and officious, character traits which had reminded Lambert of the police officer who had pulled him up when he'd been a student at the University of Brisbane for doing thirty-eight miles an hour in a built-up area where the speed limit was thirty. Having booked him for one traffic violation, the patrolman had then proceeded to examine his ancient Ford Holden to see if there were any other infringements he could charge him with. He had started by demanding to see his certificate of motor insurance, driving licence, vehicle registration document and current certificate verifying that the Holden was in a roadworthy condition. The fact that all of them had been in order had only spurred him on to greater efforts. He had checked the tread on the tyres, the brakes, the head- and sidelights, treating Lambert all the while with supercilious politeness, calling him 'sir' although he obviously held all students in deep contempt.

Lambert was no longer an undergraduate and though far younger than Uttley, was scarcely his junior in rank, but that didn't stop the older man treating him in a somewhat condescending manner.

'You'll be pleased to hear we have found Yang Bo for you,' he announced grandly when Lambert walked into his office.

We? It clearly didn't bother Uttley that all the work had been done by Special Branch; where any credit was due, he was going to make damned sure some came his way even though, as the Police Liaison Officer, he had done nothing to earn it. Police Liaison Officer, brackets Internal Security; now there was a sick joke. It was Uttley's job to brief the military authorities about the prevailing situation in the crown colony and the likelihood of communal violence between the Communist and Nationalist factions of the population. Given his knack of rubbing people up the wrong way, it was a wonder that anyone paid much attention to what he had to say.

'So where do I find him?' Lambert said, finally realising that Uttley was waiting for him to ask.

'In the Shek Pai Wan estate of Aberdeen.'

'Do you have his address?'

'Are you familiar with the estate?' Uttley asked, smiling in a patronising way.

'No.'

'You've got more than eight thousand people living in seven high-rise blocks on a fourteen-acre site. Of course, that's nothing like the density in The Walled City over by Kai Tak airport. God alone knows how many are living in that rabbit warren or what's happening inside the walls, because the law stays outside.'

'Could we get to the point?'

'The point is Mr Yang Bo lives in Building number 6, flat 1189 and you'll have a hard time finding him without a guide. The point is you had better listen to Sergeant Henry Sung and be prepared to take his advice. The Shek Pai Wan estate may be a lot more peaceful than The Walled City but you should never take anything for granted.'

Sergeant Henry Sung was twenty-four years old and was regarded as an outstanding young officer but with 1997 only three years away, he would never realise his full potential. He was a Christian, had been educated at St Stephen's Roman Catholic School and, like both his parents, had been born in Hong Kong. That combination made him *persona non grata* with Peking.

'He'll be out on his ear soon as they take over.'

'I'm sorry to hear it,' Lambert murmured.

'Yeah, it couldn't happen to a nicer guy,' Uttley said with evident satisfaction.

By any yardstick, the Chief Inspector was a first-class arsehole. Lambert supposed it was possible that somebody loved him but apart from a doting mother or a wife with rose-coloured spectacles, he couldn't think who.

'When do I meet Sergeant Sung?' he asked.

'Oh, didn't I mention it? He doesn't come off shift until 20.00 hours so he's waiting for you downstairs.' A huge smirk appeared on his face. 'I was given to understand you wanted to see Yang Bo as soon as possible, but if it's not convenient . . .'

'You're right, I do want to see him a.s.a.p.' Lambert reached for the phone on the Chief Inspector's desk and drew it towards him. 'You don't mind if I ring my colleague, do you, sport?' he asked without bothering to wait for a reply.

Lifting the receiver, he punched out the number of the Hong Kong Hotel and asked the switchboard operator to put him through to Room 528. When Ashton answered, he passed on everything he'd learned from Uttley and arranged to meet him at the Star Ferry terminal in Victoria.

The Star Ferry Pier in Kowloon was less than two hundred yards from the hotel. Four minutes after Lambert had phoned him, Ashton was on his way across the harbour, having just missed an earlier sailing by the skin of his teeth. The vehicle tunnel and the Mass Transit Railway system had, it seemed, done very little to diminish the popularity of the big green and white boats. Both the first- and second-class decks were jam-packed with people on their way to the Central District, the few tourists among the crowd easily identifiable by the interest they took in everything going on around them as the ferry weaved through the junks, sampans and other craft to reach the far shore in seven minutes.

The exodus started the instant the gangways were lowered. Ashton followed the crowd, ignored the pedestrian footbridge and made his way down the stairs leading to the General Post Office and the street below. Lambert was waiting for him with a Land Rover in Edinburgh Place. He was accompanied by a Chinese police sergeant.

'This is Sergeant Henry Sung,' Lambert said. 'He's going to guide us through the Shek Pai Wan estate.'

Ashton estimated the Chinese sergeant was about five feet eight and weighed no more than a hundred and thirty pounds. He looked immaculate in his khaki drill uniform that had knife-edge creases. Over the shirt, he wore a highly polished black Sam Browne belt and pistol holster; the .38 calibre revolver had been further secured with a black lanyard which had been passed through the D-ring in the base of the pistol grip and looped around Sung's right arm under the shoulder boards of his KD shirt. No guardsman could have looked smarter nor carried himself more erect.

'It's a pleasure to meet you,' Ashton told him as they shook hands.

'And you, sir.' Sung opened the nearside door of the Land Rover for him, then walked round the front of the vehicle and got in behind the wheel. Lambert jumped into the back.

They headed west on Connaught Road Central, Sung pointing out the various landmarks in flawless English as they swept on through Kennedy Town. At 6.30, the sun was sufficiently low down on the horizon to make the sea appear flourescent.

'Have you been to Kong Hong before?' Sung asked Ashton.

'No, this is my first trip.'

'Pity you had to come in early March, it's very cold and grey.'

'I find it pretty warm after England.'

'Today was exceptional, tomorrow it will be chilly.' Sung leaned forward over the wheel and looked up at the sky. 'And we can expect it to rain very soon.'

'Terrific.'

'Autumn is the best time. The skies are clear, there is very little humidity and it's sunny.'

'I'll be sure to bear that in mind next time,' Ashton said drily.

Aberdeen was famed for its floating restaurants, sampan population, water taxis, junks and boatyards; it was doubtful if the Shek Pan Wai estate would ever find its way into the guidebooks. Seven tower blocks on a hilltop that had been hacked off to form a small plateau, the displaced soil dumped into the sea to create yet more real estate. Eight thousand men, women and children living cheek by jowl in one vast intimidating barracks; Ashton hadn't seen anything quite like this city within a city.

'How the hell do you know what's going on in there?' he asked.

'We don't,' Sung told him. 'We rely on the inhabitants to tell us.'

'I wonder how long the Land Rover will be here after we've gone inside?'

'Don't give it another thought, Mr Ashton, the people who live on this estate are very law-abiding. Besides, this is a police vehicle.'

'Well, I suppose that would make a difference,' Ashton said.

Building number 6 reminded him of the tenements he had seen on St Petersburg's Tarasova Road, and Rusanova Prospekt in Moscow, except that it was much better maintained and wasn't in need of redecoration. The high-rise block also had proportionately more lifts than the equivalent building in Russia. Furthermore, all of them were in working order and responded promptly to the call button, which would have made a lot of Muscovites envious.

The car ran silently and stopped at the eleventh floor with no more than a slight tremor. Sung got out and moved back the small knot of residents who tried to push into the lift before Ashton and Lambert had alighted. Turning right, he led them to the east corridor, glanced at the directional signs on the opposing wall and then wheeled left. Flat number 1189 was halfway down the left.

It occurred to Ashton that what they were about to ask Yang Bo was highly sensitive and there was no foreseeing what would come out of the interrogation. The only certain thing was that Henry Sung didn't have the requisite security clearance to sit in while they grilled the former dock attendant. He wished he and Lambert had discussed what they should do about the sergeant, but there had been no opportunity to do so.

'Let's hang on a minute,' Ashton said, brushing Sung's hand away before he could hammer on the door to 1189. 'How well do you know Yang Bo and his family?'

'I don't. I've never met him.'

'Who briefed you?'

'Chief Inspector Uttley, the Police Liaison Officer,' Lambert said, answering on his behalf.

'That's right,' Sung added for good measure.

'So what did he tell you?'

'He said you needed a guide, otherwise you would never find the place, and I was elected for the job.'

'What else? I mean, do you have any idea why we want to question this man?'

'No. Chief Inspector Uttley neglected to inform me.'

Ashton nodded. It seemed the Chief Inspector had exercised a proper regard for security and was mindful of the need-to-know principle.

'But I was told you might need the services of an interpreter,' Sung continued.

'No, that's not correct. Mr Lambert here is fluent in both Cantonese and Mandarin. What I would like you to do is introduce Mr Lambert and myself as two police officers and then wait for us outside.'

'By the Land Rover.'

'No, I think it would be better if you were near at hand just in case something came up and we wanted to consult you.' He couldn't imagine why they should need to consult Sung but face was all important to the Chinese and he didn't want the sergeant to feel slighted. 'Will you do that for me?'

'Of course.'

'Thank you. Now let's see if anyone is at home.'

Sung raised a clenched fist and hammered on the door until it was opened by a thin Chinese wearing Levis and a white cotton shirt under a blue sleeveless pullover. He did not appear to be intimidated by the sight of a uniformed police sergeant and two Europeans on his doorstep; if anything, his demeanour was truculent. If it were possible, his attitude became even more hostile when Sung told him what they wanted. It made no difference; in the end, he had to let them in to his apartment.

'Shall I go ahead?' Lambert asked after Sung had left.

'He's all yours.' Ashton produced the much-handled photocopy of the photograph of Bernice Kwang which had appeared in the *South China Morning Post*. 'Get Yang Bo to describe her first before you show him this. Okay?'

'Yes.'

'But first of all, persuade him to repeat the evidence he gave at the inquest and let's see if he changes his story.'

'Fine. Anything else?'

'If I think of anything, I'll let you know,' Ashton said.

Leaving the younger man to get on with the interrogation, he wandered around the living room, conscious that Yang Bo was following him with his eyes. Twenty-six-inch television, video recorder, solid-looking dining table and chairs, bamboo couch with plump cushions, rugs on the tiled floor; it was furnished better than either of the two low-cost apartments he had seen in Russia. It was also much bigger; kitchen, bathroom and two bedrooms, but no photogrpahs, no wife and no children.

Ashton returned to the living room. There were no pictures there either, but there was something infinitely more interesting on top of the TV. What at first glance he had assumed was a remote control unit was, on closer inspection, a Cellnet phone. He looked at Yang Bo and thought how kind the years had been.

'Ask him when he was born,' he said abruptly.

'You want to know his date of birth?' Lambert asked in a puzzled voice.

'Yes. I'd like to be sure we're talking to the right man.'

CHAPTER 15

L ambert stood there, glassy-eyed like a prize fighter caught by a sucker punch that had stunned him. It took him longer than a compulsory standing count of eight to recover his wits.

'Are you saying this man is an imposter?' he asked eventually.

'In 1970 Yang Bo was your age.' Ashton pointed to the Chinese. 'How old do you think he is?'

'I don't know. I'm no good at judging a person's age.'

'Yang Bo is a few weeks short of his fiftieth birthday.'

'I have to admit he doesn't look it,' Lambert said. 'I would put him in his early forties, if that.'

Ashton nodded. 'Any idea what size family a man would need to have before he was allocated a two-bedroom apartment?'

'A wife and two children, minimum.'

'Well, they're not here and there are no pictures of them in evidence either.'

Lambert rounded on the Chinese and rapidly worked himself into a cold fury. The longer the tirade went on, the more strident he sounded. It wasn't all one-sided; Yang Bo also got pretty heated and started waving his arms around. Then suddenly he shoved Lambert in the chest, propelling him towards the door as if he intended to throw him out of the flat. As Ashton moved across the room to separate them, Lambert turned his back on Yang Bo and yanked the door open. In that same instant, the Chinese slipped past him, ran out into the corridor and collided with Sergeant Sung.

Both fell heavily, arms and legs entangled. The man who claimed to be Yang Bo ended up on top and was therefore on his feet that much quicker. He started towards the bank of lifts, then changed his mind and turned about. Ashton caught a brief glimpse of him over Lambert's shoulder as he doubled back and ran past the flat towards the emergency exit at the far end of the corridor. Sung made no attempt to intercept him; instead, he looked the other way, apparently mesmerised by something only he could see. Still rooted to the spot, he slowly unfastened the holster on his right hip and fumbled for the .38 calibre revolver.

The gunshots were muted and sounded about as menacing as a bunch of fire-crackers. For Sergeant Henry Sung they were anything but harmless. A bullet exited between his shoulder blades, taking with it fragments of the KD shirt he was wearing. He turned and lurched towards Ashton, his right arm stiff at his side, the Smith and Wesson revolver slipping from his grasp to hang suspended by the lanyard. He was hit again, the bullet smashing through the left arm just above the elbow to enter the ribcage. He made a huge effort to hold himself together, as if by standing erect, death would not come for him. Still rigid, he fell like a tree.

Ashton caught him in his arms before he hit the floor, the momentum of the fall making him seem far heavier than he was. Taken by surprise, Ashton staggered under the sergeant's weight and almost sat down. He had no choice but to lay Sung on his stomach, not that it made any difference because there was nothing he could do for him.

The fusillade continued, louder now than any firecracker. Ashton didn't know whether they were firing at Yang Bo or simply blazing away to frighten off any would-be heroes among the neighbours. But the sheer volume of fire told him there were at least two or three gunmen armed with semiautomatics, all of whom were advancing down the corridor towards the flat.

The .38 Smith and Wesson was Ashton and Lambert's only means of defence and it was underneath Sung. One eye on the open doorway into the corridor, Ashton frantically unbuttoned the epaulette on Sung's KD shirt and worked the lanyard down his limp right arm, then used it to pull the revolver out from under him. Although the cylinder was chambered for six rounds, some law enforcement agencies insisted that the one directly under the hammer should be left empty as a safety precaution. There was, however, no time to swing the cylinder out from the frame and check just how many rounds the pistol had been loaded with. Ashton told himself it was better to count on only five and use them well.

Surprise was the one thing he had going for him and even that required an element of luck. There was, he calculated, a good chance that the gunmen would expect to be confronted with an upright target. Hugging the floor, he crawled forward, transferred the revolver to his left hand and, exposing only his shoulder and the left side of his face round the jamb, snapped off a shot at the nearest of what happened to be three gunmen. He aimed upwards at the man's stomach; the kick when he squeezed the trigger lifted the barrel a fraction so that the bullet struck the breastbone. One down, two to go; he picked the next target, fired again and missed. The return fire was uncomfortably close and forced him to back off. Several rounds gouged lumps of plaster and breezeblock from the wall a few inches above his head, the ricochets buzzing about the corridor like angry bees.

'Looks like someone's mad at us,' Lambert said with a nervous laugh.

'Never mind the jokes.' Ashton jerked a thumb over his shoulder. 'Go and raise the alarm.'

'If you insist.'

There was a fatal misunderstanding. Ashton had meant him to use the Cellnet phone on top of the television set; Lambert hadn't seen it and assumed he had something more dramatic in mind. Like a sprinter leaving the blocks in a 100-metre dash, he shot past Ashton and ran out into the corridor.

There was a curious lull; either the gunmen couldn't believe their luck or else they were too busy reloading to take advantage of what was a golden opportunity. Ashton knew the ceasefire wouldn't hold and did what he could to distract the opposition; scrambling to his feet, he grabbed hold the jamb with his right hand and swung out into the corridor, left arm extended like an eighteenth-century duellist. The gunmen were on either side of the corridor, ready to cover each other as they inched towards the flat. Selecting the one diagonally opposite him, Ashton got off a snap shot before they opened up. He fired one further round at each gunman in turn, squeezed the trigger once more and heard a faint click as the hammer struck an empty chamber. With a natural instinct for survival, he literally swung himself back inside the flat.

It was Lambert who saved the day. A split second before he was hit in the right kidney, he reached the nearest fire alarm, smashed the protective glass cover with his fist and pressed the button. The bell above started ringing and triggered every other alarm on the eleventh floor. No symphony had ever sounded so uplifting as that discordant cacophony which was now being repeated on the floors above and below; no composer could have moved so many people to act in concert. Doors opened, heads appeared, voices were raised questioningly, then some people began to move towards the emergency exits at either end of the corridor. What started as a trickle, rapidly became a flood. Smiling to himself, Lambert sank down on to his haunches, leaving a bloody smear on the distempered wall.

Ashton barged through the crowd and stood over Lambert, shielding him with his body so that he wouldn't be tramped underfoot. As soon as the crush had dispersed, he collected the Cellnet from the flat, punched up 999 and told the bilingual operator he wanted the police and ambulance service. The operator, of course, wanted to know his name, where he was calling from and phone number. It was standard procedure and she was highly efficient but Lambert was in a bad way and the emergency call seemed to take for ever.

'They'll be here in a minute,' Ashton said with forced cheerfulness.

'Who will?'

'The paramedics. We'll have you in hospital in no time.'

'Don't worry about me, Peter,' Lambert said with tremendous effort. 'I'm okay.'

When his face was bathed in sweat and the colour of old parchment and the skin was tight across his cheekbones? Ashton looked away. What Lambert had done was one of the most foolhardy yet courageous acts he had ever witnessed. He had braved a hail of fire to set off the alarm in the hope that it would frighten off the gunmen. And Lambert had been proved right, they'd got the hell out of it before the building had begun to empty, taking with them the body of the man he had shot.

'I've got a nasty backache, that's all.'

'Looks like you're due for a spell of sick leave then,' Ashton said, forcing a smile.

Hazelwood read the signal from Hong Kong a second time, then buzzed the DG on the intercom and asked Dunglass if he could spare him a few minutes. It was, of course, a figure of speech; what they needed to discuss would take much longer than a few minutes. Life was never peaceful once Ashton started digging and this particular signal with its bland recommendation about the CIA was likely to cause a number of headaches.

'I see Ashton has not put his name to this,' Dunglass said, looking up from the signal, 'but there's no doubting who drafted it.'

Hazelwood nodded. The fact that it had been addressed for his personal attention was confirmation enough.

'You obviously trained him well, Victor. He's very sparing with his information.'

'He's telling us Ingolby was persuaded to fudge the inquest, Director.'

'Because there had been some horrific cock-up and Reeves knew there would be hell to pay if the jury returned an open verdict on Bernice Kwang?'

'That would be my interpretation,' Hazelwood said carefully.

'So how can we possibly go to the CIA twenty-four years later and ask them to confirm that she was one of theirs without leaving ourselves open to a barrage of embarrassing questions?'

Hazelwood didn't say anything. The DG knew the answer to that question as well as he did. What mattered in their world was not so much what they knew but who they knew. And what did friendship mean if you couldn't ask an old chum to do you a favour off the record? Dunglass had not only cut his teeth in the Far East, he had spent the greater part of his service out there and had made a large number of contacts, some of whom were now to be found among the top strata at Langley, Virginia.

'Anyway, why do we want to go to the CIA when we've already been told that she had been one of their agents? You don't suppose Lloyd Ingolby made it up, do you? He got it from Reeves.'

'I wouldn't quarrel with that assumption,' Hazelwood said. 'But it doesn't prove anything. The only thing we really know is that Bernice Kwang was an American citizen. Now, if she was killed in error, Reeves would have every reason to trash her. Take it from me, Ashton is on to something.'

'He's a loose cannon.'

'No, actually he's the reverse. He likes to be sure of his facts before showing his hand.'

'I still don't see what good will come of going to the CIA,' Dunglass continued obstinately. 'We'll only end up with egg on our faces.'

'There's an even better chance we'll discover the present whereabouts of Lenora Vassman.'

Dunglass looked as if he was about to pooh-pooh the whole idea, then had second thoughts and realised what the SIS would have done in the same situation. Had Bernice Kwang been working for them, British Intelligence would have taken a very keen interest in her flatmate. The Security, Vetting and Technical Services Division would have compiled a dossier on Ms Lenora Vassman in order to satisfy themselves that she was squeaky clean. In the course of doing this, they would have ended up knowing her better than her own parents did. If Bernice Kwang had subsequently fallen under a cloud, their interest in her flatmate would have become everlasting. Long after Kwang's death, the SIS would have kept tabs on Lenora Vassman, if necessary passing the job on to MI5 when she returned to the UK. In America it was possible that the CIA had turned their case notes over to the FBI despite the mutual antipathy which existed between the two organisations.

'I'm still not happy about it, Victor. Life's difficult enough as it is.'

Hazelwood sympathised with his predicament. The news story they'd dreaded had appeared in the *Daily Telegraph* the day after Ashton had left for Hong Kong. Although they had both known it was only a question of time before some bright journalist discovered that the two Chechans who'd died in the traffic accident had murdered Louise Oakham, it had still been a shock to see it in print. Other newspapers had taken up the story and had alluded to the husband who had absented himself without leave from his unit, but not in terms which could result in a libel action should Oakham return.

'Things could be a lot worse,' Hazelwood pointed out.

So far, no one had connected Simon Oakham with Cosgrove, the SIS wasn't in the frame and the police were still fielding all the questions. By the weekend, the story would be dead unless something happened in the meantime to give it a new lease of life. And that was precisely why Dunglass was reluctant to do anything which might bring that about.

'What could we expect to get from Lenora Vassman?' Dunglass asked.

'I would hope she could tell us something about the mystery man whom Reeves apparently recruited, who went to the barbecue with Bernice Kwang and was of considerable interest to Warrant Officer Jackson. No one else can; they're all dead.'

'She may also be dead.'

'Well, we shan't know that unless we ask about her.'

There was a lengthy silence, then Dunglass supposed he could always invite Walter to supper one evening. There was, as far as Hazelwood was concerned, only one Walter and that was Walter Maryck, the CIA's Station Chief in London.

Ashton did not make the acquaintance of Detective Superintendent George Quigley until a good two hours after he had been taken to the police station on Heung Yip Road two hundred yards from the Aberdeen Technical School. Judging by his rank, he assumed Quigley must be over forty, but if you weren't aware that he was a police officer, you could be forgiven for thinking he was no older than thirty-five. The Superintendent had short blond hair, blue eyes and a round, rather smug-looking face.

'I've read the statement you made to the duty officer,' Quigley said after introducing himself and his Chinese Detective Inspector. 'Very lucid.'

'Thanks.'

'I see you waived the right to have a solicitor present.'

'I didn't think I needed one,' Ashton told him.

Quigley stared at him, his eyes unblinking. Ashton assumed he was supposed to feel intimidated and was faintly amused. While serving with the SAS, he had been trained to resist interrogation. He had also been given a refresher course by the KGB after they had lifted him off the street in Sofia. Compared with Moscow's finest, Quigley was a rank amateur.

'Do you now require an attorney to be present?' the Superintendent asked, finally giving up the unequal struggle.

'Not unless you're thinking of charging me with some offence.'

'Why one earth should I want to do that?' Quigley smiled as though highly tickled by the whole idea. 'It's just that there are one or two points I'd like to clear up and I wouldn't want there to be any misunderstandings later. Okay?'

'Yes. What is it you wish to know?'

'Well, first of all, what were you and Mr Lambert doing on the Shek Pai Wan estate? It's hardly on the tourist beat.'

'We aren't tourists. We were accompanied by Sergeant Henry Sung.'

'No.' Quigley jabbed a finger towards him in a show of annoyance. 'Don't evade my question.'

'You should have let me finish. We were there on official business to question a man called Yang Bo.'

'Are you and Mr Lambert police officers?'

'No.'

'Civil servants from the Home Office in London?'

Ashton hesitated, wondered if he should confirm Quigley's assumption, then decided that a simple 'yes' was unlikely to satisfy him. 'I think you should have a word with Chief Inspector Uttley.'

'The Police Liaison Officer?'

'Yes.'

'Don't think I won't.' Quigley took out a packet of cigarettes and lit one. 'What's Yang Bo done?'

'He used to be a landing dock attendant, worked for the Hong Kong Yacht Club.'

'And?'

'The rest is classified,' Ashton said calmly. 'That's why Sergeant Sung remained outside in the corridor.'

'Where he got himself killed by three gunmen.'

'Yes, unfortunately.'

The Chinese Detective Inspector looked up from his notebook. 'Was an armed robbery in progress?' he asked in a slight American accent.

'I don't think so. Would it make any difference?'

'Well, it might explain why the gunmen immediately opened fire on Sergeant Sung when they saw him in the corridor. As it is, we must assume they were after you and Mr Lambert.' The Detective Inspector paused, then added, 'Or Yang Bo.'

'I can't answer for him but I don't like the idea that we were deliberately targeted.'

'So you can't think why these men should be stalking you?'

'You're wasting your breath,' Quigley told him. 'Mr Ashton knows exactly why they were after him, but he isn't going to tell you. It's a bloody State Secret.'

The Chinese police officer ignored his superior's outburst and ploughed doggedly on. 'Looking back now, can you recall anything suspicious? Could they have followed you out to the Shek Pai Wan estate?'

'If they did, I wasn't aware of it. I'll tell you something else. After we got there, we had to wait for a lift and I don't remember hearing another vehicle stop outside the entrance. Furthermore, no one entered the building before we went on up to the eleventh floor.'

'Perhaps they didn't need to follow the police Land Rover because they knew where you and Mr Lambert were going?'

Quigley didn't like the hypothesis, cared even less for the implication which stemmed from it, and moved to dispel the notion that the gunmen had a bent police officer on their payroll.

'You got it right the first time,' he told the Detective Inspector, 'They were after Yang Bo and knew where he lived.' He reached out and flicked his cigarette over the ashtray. 'So let's get down to basics and see if we can't improve on this vague description you gave the station duty officer.'

'That's easier said than done,' Ashton told him. 'The truth is I can't add anything to what I've said in the statement.'

The firefight had seemed to go on for ever at the time, but, in fact, it had lasted barely a minute. He had fired at each gunman in turn, aiming at the centre of the visible mass. To Ashton they had simply been targets and he had paid scant attention to their faces. In the event, he had also been concerned to make sure they saw as little of him as possible which, of course, worked both ways. Quigley, however, was not convinced.

'How close did you say the nearest gunman was? Forty feet?'

'Roughly speaking,' Ashton agreed.

'And what can you tell us about him? Apparently he's average height and weight for a Chinese, has black hair brushed back from the forehead, a narrow pointed face and was wearing blue slacks and a thigh-length tunic buttoned at the neck. I ask you, what sort of description do you call that?'

'Better than most you get,' Ashton snapped back. 'And while we are comparing notes, you omitted to mention that I hit him low down in the chest. Naturally, he didn't wait around for you people to show up, but if you look real hard, you might just find him lying in a hospital somewhere.'

Quigley looked as if he were about to explode. The high colour started in his neck and spread rapidly upwards. 'That's all you know,' he grated. 'They won't take him to any hospital, some half-baked pharmacist will render first aid and he will either recover or snuff it. If you hit him in the gut, chances are he's already dead and six feet under the sod some place out there in the New Territories.'

The outburst was followed by a hostile silence which would have continued indefinitely had the Chinese Detective Inspector not moved to defuse the situation.

'I'd like to hear more about Yang Bo,' he said quietly. 'You told the duty officer that, after talking to him for some minutes, your friend, Mr Lambert, opened the door as if to ask Sergeant Sung to step inside. However, before he could do so, Yang Bo pushed him aside and ran out into the corridor.'

'That's correct.'

'Do you know what Mr Lambert said to him?'

Ashton shook his head. 'Apart from memorising the odd phrase in the *Berlitz Travel Guide,* I don't speak a word of Cantonese.'

And afterwards, while they had been waiting for the ambulance to arrive, he had been too worried about Lambert to ask him what he had said to Yang Bo.

'But I think I'm probably the one who spooked him. Yang Bo was twenty-six years old when he was employed as a landing dock attendant by the Hong Kong Yacht Club in 1970. The man we saw in flat 1189 was under forty. There was no sign of his family either.'

'Does he have one?' Quigley asked, suddenly taking an interest.

'Your guess is as good as mine,' Ashton told him. 'But flat 1189 has two bedrooms and I understand that a single man wouldn't be allocated an apartment of that size.'

Quigley said he had no quarrel with that assumption; his attitude and friendlier tone of voice suggested he no longer had a quarrel with Ashton either. 'We'll be in touch as soon as we find him,' he added.

'You mean I'm free to go?'

'Whenever you like.'

'Good. I'm anxious to find out how Lambert is doing.' Ashton paused, then asked if there was any chance of a lift to the Grantham Hospital.

Quigley said he would see what he could do and eventually produced a Land Rover and driver. Just as Sung had said it would, it started raining before they reached the hospital, gently at first but then with rapidly increasing ferocity.

CHAPTER 16

T he rain beat down on the roof, slashed against the windscreen, ran off the road into the gutters and turned the storm drains into raging torrents. Even though the driver of the police Land Rover dropped Ashton off a mere ten feet from the entrance to the Casualty Department, his jacket and trousers still got a soaking. The night nurse on duty in Casualty didn't know anything about a Mr Brian Lambert and directed him to Enquiries in the main hall, who then sent Ashton to Men's Surgical. Except for the eyes, the unusually tall Chinese sister in charge of the ward reminded him of Harriet before she became pregnant and was, he thought, about her age. Her warm smile quickly faded when he identified himself and asked after Lambert.

'I'm so sorry,' she said quietly, 'your friend is dead, he died on the operating table almost an hour ago. The police have been notified.'

Dead. Ashton couldn't take it in. He felt numb, sick at heart, angry at the waste of a good man, and racked with guilt. He should have given Lambert explicit instructions instead of jerking a thumb over his shoulder in the general direction of the Cellnet phone. 'Go and raise the alarm,' he'd told him and the Australian hadn't hesitated for a second. He'd run out of the flat into a hail of small-arms fire because he was the stuff heroes were made of. But apart from that, what did he really know about Brian Lambert? His date and place of birth, the university he'd attended in Australia and the fact that his exchange appointment equated to a Third Secretary in the Diplomatic. He didn't know where Lambert lived in London, whether his parents were still alive or if he was engaged, married or divorced. But if he hardly knew him, why did he have this lump in his throat?

'Do you mind if I use your phone?' he asked huskily.

'Please do,' she said and vacated her chair at the desk. 'I have to look in on the ward again.'

Ashton took her place, lifted the receiver and rang the Joint Services

159

Intelligence Staff, one of the few establishments which was manned twenty-four hours a day, seven days a week. Their phone number was one useful piece of information he'd wormed out of Lambert before they had left for Hong Kong.

The watchkeeper who took the incoming call didn't identify himself by name but merely gave the room number of his office. There was no easy way to tell him what had happened and Ashton imagined Maurice Yule, the SIS Head of Station, would have a fit when it eventually reached his ears. Ashton knew he should have called Yule to give him some kind of fore-warning while they had been waiting for the ambulance, but he had been too busy doing what he could for Lambert, and once the police were on the scene, he'd had no opportunity to ring the Joint Services Intelligence Staff.

The watchkeeper took the news in his stride, indicated that he would inform Head of Station soonest and then asked Ashton for his movements.

Movements? He hadn't really given much thought to what he was going to do next. Somebody would have to identify the body formally and he couldn't see how he could possibly duck out of that. There was also the matter of Lambert's effects, such as they were.

'I'll be here at the hospital for at least another hour,' Ashton told him. 'After that, you can reach me at the Hong Kong Hotel.'

He put the phone down and was about to go looking for the ward sister when she returned to her office accompanied by a thin, near-sighted Chinese man with greying, wire-brush hair whom Ashton learned was Mr C. K. Yen, deputy hospital administrator. He also learned that Mr Yen required his assistance in order to complete the usual formalities.

The mortuary was a windowless concrete blockhouse tucked out of sight in a deep re-entrant behind the hospital. It was approached by a narrow covered walkway, which was just as well because it was still raining. Like all the others Ashton had seen, the mortuary was damp, cold, harshly lit by fluorescent tubes in the ceiling and smelled strongly of disinfectant. Three slabs of stone raised on pedestals served as tables for the morticians. Two were unoccupied; Lambert's naked body lay face up on the centre one. He looked older, thinner and shorter than in life.

'That's him,' Ashton said in a voice enhanced by the accoustics to the point where it seemed unusually loud.

'His name please, for the record.'

'Brian Lambert.'

'Thank you,' C. K. Yen said gravely.

In Admissions, they produced Lambert's personal effects and invited

Ashton to sign for them. They consisted of a passport, an Omega wristwatch, a fountain pen and a gold signet ring with the engraved initials 'JTL', which Ashton guessed had originally belonged to Lambert's father. Finally, there was a leather wallet containing eight hundred and seventy-five Hong Kong dollars, Diners Club and American Express credit cards and a photograph of a very pretty brunette in a polka-dot bikini. Girlfriend? Fiancée? An Australian for sure judging by the sand, sea and surf in the background.

The property clerk looked aggrieved and spoke loudly to C. K. Yen who nodded several times and then rounded on Ashton.

'This man wants to know if you think something is missing?'

Ashton felt like a peeping Tom caught in the act and hastily closed the wallet. 'No. Please tell him that's the last thing which entered my mind.'

The apology led to a further verbal exchange between the two Chinese which did little to clear the air. The property clerk still looked disgruntled when he reached below the counter and brought out a large paper sack bulging at the seams.

'Mr Lambert's clothes,' Yen told him before he could ask. 'You have to take them.'

The clerk up-ended the bag and tipped the contents out on to the counter. Bloodstained jacket, tie, shirt, slacks, soiled underwear, socks and shoes. It wasn't difficult to imagine the kind of distress the clothes would cause his family if they received them in their present state. Having them dry-cleaned wouldn't remove the bullet holes in the jacket and shirt or totally obliterate the brown stains.

'Burn them,' Ashton said. 'Put the clothes in the incinerator or whatever.'

'We can't do that, Mr Ashton, at least not without written authority.'

'Got a sheet of writing paper?'

'In my office,' Yen told him.

'Well, lead the way. The sooner we get this settled the better.'

'You have other clothes?'

'What?'

'For the undertaker.'

'I'll look some out and send them round.'

Ashton scrawled his signature on the docket acknowledging receipt of the effects belonging to the deceased and shoved the passport, wristwatch, gold ring, fountain pen and wallet back inside the Manilla envelope. Leaving the property clerk to dispose of the clothes, he accompanied Yen to his office on the ground floor of the East Wing. In measured tones, the Deputy Hospital Administrator dictated the authority he needed to cover himself which Ashton then signed and dated.

'You have transport?' Yen asked.

'A friend is picking me up.'

'Good. Not many taxis come here at this hour.'

It was just the fillip Ashton needed. Returning to the main entrance, he made himself as comfortable as possible on one of the hard wooden benches in the hall while he waited for the Head of Station to put in an appearance.

Maurice Yule arrived a few minutes after 10.30 wearing DJ trousers and a white tuxedo which suggested the watchkeeper at JSIS had dragged him away from a dinner party. Since the tuxedo was also bone dry, Ashton assumed it had now stopped raining.

Ashton remembered Yule from the Induction Course he had attended in September 1982 at Amberley Lodge, the SIS training school outside Petersfield. Yule had been the desk officer responsible for the Philippines, Indonesia, Borneo, Sarawak, Sabah and Brunei in those days and had delivered what most of the course had felt was easily the best lecture they'd attended. He had come across as a dynamic, intelligent, extrovert personality, a man in short who was going places. Twelve years later, he looked tired and a little frayed round the edges.

'This is a bad business,' he said without preamble. 'What have you told the hospital authorities?'

'Nothing. The administrator I saw was only interested to know what arrangements were being made for an undertaker to collect the body.'

'That's already in hand.' Yule steered him towards the Audi parked outside the entrance. 'Get in,' he said curtly, 'we have things to discuss.'

Nothing more was said until they were on the road to Happy Valley when Yule asked him to explain exactly what had happened. Ashton gave him the whole story in a few brief sentences, then waited for the inevitable interrogation. Yule didn't keep him in suspense for long.

'Who have you talked to apart from the police and the hospital administrator?' he asked.

'A nurse in Casualty, one of the porters on the information desk, the property clerk and the sister in charge of Men's Surgical.'

'What about the press?'

'They still hadn't arrived on the scene when I left the estate. And I've not seen any reporters since then.'

'Thank God for small mercies. What did you tell the police?'

'No more than I had to.' Ashton paused, then corrected himself. 'At least, to begin with.'

The duty officer at Aberdeen Police Station had given him an easy ride. All he had wanted was a detailed account of the fire fight on the eleventh floor of Building number 6 and having got it, had asked very few questions.

'I told him Lambert was an Australian. Good thing I did because, unknown to me, he had his passport on him.'

'When did things start to get sticky?'

On reflection, Ashton supposed it had begun when the duty officer had asked him to remain at the station while additional copies of his statement were made for his signature. But Yule was concerned with facts, not suppositions, and the interrogation had really got underway when the Detective Superintendent had arrived.

'Quigley wanted to know what we were doing on the Shek Pai Wan estate. I had to stonewall him by retreating behind the Official Secrets Act.'

'You told him you were SIS?'

'As good as.'

Yule digested the news in silence. By the time he was ready to disclose what he had in mind, they had passed through the Aberdeen tunnel into Happy Valley.

'The newspapers won't get anything out of the police until they are ready to issue a statement. By that time, Quigley will have been warned to keep his mouth shut and stick to the official line.'

'And what's that?'

'It was a Triad killing, drugs related. Lambert was an Australian customs and excise officer; acting on information, he and Sergeant Sung went to the estate and walked into an ambush. Of course, I'm just extemporising at the moment.'

'Right. Am I another customs officer?'

'You weren't there,' Yule told him. 'This time tomorrow night you'll be well on your way home. Until then, you are to keep your head down. I've got enough trouble on my hands as it is without you causing me extra grief.'

Yule couldn't think what Canberra were going to say when they learned that their exchange officer had been gunned down. Somebody in London had a lot of explaining to do and the sooner the DG got his finger out the better because he was damned if he was going to break the news to the Australian Consulate on Harbour Road. He was also faced with the bi-annual security inspection. For reasons which had not been explained to him, the Mid East embassies had been rescheduled for September and his establishment, plus the high commissions in Singapore and Kuala Lumpur, had been brought forward. This meant the insufferable Mr Hicks from the Technical Services Division would be arriving on the Cathay Pacific flight tomorrow afternoon.

There was a lot more in the same vein. In view of the number of crosses Yule already had to bear, Ashton saw no reason to add to them by pointing out that, even if the police were willing to let him go, he had no intention of leaving Hong Kong until someone paid for what had happened to Lambert.

Yule drove on through Wanchai, dropped Ashton off outside HMS *Tamar* and left him to make his own way to the Star Ferry from there. Arriving back at the hotel, Ashton dined in the Bauhinia Room which was still open. He wasn't really hungry and picked at his food even though he hadn't eaten a thing since breakfast. He had a double Scotch on the rocks with the prawn cocktail and sank two more with the filet mignon, half of which he left on the plate. Still depressed, he called it a night and went up to his room with its less than inspiring view of the alleyway between the hotel and Star House.

He thought of calling Harriet, but the dead Australian was uppermost in his mind and anything he said to her would only sound maudlin. He settled for the mini bar instead and sampled all the miniatures; two Johnnie Walkers, two Martell brandies, two Gordons gin, one Cointreau and a Grand Marnier. When he finally crawled into bed, the whole room was revolving like a carousel.

The signal from Hong Kong was graded Top Secret and carried an Emergency precedence which guaranteed it would be given top priority by the cipher operators at Vauxhall Cross. It was addressed 'For Attention Assistant Director, Combined Pacific Basin and Rest of the World Department'. The opening sentence which read, 'Regret to inform you Brian Lambert died from gunshot wounds 16 March 20.05 hours local time' ensured the contents of the signal were brought to the DG's attention in record time by Roger Benton, the department head. On the basis that three heads were better than one, Dunglass then sent for his deputy and showed him the cable from Maurice Yule.

'Seems to me our Head of Station hasn't been too clever,' Hazelwood said after reading it. 'This nonsense about Lambert being a customs officer isn't going to hold water for one minute.'

'Maurice didn't have much time. He only heard about the incident three hours after it had happened and there was a chance the press had already got wind of it from the hospital. Anyway, he had to come up with some story to explain why an Australian citizen and a Chinese police sergeant were gunned down which would satisfy the media.'

'Pity he didn't remember what KISS stood for.'

Hazelwood would never forget the acronym. Back in 1967 when he was a probationer, the head of his section had drummed it into him that the trick in making any kind of plan was to Keep It Simple Stupid. It was a dictum Hazelwood had subsequently passed on to his subordinates.

'The story has got to hold up,' Dunglass said forcefully, 'and it will, provided news of the incident doesn't travel beyond the boundaries of Hong Kong.'

'What if one of the local stringers faxes the story to London?'

'At worst, it will rate a small paragraph on the inside pages, at best, it will be spiked. Face it, Victor, the great British public won't be interested to read about the death of a Chinese police sergeant and an Australian customs officer. The only problem is Ashton. If it gets out that he was there when the ambush was sprung, then we're really in trouble.'

'Peter won't talk to the Press,' Hazelwood said. 'I'd bet my last penny on that.'

'Let's hope you won't lose it then.' Dunglass checked his wristwatch and quickly subtracted the eight hours' time difference between the two zones. 'Ashton will be leaving Hong Kong tomorrow at 13.30 our time; when he arrives at Gatwick sixteen hours later, he becomes your problem, Victor. You are responsible for ensuring he remains as silent as a Trappist monk.'

'You'll have no worries on that score, Director.'

'The question we have to decide now is precisely what we are going to tell the Australian Government.'

'The truth,' Hazelwood told him bluntly. 'We've got nothing to hide, we didn't knowingly send him into danger, we didn't have to twist his arm, Lambert wanted to go.' He looked pointedly at Benton, the Assistant Director of the Combined Pacific Basin and Rest of the World departments. 'Isn't that right, Roger?'

'Yes. In fact, he practically begged me, said he hadn't been given a worthwhile job since he joined us.'

There was an audible sigh of relief from Dunglass and something akin to a faint smile appeared on his mouth. 'All right, Roger,' he said, suddenly decisive, 'I'll break the news personally to the Australian High

Commissioner this evening. Before I do so, I want you to draft a signal to Canberra for my approval.' Dunglass opened the top right-hand drawer of his desk and took out the slim Filofax in which he recorded the personal details of his staff. 'Brian Lambert,' he read, 'born Brisbane, Queensland, on 25 November 1962. Single, parents deceased, next-of-kin, elder brother, Peter. Current address, 973 Kingsford-Smith Avenue, Woollahra, Sydney, New South Wales. I have a note here saying that the brothers weren't very close.' He looked up. 'One shouldn't say it of course but the family circumstances do make things slightly easier for us.'

'There's someone else,' Benton said, and cleared his throat. 'A girl named Hilary Lubienski, also from Brisbane. She was his fiancée, joined him in London two months ago.'

Dunglass looked dumbfounded, his mouth open as if he had been winded. 'Why wasn't I told about this, Roger?' he demanded.

Hazelwood wasn't sure whether the DG was annoyed, embarrassed or simply disconcerted. On reflection, he thought it was probably a combination of all three.

It was the mother and father of a hangover; a dozen pneumatic drills hammered his skull, his mouth was bone dry and his tongue felt as if it had been coated with a thick paste. His brain told him the phone was ringing, but when didn't it at times like these? He was however alert enough to accept grudgingly that there would be no peace until he answered the damned thing. Mustering what little willpower remained, Ashton kicked off the bedclothes and sat up. He reached out, lifted the receiver from the cradle and brought it to his ear.

'At last,' Quigley said. 'Before when I rang the hotel the switchboard operator said she couldn't raise you.'

'Well, now she has. So what do you want?'

'I want you to get your body over to Police Headquarters in Victoria soonest. There's a Mr Yang Bo I'd like you to meet. Think you're up to that, Mr Customs and Excise Officer?'

'No sweat,' Ashton told him and put the phone down.

Customs and excise: Yule had evidently already run his first attempt at a cover story past the police and had been given the thumbs down. Or at least it had failed to convince one Detective Superintendent. It was also apparent that Quigley was feeling hostile towards him again.

The pneumatic drills had eased off but his mouth hadn't improved and his legs didn't feel as though they belonged to him as he walked over to the window and opened the curtains. The sudden glare hurt his eyes and turning away, he went into the bathroom. Stupid. Stupid. Stupid. The only other time he had been this drunk he'd been a student at Nottingham University celebrating the end of Finals. What excuse was there this time? Yes, it was partly his fault Lambert had got himself killed and it was natural he should feel some guilt, but there was nothing he could do about it now and he would just have to learn to live with it.

He stood under the cold shower to freshen himself up, then shaved before breakfasting off coffee, fresh orange juice and hot rolls. By the time he boarded the Star Ferry for the short trip across the harbour, Ashton was feeling a whole lot better than when he had answered the telephone. As if to make a point, Quigley kept him waiting a good fifteen minutes after the duty officer had rung through to say his visitor had arrived. Quigley's explanation that things were a little hectic that morning fell a long way short of an apology and fooled no one.

Yang Bo was being held in an interview room on the second floor. Through the one-way glass, Ashton saw a short, roly-poly Chinese man whose grey hair was shaved close to the skull. He was clearly agitated and kept turning his head from left to right like a small bird on the look out for danger.

'Is this the man you saw last night?' Quigley asked.

'No, the one I met was much younger and roughly forty pounds lighter. Is he the real Yang Bo?'

'We're satisfied he is. He returned to the flat this morning to see if the coast was clear. Minus wife and teenage children of course; they're all spending a few days with her parents in Lai Chi Kok. Yang Bo claims this was arranged weeks ago, but he would say that, wouldn't he?'

'Can you prove he's lying?'

Quigley snorted. 'You've got to be joking. The family have been told what to say and we'll never budge them because they are more frightened of the Triad than they are of us.'

'So what happens now?'

'You and I are going to have a quiet talk.'

It was the sort of invitation which was hard to refuse. In the little time it took to reach Quigley's office at the end of the corridor, Ashton had decided just how much information he could afford to withhold from the Detective Superintendent without landing himself in the mire.

'You're a very lucky man, Mr Ashton.' Quigley waved him to a chair, closed the door and then sat down at his desk. 'First you walk away from a nasty traffic accident in the morning and in the evening you come through an ambush unscathed.'

'Actually, I would put it the other way round, the others were unlucky.'

'Li Wah Tung, Sir Lloyd Ingolby, QC, Mr Ronald Bartholomew, FRCS, Lenora Vassman and Yang Bo. I got their names from Special Branch – you want to tell me why London is so anxious to trace them?'

'You could say they were all acquainted with Bernice Kwang.'

Ashton then went on to tell him why the inquest convened to enquire into the circumstances of her death had been rigged. In what was a highly edited version of the truth, he led the Detective Superintendent to believe the Chinese American girl had been wrongly identified as a Communist agent.

'Are you saying she was killed by mistake?' Quigley said with some scepticism.

'That's what a former sergeant in the Intelligence Corps has alleged in the book he has written.'

If he was to contain the breach of security, Ashton had to explain how the affair had come to light, and Sergeant Newton made a convenient scapegoat, especially as he wasn't there to defend himself. Although the former NCO hadn't put pen to paper, it was common knowledge that a number of Intelligence officers from yesteryear had written their memoirs. And even out here in Hong Kong, Quigley would be aware of this if only because in a number of cases the authors had made headline news around the world.

'I didn't think you and your Australian friend were customs and excise officers.'

'Well, our local man was caught out and had to think up a cover story on the hoof.' Ashton smiled. 'The Firm likes us to remain anonymous if it's humanly possible.'

'A prime example being the man who killed Bernice Kwang?'

'Correction, the go-between who arranged it all. We're pretty sure the actual killer belonged to the Black Dragon Triad.'

'And this same Triad was responsible for yesterday's mayhem because of something that happened twenty-four years ago?'

'Yes.'

'Give me one good reason.'

'Because they're frightened.'

'Who are?'

'The men who murdered the Chinese American girl. My guess is that one, if not all, of them has gone up in the world since 1970. Could be they're right at the top of the pecking order.'

'I don't say it's impossible but no one is ever going to prove it.'

Quigley didn't think they would ever apprehend the men who had gunned down Lambert and Sergeant Henry Sung either. They would get nothing out of Yang Bo. Obviously he had been told to vacate the flat and had then handed the keys over to the impostor, but he was never going to confirm it, much less describe the man who had approached him. The police could charge Yang Bo with aiding and abetting and even slap him around a bit but it wouldn't do any good. He wouldn't make a statement because he had a wife and children to consider and the Triad had undoubtedly explained in graphic detail what they would do to them if he opened his mouth.

'Maybe we could try a different angle,' Ashton said and told him about the taxi driver from the Yellow Cab Company.

Quigley shook his head. 'You haven't been listening to me. This taxi driver is no different from Yang Bo; he's open to coercion and will deny everything.'

'Just knowing he was lying would be a help.'

'In what way?'

'It would give me some leverage over a man who has more reason to fear the British Government than the Black Dragon Triad.'

Quigley gazed at him with new-found interest. 'Have you got someone in mind?' he asked.

'Yes. How about Sir Lloyd Ingolby?'

'You must enjoy living dangerously.' Quigley pursed his lips. 'What was the number of that taxi driver again?'

'It was 8469,' Ashton said and watched him reach for the phone.

CHAPTER 17

The garage and dispatchers' office of the Yellow Cab Company was situated at the top end of Nathan Road in Kowloon. Before leaving Police Headquarters, Quigley had called his Chinese Detective Inspector into his office and had got him to phone the General Manager to ask if he would kindly arrange for Driver 8469 to be available for interview at 10.30 hours sharp. Quigley had made it sound like a police request when briefing the DI; listening to the Detective Inspector barking away on the phone, Ashton thought it had the tenor of an ultimatum.

'He may have twisted the General Manager's arm a little,' Quigley admitted, 'and told him what could happen if he refused to co-operate.'

The Yellow Cab Company ran a mixed fleet of Datsuns and Hondas, none more than four years old. All were exceptionally well maintained and serviced so that there wasn't the slightest chance the traffic police would find a vehicle unroadworthy in the course of a spot check. But that wasn't the point; if every Datsun and Honda belonging to the company was routinely flagged down for inspection, Yellow Cabs stood to pass up a small fortune in lost fares. Whether Quigley would have actually carried out his threat was irrelevant; the General Manager had believed he would and had made sure Driver 8469 was there when they arrived at the garage.

His name was Zhang Ke and he began to look extremely worried the moment he saw Ashton; then Quigley and the DI showed him their warrant cards and something like panic registered in his eyes. But it was Quigley's driver, a squat, ugly-looking detective constable who really made his legs turn to jelly as he retreated before them past the dispatchers office and out into the yard behind the garage.

'I owe you twenty-two dollars,' Ashton said and took out his wallet.

'No money.' Zhang Ke continued to back away from him until he ran out of space and bumped into the far wall. 'No money,' he repeated.

'I presume this is the guy who cabbied you out to Sir Lloyd Ingolby's house?' Quigley said.

'Damn right he is.'

'Maybe he doesn't understand English,' Quigley suggested.

'He understood it well enough yesterday morning.'

'I guess he's forgetful.' Quigley nodded to his DI, then placed a hand under Ashton's right elbow. 'Let's you and I go back inside,' he said.

'Why?'

'I don't speak Cantonese, do you?'

'No.'

'Then we're superfluous.'

Ashton followed the Detective Superintendent into the garage. A mechanic in greasy overalls was servicing one of the Honda fleet; beyond the inspection pit, a panel beater was knocking out a dent in the front offside wing of a second Honda Accord. Ignoring the No Smoking symbols displayed on every wall, Quigley took out a packet of cigarettes and lit up. 'We won't get anything out of Zhang Ke, you know that, don't you?' he said.

'So you keep telling me. But we already know he's lying and that's enough. While I was in the house talking to Sir Lloyd Ingolby, somebody told Zhang Ke to make himself scarce and he took off.'

'And this somebody followed you all the way from Kowloon to Big Wave Bay?'

'No, if we were being tailed I would have spotted it long before we reached Ingolby's place. Zhang Ke lost his way just beyond Chai Wan and we had to double back to the main road. That would have thrown anyone who was shadowing us.'

Quigley removed the cigarette from his lips, dropped it on to the concrete floor and crushed the butt under his heel. 'Then there's only one explanation, isn't there? The question is, who told them you were going to see the judge?'

'I could name several candidates.'

'Beginning with Ingolby himself?'

'Maybe.'

The panel beater stopped hammering at the wing and moved back to admire his handiwork. In the ensuing silence, Ashton heard the cab driver cry out. Side-stepping past Quigley to get a better view of the yard, he saw the muscular Detective Constable slap Zhang Ke across the face with a vicious backhander before grabbing him by the jaw to slam his head against the wall.

'That's enough.' Ashton rounded on the Detective Superintendent. 'Tell that bloody rock ape of yours to knock it off.'

'You're too damned squeamish,' Quigley told him. 'You think the People's Liberation Army will treat a reluctant witness like Zhang Ke with kid gloves when they are enforcing the law in three years' time? Hell, he would be lucky if they didn't string him up by his thumbs.'

'Just stop him, okay? Otherwise I'll make it my business to get you kicked out on your ear long before 1997 comes around.'

'If that's what you want.' Quigley sighed and shook his head. 'I would never have taken you for a bleeding heart but, like they say, you live and learn.' He looked over his shoulder, shouted to his Chinese officers to let go of the little creep, then faced Ashton again. 'They both understand English,' he said with a grin as though he had somehow put one over on him.

'Good for them.' Ashton took a close look at Zhang Ke as he shuffled into the garage behind the two Chinese plain-clothes men. The left side of his lower lip was split open and bleeding, and blood from his nose was running down his chin on to his shirt front. 'I think you could find yourself in trouble,' he said.

'Will I hell.' Quigley laughed derisively. 'You think he is going to make an official complaint about my officers? Look around you and tell me who's going to back him up.'

It was true. No one wanted to know, not the dispatcher in his office, the mechanic in the inspection pit or the panel beater working on the Honda. It wasn't necessary to ask, their studied indifference told him they hadn't seen or heard anything.

'Let's get out of this place,' Ashton growled.

'Why not? There's nothing here for us.' Quigley glanced sideways at him. 'Probably won't be anything at Big Wave Bay either,' he added slyly.

'Just let me off at the nearest rental agency.'

'No way. We'll drop my two officers off at Police Headquarters and then I'll drive you out to Journey's End.'

'There's no need.'

'Believe me, it will be a pleasure,' Quigley told him firmly. 'A showdown between you and Sir Lloyd Ingolby? That's something I've got to see.'

Watching television was not one of Maurice Yule's leisure pursuits but that morning over breakfast his family could have been forgiven for thinking he had suddenly become addicted to the small screen as he switched from channel to channel to catch the latest newscast. English, Cantonese; the language was irrelevant, so for the most part were the reporters. The pictures told the story in graphic detail and there had been precious little variation between the footage shown on each TV station. Almost without exception, the videos had begun with a few exterior shots of Building number 6 on the Shek Pai Wan estate before moving to the eleventh floor for close-ups of the bloodstains on the floor and wall near the shattered fire alarm as well as the gouges made by ricochets. Those residents who had agreed to be interviewed had had little to say. All had denied witnessing the murders; the most anyone had admitted to was catching a fleeting glimpse of the gunmen as they'd run towards the staircase.

Only the identity of the Chinese police sergeant had been disclosed. Lambert had been described as a customs and excise officer whose name was being withheld until next of kin had been informed. There had been one further bonus as far as Yule was concerned. None of the TV reporters had questioned the veracity of the account given by the police spokesman who'd stated that the double shooting had been drugs related.

As was the customary practice, the morning newspapers were on his desk when Yule arrived at the office. His PA had side-lined the editorials and other news items which she thought would be of interest to him. The Chinese newspapers, particularly those which followed the Peking line were usually regarded as the more important. But political attitudes and the current state of Anglo-Sino relations were not high on the list of priorities for Yule that morning. Instead of relying on his PA, he scanned every newspaper from the front page to the back and read every piece dealing with the double murder. For once, what the English-language papers had to say on the subject was paramount. In his estimation, only the editors of the *South China Morning Post*, the *Hong Kong Standard* and the *Star* were likely to sense there was a story worth digging for in the customs and excise connection. To Yule's relief there was nothing to indicate that anyone was thinking along that line as yet.

An optimist might have concluded that the situation had been contained, but Yule was by nature a hard-nosed realist. Everything depended on how the Australians reacted when they learned that their man had been killed. If they declined to support the line he'd suggested to the Director General, the consequences didn't bear thinking about. Although the watchkeeper at JSIS had phoned him in the early hours of the morning to report that London had acknowledged his cable and were taking appropriate action, he was still waiting to hear just what that meant.

He found out shortly after 10.30 when his PA walked into the office with the latest signal from Vauxhall Cross.

Addressed to him personally from the DG, it was, Yule learned in the opening sentence, for his eyes only and was to be destroyed immediately after reading. It was the first such communication he'd received since joining the SIS and he could see why Dunglass didn't want a copy to go on file. It was, however, rather galling because the Director had accepted his advice lock, stock and barrel and this fact would now go unrecorded. But as far as the immediate future was concerned, Yule did not feel quite so exposed.

Dunglass had had a pretty sticky time of it with the Australian High Commissioner in London but in the end, he had persuaded him to signal Canberra recommending that his government should accept the SIS version of events. There was a price however: the High Commissioner had only agreed to the proposal on the understanding that the Minister of State for the Foreign and Commonwealth Office would appraise Canberra of the true facts in person.

For his part, London required Yule to brief the Australian Consul in Kong Hong and ensure that Ashton was on the British Airways flight to Heathrow that evening which, at the moment, he did not regard as a particularly onerous duty. The only blot on the horizon was the impending arrival of Mr Terry Hicks from the Technical Services Division on the Cathay Pacific fight at 14.00 hours. Accommodation had already been arranged for Hicks at HMS *Tamar*, meeting him at the airport was a task Yule proposed to delegate to his assistant.

If Ingolby hadn't been exactly overjoyed to make Ashton's acquaintance yesterday, he was clearly very displeased to see him again twenty-four hours later. The cold, almost hostile reception was, however, no more than Ashton had anticipated. He was to some extent responsible for the fact that the judge had been deprived of the services of his chauffeur-cum-general handyman. There was also the damage that had been done to the Ford Willys jeep which had been his pride and joy.

Then there was Quigley; his presence at the house contributed to the strained atmosphere and it rapidly became evident that there was no love lost between the Detective Superintendent and the former High Court judge.

'Quigley and I know one another,' Ingolby said curtly when Ashton attempted to introduce him. 'We go back a long way, don't we, Superintendent?'

'We've crossed swords a few times in court.'

'Something tells me we are about to do so again.'

Ingolby deliberately kept them standing while he lounged in an arm-chair. Bad manners had nothing to do with it; Ashton recognised the discourtesy for what it was, a psychological ploy that was intended to make them feel at a disadvantage.

'There are one or two questions we would like to ask you,' Quigley said, his face suffusing with colour.

'Oh, really? Well, you can ask all the questions you like, whether I choose to answer them is another matter.'

'There's been a serious breach of security,' Ashton said before the two men were metaphorically locked in combat. 'We're hoping you can help us to pinpoint the leak . . .' He paused, then added 'sir'. Apart from it sticking in his craw, a little obsequiousness cost nothing and it could be a sight more productive than Quigley's less than tactful, heavy-footed approach. 'All we ask is for a few minutes of your time.'

'Well, I'm sure I can spare you that much.' Ingolby waved a hand in the general direction of the second armchair and the couch. 'Do please sit down, Mr Ashton. You too, Superintendent.'

'Thank you,' Ashton said and chose the armchair, leaving the couch to Quigley which was a nice way of symbolically distancing himself from the policeman, a gesture he was sure would not be lost on Ingolby.'

'A breach of security?'

'Yes.' Ashton glanced at the newspaper which was lying on the coffee table. 'You've presumably read about the double shooting at Aberdeen last night?'

'Yes, a bad business.'

'Oh, it certainly was, and you can forget that tale about it being a drug-related crime. It was a deliberate hit.'

'How do you know?'

'I was there when it happened. If it hadn't been for my partner, I would have been gunned down too. We'd gone to the Shek Pai Wan estate to question Yang Bo, the landing dock attendant who gave evidence at the Bernice Kwang inquest and we walked into an ambush.'

'Good God.' Ingolby looked and sounded genuinely shocked. 'But I don't understand why you think I can be of assistance.'

'What started out as a traffic accident yesterday morning is now beginning to look like attempted murder. In the light of what happened last night, we believe the truck driver deliberately side-swiped your jeep with the intention of either maiming or killing Mr Ashton. Naturally, the man who planned it had to know in advance where he would be going.'

Ashton gritted his teeth. Quigley had been silent for all of three minutes and had evidently felt the need to reassert himself. In doing so, he had come close to libelling Ingolby by inferring, however indirectly, that the information could have come from him. If Quigley was trying to redress some humiliation he had suffered at the hands of the former judge light years ago, he was going the right way about setting himself up for another chastening experience.

'Perhaps you would care to elaborate on that assertion, Superintendent?' Ingolby said in a dangerously silky voice.

'I believe you had a long conversation with the Attorney General who explained why I wanted to see you,' Ashton said quickly.

'You have a good memory,' Ingolby told him drily.

'Was this over the telephone?'

'Yes.'

'Could anyone have overheard your conversation? One of the servants perhaps?'

'There is only one telephone in the house and that's in my study. And I can assure you, Mr Ashton, I do not converse with someone like the Attorney General in the presence of one of the servants.'

According to the *Berlitz Travel Guide*, the air was supposed to be moderately cold from December to February. It was now the middle of March but the atmosphere in the drawing room of Journey's End was almost on a par with the South Pole. Despite the cold front moving in, Ashton was undeterred.

'This long conversation you had with the Attorney General – did he tell you then when to expect me?'

'No, he phoned me a second time three days later, at six on Monday evening to be precise. And before you ask, no one overheard that conversation either.'

There was the sound of footsteps from the hall, then the door opened and a slender, elegant woman entered the drawing room. Ashton stood up and after a momentary hesitation, Quigley followed his example; husband Lloyd however remained seated. Lady Ingolby was, Ashton judged, in her late sixties and her neatly coiffured hair was completely grey.

'Yes, Mary?' Ingolby said in an impatient tone of voice.

'I was just wondering if these gentlemen would care for a drink?'

'No, they are just about to leave. We've finished our business.'

Quigley turned an even deeper shade of pink than he had previously and looked as if he were about to contradict the judge.

'It's very kind of you, Lady Ingolby,' Ashton said warmly, 'but we really do have to be on our way.'

'You're sure?' she asked.

'You heard him, Mary.'

Ingolby was all charm; he'd embarrassed his wife, riled Quigley and given Ashton a pretty shrewd idea of how Ms Lenora Vassman must have felt when he'd rubbished her at the inquest.

'One day I'm going to nail that insufferable bastard,' Quigley said, after one of the servants had closed the front door behind them.

'You shouldn't let him get to you.'

'You know something, Ashton, you're all talk. What happened to that leverage you were going to exert on him?'

'If you want to frighten a man like the judge, you put the stiletto in when he least expects it. You do not go at him like an angry bull; that only gets his back up and stiffens his resolve.'

'Are you trying to say it's my fault this has been a wasted journey?'

'It's not been a waste of time.' Ashton walked round the Mercedes, waited for Quigley to flash a signal to the central locking system, then opened the door and got in beside him. 'He wasn't responsible for the leak. I know there is a bit of an actor in most lawyers but Ingolby wasn't giving a performance. He was genuinely outraged by your inference that he had blown the whistle on me.'

Quigley switched on the ignition, fired the engine and slammed the automatic gearbox into drive. Releasing the handbrake, he then flattened the accelerator and took off, the rear tyres leaving flecks of burning rubber on the surface of the asphalt road.

Ashton ignored the show of bad temper. 'You've got a bent copper in Chief Inspector Uttley,' he said calmly.

'Convince me.'

'Until 18.00 hours yesterday evening, neither Lambert, myself nor anyone at JSIS knew where to find Yang Bo. It was Uttley who told my partner.'

'Listen, I don't hold any brief for the guy but it was Special Branch who found the landing dock attendant. Why are they above suspicion?'

'I'm not saying they are but right now, Uttley is in the frame and I think we should stick with him.'

'We?' Quigley said.

'I can provide certain technical support. At a price of course.'

'Naturally.'

'I want the Black Dragon Triad to tell me what they know about a man called Gillespie who was close to them back in 1970. I expect you to persuade the elders of the Triad that it is in their interest to come across with the information.'

'Be your age – how the hell do you think I can do that?'

'By giving Li Wah Tung a hard time.'

'Li Wah Tung?' Quigley laughed. 'What's he done to you?'

'Nothing, but we hear he is moving a lot of money to the West Coast, buying up all kinds of commercial properties and companies in California.'

'Well, he's an entrepreneur and doesn't see much future for himself after 1997.'

'He's not the only one,' Ashton said. 'What kind of future does the Black Dragon Triad have once the People's Liberation Army is policing Hong Kong and the New Territories? A lot of them are going to be paying for the bullet they will get in the back of the neck. That's why they are looking to establish themselves elsewhere – America, Singapore, Malaya, Western Europe, the UK. Li Wah Tung is one of their bagmen.'

'Can you prove it?'

Ashton couldn't, that was the trouble. In fact, everything he had said stemmed from a gut feeling. It wasn't the best reason in the world for advocating a course of action but as Victor Hazelwood had told him more than once, sometimes you had to make things happen.

'Think about it,' he said. 'Here's a successful businessman with a snowy white reputation. You think anybody on the West Coast is going to ask Li Wah Tung how he managed to accumulate so much wealth? Hell, no. You can bet he arrived in California with an armful of references from impeccable banks like the Hong Kong and Shanghai, the Standard Bank, Bank of America and First National, all of them saying what a sterling character he is. If you're still not convinced, get a copy of the inquest on Bernice Kwang and see who found the body.'

Quigley didn't say anything. He had invited him to think about it but the Superintendent remained incommunicado all the way from the outskirts of Shek O to the Central District of Victoria. It was only when Quigley pulled up outside the Star Ferry terminal that he seemed ready to share his thoughts with Ashton.

'What exactly is this technical support you are willing to provide?' he asked, testing the water.

'You don't want to know,' Ashton told him. 'But if things go right, it will make your reputation. Play your cards right and you won't have any trouble finding another job when your contract expires in 1997.'

'I wish I could believe that.'

'Look, as of now, all I want from you is Uttley's home address. Think you can get it for me without drawing attention to yourself?'

'Yeah, no problem.'

'Good. I'll phone you around four o'clock this afternoon.'

Ashton got out of the Mercedes, walked into the Ferry terminal and paid seventy-five Hong Kong cents for the privilege of sitting on the upper deck. Yule was determined to put him on the British Airways flight departing Kai Tak at 21.30 hours that night. First thing he had to do was check out of the Hong Kong Hotel and find himself a bolt hole, the sort of place Head of Station would not dream of looking for him. Then he would need to get in touch with Terry Hicks. From his time at Benbow House when he had been in charge of the Security, Vetting and Technical Services Division, Ashton knew that as regards allowances and travelling expenses, Hicks was on the same scale as a warrant officer in the services. That meant he would be accommodated at HMS *Tamar*.

The retired telephone engineer was sixty-eight years old and lived alone with his crossbred Dalmatian in a cottage on the outskirts of Brockenhurst. Every morning, winter or summer, he left the cottage at 7 a.m. to exercise the dog in the New Forest. The Dalmatian was a natural hunter and was particularly adept at killing rabbits. This morning he had found something which was too big for him to handle and he stood pointing at some gorse bushes off the footpath until his owner caught up with him. Some other animal, possibly a fox, had been there ahead of him and had uncovered a foot which it had partially gnawed before apparently deciding the flesh was not very palatable.

The body was lying in a shallow grave, no more than eighteen inches deep. Leaves and fallen branches had been heaped on top of the earth to camouflage the soil. Unable to restrain his curiosity, the telephone engineer picked up a small branch and brushed the earth and leaves from the corpse until it was totally exposed. The man was fully dressed except for his jacket. He was lying on his back, his ankles lashed together with picture cord, his hands apparently tied behind him. Someone had put his head inside a plastic bag and strangled him with a nylon stocking.

CHAPTER 18

The Grand Emperor of China Hotel on Jordan Road catered for the passing trade. When Ashton checked in, the register showed that recent guests had included Guy Fawkes, Oliver Cromwell, Lloyd George, Mr Pearly King and Queen and Elvis Presley. One wit had signed himself in as Snow White and the Seven Dwarfs. To book a room for three nights under his real name would make it easy for Yule to trace him; following the example set by others, he signed in as Fred Astaire. The hotel was frequented by prostitutes who came in off the street with their clients – servicemen, merchant seamen of every nationality and tourists seeking the dubious pleasure of having it away with a bit of the local colour. The lobby was marginally bigger than a small backstreet hairdressing salon and beyond the reception desk in the entrance, a concrete staircase led to the bedrooms on the two upper storeys. There was no carpet on the stairs or anywhere else for that matter and the whole place smelled of wet cement.

Ashton's room was on the top floor halfway down the corridor on the left side. It was furnished with a small double bed, a free-standing wardrobe and a wooden ladderback chair. Instead of curtains, there was a Venetian blind in the window. There was a washbasin in the corner and a tooth mug with a carafe of dusty-looking water on the glass shelf above. The lavatories and two bathrooms were located at the far end of the corridor.

A woman tapped on the door as he finished unpacking, told him she was the maid and let herself in with a pass key. She was wearing high heels, black silk beach pyjamas and a thigh-length, midnight-blue satin tunic.

'You like service?' she asked in broken English with a smile that threatened to crack the heavy layer of make-up she had plastered on her face.

Ashton shook his head. 'Everything's okay,' he assured her.

'You sure you not want jig jig?' she said, pointing to his crotch and pumping backwards and forwards.

'Not today, lady, nor any other time.'

Ashton snatched the pass key from her grasp, put a wrist lock on the hooker and frogmarched her along the corridor and down the staircase. She did not come quietly; kicking and spitting, she called him all the names under the sun in a voice loud enough to be heard two blocks away. The desk clerk in the lobby appeared unfazed by the noise; it was, Ashton imagined, the kind of disturbance he had witnessed many times before.

'You see this?' he snarled and waved the pass key under the clerk's nose. 'I paid good money for one of your rooms and I expect to have a little privacy. Now, you tell this hooker to shut her mouth and stay away from me.'

It needed only one word from the lobby clerk to silence her; a couple of brief sentences in an equally low but forceful voice and she looked totally cowed.

'No trouble now,' the Cantonese clerk told him.

'Good. Pass the word to the other girls.' Ashton pocketed the pass key. 'I'm off out,' he said. 'Could be I'll be gone for several hours, but I'll be back. You'd just better make sure none of my stuff goes missing in the meantime.'

Ashton left the hotel, turned left outside and walked towards Nathan Road. He had paid the bill at the Hong Kong Hotel with his Gold MasterCard but that would not be acceptable in the kind of places he would be staying from now on. A credit card transaction was traceable and as soon as Yule discovered he had done a runner, it was likely that action would be taken at the highest level to get his piece of plastic declared null and void. While Ashton wasn't completely sure the SIS could persuade Lloyds Bank to do this, it was best to assume he wouldn't be able to use the facility in future.

Lambert had given him three hundred pounds worth of traveller's cheques before they left Heathrow and they were still untouched. Any major bank would cash them; however, the cheques had been issued by Kelso and the pay section would have a record of the serial numbers. Yule would certainly have taken possession of the traveller's cheques Lambert had retained for his own use. When the full list of numbers came through from London, he would be able to deduce the serial numbers of those in Ashton's possession and alert every bank in Hong Kong. To be really safe, Ashton figured he would have to draw what money he needed from cashpoints, using his PIN number. Meantime, he had just under two thousand Hong Kong dollars on him.

At the top of Jordan Road, he turned right into Nathan, then hailed a passing cab and told the driver he wanted to go to the South Seas Centre. Except for the names, all shopping malls in Kowloon and Victoria were pretty much alike. The South Seas Centre had the usual mix of boutiques, opal retailers, arts and crafts from mainland China, fur salons, ivory, silk emporiums, bespoke tailors, gem markets, pearl galleries, Rolex agents and camera, video and television retail outlets by the dozen. Ashton wandered into an opal showroom and looked briefly at a display cabinet before asking one of the sales assistants if he could use their phone. He called Quigley at Police Headquarters and took down Uttley's home address, then asked the Superintendent if he was married.

'What's it to you?'

'I need to know where I can find you later this evening.'

'Try 521 3462; that's if I ever get home tonight.'

'You have my sympathy,' Ashton told him and hung up.

He thanked the sales assistant for the use of the phone and left the store. With so few coin-operated booths in Hong Kong, what he had just done was the customary practice but he still half expected the store keeper to come running after him for the money. He went up a floor and did the same thing again, this time choosing an arts and crafts centre. He rang HMS *Tamar*, told the mess steward his name was Roy Kelso and asked for Mr Terry Hicks.

'Recognise the voice?' Ashton asked him when finally he came to the phone.

'Yeah.' Hicks sniffed audibly. 'Why all the secrecy?'

'We'll talk about that later. When do you start the check?'

'Tomorrow 08.00 hours.'

'Are you free this evening?'

'Well, it looks as if Head of Station has forgotten to invite me to dinner.'

'You're in luck then,' Ashton told him. 'Meet me at the upper terminus of the Peak Tram and I'll buy you a drink.'

'Now there's an offer I can't refuse. What time?'

Ashton glanced at his wristwatch. 'Let's make it half six.'

'Right.'

'And don't bring any hangers-on with you.'

He didn't have to spell it out. Hicks was no back-room electronic specialist; he had been up at the sharp end and knew when to keep an eye out over his shoulder.

*   *   *

Harry Farnesworth spotted the directional arrow on the grass verge and tripped the indicator to show that he was turning left off the main road into the New Forest. Although Brockenhurst was in the neighbouring county and therefore outside his area, liaison between the Hampshire Constabulary and his own force had always been good. While Cosgrove might or might not have been murdered, no such doubt existed about the man whose body had been found in a shallow grave earlier that morning. Both victims had been tied up and hooded with plastic bags tied around the throat and it was these two similarities that had prompted the Western Division of the Hampshire Constabulary to contact their opposite numbers.

The track came to an abrupt end less than a hundred yards into the forest. Alighting from his vehicle, Farnesworth locked the doors and guided by the directional arrows, came across a footpath which led to the taped-off area where the body had been found. Most of the scenes-of-the-crime photographers and technical services had already departed; the corpse too had been removed and taken to Southampton General Hospital for a post mortem. Only half a dozen uniformed constables were still on the ground conducting an inch-by-inch search of the immediate area under the watchful eye of a sergeant. There was also a detective inspector whom Farnesworth had met during a three-day seminar on psychological profiles fifteen months back.

'So what have you got, Wilf?' Farnesworth asked, hoping that he'd got his first name right.

'A partially decomposed body, male Caucasian, aged thirty to forty, height five feet seven, estimated weight one thirty-five pounds, light brown curly hair, no distinguishing marks, no means of identity. The medical examiner reckons he's been in the ground for at least one month.'

'What was he wearing?'

'One brown leather shoe, the remains of a pair of tan-coloured socks, cavalry twill slacks and a thin, black roll-neck sweater.'

'There was snow on the ground a month ago,' Farnesworth observed.

'Yeah, I know, no jacket, no topcoat. We figure he was murdered some place else and dumped here.'

'If it's who I think it is, Wilf, you're missing a regimental blazer and a British warm as well as a shoe.' Farnesworth took out a photograph from the inside pocket of his jacket and handed it to him. 'Would this be your body?' he asked.

The Detective Inspector studied the photograph, his eyebrows meeting in a frown. 'Could be. Like I said, the body was getting ripe and the face was bloated. But yes, I wouldn't be surprised if this wasn't the bloke.'

'Do yourself a favour. Get on to the 24th Royal Dragoons at Tilshead Camp and ask for the dental records of Captain Simon Oakham.'

'Thanks for the tip, Harry.'

'That's okay,' Farnesworth said. 'I'd be interested to hear what comes out of the autopsy.'

'I'll ring you as soon as we get the pathologist's report,' Wilf assured him. 'This Simon Oakham,' he added, frowning again, 'was he related to the woman who was murdered in Guildford?'

'Her husband. Some constable from your Eastern Division found his vehicle in the multistorey car park near the Continental Ferry Port in the North End District of Portsmouth. Probably been there since Saturday, 19 February – a dark blue Volvo estate, '88 model, registration number D147 AZX. Might be worth circulating a description of the vehicle.'

Farnesworth was suitably diffident. A little advice when it was asked for was okay but nobody liked being told how to do their job. Wilf was an experienced police officer and knew what he was doing; to point out that the killers had possibly used Oakham's car to transport his body to this part of the New Forest would have been an insult to his intelligence.

'No chance you can supply a motive too, is there, Harry?' the DI asked him with a roguish smile.

'I was hoping you were going to tell me.'

'You'll be the first to hear if we do come up with a reason, but don't hold your breath.'

'Right.' Farnesworth noticed that the uniforms had started to scour the same piece of ground again and decided there was nothing to be gained by hanging on any longer. 'Time I was going,' he said. 'Things to do.'

He couldn't specify exactly what. If the dental chart proved the dead man really was Oakham, he would have to tell Interpol they could stop looking for him, but that was some time in the future. Right now, he couldn't see the wood for the trees. Oakham hadn't gone absent because a sex game had gone wrong. Cosgrove had been deliberately suffocated and somehow, before he had been strangled, Oakham had been persuaded to write a postcard to his wife which had subsequently been posted in the South of France. The killer had certainly gone to a lot of trouble to create the impression that the Pay Corps officer had skipped the country, and that picture postcard of the Promenade des Anglais in Nice showed real premeditation.

Farnesworth stopped to light a cigarette and then continued on his way. Maybe Ashton had inadvertently got it right? Maybe the police were meant to think that Oakham had hired a couple of hit men to gun down his wife? If so, the plan had come unstuck on two counts – a grave that had been too shallow and a fatal traffic accident on the Leatherhead bypass. The body of the missing husband should never have been found and no one could be expected to believe that a captain in the Pay Corps had known how and where to go about hiring two members of the Chechnya *Mafiozniki*. Three linked murders, and two hired assassins killed in a multiple pile-up; some would say the circle was complete, and maybe it was, but it would be nice to know what the hell it had all been about. There was a fat chance of discovering that when people like Mr Clifford Peachey and Mr Peter Ashton were holding their cards close to their chests. He didn't know how to contact Ashton but the MI5 man was different; at least he had a phone number for him.

The lower terminus of the Peak Tram was situated opposite the American Consulate in Garden Road. From there, the funicular rose over thirteen hundred feet to the summit, a journey time of a little over eight minutes for the two-car tram. From vantage points on Lugard Road, sightseers could look down on Kai Tak airport across the harbour. But at half-past six, the last of the guided tours had departed and it was still too early in the evening for many people to be dining in the Peak restaurant. Consequently, instead of the usual eighty passengers, only a handful alighted with Hicks.

Ashton caught his eye, then left the upper terminal to browse the souvenir shops along the footpath above the car park.

'Did anyone attempt to follow you?' he asked when the electronics expert joined him.

'Not as far as I know, but all these Chinks look alike, don't they?'

Chinks, Frogs, Pakis, Gyppos, Krauts, Coons; the way Hicks described the various nationalities was enough to give the politically correct a fit of the vapours. There was no malice intended and he would have been mortally offended had anyone been foolhardy enough to accuse him of being a racist. He was British and proud of it; like most of the English, he had Irish, Scots and Welsh blood in the family but that didn't stop him from referring to the ethnic groups as Micks, Jockstraps and Taffies.

'Chinese,' Ashton said, gently correcting him.

'What?'

'It's insulting to refer to a Chinese as a Chink or a Chinaman.'

'Well, fuck me, squire,' he said cheerfully, 'you learn something every day.'

'That we do. How long do you expect to be in Hong Kong?'

'Two days, three at the outside, then I'm off to Singapore and Kuala Lumpur to sweep both High Commissions. Why?'

'I've got several addresses for you to bug.'

'Kosher, is it?'

'What do you think?'

'Forget I asked. Who are you after?'

'A police officer called Uttley and Li Wah Tung, a Chinese businessman.'

'What have they done?'

'Have you heard about the double shooting at Aberdeen last night?'

'I arrived at two o'clock this afternoon and I didn't get a wink of sleep on the plane last night. I haven't felt like reading a newspaper or watching TV.'

'Brian Lambert, our Australian exchange officer, was killed last night. I think Uttley and the Chinese businessman had something to do with it.'

'Lambert.' Hicks shook his head. 'I can't believe it.'

'There's something else you should know,' Ashton told him. 'Head of Station has ordered me out of the colony. I'm supposed to leave on the British Airways flight tonight. He's going to be pretty mad when he discovers I've disappeared and it could rebound on you if we are caught together.'

'I'll worry about that when it happens. Now where did you say these jokers live?'

'I'm going to show you.'

Ashton walked him back to the terminal and caught the next funicular down to Garden Road. There were half a dozen car parks within easy walking distance of the American Consulate. Ashton had left the Datsun he had rented from Avis in the one behind St Joseph's Church.

Li Wah Tung lived in Repulse Bay. Getting there via Wanchai and Happy Valley was no problem; locating Seabreeze Mansions on Belleview Road took longer than Ashton had anticipated.

'Not a bad place,' Hicks observed as they drove slowly past the building to park by the kerbside farther down the road. 'Wouldn't mind dossing down there myself.'

'Li Wah Tung owns the penthouse suite,' Ashton informed him.

'Won't be easy to effect an entrance.'

'Let's take a look at the underground car park.'

Ashton got out of the Datsun and walked back to Seabreeze Mansions. A concrete slope with a steep gradient provided access to the basement garage from the road above. A portcullis barred the entrance; TV cameras were positioned to capture anyone attempting to break in.

'There will be a security guard in the lobby,' Hicks said. 'System's no good without a backup; his presence will make it even more tricky to gain admittance to the penthouse suite.'

'You won't have to. Li Wah Tung is the proud owner of two Rolls Royce Corniches labelled "His" and "Hers"; one is lime green and the other salmon pink.'

'Jesus.'

'Yes, I know. I don't suppose Rolls Royce is too happy with the colour scheme either, but you won't have any trouble picking them out. You see, I plan on bugging the limousines not the apartment.'

It was, Ashton admitted to himself, a bit of a hit or miss affair, but the way he looked at it, Li Wah Tung was likely to do most of his business on the car phone when he wasn't in the office.

'What about the TV cameras?' he asked. 'Are they going to be an insuperable problem?'

'No, I can blank them out for the few seconds it will take me to run down the slope and into the garage. I'll give the security guard a snowstorm on his monitor; he'll think the signal is momentarily on the blink. I'll do the same coming out.' Hicks rubbed his jaw. 'The portcullis responds to a coded signal from a transmitter. Shouldn't be too difficult to buy a gizmo which will get round that.'

'Have you seen all you want to?'

'All I can from here.'

'Then let's move on.'

The House of Pearls and Gems was the registered company name for Li Wah Tung's business empire. The head office in Victoria was on the top floor of the Landmark Shopping Centre on Des Voeux Road Central and Pedder Street. The building was one of Hong Kong's shopping malls that was open until late at night. Consequently, no one paid any attention to Ashton and Hicks when they made a quick circuit of the top floor. Hicks took one look at the head office of Li's trading house and announced that picking the lock on the door would be child's play.

'Ten minutes in and out; shouldn't take longer than that to wire the place for sound.'

'Good. Now let's take a look at the policeman's flat.'

'I hope you're not expecting me to do all three in one night?'

'No, you can do Uttley's place in broad daylight,' Ashton told him.

'In broad daylight?' Hicks echoed. 'Look, I don't mind chancing my arm on your behalf but I draw the line at committing suicide.'

'He will be on duty and his wife won't be at home. I guarantee it.'

'If you say so.' Hicks followed him on to the down escalator. 'I'm going to need a load of gadgetry.'

'Give me a list of what you want and I'll buy it.'

Alighting from the escalator on the ground floor, they walked out into Pedder Street and made their way to Edinburgh Place where Ashton had left the Datsun. The Uttleys had an apartment on the eighth floor of Mirabar Court, a tower block surrounded by the Shangri-La, Royal Garden and Regal Meridien luxury hotels. Instead of taking the cross-harbour tunnel to Kowloon, Ashton chose to use the Yau Ma Tei car ferry on the grounds that it happened to be nearer. He also thought there was less chance of running into Maurice Yule.

Security at Mirabar Court was nowhere near as tight as it had been at Seabreeze Mansions. There was no electronic surveillance and the hall porter paid no attention to them. Neither did any of the residents they encountered. Each apartment had a steel reinforced front door provided with a spy hole and Hicks assumed there were draw-bolts top and bottom in addition to the usual security chain. Well over ninety per cent of the work had gone into making the occupant feel safe when at home. When the apartment was empty, the only thing to deter a burglar was the lock on the door which did not impress Hicks.

'I've seen enough,' he told Ashton.

It was not the first time Hicks had been to Hong Kong. The crown colony featured in the list of vulnerable areas and was one of the places he visited every other year. With his local knowledge, he knew exactly where to obtain the eavesdropping equipment he required. Credit cards were not in vogue with retailers who specialised in electronic surveillance, which meant the hundred pounds worth of Hong Kong dollars Ashton had drawn from a cashpoint earlier in the evening vanished. So did a lot of the original folding money he had in his wallet.

The news that Oakham's body had been found in the New Forest reached Hazelwood via Clifford Peachey shortly after 2 p.m. It was not the best start to the afternoon and it was destined to get a lot worse. While he was still assessing the implications of this latest development, his PA informed him that Head of Station, Hong Kong was on the Sky Net satellite link. Dunglass was out of the office briefing the Minister of

State at the Foreign and Commonwealth Office, and it seemed that Roger Benton, the Assistant Director in charge of the Pacific Basin and Rest of the World Department, did not feel qualified to advise him. Muttering under his breath, Hazelwood lifted the crypto-protected phone and pressed the encoding button on the cradle.

'Hello, Maurice,' he said, doing his best not to sound irritable. 'What can I do for you?'

'Ashton has disappeared,' Yule told him abruptly.

'What do you mean, disappeared?'

'Just that. He checked out of the Hong Kong Hotel at 14.00 hours our time and hasn't been seen since. British Airways flight 036 took off without him, so you needn't bother sending anyone out to Gatwick tomorrow morning.'

'Perhaps he's been injured. Have you checked all the hospitals?'

'That's already in hand. What I want to know is do we make every effort to apprehend him if it turns out he is not in hospital?'

The DG had wanted Ashton out of Hong Kong but it seemed he was doomed to be disappointed. Although Yule had not specifically alluded to the double murder on the Shek Pai Wan estate yesterday, it was obvious to Hazelwood that this was uppermost in his mind. There was not the slightest chance that Ashton would talk to the press and torpedo the cover story Yule had put about to account for Lambert's death. But if it became known that the police were looking for him, there was a good chance some bright reporter would get on to the fact that Ashton had been present when Lambert had been gunned down and then the fat really would be in the fire.

'You sit tight and do nothing,' Hazelwood told him. 'You wait for Ashton to come to you. Okay?'

'What about the DG . . . ?' Yule began.

'You leave him to me,' Hazelwood growled and severed the satellite link with the crown colony.

CHAPTER 19

For sheer numbers coming and going, the Grand Emperor of China Hotel sounded like London's Waterloo station in the peak hours except that, unlike the rail terminus, it was past three o'clock in the morning before things had finally quietened down. Up until then, Ashton had slept fitfully, woken every half-hour or so by people bawling, shouting, laughing and falling down drunk. There were two fist fights in the corridor and there would have been a third had some enraged Scandinavian managed to kick the door down and break into his room. He had paid for three nights in advance with the intention of staying two; if the equipment he'd purchased for Hicks hadn't made such a dent in his wallet, Ashton would have moved on after one night.

He woke at 6.30, washed and shaved in tepid water, then put on the last clean shirt he had, which made his much-creased jacket and slacks look slightly more presentable. The same desk clerk as yesterday was on duty in the lobby, looking even less happy than he had been when Ashton had first made his acquaintance. The lump under his right eye suggested he had been involved in one of the two fist fights that had been staged on the top floor last night and had come off worst. Taking out his wallet, Ashton extracted a Hong Kong hundred-dollar note, ripped it in two and gave the Chinese one half.

'You get the rest tonight,' he told the clerk, 'provided my gear hasn't been removed. Okay?'

'Sure thing, boss.'

'I'd also like to know if any friends come looking for me while I'm out.'

'I tell them you no here.'

No smile, just the same sullen expression, but his eyes were on the other half of the note which Ashton was still holding and he knew what was required of him if he was to get his hands on it.

'That's the idea,' Ashton said.

Leaving the hotel, he made his way up to Nathan Road and had breakfast in Jingles. Forty years ago, the restaurant had been located at the bottom end of Nathan Road opposite Whitfield Barracks, a block from the Peninsula Hotel. Now this site was occupied by Chung Ming Mansions and the army barracks too had long since vanished. All that remained of the original establishment were the autographed photos of such sporting personalities of bygone days as James J. Braddock, heavyweight champion of the world, who lost his title to Joe Louis. There was also a photograph of Jingle himself, the ex-machinist mate of the United States Navy. Taken inside the original restaurant with its ceiling fans, bamboo tables and chairs, it showed a large fat man leaning on a cane who bore an uncanny resemblance to Sydney Greenstreet, a movie star whom Ashton had become acquainted with through watching old, late-night films on Channel 4 television.

The menu was about a yard and a half long. From it, he chose grapefruit, fresh orange juice, two soft-boiled eggs with toast and coffee. The order included a free copy of the *South China Morning Post* which arrived on the table before the starters did. Lambert was still making the headlines and there was also a recent photograph of Sergeant Henry Sung on the front page which Ashton presumed had been supplied by the police. There was a much fuller report of the incident than any that had been published in yesterday's newspapers and a number of the residents on the eleventh floor of the tower block had been interviewed. None would admit to being an eyewitness but one of the Chinese had stated emphatically that he had seen a second European by the fire alarm. When questioned about the allegation, a police spokesman had expressed bewilderment and had appealed for the mystery man to come forward which Ashton thought was, metaphorically speaking, the equivalent of returning service with a passing shot down the line.

Breakfast arrived while he was reading the paper. By the time he'd finished both, he still had almost two and a half hours to kill before he phoned Quigley to learn whether it was a go or no-go situation. There was, however, a limit to the number of cups of coffee he could drink, so, paying the bill, he left Jingles and continued on down Nathan Road and collected the Datsun from the security car park in rear of the Sheraton where he'd left it overnight.

After paying the fee, he headed north and took the Castle Peak road out of town. He drove on through Tsuen Wan and Tuen Mun to the border crossing point near Fanling, then looped back to Kowloon via Tai Po and Sha Tin. The round trip of the New Territories served no purpose other than to pass a couple of hours. Back in the city, he parked the car in a side street off Nathan Road and went shopping. From a men's outfitters in the arcade of the Hyatt Regency Hotel, he bought a couple of Van Heusen shirts, then asked to use the phone and rang Quigley, only to find his extension was engaged. After two further attempts, he finally got through to him.

'So is lunch on?' he asked.

'You surely don't think Diane Uttley would turn down a freebie even at this short notice, do you?'

'I don't know the lady,' Ashton told him.

'They're meeting in the lobby lounge of the Peninsula Hotel at 12.30 before lunching in the Swiss Centre.'

'How will I recognise your wife?'

'She's blonde, has green eyes, is five feet six and a bit and weighs about a hundred and—'

'That's all very well but what will she be wearing?'

Last night he had specifically asked Quigley to find out. The pregnant silence which followed led him to conclude the Detective Superintendent had forgotten to check with his wife.

'Navy-blue two-piece woollen suit,' Quigley said after considerable thought. 'It's got some white piping on the collar.'

'I hope to God you're right,' Ashton said and hung up suddenly aware that the English-speaking sales assistant was listening to his side of the conversation.

He went into a tobacconist's farther up the arcade and bought a small box of Burma cheroots for Hazelwood before asking if he could use the telephone. He then rang the mess at HMS *Tamar* and asked the steward to page Mr Hicks to the phone.

Although Ashton hadn't laid down a rigid timetable, there was a limit to how long the electronic specialist could dally over a fifteen-minute coffee break before Yule began to wonder what was keeping him. The delay in contacting Quigley had thrown everything out of kilter and he counted himself fortunate that the abrasive Londoner was still in the mess.

'You've got a lunch date for 12.30,' Ashton told him.

'I'm happy to accept. Have you been invited too?'

'Oh yes, I'll be there.'

'See you then,' Hicks said and hung up.

Although no plan was ever a hundred per cent foolproof, Ashton was satisfied he had anticipated the things that could go wrong. Hicks had asked for thirty uninterrupted minutes to get the job done; in the event, he could count on a minimum of an hour and a half. And if lunch finished early or the lady in question failed to show up, he would ring the apartment and warn Hicks to get out. Ashton therefore couldn't understand why he should feel uneasy when everything seemed to be so nicely buttoned up.

Uttley lit another cigarette, the tenth he'd smoked since reporting for duty that morning. He had always been a twenty-a-day man but in the last thirty-six hours he had become a compulsive smoker. It was fortunate that he'd caught the newscast on TV before he went into the office yesterday otherwise he might have gone to pieces. It wasn't that he felt anything for Lambert; how could he when the man was virtually a complete stranger? The fact was he had been one of the last men to see the Australian alive and that made him feel exposed.

All day yesterday he had been like a cat on hot bricks, expecting at any moment to be visited by the investigating officers. Joe Public might think Lambert and Sergeant Henry Sung had been gunned down in a drugs bust but the Assistant Commissioner in charge of Special Branch knew different. Even if Quigley hadn't figured it out for himself, the Assistant Commissioner would have told him that the two men had walked into an ambush.

But Quigley hadn't been anywhere near him. Instead, his wife, Ellen, had rung Diane last night and invited her out to lunch. Said she was coming over to Kowloon to do a little shopping and wouldn't it be nice if they could get together? Anyone would think they were close friends, which was one hell of a joke because he and Quigley couldn't stand the sight of each other. While they had never had a stand-up row, everyone knew there was an atmosphere between them and they had never socialised. So why the sudden and unexpected invitation from Ellen Quigley? What was behind it? Diane hadn't wanted to accept and maybe he shouldn't have talked her into it, but at the time he had wanted to know the answers to both questions. He still did, but wished there was some other way to find out.

'You got a minute, Steve?'

Uttley almost jumped out of his chair. Absorbed in his dark thoughts, he'd not heard Quigley enter the room. 'Yes, of course. What can I do for you – George?'

They had never been on first-name terms; usually he addressed the Superintendent as 'sir' and he was hesitant about calling him George. He did so now because he wanted Quigley to think he didn't have a care in the world.

'Well, I'm hoping you can tell me just how many officers knew the Foreign and Commonwealth in London had asked us to find Yang Bo?'

'You mean apart from the Commissioner?' Uttley managed to raise a smile even though his stomach was churning.

'And yourself,' Quigley said with brutal directness.

'Well, I am the Police Liaison Officer,' he said and stubbed out his cigarette in the already overflowing ashtray.

'And it was your job to pass the information on to Lambert.'

It was a bald statement of fact, not a question. The trouble was it sounded like an accusation the way Quigley put it.

'Looks bad for me, doesn't it?' Uttley said in what he hoped was a jocular tone.

'Did I say that?'

'No.'

'Then why are you being so defensive?'

'I'm not. Look, I first became aware that we were looking for Yang Bo when I saw a copy of the internal memo on the float file.'

'Who was it addressed to?'

'What – the internal memo?' Uttley cursed himself for being an idiot. Answering a question with a question was the standard response police officers had come to expect from a suspect who had something to hide and needed a breathing space to come up with a plausible explanation.

'That will do for starters,' Quigley said tersely.

'That memo was addressed to the ACP in charge of Special Branch from the Commissioner. The float file is seen by the Commissioner and the Assistant Commissioners responsible for Special Branch, the Criminal Investigation Department, Operations and Administration.'

'And their respective clerks,' Quigley added.

'That goes without saying. You should also bear in mind that a number of Special Branch officers knew London was interested in finding Yang Bo. I haven't the faintest idea how many were told about it; only their head man would know that.'

'Don't worry, I'll make a point of asking him.'

Quigley started towards the door, then turned about, his forehead creased in a puzzled frown as if something he had been told no longer made sense to him. It was, Uttley thought savagely, a trick he must have acquired from watching *Columbo* on television.

'Do you trust your clerk?' he asked.

'Implicitly,' Uttley told him. 'I have no reservations about her whatsoever. She's loyal, discreet, hard working—'

'The Assistant Commissioner, Special Branch called you into his office the day before yesterday and gave you Yang Bo's address. Correct?'

'Yes. He also said I was to pass the information on to Lambert and arrange for an English-speaking police officer to accompany him to the Shek Pai Wan housing estate.'

'And you said nothing about this to your loyal, discreet and hardworking clerk?'

Quigley's voice dripped with sarcasm and touched a raw nerve. 'Of course I didn't, that would have been a gross breach of security.'

'So it would be true to say that only the ACP, Special Branch, Sergeant Henry Sung and yourself knew exactly when Lambert would be calling on Yang Bo?'

'What are you inferring?'

'Nothing,' Quigley said airily. 'I merely wanted to be sure of my facts. Not that we'll ever find the killers, you never do when a Triad is involved.'

The bastard had him pegged as the informer, but Quigley would have a hard time proving he was on the payroll of the Black Dragon Triad. He and Diane lived modestly, some would say frugally. They were the only couple he knew who didn't employ a Chinese houseboy, never mind a cook housekeeper, and Diane had a part-time job too. Double income, no kids, mean as hell and salting the money away; Uttley knew what they said about him behind his back and it suited his purpose to let them think he was saving for that rainy day in 1997. Let Quigley do his worst, he'd never be able to prove a damned thing. Or was he simply indulging in wishful thinking? Uttley reached for another cigarette and lit it with a hand that trembled.

Hicks took the Star Ferry to Kowloon and started walking. As far as Yule was concerned, he was having an early lunch in HMS *Tamar* and would be back at 13.45 hours. In theory, he had plenty of time in which to effect an entry and bug any room in the Uttleys' apartment and return to Victoria with almost half an hour to spare. In theory, it was a soft target, no children, no servants, a foolproof early warning system and a lock a child could pick. But it only needed a chance encounter with one of the neighbours as he was leaving the flat for the whole business to end in tears.

There was a different hall porter on duty in the lobby of Mirabar Court but he was no more inquisitive than the one who had been there last night. Hicks wished him a cheerful good morning and recieved an equally cheerful greeting in return as he walked on past the desk towards the lifts. An empty car on the ground floor was another bonus; entering it, he pressed the button for the eighth floor. When he alighted, the corridor was deserted and remained so while he picked the lock on 823 and let himself into the apartment.

Although the flat was comfortably furnished, there was nothing ostentatious about it. The pictures on the walls were not originals, the cutlery was EPNS and the bone china was commonplace and inexpensive. From previous occasions when he had been in Hong Kong, Hicks knew how relatively cheap it was to have a bespoke tailor run up a made-to-measure suit. Because of this, he did not attach much significance to the number of suits hanging in Uttley's closet. What did impress him was the absence of any designer labels in Diane's fitted wardrobe. Ashton believed the Chief Inspector was on the take; from what he had seen of their life style, there was no evidence to support the contention. Whether or not Ashton was barking up the wrong tree was no concern of his; the former head of the Security, Vetting and Technical Services Division had asked him to bug the place and he had better get on with it.

The accommodation consisted of a hall, lounge-diner, kitchen, utility room, lavatory and bathroom and two bedrooms, the smaller of which Uttley used as a study. To bug the place he had two miniature transmitters with an operating range of a mile and a half. The microphone was no thicker than a strand of fuse wire and the battery-powered transmitter was roughly the size of a five-pence coin. The locations of the two telephones in the apartment dictated that one would have to be installed in the study, the other in the lounge-diner. Just where he could conceal them however was a more vexing problem. If Uttley was bent, he would almost certainly make a point of checking the phones at regular intervals. He would also run his eye over the rest of the room but few people, and that included experienced police officers, ever looked up at the ceiling. The snag was that the Uttleys hadn't bothered to have their ceilings papered. Anything he fixed to the distempered surfaces would therefore attract immediate attention. That meant he would have to lodge the transmitters under the coving in both rooms, a job that would take him a lot longer than he and Ashton had allowed for.

Five minutes to one; Quigley thought it was about time he looked in on Uttley again and put a little more pressure on him. Ashton was right; the Police Liaison Officer was on the payroll of the Black Dragon

Triad, probably had been ever since he joined the force. How they went about proving that was where he and Ashton differed. The SIS man was prepared to rely on an electronic and visual surveillance to obtain the necessary evidence, but that could take for ever and tie down a lot of police officers who already had a heavy enough case load as it was. No, the answer was to speed things by spooking him; once Uttley twigged that he was regarded as a prime suspect, he would panic and make the kind of wrong move which would ultimately bring him down.

But Uttley wasn't in his office. The desk was clear, the filing trays had been locked away in the safe and the contents of the ashtray emptied into the wastebin. Only the blue-grey haze of cigarette smoke remained.

Quigley turned about and walked into the clerk's office next door. 'Where is Chief Inspector Uttley?' he asked the Chinese secretary.

'He's gone home, sir,' the girl told him. 'He wasn't feeling well.'

'What time did he leave?'

'About half an hour ago.'

Quigley thanked her and returned to his own office. He thought it significant that Uttley had begun to feel queasy some time after he had grilled him in his own office. It showed the bastard had got the wind up and it was tempting to speculate how he would feel in a few minutes from now when he walked into his flat and found Ashton's technician hard at work. But he couldn't allow that to happen. It wasn't just a question of the electronic surveillance going down the toilet. If Uttley succeeded in apprehending the intruder and found that his apartment had been bugged, all hell would be let loose. Internal Affairs would be dragged in and it wouldn't be long before someone began to wonder out loud how it was that on that particular day, Diane Uttley had been invited out to lunch by Ellen Quigley for the first time ever. Lifting the receiver, he rang the flat in Mirabar Court.

The strident summons of the telephone sent a charge through Hicks like an electric shock and he nearly fell off the chair he was standing on. Heart in his mouth, he waited for the phone to stop after it had rung six times. There would then be a brief pause while Ashton redialled and subsequently allowed the number to ring out just twice. But this was no alarm signal; either the caller was a friend of Diane Uttley and was not aware that she was out to lunch or else it was a wrong number. Satisfied with the explanation, Hicks went back to work.

Planting a transmitter in the study had been a relatively simple task. There had been a couple of hairline cracks where the coving had come unstuck from the ceiling and he had been able to insert the blade of his penknife into the gap and enlarge it just enough to accommodate the bug without leaving any telltale traces. The lounge-diner was a different proposition altogether. The coving was flush with the ceiling and the only suitable hiding place, which wasn't regularly dusted or polished, was the top surface of the door frame.

An upright chair from the dining alcove had served as a stepladder and using his penknife again, he had carefully dug out a shallow trough for the transmitter. The job now completed, Hicks put the chair back where he had found it and fetched a dustpan and brush from the broom cupboard. He was on his hands and knees making sure every sliver of wood and flake of paint was removed from the carpet when the phone rang again.

One, two, three, four, five; he counted the number of rings and sighed with relief when it went on past six, then became tense when the phone stopped after eight. You didn't usually get two wrong numbers in a row barely five minutes apart, and the odds against the caller being another friend of Diane Uttley had to be pretty astronomical. He went into the kitchen, tipped the contents of the dustpan into the sink and flushed the debris down the waste outlet, then returned the brush and pan to the broom cupboard. The phone rang a third time as he was passing the study. Thoroughly unnerved, Hicks ducked into the room and lifted the receiver.

A man said, 'Is that you, Steve?'

'I think you must have the wrong number,' Hicks told him in a voice that quavered.

'Get the hell out of there whoever you are, Uttley's on the way home. He left here nearly forty minutes ago.'

Hicks slammed the phone down, ran towards the front door, then ran back into the study twice as fast when he heard a key turn in the lock. Back pressed against the wall, he waited to see what Uttley would do.

'Anyone at home?'

Anyone? He wondered why Uttley had said that when they were a twosome, no kids, no live-in servants and not in the social swim either. Was it because Uttley suspected there was an intruder in the apartment? Had the door to the study been open or closed before he entered the room the first time? Whatever the answer, he hoped to God the Chief Inspector wasn't carrying a revolver. A very tentative push swung the study door back towards Hicks as Uttley entered the room.

In his formative years, Hicks had been a promising amateur welter-weight and had had thirty-odd bouts before giving up the sport. Although decidedly ring rusty, there was nothing wrong with his timing and before the Chief Inspector saw him, he caught Uttley on the jaw below the left ear with a vicious right-hand jab that poleaxed him. Stepping over the unconscious police officer, Hicks went into the master bedroom and racing against time, tipped everything out of the chest of drawers and dressing table on to the floor to give the impression that the place had been ransacked. Then he left the apartment and walked down to the seventh floor before summoning the lift. His heart didn't stop pounding until he boarded the Star Ferry ten minutes later.

CHAPTER 20

Ashton paid his bill and left the Swiss Centre while Ellen Quigley and Diane Uttley were still lingering over coffee. From a vantage point in the lobby of the Peninsula where he could watch both the staircase and the lifts, he waited for the two women to leave the hotel and go their separate ways. It was not a long vigil; he had been sitting there for rather less than five minutes when they appeared from the direction of the elevators and walked right past him towards the main entrance on Salisbury Road. Watching them as they kissed each other on the cheek in a perfunctory manner, he got the impression that their luncheon date was not likely to be repeated.

When they parted company, Diane Uttley turned left and walked towards the junction with Nathan Road while Ellen Quigley moved off in the opposite direction to make her way to the Star Ferry. Ashton got to his feet, walked through the arcade on the south side of the hotel and left by the side entrance in Hankow Road where he had parked the Datsun. Opening the boot, he took out a brown paper package about the size of a shoebox and set off in pursuit of Ellen Quigley. He kept her in sight, gradually closing the distance between them to ensure he caught the same ferry sailing. Once on board the cross-harbour boat, he waited until the crew had cast off the hawsers before accosting her.

'Mrs Quigley?' Ashton said, smiling.

'Yes. Do I know you?'

She had a pleasant voice with a slight regional accent which he couldn't place. 'My name's Ashton. We've never met before but I'm the man who was responsible for your lunch date.'

'I'm surprised you admit to it,' she said with a faint smile.

'As bad as that, was it?'

'I don't actually like Diane very much so it was a bit of an ordeal.'

'I'd like to say this is a little something to make up for it,' Ashton said and gave her the package. 'Unfortunately, I'm afraid it's for your husband.'

'It would be. Am I allowed to know what it is?'

Ashton didn't see why not. Ellen Quigley had already been told why she had to invite Uttley's wife to lunch and the contents of the package would be openly on display once Quigley set up the monitor in their flat on Harcourt Road overlooking the waterfront.

'It's what we call an audio sentry,' he told her. 'The receiver is tuned to a certain wavelength and activates the built-in tape recorder when it picks up a signal.'

'From inside the Uttleys' flat in Mirabar Court,' she added quietly.

'Yes.'

'And by a signal, you mean his voice?'

'Or hers. The receiver is pretty indiscriminate in that respect.'

'Will George know how to operate it?'

'I imagine so. If he doesn't, there's a broadsheet inside.'

'I hope it's straightforward. My husband is not a very practical man. If a plug needs changing in our house, I have to do it.' Ellen Quigley leaned against the rail, arms loosely folded across her chest and gazed at the closing shoreline of Victoria as if she had never seen it before. 'You're not a police officer, are you, Mr Ashton?' she asked in a low voice.

'No, I'm not.'

'And what you and my husband are doing is completely unlawful, isn't it?'

'Don't worry about it,' Ashton told her in an equally low voice. 'Whatever happens, your husband won't be implicated.'

'But I had lunch with Diane . . .'

'So what? You two have never got on and you decided to do something about it. That's the line to take should anyone ask why you invited her out, which they won't.'

'You make it sound as though there's nothing to it.'

'Well, there isn't. Just tell your husband to make sure the monitor is up and running by tonight.'

The captain brought the ferry alongside the pierhead with all the deftness of a cab driver picking up a fare from the kerbside. The gangways went down and the passengers on the lower deck streamed ashore, jostling for position like competitors at the start of the London Marathon. Those on the upper deck disembarked at a more leisurely pace but in the general exodus, Ashton still became separated from Ellen

Quigley. Swallowed up in the crowd, he caught one last glimpse of her as she descended into Pedder Street.

Ashton turned about, went through the turnstile and caught the next ferry back to Kowloon. When he collected the Datsun from Hankow Road he still had four hours to kill before meeting Hicks.

Uttley was on his fourth double whisky and was more than a little inebriated when Diane let herself into the flat. He had the telephone in the lounge in pieces and was trying to reassemble it on the dining table with fingers that were all thumbs. He also had difficulty in getting his tongue round any word of more then two syllables.

'We've been burgled,' he announced in a slurred voice when she walked into the room.

'And you've had too much to drink.'

'That's as may be,' he said owlishly, 'but it doesn't alter the fact that someone broke into the flat while we were both out. If you don't believe me, take a look at the state of our bedroom.'

'Don't think I won't,' Diane said and turned on her heel.

Uttley got to his feet and lurched after her. Although unable to walk a straight line, he somehow managed to keep his balance despite an undulating floor in the hall.

'My God, what a mess.'

Diane stared at the scene that confronted her. All the drawers had been removed from the dressing table and the contents tipped out on to the floor. Foundation garments, bras, slips, panties, nightdresses, stockings and tights were piled in a heap. Lipsticks, nail varnish, face powder, eye shadow, bottles of perfume and a jewellery box had also ended up on the floor when the intruder had deliberately swept everything off the dressing table. It had been done with such force that a bottle of perfume had lost its stopper and was leaking into the carpet. The face powder container had burst open, covering everything in the near vicinity with a fine dust. Although Uttley's own belongings had been treated with similar disregard, his wife was far too preoccupied to notice.

'What disgusting animal did this to me?' she said and rounded on him, her face contorted with fury. 'I'd like to get my hands on him, whoever he is.'

'Never mind that. Is any of your jewellery missing?'

The question had Diane on her hands and knees checking the contents of the small, red leather box. It didn't take her long; apart from a pair of diamond earrings, a garnet brooch and a string of pearls, the rest was on her fingers.

'It looks as if nothing has been stolen,' she said, looking up at him with a puzzled frown.

'That's what I thought. The intruder was still on the premises when I came home . . .' Losing the thread of what he was about to say, Uttley shook his head in an effort to clear the cobwebs from his brain. 'Bastard was lurking in the study,' he continued in a voice little above a mumble. 'Caught me with a lucky punch on the jawbone as I walked into the room. Never knew what hit me.'

'Have you reported this to the police?'

Uttley sniggered. 'I am the police.'

'You're drunk,' Diane said contemptuously and got to her feet. 'I can see I shall have to do it myself.'

'You can't, the phone's out of order.'

'What do you mean, it's out of order?'

Uttley didn't say anything. Instead, he grabbed hold of a wrist and dragged her, kicking at him and screaming at the top of her voice, into the bathroom. Still holding on to Diane, he reached out with the other hand and turned on both taps of the washbasin before telling her the phones were probably bugged.

'Bugged?' Her voice rose a full octave. 'Who would want to do a thing like that?'

'Quigley.' He could tell from her expression that she thought he had taken leave of his senses. 'Think about it,' he urged her. 'Why do you suppose Ellen Quigley invited you to lunch?'

'Because she thought it was about time we got together.'

'Wrong. Her husband wanted to make sure the flat was empty before he put one of his goons in to bug the place.'

'I didn't want to have lunch with Ellen Quigley,' Diane reminded him. 'It was you who wanted me to accept the invitation.'

'I had to know what Quigley was up to.' Despite the precautions he had taken to ensure no eavesdropper could pick up their conversation, Uttley instinctively lowered his voice. 'He's in charge of the murder investigation and I was the last person to see Lambert alive.'

'Does he suspect you were involved?'

'Oh, yes.'

Uttley told her what had happened that morning and why the grilling he'd had from Quigley had convinced him the Detective Superintendent believed he was the source who had tipped off the Black Dragon Triad.

Uttley wasn't always coherent, nor was he entirely accurate. Rather than admit to Diane that the interrogation had literally made him sick with fear, Uttley pretended he had left the office early because he suspected Quigley's people were about to effect an illegal entry with the intention of bugging their apartment.

'Good thing I did; another few minutes and the intruder would have completed his task and we would never have known he'd been here.'

'So this man who hit you didn't have time to plant anything?'

'Well, the phones haven't been doctored, but that isn't saying much.' Uttley shrugged, affecting a sang-froid he did not feel. 'I mean, he must have had upwards of half an hour to himself before I arrived on the scene.'

'Are you telling me our home isn't safe?'

'I don't know.'

'Then you'd better find out, Steve. If the task is beyond your limited talents, you'd better ask your friends to help.'

'My friends?' he repeated blankly.

'In the Triad,' Diane said impatiently.

'Are you mad? You think Quigley doesn't know what happened here this afternoon? From now on he will have me watched round the clock. I won't be able to break wind but what he knows about it. And if he ever gets wind of our joint account in the Bahamas—'

'What joint account?' she asked, interrupting him.

Uttley stared at her in disbelief, his mouth open. 'The one we've got with the Union Bank of Grand Bahama,' he said, recovering.

'That's the first I've heard of it.'

The implication of what Diane was saying didn't register at first. When it did, a terrible rage began to boil within him. It was fuelled by all the wounding things, real and imagined, that she had said about his supposed inadequacies over the years. It was Diane who had urged him to line his pockets when the opportunity had arisen and now, at the first hint of trouble, she was planning to dump him.

'You bitch.'

He punched her in the face, splitting the bottom lip and followed it up with two more to the head, inflicting a nose bleed and closing the left eye. When she threw up her hands to ward off any further blows, he jabbed a fist into her stomach. For the first time in their life together, he heard her sobbing and knew she was frightened of him; for the first time in their life together, he heard her beg for mercy and exulted in the sense of power this gave him.

*   *   *

Ashton squeezed the Datsun into a vacant space at the kerbside just beyond the King's Cinema on Queen's Road Central and kept the motor running while he waited for Hicks to join him. One look at the surly expression on his face when he got into the car told him that the king of electronics had not had a good day. Shifting into drive, Ashton checked the rear-view mirror and then pulled away.

'So what happened?' he asked.

'I nearly got caught, didn't I?'

'I don't know, I was hoping you were going to tell me.'

'Uttley came home while I was still inside the bloody flat.'

Ashton made two right turns in quick succession and headed back in the direction of the Star Ferry. 'Did he see you?'

'The only thing Uttley saw was a lot of stars,' Hicks said tersely. 'When he walked into the study, I lashed out, caught him with a real belter to the side of the jaw before he could look round. Went down like a felled tree.'

'When did this happen?'

'You mean what time of day?' Hicks shrugged his shoulders. 'One fifteen? One thirty? Who knows? Is it important?'

'It was getting on for three o'clock when Diane Uttley left the Peninsula Hotel.'

'The telephone in their flat rang three times before that. I knew it couldn't be you because it went on ringing. When I finally did pick up the phone, some guy asked if that was Steve. I made some excuse about him having got the wrong number and he told me to get the hell out of the flat because Uttley was on the way home. Said he'd left forty minutes ago. I figured the caller had to be Quigley.'

'You're right,' Ashton told him. 'It couldn't have been anyone else; only Quigley knew what was going down.'

From what Hicks had said, there were grounds for thinking that for reasons best known to himself, the Superintendent had tried to apply a little psychological pressure on Uttley and had botched it.

'We shan't get anything from the flat now,' Ashton said.

'Oh, I don't know about that. I turned the bedroom over, made it look as though Uttley had disturbed a burglar.'

Uttley was an experienced police officer and it would take a lot to fool him. 'Did you lift anything valuable?' Ashton asked.

'What do you think I am?' Hicks said indignantly. 'A thief?'

That did it. Uttley would twig it was a put-up job and would go over his apartment with a fine-tooth comb looking for the transmitters.

'You can drop me off here,' Hicks said. 'I can walk the rest of the way to HMS *Tamar*.'

'What are you talking about? We haven't taken care of Li Wah Tung yet.'

'And I'm not going to, Mr Ashton. I've had enough excitement for one day.'

The way Hicks saw it, in doing Ashton a favour he had gone out on a limb and had been lucky to get away with it. If he had been arrested by Uttley, the SIS wouldn't have stood by him and he would have been thrown out on his ear, sans pension, sans terminal grant, sans testimonial.

'Enough's enough.'

'I agree.'

'You do?' Hicks said, obviously expecting some argument.

'I wouldn't say so if I didn't mean it.'

Without Hicks noticing it, they had gone past the shore establishment known as HMS *Tamar* and were now in the Wanchai District. Ashton didn't know Mexican Pete's Place from any other bar or disco in the neighbourhood but a cab happened to pull out from the kerb by the entrance and he nipped into the vacant space before any other driver could grab it.

'Why are we stopping here?' Hicks asked.

'I'm going to buy you a drink. Okay?'

'Fine by me.'

Ashton got out of the Datsun, waited for the electronics specialist to join him then simultaneously locked all the doors and activated the alarm system with the remote control before leading the way into the disco.

Mexican Pete's Place was all flashing lights and a decibel count guaranteed to make the hearing seriously impaired in later life. The bar girls wore high-heeled boots with silver-coloured spurs, brown leather skirts with a six-inch long fringe, white satin blouses with bootlace tie, waistcoats and sombreros which instead of adorning the head, nestled between the shoulder blades. The Mexicans came from Canton, the clientele came from the four corners of the globe, were in their early to mid-twenties and gave a convincing impression of being comatose as they jigged to the music. Ashton fought his way through the crush, reached the bar and ordered two Scotch on the rocks, then borrowed the phone and rang Quigley.

There was no chance of anyone being able to eavesdrop on their conversation. The din was such that Ashton could scarcely hear himself speak and had to press a finger to his left ear in order to catch what Quigley was saying. Even so, he still couldn't afford to be indiscreet.

'It was a lousy party,' Ashton told him in guarded language. 'A gatecrasher showed up, there was a brief fistfight and the guest of honour was forced to leave early. On top of that, the hi-fi system broke down.' He waited for a reaction and when none came, he added, 'I think someone ought to keep an eye on the equipment in case it goes missing.'

Quigley said he would see what he could do and put the phone down. It was not the whole-hearted commitment Ashton would have wished for but since he was in no position to twist Quigley's arm, he just had to accept the situation. He paid the bar girl for the drinks and holding a glass in each hand, eased a path through the crush to join Hicks near the fire exit at the rear of the disco. What few booths there were in the place had already been taken.

'I was beginning to wonder what had happened to you,' Hicks told him in his usual lugubrious fashion.

'I rang Quigley, told him what had happened and suggested he put some men on the street to watch our friend round the clock.'

'And?'

'He's thinking about it.' Ashton raised his glass. 'Mud in your eye.'

'And yours.'

'Now suppose you tell me how to use the gizmo I've got in the boot of the Datsun.'

Hicks stared at him, the whisky halfway to his mouth. 'Let's get this straight,' he said slowly. 'You're planning to go into the basement garage of Seabreeze Mansions and bug the two Rolls Royce Corniches?'

'And Li Wah Tung's office in town,' Ashton said cheerfully.

'You must be off your bloody trolley. When was the last time you installed a snooper?'

'That's beside the point. The job has got to be done and you've made it clear that you are not available.'

'Aw, shit.' Hicks tossed his whisky back and placed the empty glass on top of the wall-mounted fire extinguisher. 'I'll do it.'

'You don't have to.'

'Oh yes I do. You'll get caught sure as eggs are eggs and while Yule may not be the brightest Head of Station we've ever had in Hong Kong, it won't take him long to work out who advised you what equipment to buy. So I might as well get hung for a sheep as a lamb.'

As homespun philosophies went, Ashton thought, there was a good deal of truth in that old adage. Inviting Hicks to follow him, he shouldered a path towards the entrance where he blithely handed his empty glass to one of the bouncers before exiting into the street. Neither man said anything during the fifteen-minute drive to Belleview Road in Repulse Bay.

Dunglass did not look round when Hazelwood entered the office but remained standing at the window, his back to the door, arms loosely folded across his chest. At the morning conference with heads of departments, Hazelwood had thought the DG was preoccupied and it seemed he still was. Yet on the intercom only a few moments ago Dunglass had sounded alert enough, even a touch abrasive. Hazelwood wondered if Yule had called the DG from Hong Kong to complain that his deputy had countermanded the instructions he had received and what was he supposed to do about Ashton please? When a polite cough failed to attract his attention, Hazelwood reminded Dunglass that he had asked him to step into his office.

'Sorry, Victor, I was deep in thought.' Dunglass returned to his desk, waving Hazelwood to a chair as he did so. 'Yesterday was rather difficult for me,' he added.

'It can't have been easy briefing the Minister of State about Lambert.'

'No, he was all right. Naturally he asked a number of penetrating questions but the Minister merely wanted to get his facts straight before flying out to Canberra.' Dunglass played around with the blotting pad on his desk, lining it up until it was exactly parallel with the old-fashioned pen and ink stand he'd purchased from an antique shop in Chester. 'Actually, I'm sorry to say my problem is more of a personal nature.' He cleared his throat before continuing. 'Bit of trouble with the old prostate. I'm afraid it means an operation.'

'Have they given you a date?'

'I'm being admitted this coming Monday, the surgeon goes to work on me the following morning.'

Hazelwood didn't know what to say that wouldn't sound trite. A part of him was also conscious of just how much fate had shaped his career, and to no small degree. He could not forget that he would probably have risen no higher than head of the Russian Desk had the then Assistant Director, Eastern Bloc not suffered a fatal coronary. He had stepped into the dead man's shoes and had been confirmed in the appointment after the department had been restructured to take account of the new political situation in Eastern Europe following the break up of the Warsaw Pact. Although Dunglass had been favourite to succeed the previous DG, the appointment of Deputy Director General had been regarded as wide open.

Content with his lot, it hadn't occurred to Hazelwood that he might be in the running for the post. He owed his unexpected advancement to Dunglass who had evidently felt that, having spent the greater part of his service in the Far East, he needed an expert on the Eastern Bloc he could turn to for advice.

Now it seemed fate had intervened yet again and he was about to go all the way to the top. Sir Victor and Lady Hazelwood; Alice would like that, he thought, and was immediately overwhelmed by a sense of guilt.

'I'm sorry, Stuart,' he murmured.

'What for?' Dunglass smiled. 'I'm not planning on dying in the near future. You'll just be keeping the chair warm for me while I'm in hospital and convalescing.'

Hazelwood groped for the right words. 'Let's hope that won't be long,' he said feebly.

'Yes, indeed. However, there are a number of matters we need to discuss.'

Amongst them was the line Dunglass wanted him to take when resisting the Treasury's latest demand for a further twenty per cent reduction in the SIS budget. The Cabinet Secretary had also set up a working party to consider whether, as a cost-cutting exercise, the training school at Amberley Lodge shouldn't be amalgamated with the MI5 establishment in the Thames Valley. Dunglass thought he might be prepared to accept that option but in return, he expected a more realistic assessment of their needs by the Treasury.

'I think that about covers it, Victor, except for one thing.'

'What's that?'

'I hope you and Alice are free to have dinner with us tonight?'

'Well, that's very kind of you but—'

'No buts, Victor,' Dunglass said, interrupting him. 'Walter Maryck, the CIA Station Chief in London is coming. If you want to ask him about Bernice Kwang, you'd better be there.'

CHAPTER 21

Ashton dropped Hicks off at HMS *Tamar* and continued on to Causeway Bay and the cross-harbour tunnel to Kowloon. The operation ought to have been a hundred per cent successful because the plan had been simple, effective and well-executed. It was destined to be a total failure because Quigley had stuck his oar in and spooked Uttley and that capricious element called luck had favoured the opposition. Hicks had burgled his way into and out of the underground garage of Seabreeze Mansions in the space of a few minutes. Unfortunately, the Rolls Royce labelled 'His' wasn't there and the World's End shopping centre where Li Wah Tung's office was located had closed by the time they got back to Victoria.

Emerging from the harbour tunnel, Ashton drove across town and left the Datsun in a car park off Kansu Street, six blocks north of the Grand Emperor of China, then slowly walked back to the hotel carrying the Van Heusen shirts and the box of cheroots he'd purchased in a shopping bag. It was only a couple of minutes short of ten o'clock and he hadn't eaten anything since lunch but just the thought of food made him want to throw up. So did the fact that everything Hicks had done had been in vain. There would be no end result; worse still, Ashton had no idea what to do next. It seemed to him that for all the good he was doing, he might as well get himself on the first plane leaving for England.

The night clerk was on the reception desk when he walked into the hotel. In the short time he had been staying there, Ashton had assumed the Grand Emperor of China got by with a staff of two lobby men, each working a twelve-hour shift, but he hadn't seen this man before. However, the liaison between the day and night staffs could not be faulted.

'Your things okay,' the clerk told him.

'Good.'

'My friend say you give me rest of money now.'

'Why?'

'He come here later for it.'

'Well, okay.' Ashton placed the shopping bag on the desk. Pulling out his wallet, he found the other half of the hundred-dollar note and gave it to the night clerk. 'Tell him not to spend it all at once.'

Ashton picked up the shopping bag and moved on towards the concrete staircase. At the top of the first flight he passed one of the short-term guests on his way out of the hotel. He turned the corner, started up the next flight, then stopped dead. How the hell had the night clerk known who he was? If Westerners found it difficult to describe most Chinese in other than mundane terms, wouldn't the same generalisation apply in reverse? Ashton didn't like it. If the night clerk was guarding the entrance and a reception committee was waiting for him on the top floor, he was the meat in the proverbial sandwich. Had Yule gone to the police and asked them to apprehend him? Was the man in the lobby a plain-clothes officer? Ashton discounted the possibility. Turning about, he charged downstairs.

The night clerk had deserted the reception desk and was waiting for him at the foot of the staircase, a semiautomatic pistol in his right hand. One fleeting glance at the noise suppressor attached to the barrel was enough to convince Ashton that the clerk wasn't a police officer. They were just two steps apart when Ashton dropped the shopping bag and deliberately jumped into him. He cannoned into the Chinese like a runaway train and heard his skull hit the concrete floor with a sickening thud as he landed on top of him. The semiautomatic flew out of his hand and skidded across the floor. Ashton went after it on hands and knees, curling his fingers round the butt, then sprang to his feet and ran out into the street.

He sprinted towards the bright lights and gaudy neon signs in Nathan Road, the gun in his right hand cleaving a path for him on the crowded pavement. Anxious not to give any pursuer a clear shot at his back, he suddenly cut across the road, honked at by every driver who was forced to brake in order to avoid him. Approaching the brightly lit junction up ahead, he slowed to a walk and tucked the automatic in the waistband of his slacks and buttoned the jacket to make sure it stayed hidden.

The handgun was a 7.65mm type 64 pistol made in the People's Republic of China. Ashton recalled what the weapon training instructor from the SAS had told him and his fellow students on the Induction Course at Amberley Lodge back in September '82. Manufactured solely for assassination purposes, the type 64 could be used in either a manually operated single shot mode or as a self-loader. Single shot achieved the maximum silencing effect but reduced the muzzle velocity to the point where the bullet lost a great deal of its penetrative force. When used as a semiautomatic, the weapon was noisier but had greater stopping power. Whether the pistol was set for single shot or self loading was immaterial; given half a chance, the night clerk would have killed him.

He followed the signs for Jordan station on the Mass Transit Railway, fed the ticket vending machine in the entrance hall with three dollars fifty and caught a train to Admiralty on the Island. From there he started walking towards the Wanchai District and turned into the first bar he came to. As far as he could tell, nobody had been following him.

There was, he thought, nothing like a large tot of Chivas Regal on ice to set you up and put the world to rights. The first question he needed to answer was how the Black Dragon Triad had traced him to the hotel on Jordan Road? To know his name wasn't enough, they had to be able to describe his appearance to God knows how many desk clerks in Kowloon and probably Victoria as well. What they really had needed was an up-to-date photograph.

No one would have given them one; they must have taken his picture without him being aware of it. Where and when? At the airport? Or outside the hotel that first morning? No, it had to be later on, after he had become more than just a name to them. Lloyd Ingolby; they had known in advance that he intended to question the former judge. They could have been watching the house from somewhere on the hillside above it. And they had seen him arrive at Journey's End and had taken his picture with a long lens camera.

It also wasn't too difficult to figure out why the Triad had decided to eliminate Lambert and himself. The Triad were investing all their money in California against that rainy day in 1997 when the People's Republic of China took over. If the CIA learned that one of their agents had been murdered by them, the leaders of the Triad believed the US Government would take steps to seize their investments. So once it became apparent that he and Lambert were close to proving that Bernice Kwang hadn't been accidentally drowned at sea, the leadership had decided to have them both killed. But in the end, it all came back to Uttley.

Ashton finished his whisky, left the bar and walked back to the Central District of Victoria. The big shopping centres had closed long ago but many of the small retailers and backstreet traders remained open all hours. He scoured the area between Connaught and Des Voeux bounded by Pedder Street in the east and Jubilee to the west. Amongst those shops that were still open he eventually found one which sold all kinds of electrical goods. After purchasing a Sony tape recorder, he made his way back to the Star Ferry and returned to Kowloon.

Although Mirabar Court was no distance from the ferry terminal, he hired a cab because he had to assume the Triad were still looking for him in Kowloon and there was no point in taking unnecessary risks. Short of threatening to shoot the lock off, there wasn't much he could do should Uttley refuse to open the door to him but that was a problem he preferred to shelve until it happened. When he walked into Mirabar Court after paying off the cab, the doorman paid no more attention to him than he had yesterday evening. The Uttleys didn't pay much attention to their own doorbell either and he had to keep his thumb continuously on the button for a good minute before there was any kind of response from within.

'Who is it?' a woman asked in a muffled voice.

Ashton produced his passport, held it up to the spyhole in the door, turned the pages to his photograph and waited for her reaction. Presently he heard her withdraw the top and bottom bolts and unlock the door which she then opened as far as the security chain would allow.

'My name is Ashton,' he told her through the gap. 'I'm a senior civil servant from London and you would be well advised to let me in, Mrs Uttley.'

How pompous can you get? he thought. But it did the trick because she slipped the security chain and opened the door. It was only when Ashton stepped into the hall that he saw that someone had been knocking her around. The left eye was closed to a narrow slit, the cheekbone below was badly bruised, her nose was swollen and the bottom lip was twice the size of the upper.

'Who did that to you?' he asked.

'Who do you think?'

'Your husband?'

'Right first time,' she said bitterly. 'The swine had been drinking and was full of Dutch courage.'

'So where is he now?'

'Steve went out a few minutes ago, said he wouldn't be long.'

'He's in serious trouble . . .'

'It could be Superintendent Quigley who's in trouble,' she said defiantly. 'He had one of his men break into our flat while we were out. Steve found two—'

'Why are you defending him?' Ashton said, cutting her short. 'Do you like being used as a punchbag?'

'Don't be stupid.'

'So what are you going to do about it?'

'That's none of your business.'

He was going down the wrong path, getting nowhere, and Uttley might return at any moment. Diane wouldn't give him what he wanted merely to spite her husband. He had to convince her that she owed it to herself to come clean.

'I'm not sure what the sentence is for being an accessory to murder but at a guess I would say you are looking at ten years minimum.'

'I don't know what you are talking about,' Diane said and tossed her head.

'It was on TV; don't tell me you never watch it.'

'We look at the news.'

'Then you will know I'm talking about the murder of a customs officer on the Shek Pai Wan estate, except that Lambert was in the Australian Secret Service and your husband set him up.'

'Nonsense.'

'Forget the burden of proof,' Ashton told her. 'I'm not a policeman and no charges will be brought against your husband, but I am telling you he will end up dead on a slab because we don't play by the rule book in our world.' He reached inside his jacket and took out the semiautomatic pistol. 'You see this? It's a type 64 purpose-built assassination weapon designed and manufactured in Communist China. I don't know how the Triad got their hands on this type of pistol but you can bet they've got plenty more like it.' He tucked the pistol back inside the waistband of his slacks. 'Should word get around that Steve is being very co-operative, they will come looking for him with one of these. And you had better not be there when it happens because they will put you down too.'

He did not say who was going to spread the word; he thought Diane was intelligent enough to draw her own conclusion. His assumption was rapidly justified when she asked him what she should do. What he wanted from her was a statement telling him what she knew about the money her husband had received from the Triad and where he had salted it away. It was obvious that Diane didn't like the suggestion and he had a hard time persuading her that nothing she said could be used in evidence against her or Steve.

'I'm not worried about that louse.'

Ashton had wondered why she had seemed determined to protect her husband despite what he had done to her. Now it was clear that her previous reluctance to tell him what she knew had had nothing to do with loyalty. Diane Uttley had only been concerned to protect herself.

'Does that mean you are willing to make a statement?' he asked.

'Why not?'

She opened a door off the hall and showed him into the lounge diner. There had been moments when Ashton had felt he was butting his head against a brick wall but the barriers were down now and she made no objection when he produced the Sony tape recorder.

Ashton told her to start by giving her full name, date and place of birth, date of marriage and full particulars of husband Steven. He also wanted the sort of personal detail only she would know just in case somebody tried to claim the statement had been faked. After that, he let Diane have her head.

The end product wasn't the most lucid account he'd ever heard but it was a strong contender for one of the most damaging. In all, she spoke nonstop for the best part of twenty minutes and there was still no sign of Uttley when she finally ran out of things to say.

'What happens now?' she asked.

'Well, first of all I would like someone in authority to hear this . . .'

'Not Quigley.'

'No, not him.' Even if she hadn't objected, Ashton wouldn't have contacted the Detective Superintendent. Quigley had had his chance and he wasn't about to give him a second bite at the cherry. 'Matter of fact,' he continued, 'the man I'm thinking of is in a different line of business altogether.'

'Well, I guess that's all right then.'

'So may I use your telephone?'

'Be my guest,' Diane told him.

Ashton walked over to the phone, lifted the receiver and dialled Yule's home number.

Maurice Yule and his wife, Jennifer, rarely went to bed much before midnight and even then usually had their noses in a book for a good half-hour before they switched off the light. There were occasional exceptions to this routine and that evening they had turned in shortly after 10.30. One way or another, Ashton had given him a couple of sleepless nights and Jennifer had insisted they retire much earlier than was their normal practice. Fast asleep when the phone rang, Yule was slow to surface. When he did come to, he instinctively reached out to shut off the alarm and in the process managed to sweep the clock on to the floor. The telephone nearly followed suit when he finally got around to lifting the receiver. A cheerful voice in his ear told him that he sounded dead to the world after he had grunted into the mouthpiece.

'Who is this?'

'Ashton.'

Wide awake now, Yule sat bolt upright in bed. 'I've got a bone to pick with you,' he said angrily.

'That will have to wait. Right now I want you to listen to this . . .'

There was a brief pause before a woman said, 'My name is Diane Mary Uttley. I was born in the South London Borough of New Malden on 11 August 1952. When I was five, my parents moved to Sevenoaks in Kent where I was married in St Paul's church on Saturday, 15 May 1971. My husband is Chief Inspector Steven Uttley. To my certain knowledge he has been receiving money on a regular basis from the Black Dragon Triad for the past six years . . .'

The woman stopped abruptly. 'Did you get all that?' Ashton enquired.

'I did,' Yule told him, 'but why are you telling me?'

'Just listen and you'll find out.'

There followed a whirring noise punctuated at irregular intervals by the odd few words as the tape recorder was run fast forward while Ashton searched for the part he wanted him to hear. In a detached voice, Diane Uttley went on to state that her husband had warned the Triad that London was anxious to interview certain witnesses who had given evidence at the inquest on Bernice Kwang. She also claimed that he had subsequently kept the Triad informed concerning the movements of Brian Lambert. Then the tape stopped again and Ashton came back on the line.

'I think we've got Uttley where we want him, don't you?' he said.

'I'm no lawyer,' Yule told him, 'but in my opinion what you have on tape is inadmissible evidence.'

'Who said anything about using it in a court of law? I'm aiming to turn Uttley round and that statement gives us the necessary leverage.'

'Us?' Yule echoed indignantly. 'I don't know what you have in mind but I won't have anything to do with it. This is a matter for the police.'

'They can have Uttley after we have finished with him.'

Yule listened incredulously as Ashton outlined what he planned to do. What he proposed would undoubtedly destroy the harmonious relationship with the Hong Kong police which successive Heads of Station had carefully nurtured down the years, but that didn't seem to bother him in the least. He had a fixation about a man called Gillespie and was convinced Uttley would be able to persuade the Black Dragon Triad they should tell him what they knew about the man.

'Who the hell is Gillespie?' Yule asked and immediately wished he hadn't when the younger man mentioned Reeves and the Asia and Pacific Travel Agency in the same breath. 'For God's sake,' he snapped, 'watch what you're saying. This is an open line.'

'Then get your skates on and come over here.'

Yule was lost for words. Ashton's nerve was breathtaking. In the SIS he had been a middle-ranking desk officer and out of it he was nothing, but anyone who had heard both sides of their conversation could be forgiven for thinking Ashton was his superior officer. If it didn't sound quite so pompous, Yule would have asked him who he thought he was talking to.

'I'm staying where I am,' Yule said firmly. 'I've already told you this is a matter for the police.'

'Try telling that to Victor Hazelwood,' Ashton said bluntly.

Yule froze, gripped the combined microphone and receiver even tighter. He couldn't think how Ashton knew that Hazelwood was in the chair when the ciphergram from London addressed to all Heads of Station worldwide had only arrived just as he was about to leave the office. The short answer was that he couldn't possibly have heard the news, but it might be wise to proceed on the assumption that he had. What was it Lambert had said when they were gossiping over dinner the night he had arrived in Hong Kong? Hazelwood and Ashton; they're like David and Jonathan? As he recalled it now, those had been his exact words.

Yule cleared his throat. 'Where did you say you were calling from?' he enquired politely.

'I didn't, but I'm at the Uttleys' apartment in Mirabar Court. It's on the eighth floor and the number is 823.'

'I'll be there in half an hour.'

'Good. Make sure you bring the Assistant Commissioner in charge of Special Branch with you. We've got to offer Uttley something or we won't get a damned thing out of him.'

For sheer gall, Ashton was in a class of his own. He seemed to think he had only to snap his fingers and the Assistant Commissioner would came running.

'Incredible,' Yule muttered to himself as he slowly replaced the receiver.

'Who was that, darling?' Jennifer asked in a drowsy voice.

'A lunatic,' he told her, but she had already drifted off to sleep again and did not hear him. Taking care not to disturb her, Yule got out of bed and started dressing in the dark.

*　　*　　*

Uttley did not sneak back into the apartment like a man who had spent the night carousing with friends and wanted to avoid a tongue-lashing from his wife. Instead, he let himself into the hall and boldly announced that he was home as though he hadn't beaten his wife almost senseless only a few hours ago. Ashton raised a finger to his lips urging Diane not to answer him, then left the chair to stand behind the door, his back to the wall.

'I'm home,' Uttley repeated and walked into the lounge/diner.

'Welcome back,' Ashton said behind him.

Uttley jumped, not metaphorically speaking but literally, his feet parting company with the floor. Although he didn't actually rotate in midair, he came pretty close to it.

'Jesus Christ.' Uttley placed a hand on his chest as though he was having palpitations. 'Who the hell are you?' he gasped.

'Well, I'm either going to be your best friend or your worst enemy. The choice is yours.'

'Get the fuck out of here, whoever you are.'

'Ashton. My name is Ashton, and you would do well to remember me because I'm the other man you betrayed to the Black Dragon Triad.' Dipping into his jacket pocket, he brought out the Sony recorder. 'I want you to hear this,' he said calmly.

Ashton ran the tape forward until he judged Diane Uttley had finished giving her personal details, then pressed the play button to come in where she was talking about the Union Bank of Grand Bahama. The effect on Uttley was explosive.

'You stupid bitch.' His face contorted with rage, he advanced towards his wife. He managed all of two paces before Ashton moved in and kicked his legs from under him.

At five feet eight, the Chief Inspector just exceeded the minimum height for a ranking officer in the Hong Kong police. Before the night was out, he would be wishing he had been half an inch under if Ashton had anything to do with it. Planting a foot between Uttley's shoulder blades, Ashton pinned him down.

'You're in enough trouble as it is,' he said in a conversational tone of voice. 'Don't make things worse for yourself. Of course you are going to tell me the prosecution can't make Diane go into the witness box but I doubt they will need her evidence to secure a conviction of corruption. I'm also sure you will get the maximum custodial sentence, which is what? Seven years? Whatever it is, I guarantee you will still be languishing in

Stanley Prison when the colony reverts to Communist China. So what are the options? you may ask.'

Uttley didn't ask but that didn't stop Ashton from spelling them out just the same. He wanted it clearly understood that there was no way Uttley could hang on to the money he had stashed away in the Union Bank of Grand Bahama, nor could he avoid a custodial sentence. What Uttley might anticipate was a minimum term of imprisonment and transfer to the UK before 1997.

'You couldn't deliver it,' Uttley told him.

Ashton wasn't sure he could either but that little problem could only be resolved when Yule arrived with the Assistant Commissioner in charge of Special Branch. 'There's a price of course,' he continued. 'You don't get anything for nothing in this world. You want to hear what it is?'

'You'll be wasting your breath.'

As an act of bravado it lacked conviction. Ashton doubted if Uttley even succeeded in fooling himself. Removing his foot, he told the Chief Inspector to sit down on the couch and behave himself.

'You're going to work both sides of the street,' Ashton told him, then explained exactly what that entailed.

Uttley's first task was to offer his superiors a sweetener. That meant telling the Assistant Commissioner everything he knew about the Triad, particularly their business interests and the identities of his contacts in the organisation. Once the Drugs and Vice Squads had made life sufficiently difficult for the Triad, he would then be required to pass the word through his contact that things could get a little easier in return for all the information they had on a man called Gillespie. When Uttley was finally arraigned, tried and convicted, his sentence would be commensurate with his success or failure as a double agent. When he had finished laying it out, Uttley invited him to try selling the package to the Assistant Commissioner, Special Branch.

Ashton did exactly that when Yule eventually arrived with the Assistant Commissioner in tow. Overcoming their objections took him the best part of two hours and even then the scheme was subject to the approval of the Commissioner of Police, the Attorney General and His Excellency the Governor.

Their consent was still being awaited when Yule, having moved heaven and earth to do so, personally put Ashton on the first available flight to London.

CHAPTER 22

Ashton flew into London Heathrow on the Sunday morning with the rain bucketing down from an inky black sky. He guessed Yule would have signalled Vauxhall Cross to let them know that he was on the way home but Roger Benton, Head of the Pacific Basin and Rest of the World Department, was the last person Ashton had expected to see when he emerged from Customs and Excise into the main concourse of Terminal 4. The Assistant Director looked down in the mouth; Ashton thought it could be on account of the weather or because he had been dragged out of bed on a Sunday morning at the unearthly hour of 5 a.m. A much more likely cause however was the fact that Benton had evidently been made responsible for him, an obligation which clearly was not to his taste.

'Hello, Roger,' Ashton said cheerfully, 'this is an unexpected pleasure.'

'It's certainly unexpected,' Benton said mournfully, then added that his Ford Granada was in the short-term car park.

'There was really no need for you to meet me,' Ashton told him as they made their way towards the exit.

'Hazelwood said there was, and he's running The Firm now.'

'What?'

Benton glanced sideways at him. 'You obviously haven't heard the news. Dunglass has prostate trouble. Nobody knows how serious it is but rumour has it that the Director has cancer of the bowel and is not expected to return. Anyway, Victor's in the chair and enjoying every minute of it.'

Ashton thought it wouldn't be permanent because Hazelwood liked to make things happen. There was nothing wrong with a little bit of aggression but he was the apostle of the high-risk strategy which was anathema to the Foreign Office and politicians on both sides of the House. Victor was okay as a temporary stand-in but if Dunglass was forced to retire on grounds of ill health, the Permanent Under Secretary of State for Foreign Affairs would advise the politicians to look elsewhere when choosing a successor. What was needed was a safe pair of hands, a description which didn't readily apply to Hazelwood.

'Oakham has been found; his body was lying in a shallow grave just outside Brockenhurst in the New Forest.' Benton erected his large golfing umbrella and held it partially over Ashton to shield him from the rain as they crossed the road outside the terminal building and walked into the short-term car park. 'The police identified him from his dental records. According to the pathologist who performed the autopsy, he was murdered around the same time that Cosgrove met his death. It seems Detective Chief Inspector Farnesworth is anxious to see you.'

'Surprise, surprise.'

Benton stopped by a dark blue Ford Granada and unlocked the doors, then lowered his umbrella and stowed it in the boot. 'So is Clifford Peachey,' he added.

Ashton dropped his suitcase into the trunk. 'Well, there's another surprise.'

Benton had a few more in store for Ashton as he brought him up to date. Hazelwood had met Walter Maryck at a dinner party hosted by Dunglass at his house in Montrose Place on Friday night and had asked the CIA Station Chief what he could tell him about Bernice Kwang and Lenora Vassman.'

'When can we expect to hear something?'

'Middle or end of next week.'

Ashton got into the car, pulled the seat belt from the inertia reel across his chest and clipped it into the housing. 'Middle or end of next week,' he repeated thoughtfully.

'That's what Maryck said.'

'They must be taking time out to think about it.'

'You've got the most suspicious mind of anyone I know.' Benton started up, shifted into reverse and backed out of the parking slot, then made for the exit. 'You think the CIA has that kind of information on tap?'

'They are bloody inefficient if they haven't got it on a disk.' Ashton looked about. Instead of taking the A4 into London, Benton was heading in the opposite direction towards the M25 orbital. 'You mind telling me where we're going?' he asked.

'Amberley Lodge. We've got a lot of ground to cover before we let Farnesworth anywhere near you.'

'I'm going to need a change of clothing if I'm staying overnight.'

'What have you got in the suitcase?'

'A lot of dirty washing plus a jacket and a pair of slacks in need of urgent attention from a good tailor.'

Yule had not allowed him to return to the Grand Emperor of China. What was left of his gear had been collected by an RAF warrant officer from the Joint Services Intelligence Staff. The Van Heusen shirts he'd purchased in the shopping arcade of the Hyatt Regency had disappeared, so had the box of Burma cheroots he'd intended to give Hazelwood.

'I'm not turning back,' Benton told him. 'You'll have to make do with what you've got.'

'Why do I get the feeling I'm going to be held incommunicado?'

'Because, as I said before, you've got a suspicious mind.'

After that exchange, their conversation got a little strained and died altogether before they picked up the A3 to Petersfield.

Except for the duty cook, a barman-cum-waiter and a bachelor member of the permanent staff who lived in, Amberley Lodge was deserted. There was however nothing unusual about that. Even when a training course of one description or another was in full swing, the house was always empty over a weekend after the student body had departed on Friday afternoon until they reassembled for the first lecture at nine o'clock on the Monday morning. Following the collapse of the Warsaw Pact, courses were now few and far between and there had been none since the end of November.

Clifford Peachey arrived shortly after nine o'clock and joined Ashton for coffee in the library while they waited for Benton to finish breakfast. As always, he asked after Harriet and wanted to know how she was.

'Still pregnant,' Ashton told him bluntly.

He could have added that she was still mad at him except that it wouldn't have been strictly true. When he had telephoned her a few minutes ago, she had been in turn, happy, apologetic and then coldly angry. Happy because she had believed he was at last responding to the message she had left on his answer machine and apologetic because she was sorry for being so bitchy to him last Sunday. She had only become coldly angry when she learned that he had been in Hong Kong all week and had not, as yet, checked his answer machine. Ashton couldn't understand her attitude. Apparently, all would have been well had he ignored her message, sulked in his tent and passed up the opportunity to spend the weekend with her in Lincoln. What she couldn't forgive was the fact that he had gone away without saying goodbye and hadn't bothered to phone her until he was back home again. Trying to explain that it hadn't been like that had been a waste of time.

'When are you two going to get married?'

Peachey meant well. He thought of himself as a proxy father to Harriet and wanted nothing more than her happiness, but his tone suggested that he thought Ashton was behaving in what he regarded as a thoroughly dishonourable way.

Tersely, Ashton gave Peachey Harriet's parents' telephone number. Peachey frowned. 'In a roundabout way you are telling me that it's up to her?'

'I always did think you were the best DG MI5 never had,' Ashton told him acerbically.

'Point taken. I'll mind my own business in future.'

'I'm sorry to hear that,' Benton said, and closed the library door behind him. 'I was hoping we could have a full and frank exchange of information.'

'It's why I am here,' Peachey said.

Benton caught Ashton's eye and put on his anxious I-trust-you-are-not-going-to-rock-the-boat expression.

'No need to look so worried, Roger,' Ashton said reassuringly. 'You caught the fag end of a different conversation. It was a private matter, nothing to do with business.'

'Well, that's a relief.' Benton moved an armchair closer to the two men and sat down. 'So who's going to start the ball rolling?' he asked, and gave the MI5 man an encouraging smile.

'Harry Farnesworth is making a nuisance of himself,' Peachey said, coming straight to the point. 'He seems to think we are deliberately withholding information from him and we would like you to satisfy his curiosity. Call it a quid pro quo.'

'How's that?' Benton asked, looking genuinely puzzled.

'I asked Clifford to put me in touch with him,' Ashton said, 'and things sort of snowballed from the moment he learned that Cosgrove and Oakham had known one another from way back and were probably still enjoying a homosexual relationship when the major ended up with his head in a plastic bag.'

'I see.' Benton gazed at the view beyond the window, apparently mesmerised by the pools of water lying on the surface of the rain-sodden lawn. 'And what does Farnesworth think we can supply?'

'A motive,' Peachey said and then promptly took out his pipe and began to fill the bowl with Dunhill Standard Mixture from his much-used pouch.

'He believes it is more than likely that the two Chechen gunmen who shot down Louise Oakham also murdered her husband and Richard Cosgrove.' He struck a match and held it over the bowl. 'If Farnesworth's supposition is correct, he can wrap everything up, always provided he can explain why these two gangsters from Grozny should want to kill them.'

'I saw an article in the *Sunday Times* a week ago which claimed Afansiev and Ovakimyan were over here to buy two thousand Stinger anti-aircraft guided missiles.' Ashton smiled. 'I was just wondering if there was any truth in the story.'

'We had heard that representatives of the Chechnya Republic were in the market for such weapons,' Peachey admitted. 'But the information was from a low-grade source. It's also a fact that neither Afansiev nor his half-brother Ovakimyan came to our notice before they were killed in that traffic accident on the Leatherhead bypass.'

'What about arms dealers?'

'The locals are known to us and their activities are monitored pretty closely. Special Branch keep tabs on those arms brokers from overseas who are in this country on business.'

'Assuming you are aware they are in the trade.'

'Well, naturally we wouldn't pretend to know every face,' Peachey said.

'Does the name Gillespie ring a bell with you?'

'Who's he?' Benton interjected.

'I'm surprised you don't know,' Ashton said. 'Considering the number of cables Maurice Yule fired off to London during the last forty-eight hours, I thought he would have included that titbit.'

'Well, he didn't.'

Peachey looked from one man to the other like a spectator watching a rally between two power players on the centre court of Wimbledon. Spittle bubbled in the stem of his pipe as he puffed away contentedly.

'Gillespie is the man who was photographed with Bernice Kwang at a barbecue in the New Territories,' Ashton continued. 'He ran the Asia and Pacific Travel Agency for Reeves and almost certainly had the Chinese American girl murdered by the Black Dragon Triad.'

'Gillespie?' Peachey shook his head. 'I can't say the name strikes a chord.'

'For all I know he could be using a different one these days.'

In fact, he only had Lloyd Ingolby's word for it that the mystery man had called himself Gillespie back in 1970. He had asked Lambert to check the local tax records and the audited accounts of the travel agency to see what they could learn about him but the Australian had been killed before he'd had a chance to do anything about it. And Yule had told him the local tax office would not have kept any of the returns which Gillespie might have filed twenty-four years ago.

'This is a waste of time,' Benton said irritably. 'For all we know, the man could be dead.'

'I don't think so,' Ashton told him. 'I believe he has changed his occupation and is now an arms broker. Furthermore, I'm prepared to bet he isn't one of the home-grown variety either.'

'This man is in and out of the country like a Eurocrat from Brussels, is he?'

'Yes. He goes where the money is and right now, there are a lot of trade delegations from the newly independent republics in London who are on a shopping spree.'

'Well, it's an interesting theory,' Benton said dismissively, 'but how will it satisfy DCI Farnesworth?'

'Cosgrove ran into Gillespie on one of his periodic trips to London and knew he had seen him somewhere before. Once he recalled the circumstances, he and Oakham decided to try their luck with a spot of blackmail.'

'Demanding money with menaces.' Peachey clucked his tongue. 'Farnesworth will want to know why this man felt so threatened that he had Cosgrove and the Oakhams killed.'

'In 1975 while staying at a *Gasthof* in Winterberg, they saw Gillespie murder a warrant officer in the army's Special Investigation Branch of the military police.'

'That would be a good enough motive for Harry Farnesworth.'

'I'm not sure we can be quite so open with him as that,' Benton said.

'I don't see why we can't. It's the Bernice Kwang episode that can really hurt us and we are not going to tell Farnesworth what happened in Hong Kong twenty-four years ago. If we convince him the whole thing started in Winterberg, he'll stop digging.'

'I wish it was as simple as that, Peter. My gut tells me Farnesworth won't rest until he feels Gillespie's collar. And the first thing he will ask for is proof that Gillespie is an arms broker.'

'Indeed he will,' Ashton said, 'and it will be up to Clifford to furnish him with the necessary proof.'

Peachey removed his pipe and gaped at him open-mouthed. 'Me?' he said incredulously.

'Why not? You said Special Branch tried to keep an eye on visiting arms dealers and we've got a colour snapshot of Gillespie taken when he was on a fishing trip with the SIB detachment in Hong Kong. Hicks can run off a few more copies and you can give them to Special Branch and maybe one of the officers will remember seeing him.'

'Gillespie was a young man when that picture was taken,' Benton said. 'He could have changed out of all recognition since those days, he might even have been to a plastic surgeon and had his face altered.'

Ashton told himself to cool it, that losing his temper with the Assistant Director would only be counterproductive but the admonition was only partially effective. 'It seems to me you are looking for an excuse to do nothing,' he said tartly.

It was Peachey who nipped a potentially explosive row in the bud by calmly pointing out that they had nothing to lose, adding that he personally was happy to go along with the suggestion. He was also firmly of the opinion that Farnesworth would not question the information they proposed to give him.

'So when do I renew my acquaintance with Harry Farnesworth?' Ashton asked.

'After I've cleared it with the acting DG,' Benton told him. 'And after Clifford and I have come up with a convincing story to explain why it has taken the best part of a week to put you in touch with the Detective Chief Inspector.'

Warren Treptow was twenty-eight years old, hailed from Redondo Beach, California and had graduated from UCLA in 1988. He was five eleven, weighed a hundred and fifty-eight pounds, had light brown hair and eyes to match. When asked to describe him, most people recalled that he had a nice smile but could remember little else about his features. He had been drawn to the Central Intelligence Agency like metal to a magnet. It had been a calling; where some had always wanted to be a soldier, sailor, doctor, astronaut, pilot, lawyer, fireman, train driver or policeman from childhood, Warren Treptow had wanted to be a spy. In his early teens, he had amended this to Intelligence Analyst, a more accurate if less glamorous job description.

With the benefit of hindsight, Treptow had come to see that he could not have joined the CIA at a worse time. Eighteen months after completing the officer training programme at Camp Peary near Williamsburg, Virginia, the Wall had come down, the Warsaw Pact was defunct and the Soviet Union had broken up. Treptow had seen himself as one of the sentries who stood watch ready to warn the garrison within; now there was no enemy outside the gates and a lot of the self-motivation had gone. He had always enjoyed the theatre, liked going to the movies and was an avid reader of fiction. Contemplating a change of career, he had recently signed up for a course on creative writing.

It hadn't only been the lack of a credible threat to the United States that had raised doubts in his mind. Assigned to the élite Directorate of Operations after training, he had been posted to Bonn, the largest CIA station in Europe with an establishment of sixty case officers. Before leaving for Germany, he had been told he'd better be blessed with a fast learning curve because the station was a real boiler house. In the event, his fast learning curve hadn't been up to speed and it had taken him a full year to discover that his immediate superior was totally corrupt. Eighty per cent of agents he had supposedly recruited were imaginary, so were the Intelligence reports they filed. Before his superior was caught, the scam had enabled him to pocket several hundred thousand dollars, financial rewards which had allegedly been paid to the mythical agents. There had been other pinpricks which had dented Treptow's morale, like the in-fighting with State Department officials who'd claimed CIA officers were poaching their sources. But the biggest let-down of all had been the fact that master Soviet spy Aldrich Ames had twice been promoted while serving with the Bonn station.

He hadn't been too sorry when his tour of duty had been cut short in the fall of '91 after the establishment of the Bonn station had been reduced. Home again, he had been reassigned to a desk job in the East Asia Division. Some thirty months later, he was still pushing paper at Langley and was still unsure what he was going to do with the rest of his life. The one certain thing was the realisation that he lacked the creative ability to become a successful writer. Treptow figured he would discover job satisfaction if only he could get a transfer to Counter Narcotics. That desired goal was however some way off. As of today, he was engaged on a public relations mission to Chicago. Departing Washington National Airport on a United Airlines 727, he had flown into O'Hare and taken a cab to 841 Lawn Green Drive between Ashland Avenue and Wrigley Field.

Treptow was no realtor but he thought the house where Lenora Vassman lived couldn't be had for under seven hundred and fifty thou. He paid off the cab, walked up the drive and pushed the bell button. The chimes played a melody he couldn't place. A few moments later, the speaker above the bell button crackled and a metallic-sounding voice asked him who was calling.

'My name's Warren Treptow,' he said, bending close to the mike. 'Ms Vassman is expecting me.'

The woman who opened the door to him was wearing a blue and white striped shirt with broad white lapels and double cuffs fastened with gold links, a mid-calf black skirt with eight military-style gold buttons arranged in two vertical rows from waist to thigh, and high-heeled slippers. Diamond earrings and a gold Cartier wristwatch completed the designer label outfit. But it was the woman who made the clothes. She had black curly hair which just touched her ears, the bluest eyes he had ever seen and a remarkably attractive face.

'Ms Vassman?' he said in disbelief.

'The same,' she said and closed the door behind him.

He couldn't believe it. In a few days' time, Lenora Vassman would be celebrating her forty-ninth birthday, yet here she was looking no more than a woman in her late thirties. If she had had a facelift or any other cosmetic surgery, he thought she must have been to the best damned surgeon in the world. Full of admiration, he followed her into a large sitting room on the east side of the house.

'Now what is it you want to see me about, Mr Treptow?' she asked after inviting him to sit down.

'The Brits are reviewing the inquest on Bernice Kwang,' he told her.

'The Brits?' she repeated.

'Yeah. Well, their Secret Intelligence Service to be more exact.'

'After twenty-four years,' she mused. 'A little late in the day, wouldn't you say?'

'Seems a lifetime to me,' Treptow said, which was almost literally true.

'Better late than never, I guess.' Lenora Vassman uncurled herself from the couch and walked over to a small cocktail bar in the far corner of the room near the large picture window. 'I need a drink; will you join me?'

It was a little early in the day for him but he didn't want to appear unsociable. 'Have you got a beer?'

''Fraid not. My husband used to drink it but I never acquired the taste.'

Lenora had married an attorney in 1972 whom she had divorced nine years later on the grounds of physical abuse. The house on Lawn Green Drive had been part of the settlement; the rest had consisted of a lump sum of a hundred and fifty thousand dollars in lieu of alimony. She had used the money to start a chain of beauty salons which had eventually made her a wealthy woman.

The details were recorded in her security file at Langley which he had read before leaving for Chicago.

'How about something stronger instead? Bourbon, gin, brandy, whisky . . . ?'

'No thanks. Don't worry about me, I'm fine – really.'

'A soft drink then?'

'Thank you, that would be nice.'

'Coke, Pepsi, Seven-Up . . . ?'

'Seven-Up.'

'You got it.'

Treptow looked round the room while she poured a can of 7-up into a glass and then fixed herself a bourbon and branch water. There were photographs everywhere, too far away for him to identify the people, but he could make a pretty accurate guess. Lenora Vassman had had it pretty rough over the years. Father died of malnutrition while a prisoner of war in North Korea before she was six, elder of two brothers k.i.a. in Vietnam. Mother a confirmed alcoholic in and out of clinics from San Diego to San Francisco, no contact with her other brother since 1973. And if that hadn't been bad enough, Lenora's daughter and only child had died of leukemia aged ten, eleven months after the divorce.

'Your drink,' Lenora Vassman said.

Lost in reverie, Treptow had thought she was still behind the bar and looked up startled to find her leaning over him.

'Your drink,' she repeated and handed him the glass.

'Thanks.'

'My pleasure.' Lenora Vassman returned to the couch and sat down. 'You know something?' she said. 'I still feel bad about Bernice.'

'Yeah, I guess the memory must be painful.'

Treptow hadn't the faintest idea what he was talking about. His superiors at Langley had not taken him fully into their confidence and all the way to Lawn Green Drive he had been wondering how he was going to put it to her, and now she had presented him with the launch programme he needed. Choosing his words carefully, he told her it was possible the Brits might want to send one of their operatives over to the US to ask her if there was anything she would like to add to the evidence she had given at the inquest.

'My God, they've got a nerve.'

'It may not happen,' Treptow said hastily, 'and even it if does, you're under no obligation to see the guy.'

'Really?'

'Yeah, really. My superiors were very adamant about that.'

'Well, that was very considerate of them,' Lenora Vassman said after some thought. 'But I would like to set the record straight. Besides, I'd welcome the opportunity of giving one of Her Majesty's representatives a piece of my mind.'

Observing the baleful look in her eyes, Warren Treptow almost felt sorry for the emissary.

CHAPTER 23

A shton had spent the whole of Sunday cooling his heels in Amberley Lodge while Benton returned to London and cleared the story they had rehearsed with Victor Hazelwood. Ashton had given Benton the keys to his flat and the car because he needed a change of clothing and hadn't wanted to be dependent on public transport. With only one suit in the wardrobe and two clean shirts in the chest of drawers, Benton couldn't go far wrong. He did, however, manage to put a dent in the bodywork and smash the nearside tail-light assembly when manoeuvring the Vauxhall Cavalier out of the parking space by the kerb.

The damage to the car was more than annoying. Between Amberley Lodge and Poole, Ashton was flagged down twice and warned that it was an offence to drive a vehicle on the public highway with a defective indicator and tail-light assembly. Figuring he wouldn't get away with it a third time, he parked the Vauxhall in the Dolphin Centre and walked the rest of the way to the central police station. Although he hadn't expected Harry Farnesworth to be overjoyed at seeing him again, the perfunctory greeting he received from the Detective Chief Inspector was one more irritant he'd had to put up with since arriving home in the early hours of yesterday morning.

'What are you giving me this time?' Farnesworth growled. 'Another load of bullshit?'

'Not on your life,' Ashton told him, 'you're due for some Grade A liquid manure.'

'I hope you're joking.'

'Of course I am. From here on, it's a hundred per cent kosher.'

What Hazelwood had said he could tell Farnesworth was a long way short of the whole story, but Ashton fancied it would satisfy his curiosity. Cosgrove and Oakham had orchestrated their own violent deaths because they had been witnesses to a murder and nineteen years later they had run into the killer again and had tried to blackmail him. What had happened to Bernice Kwang had no bearing on their ultimate fate and therefore it wasn't necessary for Farnesworth to know about the Hong Kong connection. The DCI heard him out, saving the jackpot question until he had finished.

'One thing puzzles me,' Farnesworth said quietly. 'If Gillespie is the man who ordered the hit, how did your lot manage to identify him? I mean, to my way of thinking, the only people who knew Gillespie were his victims.'

'We arrived at his name by a process of elimination,' Ashton said blandly. 'We started with Warrant Officer Jackson and looked at every case he had ever been involved with. That was one angle; the other was Afansiev and Ovakimyan. They came to London to buy weapons for the Chechnya Republic, they also killed Louise Oakham as a favour to somebody, and that somebody had to be the arms broker who was going to sell them the Stinger missiles they wanted. Special Branch had heard whispers about a shady arms dealer called Gillespie who was willing to cut a few corners for the right kind of money, and what do you know, a Sergeant Gillespie had featured in one of the investigations Warrant Officer Jackson had carried out.'

'What crime had Gillespie committed?'

'Murder. At least he was thought to have murdered a corporal in the Medical Corps.'

'Thought?'

'The corporal was found hanging from the rafters in the attic of the Out Patients Department at the British Military Hospital, Holzminden. He had a duplicate set of keys to every poison cabinet in the BMH and a lot of morphine had gone missing during the eight months prior to his death. The army's Special Investigation Branch believed he had been supplying drugs to Sergeant Gillespie and others who had then sold them on to local civilians at a profit. The investigation never came to anything because the corporal left a note to say he had committed suicide.'

'But Jackson didn't believe it?'

'That's the conclusion we came to.'

No corporal in the Royal Army Medical Corps on the staff of BMH Holzminden had committed suicide by hanging himself from the rafters. There had been no drugs ring and no investigation by the SIB of the military police. But if the beginning of the story was a complete fabrication, there was no reason for Farnesworth to query it when the rest was as close to the truth as anyone was likely to get.

'Do we have a description of Gillespie?'

'We've got a photograph of him,' Ashton said. 'Admittedly it is twenty years out of date but any picture has got to be better than an artist's impression. At least that's what Special Branch told us when they asked for copies.

'Are they involved now?'

'Well, Special Branch know most of the legitimate arms dealers in this country and they are likely to be the only people who can give them a line on Gillespie.'

'What a bloody mess,' Farnesworth snorted. 'We're really getting our wires crossed.'

He had Ashton's sympathy. The Dorset, Hampshire and Surrey Constabularies were already involved, now they had to contend with the Special Branch of the Metropolitan Police. Just keeping the chief constables appraised of developments was almost a full-time job in itself.

'Did I ever tell you I saw Louise Oakham the day she was murdered?' Farnesworth said seemingly apropos of nothing.

'Not directly, but I guessed you had when you produced the postcard from Simon Oakham.'

'She had been going through her diaries for this year and last and was able to give me a list of dates when her husband was supposed to have been on duty over the weekend.'

Farnesworth had subsequently checked the dates with the adjutant of the 24th Royal Dragoons and to his surprise had found that up to and including the weekend of 9 and 10 October '93, Oakham had had a valid excuse for not going home. It had only been after that date that he had consistently lied to his wife.

'The Regiment organised a point-to-point at Larkhill on Saturday, 9 October,' Farnesworth continued. 'As the unit paymaster, Oakham was the ideal man to run the tote for the regiment. One of the horses entered for the meet was part-owned by Major Richard Cosgrove.'

It was a missing piece from the jigsaw. The question of how, where and when the two men had got together again, which had puzzled Ashton, had finally been answered.

'The discovery of Oakham's body generated a lot of publicity, especially when one of the tabloids disclosed that he and Cosgrove had been on intimate terms.' Farnesworth emptied the ashtray on his desk into the wastebin, then lit another cigarette. 'It also prodded the memory of one witness and the conscience of another.'

A businessman who hadn't wanted his wife to know that he had been out on the tiles with his secretary had come forward to say that late one Friday evening about five weeks ago, he had been following a Volvo estate towards Wareham which had suddenly turned off the A35 into a narrow lane in the vicinity of Oak Tree Cottage. A ticket collector at Bournemouth station who knew Cosgrove by sight, recalled seeing him meet a stranger off the 4.45 train from London.

'He thought it was a Friday but couldn't be sure. He gave us an equally vague description of the stranger which could fit almost anybody.'

'You can have a copy of the photograph we gave Special Branch,' Ashton said.

'Can't do any harm, might even jog his memory a bit more.'

It was Gillespie who had been on the London train and his intended victim had picked him up from the station. If the errant businessman was right, they would have arrived at Oak Tree Cottage at least an hour before Oakham showed up. Time enough for Gillespie to force Cosgrove to change out of his clothes into women's underwear and lie down on the bed when he had then passively allowed himself to be tied up. Although a neat hypothesis, Ashton couldn't bring himself to accept it. Whatever else he might be, Cosgrove was no fool; he had seen Jackson murdered in cold blood and even if all the tea in China had been at stake, there was no way he would have gone to meet Gillespie on his own. The ticket collector might only have seen Cosgrove but Oakham could have been waiting outside the station with his Volvo.

'This businessman and his secretary bird—' Ashton began.

'I wouldn't attach too much weight to his statement,' Farnesworth said, cutting him short. 'He was pretty woolly about the date, time and place. Got the wrong colour Volvo too – swore it was red.'

Oakham had owned a dark blue estate, but that didn't necessarily mean the businessman's statement was worthless. Knowing who they were up against, Cosgrove and Oakham would have been on their guard and Gillespie might well have had a hard time subduing them on his own. But he would have had no problems at all if a couple of business acquaintances like Afansiev and Ovakimyan had arrived to lend him a hand. Their presence at Oak Tree Cottage would explain why there had been no signs of a struggle.

'You want to share them?' Farnesworth asked.

'What?'

'Your thoughts.'

'I was just wondering if we would ever know what really happened that night.'

'I think that rather depends on you people.'

It was the kind of remark that could be taken in two ways. Ashton played it safe and didn't rise to the bait. Instead, he promised Farnesworth a photograph of the wanted man would be on his desk first thing in the morning, then said it was time he was moving on.

'I owe you an apology,' Farnesworth told him before they parted company.

'How's that?'

'I had Forensic take another look at the postcard Louise Oakham was supposed to have received from her husband. And you were right, his thumbprint wasn't on the stamp.'

'Well, it's all water under the bridge now, isn't it?' Ashton said.

Leaving the police station, he called Benton from the nearest pay phone to report what had happened, then collected his car from the shopping centre. There was nothing for him to do in London other than submit a claim for travelling expenses, but since Kelso would take for ever to approve it, he was in no hurry to fill out the appropriate form. As he had done on the previous occasion, he headed out of town on the A348 to Ringwood, then made tracks for Lincoln, and Harriet. If the police pulled him up for the defective taillight, he would give them some cock and bull story. He'd certainly had plenty of practice at that lately.

Walter Maryck was a man to gladden the hearts of every tailor in Savile Row. He did not care for loud checks or clothes which were supposed to make some kind of statement about the wearer. Instead, he affected a style of dress much favoured by senior officers in the Brigade of Guards which meant that, in addition to being extremely well cut, his suits were of varying shades of grey. He looked especially at home in green wellingtons, corduroys, a Barbour jacket and a peaked cap when invited to join a shoot or attend a point-to-point. Aged forty-five, he was by any standard a handsome man who, as it happened, was also married to an extremely attractive woman. To make them the perfect nuclear family, they had a nine-year-old boy and a girl of eight. They were, in fact, the sort of people you would expect to appear in such quintessentially English publications as the *Field*, *Country Life* and *Harpers and Queen*.

It was common knowledge in London that Walter's enemies within the CIA frequently accused him of being too pro-British, a charge so far removed from the truth as to be laughable. In fact, as Hazelwood and others could testify, whenever a possible conflict of interest arose, there was no doubt in their minds concerning his allegiance. Maryck was a patriot through and through; he had enlisted in the army straight from college and had completed two tours of duty in Vietnam with the Green Berets, winning a Distinguished Service Cross and Silver Star in the process. With the end of the Vietnam War, a sideways move into the CIA had followed as naturally as night follows day.

In 1982, he had been transferred from the Agency's East Asia Division to Europe. Nine years later he had been appointed Chief of the London station. In those days, Hazelwood had been the Assistant Director in charge of the Eastern Bloc Department. As such, he had been one rung down the ladder from the American and consequently Hazelwood had always gone to Maryck's office in Grosvenor Square whenever he had found it necessary to liaise with Walter. Although he was now the acting DG, it seemed that Maryck still expected him to observe the same practice, and indeed that had been the impression his PA had formed when Maryck had phoned while he had been holding morning prayers.

Maryck's office was on the second floor of the embassy in the ultra high security area. Although spacious, it had no outlook whatsoever, a protective measure dating back to the seventies when CIA chiefs throughout Europe had been targeted by such diverse terrorist organisations as Black September, the Red Army Faction and the Popular Front for the Liberation of Palestine. How anyone could bear to work in artificial light day in, day out was beyond Hazelwood. As a visitor, he wanted nothing more than to complete his business in the shortest possible time.

'So what have you got for me, Walter?' he asked once his Marine escort had departed and they were alone.

'You want the bottom line?'

'What else?'

'Then the answer is, not a lot. Sure, Bernice Kwang worked for us but she was a very junior officer and did little more than run errands for her boss.'

'Who was?'

'I haven't the faintest idea; you never asked me to find out who was running the base.'

'Base?' Hazelwood queried. 'Are you telling me Hong Kong was not a fully fledged station?'

'I certainly am. In those days it was regarded as a minor post, a backwater even.' Maryck smiled. 'Now, are we going to talk about this lady, Victor, or the number of officers assigned to the base?'

'I'll stick to Bernice Kwang.'

'Well, like you already know, the newspapers regarded her as a socialite and in a sense, that was true. Her father was into fruit and vegetables and owned a chain of restaurants on the West Coast which is why Bernice had money of her own and wasn't dependent on the salary she received from the Agency. If her performance-related assessments are anything to go by, perhaps that was just as well because she clearly wasn't going places in the CIA. Every superior officer Bernice ever had said she was a romantic. "Inclined to be naïve at times and occasionally shows signs of immaturity" were among other detrimental remarks which appeared in the assessments from time to time.'

'In other words, Bernice Kwang was a very indifferent officer.'

'Hey, I wouldn't go that far, Victor. She cultivated the leading lights among Chiang Kai-shek's most ardent supporters in Hong Kong and also got close to the monied Chinese. What I'm saying is that Bernice provided some good political Intelligence but nothing that was likely to get her killed as you seem to think she was.'

'I'm not the only one. Lenora Vassman did all she could to convince the inquest jury that her friend had been murdered.' Hazelwood paused, hoping the American would automatically respond and tell him what he wanted to know about the girl who had once shared an apartment with Bernice Kwang. When Maryck remained obstinately silent, he was forced to ask him point-blank if the Agency knew the present whereabouts of Lenora Vassman.

'Let me ask you a question,' Maryck said. 'What do you hope to get from the lady?'

Walter had the information at his fingertips; Hazelwood was equally sure he would have to give the American a blow-by-blow account of everything that had happened from the moment Oakham had deliberately sabotaged his chance of working for the SIS. Throughout the long briefing, it was impossible to guess what Maryck was thinking. His face gave nothing away which was a good enough reason for Hazelwood to make a mental note never to play poker with him.

'It's an interesting story,' Maryck said when he had finished, 'but where's it taking you, Victor?'

'To an arms broker called Gillespie who may or may not have had Bernice Kwang murdered.'

'Well, as I see it, you're locked into a homicide investigation which the police are better equipped to handle.'

'Maybe, but you have been around long enough to know that in our line of business, nothing is ever what it seems. That's why I've a hunch Lenora Vassman can point us in the right direction.'

There was another prolonged silence before Maryck told him there was no way the Agency would permit British Intelligence to question her without one of their officers being present.

'Quite right too,' Hazelwood said. 'I believe we should work together on this one.'

'I'm glad to hear it. For your information, the lady is living in uptown Chicago, 841 Lawn Green Drive between Ashland Avenue and Wrigley Field.'

'Thanks.'

'So when can we expect to see your guy, Victor?'

'As soon as I've cleared it with the Cabinet Office.'

Ever since they had been caught trying to help George Bush get re-elected for a second term, the Government and the Foreign and Commonwealth Office in particular were leery of offending Washington. And with some justification. Hazelwood thought there was a good chance the Bernice Kwang affair could become highly political.

Ashton parked the Vauxhall in the multistorey near the city hospital, used the underpass to cross Maid Marian Way and then walked on down Friar Lane to the offices of Vanguard Security in Nottingham. He had no idea whether Newton would be in the office or out looking at one of the sites his company was responsible for protecting. The decision to break the journey to Lincoln had been taken on the spur of the moment and it wouldn't be the end of the world if nothing came of it.

He pushed the street door open, climbed the concrete staircase to the waiting room off the second floor landing and used the buzzer to summon one of the clerks. The same frizzy blonde who had greeted him on the previous occasion opened the hatchway in the frosted-glass partition. She treated him like a favoured client with a promise that Mr Newton would be free in a moment or so and meantime would he like to take a chair and maybe have cup of coffee, an offer he politely declined. A presentiment that she had mistaken him for someone else was confirmed when he was shown into the MD's office and the welcoming smile on Newton's face disappeared even quicker than he could lower his extended right hand.

'Oh no, not you again,' he said wearily. 'What are you after this time? A job?'

'I'd sooner have five minutes of your time.'

'I know your five minutes, they're like a countryman's mile.'

'I think that's a bit of an exaggeration,' Ashton said, then pulled a chair up to the desk and sat down.

'Make yourself at home,' Newton told him drily.

'Thanks. About this man you saw with Reeves a couple of times, the one you said was called Tom something or other? Could his last name have been Gillespie?'

'It could have been Smith or Jones for all I know. I was never introduced to the guy.' Newton made a big thing of consulting his wristwatch. 'You've got four minutes left.'

'I'd like to pick your brains.' Ashton shrugged. 'Who knows, maybe we will finish with time to spare.'

'Not the way you're going.'

'What can you tell me about arms trafficking from your days in the Intelligence Corps?'

'Very little. I never served in Northern Ireland before I left the army in '71. My first-hand knowledge concerning the methods used by the IRA is zero.'

'Forget the IRA; it's too easy for them to get what they want from Libya or their friends in the US. Let's say that the Chechnya National Liberation Army wanted to buy two thousand Stinger missiles off the shelf without going through the usual channels. How would they go about it?'

'You're asking the wrong man,' Newton said woodenly. 'I spent the last two years of my service on the drill square at the depot.'

'You had separated from your wife,' Ashton told him, 'and you were living in the sergeants' mess. There were guys coming and going all the time on courses, between postings and so on. Don't tell me you didn't hear things over a few drinks in the bar.'

'I'd had my security clearance taken away. Remember?'

'Of course I do, but nobody hung a placard round your neck saying this NCO is only cleared for material graded no higher than Confidential. Only the Director Intelligence Corps and the Commandant of the Depot were aware of that restriction. So please, no more shillyshallying, just give me your informed guess.'

'Two thousand Stinger missiles on the q.t.' Newton rubbed his jaw. 'Kuwait or Saudi Arabia would be the best place to look for them. Must have been thousands left out there after Desert Storm. The Yanks put how many divisions into the field? Eight?'

Ashton nodded. Two marine, two armoured, two mechanised infantry, one cavalry and one airborne, all of them lavishly equipped to deal with any contingency, especially from the air. The planners would have made sure the ground troops never ran short of man-portable missiles and it wasn't their fault that the weapons system had not been required because no one could have foreseen that the Iraqi Air Force would seek refuge in neighbouring Iran. Most of the anti-aircraft missiles would eventually have been back-loaded to the States but a substantial number would have gone to re-equipping the Kuwait armed forces and a hell of a lot would have simply disappeared.

'I'd buy that supposition, Mr Newton,' he said. 'Now tell me how you would get the Stingers to Chechnya in the foothills of the Caucasus.'

'Overland by truck?'

'To avoid Iraq they would have to route the vehicles via Saudi Arabia, Jordan and Syria – lousy roads all the way. Then there's the onward journey through Turkey and across Georgia with every chance the consignment would disappear along the way.'

'You got a better idea then?'

'I think I would ship the missiles to Istanbul, truck them on through Bulgaria to Varna on the Black Sea and thence by freighter to Odessa where I would get the Ukranians to airlift the consignment to the final destination. Ferrying arms to the breakaway Republic of Chechnya would be an opportunity to put one over on the Russians they couldn't resist.'

'You reckon?'

'Yes.'

'Well, in that case, I don't see why you needed my help.'

'You pointed me in the right direction,' Ashton told him. 'You could say we complemented one another.'

'Maybe I should offer you a job after all.'

'I might just hold you to that,' Ashton said.

The *Tristan da Cuhna* was a 6,000-ton, flag of convenience, rust bucket registered in Panama and owned by the Bombay, Calcutta and South East Asia Line. The ship's crew, with the exception of the master, first mate and chief engineer were Filipinos. Since leaving Pusan in South Korea with a cargo of electrical goods, the freighter had called at Kuwait, Bahrain and Aden before arriving at Istanbul.

A LETHAL INVOLVEMENT

The fatal mishap occurred while discharging cargo into a lighter off Harmet Point in the Sea of Marmara. It was the owners' misfortune that a Turkish customs officer was on board when the brake on the 15-ton derrick suddenly failed. The wooden crate, which measured 25 by 9 by 8 feet, was at the maximum elevation directly above the lighter and the derrick operator was in the process of lowering the cargo when it went into free fall, crushing one of the stevedores on the lighter. The crate shattered on impact, disgorging dozens of containers into the hold, each one stencilled with the lot and batch number of the man-portable, shoulder-fired guided missiles manufactured by General Dynamics, Valley Systems Division, PO Box 50-800, Ontario, California.

CHAPTER 24

A shton rubbed both calves, then stretched out his legs as far as the seat in front would allow. The relief this gave him was purely temporary; within a few minutes, all the numbing aches associated with sitting in a cramped position for endless hours had returned. A little over a week after returning from Hong Kong, he was on the move again, having spent six happy days in Lincoln with Harriet and passed another three divided between Amberley Lodge, Poole and London. In that time, he had managed to get his claim for travelling expenses past Kelso, a minor triumph in itself, but more importantly, he had persuaded Harriet to set a date. It wasn't public yet but on Saturday, 9 July, approximately ten weeks after their child had been born, they would cement a relationship that had had more than its fair share of ups and downs.

He reached behind his back for the pillow, shoved it under his head and closed his eyes. Any long haul was a test of endurance but this particular one to Chicago seemed to be taking for ever, mainly because the in-flight movie hadn't been up to much. He felt himself sinking back into oblivion and surrendered gratefully, then a bell pinged and the engines were roaring in reverse thrust and he wondered why one of the stewardesses hadn't woken him before the plane touched down. Reacting instinctively, he sat bolt upright and tried to fasten the seat belt but was unable to find the damned thing and he couldn't think what a couple of armchairs and a round table were doing on board a 747. Then suddenly everything fell into place. The pinging noise was in fact the continuous buzz of the wake-up alarm he had set last night and the roaring noise was a train on the elevated railway a block away. And this great cabin was his hotel room in the Palmer House Hilton on Monroe Street, not a wide-bodied 747.

So how much was real, and what had been merely a dream? Well, he had got his claim for reimbursement past Kelso but not before the Admin King had deleted the cost of the Van Heusen shirts he'd purchased in Hong Kong on the grounds that he should submit a claim to his insurance company for all items of a personal nature. And Harriet had set a date, though it was not as clear cut as he had fondly imagined in his dream.

Warren Treptow was real. The American had been waiting for him in the arrivals hall at O'Hare nursing a placard to his chest with Ashton's name on it. He looked incredibly young, innocent and wholesome, like a rôle model for a Norman Rockwell picture on the front cover of the long defunct *Saturday Evening Post*. He was also very helpful; all the way into town on the John F. Kennedy Expressway, he had bent Ashton's ear telling him everything he knew about Lenora Vassman and what a lousy deal she had had out of life. There had been a brief interlude while he registered, unpacked, freshened up and changed before Treptow had continued the saga of Little Orphan Annie over dinner. By the time they parted company for the night, Ashton had also learned that Lenora Vassman was no Anglophile.

Ashton rolled out of bed, walked over to the window and opened the curtains to a fine bright morning. The sunlight was deceptive, creating the impression that, like his hotel room, the temperature outside was touching seventy. However, most of the men on Monroe Street weren't walking around in shirtsleeves and the ladies hadn't left their spring coats at home either. He took a leisurely bath before shaving, then put on a worsted two-piece. After breakfast, he returned to his room to collect a Burberry trenchcoat and was waiting in the lobby when Treptow arrived in a rented Ford compact to collect him on the dot of 10.30.

Treptow was the talkative kind of driver. Ashton thought he could always find a niche for himself as a tour guide if ever he tired of the CIA. Listening to him, few people would have guessed Chicago was not his home town. The running commentary started as they headed east on Monroe across Wabash and thence north on Michigan Avenue. It did not end until they had left Lake Shore Drive and were passing Wrigley Field when he returned to the subject of Lenora Vassman and why it was necessary to handle her with kid gloves.

'You've already told me I'm not likely to be the flavour of the month,' Ashton said mildly.

'Just so long as you keep that in mind.'

'Listen, if it will make you any the happier, I promise I won't bite her ankles unless she bares her teeth at me. Okay?'

'I just know the next hour or so is going to be very difficult,' Treptow said plaintively before making a sharp left turn into an asphalt drive fronting a large, split-level, ranch-style house. 'Some place, huh?'

'I think it would do me,' Ashton agreed.

Treptow had told him that Lenora Vassman was the kind of glamorous woman you only found between the pages of *Vogue*. When she opened the door to them, he could see the American hadn't been exaggerating. She was wearing a pair of natural suede hipster jeans, a white silk chiffon shirt and a pair of gold leather sandals. Ashton had no idea what she would have had to pay for such an outfit from Marshall Field but in London she wouldn't have seen much change from a cool eight hundred pounds. If life hadn't exactly been a bed of roses for her, he thought there had certainly been a few compensations along the way.

'Mr Ashton,' she repeated coolly when Treptow introduced him. Nothing else, not even a meaningless 'nice to meet you'.

After they left their coats on a chair in the entrance hall, she led them into a sitting room large enough to be a bowling alley and waved a hand in the direction of a three-piece suite. It was the nearest Ashton got to an invitation to make himself comfortable.

'Warren tells me you people have reopened the inquest on Bernice Kwang?'

It wasn't entirely accurate but there was nothing to be gained from disabusing her of the notion. 'We've had another look at the proceedings,' he said.

'Why did you do that?'

'Because a man called Gillespie reappeared on the scene. This is a photograph of him taken twenty-four years ago.' Lenora Vassman was leaning against the stone fireplace. To pass the snapshot to her, Ashton had to leave his chair and take a couple of paces forward. 'Here's another one of him at a barbecue with your flatmate.'

'Very interesting,' she said and returned the snapshot and press cutting after no more than a cursory glance.

'You want to tell me why you think Bernice was murdered?' Ashton said in a level voice.

'I'd like to hear what converted you first.'

'I read the transcript of the inquest and it was obvious the coroner had been determined to gag you. And it wasn't pure conjecture either. I saw Lloyd Ingolby in Hong Kong recently and he confirmed he'd had orders to ensure the jury brought in a verdict of Death by Misadventure.

Ingolby claimed he had been told it was a matter of national security and I don't think he was lying.'

'So what are you doing about it? Is this Mr Ingolby going to be charged?'

'He was given immunity from prosecution,' Ashton told her. 'Without that, he would never have talked to me.'

'I might have guessed you people would be only too happy to sweep the mess under the carpet.'

'I don't think you can hold Mr Ashton responsible for something that happened twenty-four years ago,' Treptow said in a mildly reproving voice.

Lenora Vassman glared at her fellow countryman. 'Did I ask for your opinion?' she enquired witheringly.

'For Christ's sake, Ingolby's an old man,' Ashton snapped. 'What good will come of banging him up? You think it will resurrect Bernice Kwang?'

'Don't you yell at me.'

'You're right, I shouldn't have done that and I apologise. Now, can we try again? I mean, the really important thing is to discover the truth – right? It's not necessary that we should like one another.'

Treptow bit his lip. In the short time Ashton had known him, he had come to the conclusion that the CIA man had three basic expressions – sincere, earnest and anxious. Right now he was doing his anxious bit.

'You're very direct, Mr Ashton,' Lenora said with a faint smile.

'One of my many failings,' he agreed.

In some circumstances it was also one of his strengths. It had worked with Harriet when he'd told her point-blank that he'd had enough of their on-off relationship and would she finally make up her mind what she wanted? And to his surprise, Harriet had told him she supposed he had better get a special licence or something after their child had been born.

'What have you been told about Bernice?' Lenora asked softly.

'That she had money of her own and worked for the CIA. Apparently, she wasn't very highly regarded by her superiors who thought she was naïve and immature. I got the impression she was a well-meaning amateur.'

'Evidently the people who killed Bernice saw her in a different light.'

'I guess they did,' Ashton said.

'I don't know why they wanted to kill her but I can tell you how it was done.'

Lenora Vassman began the way she had at the inquest with a clearly reasoned argument proving why Bernice couldn't have been on the landing dock when Yang Bo claimed to have seen her there. However, from there on, what she had to say was all new ground for Ashton.

'Bernice was not a tidy lady. Usually, she never put her clothes away until the last thing at night. Whenever she was going out for the evening, she'd drop her workday outfit on the bed. So I was kind of surprised to find her room neat as a new pin when I returned from the bank that evening. Also her bedroom window was open.'

'And that struck you as odd?' Ashton said.

'This was May,' Lenora Vassman explained patiently, 'the temperature was rising, so was the humidity. All the apartments in Belmont House had air conditioning. Open a window and you might just as well switch the plant off. I remember there was a funny smell in the room. I couldn't place it at first but after the police informed me that Bernice had been drowned at sea, I suddenly realised the odour had to be either chloroform or ether.'

If traces of either anaesthetic had still been present to any degree, she would have known it at once. It had been a deduction on her part, not a recollection. All the same, Ashton thought she was probably right.

'The last time I saw Bernice alive was over breakfast that morning when she had been wearing a green silk dress. I could find no trace of it in her wardrobe.'

Lenora Vassman didn't know about the clothes Bernice was wearing when she had been fished out of the sea. They might or might not have belonged to her. The fact was it hadn't only been the missing silk dress which had convinced her that Bernice had been kidnapped. There had been another, far more sinister reason.

'One of the residents on our floor saw two Chinese wheeling a big laundry basket towards the service elevator. This was shortly after I had telephoned Bernice from the bank to say I wouldn't be able to make the party on time. But you want to know what was really scary? I couldn't find a single resident on our floor who'd sent anything to the laundry on that particular Friday. I did however find someone who recalled seeing a Transit van from the dry cleaners in the underground garage.'

Ashton was about to ask what was so significant about this when she told him that the dry cleaners called three times a week on Tuesday, Thursday and Saturday. The longer Lenora went on, the more animated she became, striding up and down in front of the fireplace one minute, then throwing herself into a vacant armchair only to get up again a few moments later. The only thing she couldn't explain was why Bernice had opened the door to her kidnappers. But otherwise, she knew just what had happened to her friend from the moment they had chloroformed Bernice and then dumped her into the laundry basket trussed up like a chicken.

'They made Bernice change into those ridiculous shorts and knitted cotton sweatshirt, then the bastards calmly held her head under water until she drowned.' Lenora stopped pacing and turned on Ashton, her face contorted with anger. 'Tell me something, did you people have her murdered?'

'I wouldn't know, but I don't think William Reeves lifted a finger to stop it.'

'I hope he burns in hell.'

'He collapsed and died on the Fanling golf course barely four months after your friend was drowned.'

'I can't say I'm sorry; he had it coming. Does that shock you?'

'No. What puzzles me is how you two got together.'

'We met at the reception hosted by the US Consulate to celebrate the Fourth of July. Two single, unattached American women living in a claustrophobic place like Hong Kong; it was almost inevitable that we would become good friends once we discovered we had similar outlooks on life and shared similar tastes.'

When the Chinese American girl had learned that Lenora Vassman was looking for somewhere cheaper to live, she had invited her new-found friend to move into her apartment in Belmont House.

'I was only too happy to accept her invitation. The lease on my apartment was up for renewal and I couldn't afford the rent the agents wanted.'

'Did the CIA check you out before you moved in with her?'

'If they did, I wasn't aware of it. Hell, I didn't even know Bernice worked for the Agency until after she had been murdered. I guess The Company has been keeping tabs on me ever since. How else would you guys have known where I was living?'

Ashton ignored the question. 'Was Bernice a secretive person?' he asked.

'Only about her job.'

'She told you about her boyfriends?'

'Yeah. It was no big deal, she wasn't serious about anybody.'

'How about Gillespie?'

'As far as I know, she only dated him a couple of times.'

Ashton sensed Lenora Vassman was holding something back. At least he hoped she was, because every other source had dried up. The Hong Kong police intended to make full use of Uttley and would no doubt inflict grievous harm on the Black Dragon Triad but that was as far as the undercover operation would be allowed to go. There would be no deal with the Triad, no promises to go easy on them in return for information on Gillespie. His Excellency the Governor, the Attorney General, the Chief Justice and the Police Commissioner were not prepared to turn a blind eye to their criminal activities in return for favours rendered. That in a nutshell was the gist of the message they had received from Maurice Yule. It was the reason why Hazelwood had managed to browbeat the Cabinet Secretary and the Permanent Under Secretary of State for the Foreign and Commonwealth Office into agreeing that Victor could send him out to Chicago to sniff around.

'We heard Gillespie's first name was Tom. He's also said to be an American.' Ashton smiled. 'Any truth in that?'

'His first name was Tad.'

'Tad?' Ashton repeated blankly.

'Yes. It was probably Tom to begin with and he changed it, part of the image he wanted to create for himself.'

'Was he an American?'

'I was told that he was born in Southampton, England and that his parents brought him to this country when he was a year old. I was also told that he was a Canadian by adoption and had spent most of his formative years in Toronto. Personally, I thought the guy was a fink but Bernice liked him well enough. He had a travel agency, used to give her a hell of a discount on her air fares. Maybe that was the attraction for her. Although Bernice might not have been short of a dollar or two, she loved a bargain.' Lenora paused. 'Can I get you guys a cup of coffee?' she asked, pointing to the bar. 'It's no trouble, the Cona's bubbling away on the electric ring.'

Treptow said he could certainly use one and opted for black with no sugar and insisted on helping her. Ashton said he preferred white and got cream instead of milk. The interlude was a distraction with Treptow making small talk, seemingly determined to keep Lenora off the subject of Bernice Kwang.

'Bernice did a lot of travelling around the Far East then?' Ashton said after coffee had been served.

'A fair amount. She was a freelance doing articles for the Chinese language newspapers back in the States. It never dawned on me that this was probably a cover for her real job.'

'If I might butt in a moment,' Treptow said. 'Apropos of work, how did the bank react to your involvement with Bernice Kwang?'

'After she'd been murdered? They didn't like the attendant publicity. I was their corporate finance broker in Hong Kong and they took the view that it was bad for business.'

Lenora Vassman had resolved their predicament by asking for a transfer. She had been unhappy with the jury's verdict and believed she had failed to get justice for her friend.

'I got to hate the damned place; it got so bad I didn't want to hear another English voice for the rest of my life. That's the bottom line, Warren.' A mechanical smile appeared. 'Present company excepted, Mr Ashton,' she added.

She called him mister but Treptow was Warren. Ashton wondered how much significance he should attach to that.

'So when did you leave Hong Kong?' Treptow asked her quickly.

'Friday, July 24, 1970.'

They were back on what the American obviously considered was safer ground. Ashton went along with it because he was satisfied Lenora Vassman had told him all she knew about Gillespie. Fact was, it hadn't been a bad morning's work. He had been given Gillespie's place of birth and judging by his colour photograph, he must have been between twenty-eight and thirty-two years of age when he went fishing with members of the SIB detachment in Hong Kong. Maybe the information was a little skeletal, but it would be enough for the Security, Vetting and Technical Services Division at Benbow House to get their teeth into.

'I think we have just about covered everything, haven't we?' Treptow said, catching his eye.

'We have,' Ashton said, 'and I can't thank you enough for being so helpful, Ms Vassman.'

Lenora Vassman told him he was welcome and urged them to have a nice day when they said goodbye in the hall. The front door closed before they were halfway to the car.

Ashton waited for the American to unlock the Ford compact, then got in beside him.

'You don't know how lucky you were.' Treptow checked to make sure the road was clear, then reversed out of the drive to head back the way they had come. 'The Brits aren't popular with Lenora and she is really mad about the way the inquest had been rigged. I thought she was going to give you a hard time but there was only one sticky moment.'

Ashton listened to him with only half an ear. Some things didn't add up. Lenora Vassman had left Hong Kong in July, two months before

Reeves had died; no one would have told her that he had been the SIS Head of Station but she held him responsible for the cover-up. So just who was Lenora? What was it she had said? 'I guess The Company has been keeping tabs on me ever since.' In England, the SIS was known by insiders as The Firm; in the US, the CIA was The Company.

'Turn around,' Ashton said loudly.

'What?'

'You heard me, we're going back.'

'You mind telling me why?'

'Vassman was CIA, her job with the Bank of America was her non-official cover.'

'So what was Bernice Kwang?'

'The decoy duck,' Ashton told him.

Hazelwood actively disliked the Assistant Director in charge of the Mid East Department. Ambitious, selfish, inconsiderate of others and motivated by self-interest were but a few of the choice phrases which instantly came to mind whenever they were in the same room. The fact that the Assistant Director happened to be a woman had nothing to do with his antipathy; the fact that at one time Jill Sheridan had been engaged to Peter Ashton before dumping him like excess baggage was also irrelevant.

Although Jill Sheridan was now married, she preferred to retain her maiden name for professional reasons. This was readily understandable by anyone who had met her husband, pompous old Henry, whom she had met in the Persian Gulf and who was nearly old enough to be her father.

Jill Sheridan had been in the fast lane from the day she had joined the SIS. Her father, until he retired in 1993, had been an executive with the Qatar General Petroleum Corporation and she had spent most of her childhood and adolescence in the Persian Gulf. Arabic had been her second tongue; Persian or Farsi was an additional language she had acquired at the School or Oriental and African Studies. In October '89, she had been appointed to run the Intelligence network in the United Arab Emirates from Bahrain. Unfortunately, in that part of the world a woman was definitely a second-class citizen. In order to function at all, it had therefore been necessary to disguise her true status and on the Embassy staff list she had been shown as the Personal Assistant to the Second Secretary Consul.

It had not been a happy arrangement, but she had stuck it out for twenty-one months before requesting a transfer. Posted back to London she had been given the Persian Desk, a sideways move rather than a demotion. She had still been regarded as a rising star though her peers had been convinced that her chances of becoming the first woman DG had gone for ever, thanks to the Arabs. But in addition to all her other qualities, Jill Sheridan was a survivor. She had caught the eye of Stuart Dunglass and now she was the newest and youngest Assistant Director, promoted over the heads of many of her more senior male colleagues.

The signal from Head of Station, Istanbul reporting the discovery of a large number of Stinger missiles on board the *Tristan da Cuhna* had gone straight to the European Department on the grounds that Turkey was a member of the North Atlantic Treaty Organisation. Hazelwood had decided however that the follow-up would be handled by the Mid East Department because he was satisfied the shoulder-operated air defence weapon had come from Kuwait which was very much a part of Jill Sheridan's bailiwick.

For someone who had only been in the chair five minutes, Jill Sheridan was remarkably confident, even arrogant. Hazelwood prided himself on being the least pompous of men; he did not object to her calling him Victor but the almost impudent way she marched into his office without knocking first to ask if he could spare her a few minutes and promptly sat down before he could utter a word was breathtaking.

'Feel free,' he murmured.

'The lot and batch number of these Stinger missiles,' she began. 'I faxed them to Langley and requested they check the data with the Pentagon. We've just had their reply; according to the CIA, the US Army is unable to say which units or formations received them or how they were disposed of.'

'But that's nonsense—'

'Of course it is, Victor. The whole idea of a lot and batch number is to make every consignment from an ammunition depot traceable. If any missiles from a production run are found to be defective, the Pentagon has to know where they were manufactured and which units are holding a batch.'

Hazelwood could guess where and how Jill Sheridan had acquired her expertise. She had got the Armed Forces Desk at Vauxhall Cross to seek advice from the Ministry of Defence and had then mugged up the answer before seeing him.

'The Americans are being deliberately obtuse,' he said irritably.

'It's not the first time they have treated us this way. We had a similar problem in 1957 when John Foster Dulles was in charge of the State Department.'

Another slice of research, Hazelwood thought wearily, and steeled himself to listen to an account of the Saudi-backed insurrection in Oman and how, under cover of darkness, the rebels would come down from their mountain stronghold on the Jebel ash Shan to mine the tracks around Nazwa where the Sultan of Muscat's Northern Frontier Regiment was based.

'We recovered a significant number of M6 anti-personnel and M7 anti-tank mines, all of them clearly stamped with the lot and batch number. But on instructions from the State Department, the CIA kept on saying they were old World War Two stock and couldn't be traced. Of course it was all about oil; the Americans were concerned to protect their investments in Saudi Arabia and didn't want the British Government upsetting the Saudis. It didn't go down too well with us because the Sultan of Muscat had asked for military assistance and a lot of army officers and Royal Marine NCOs who were serving with the Northern Frontier Regiment were at risk. Finally we retrieved an M7 anti-tank mine which was overstamped "Supplied to Saudi Arabia" and they had to come down off the fence and do something about it.'

'Is this really relevant today?' Hazelwood asked when she finished lecturing him.

'Well, I thought you could use the story to embarrass Walter Maryck when you see him again. Could help to twist his arm.'

Hazelwood began to wonder exactly who was running The Firm in the enforced absence of Stuart Dunglass. But she was right, that was the annoying thing. They had to know exactly where those missiles had come from and that would mean going cap in hand to Maryck.

'Last time this sort of thing happened, American Intelligence felt so bad about it, they showed us Top Secret State Department papers which were headed "FOR US EYES ONLY".'

Why was he in doubt? The day would surely come when Jill Sheridan was running the show.

'What has Head of Station, Washington, been told about this business, Jill?'

'Nothing so far.'

'Then see he is briefed as soon as possible.'

'I'll get a signal off—'

'Phone him on the scrambler this afternoon.'

'It's not as secure as a cryptoprotected transmission, Victor. The Americans may record our conversation and unscramble it.'

'I hope they do,' Hazelwood told her. 'I want to embarrass them.'

'I wish I had thought of that,' she said, frowning. 'It's a clever way of exerting pressure on them.'

'Well, don't let me detain you. Ashton has been told to keep in touch with the embassy and I want him to be aware of this situation. It will give him some ammunition to use on whoever has been detailed to hold his hand.'

'With respect, Victor, I don't think Peter should be told about this. Much as I admire him, he's not the most subtle of men and he is likely to—'

'He's subtle enough for me,' Hazelwood growled, interrupting her, 'and that's all there is to it.'

Lenora Vassman stared at the telephone, willing it to ring. What the hell was the matter with Brad? Well over an hour ago, she had rung his home number and left a message asking him to contact her as soon as possible. Didn't he and his goddamned wife talk to one another? Deep in thought, Lenora allowed the cigarette she was smoking to burn down between her fingers and scorch the flesh. More startled than hurt, she leaped to her feet and threw the offending stub into the fireplace. Then the phone rang and in her haste to answer it, she knocked the instrument on to the floor as she snatched the receiver from the cradle.

'Is that you, Brad?' she asked, her voice on edge.

'Yes. What's the matter? You sound very uptight.'

'I am. Ashton and that dummy Treptow came back.'

'What do you mean, they came back?'

'Don't you understand plain English? They talked to me, they went away and then they returned. I must have said something that made Ashton suspicious. Anyway, I'm telling you he knows I was running Bernice Kwang and he suspects a great deal more.'

'What if he does, Lenora? He can't prove anything.'

'Ashton is one hard-nosed son of a bitch and he is going to keep on coming back at me until he can. So you had better do something about him, Brad, because I am not having my life messed up again.'

'Take a vacation.'

'What?'

'Pack a bag, leave the answerphone on, and walk out of the house. Go where you like but stay in touch. I'll have this bastard Ashton out of the country inside a week. Okay?'

'Yes.'

'Do it then,' Brad said and put the phone down.

CHAPTER 25

T he more Ashton thought about it, the more he was convinced Lenora Vassman had been throwing dust in his eyes. His only lingering doubt was whether Warren Treptow had been her willing accomplice. The CIA man had been reluctant to question her again so soon after leaving the house and had been positively against the idea of interviewing her a third time yesterday afternoon. But, in the end, Treptow had accompanied him to 841 Lawn Green Drive and had been more than a little relieved to find that she was out.

Ashton had insisted they wait outside the house but by six o'clock there had still been no sign of Lenora Vassman. Their presence on the street however had not gone unnoticed by other residents in the neighbourhood and much to Treptow's embarrassment, two police officers had arrived in a prowl car to check them out. His guilty reaction had immediately aroused their suspicions and they had ordered him and Ashton out of the car, and had become downright hostile when one of the officers had discovered that Treptow was carrying a .357 Ruger General Purpose revolver in a shoulder holster. They had ended up with their wrists handcuffed behind them and Treptow had had to use all his diplomatic skills before they agreed to look at the ID in the breast pocket of his jacket. Even after they had done so, all had not been sweetness and light. The two patrolmen couldn't understand why a CIA officer should need to carry a revolver on the streets of Chicago and had considered taking him in for further questioning. Only some fast talking by Treptow and an undertaking that they would leave the neighbourhood immediately had persuaded them to change their minds.

Relations had been a little strained when Ashton and Treptow had parted company last night. He wondered if peace would break out over breakfast. After checking to make sure he had his room key before closing the door behind him, Ashton went down to the coffee shop to find the American had beaten him to it and had grabbed a table for two.

The cheery smile and handwave suggested that all had been forgiven.

'Hi there,' Treptow said and snapped his fingers to attract a waitress. 'I haven't ordered yet, thought I'd wait for you.'

Two menus, coffee and fresh orange juice arrived in next to no time. Treptow ordered pancakes, Canadian bacon and two eggs sunny side up. Ashton went for a mushroom omelette and toast and was offered a dozen different types of bread, half of which he'd already forgotten by the time the waitress finished reciting them, which was why he chose brown.

'Listen, I'm sorry about yesterday,' Treptow said after their waitress had moved away.

'I don't think you should apologise, Warren. For one thing, it's not necessary, and for another, you might regret it. You see I rang Lenora Vassman late last night and all I got was the answer machine.'

'Me too. "You have reached 777-9000",' Treptow continued, mimicking her voice. ' "I'm sorry I'm not here to take your call but if you would like to leave a message after the tone, I'll get back to you as soon as I can." '

'I tried her number again this morning,' Ashton said, 'and she's still not there.'

'Did you leave a message?'

'No.'

'I did. I told her where I was staying and said it was important she contacted me.'

'So what do you make of it?'

'I'd like to think she stayed the night with friends in Chicago but I'm inclined to doubt it.'

'Yesterday morning I got the distinct impression that Lenora Vassman was racked with guilt.'

'Boy, that's a good one.' Treptow smiled and shook his head. 'She gets mad at you because she's hurting?'

'I happened to be a convenient target for her anger.'

'Man, you were like a red rag to a bull. First you tell the lady she was CIA, then you calmly infer she was responsible for what happened to Bernice Kwang.'

'Lenora, Bernice and Gillespie,' Ashton said, ignoring the accusation the American had levelled at him. 'There was an involvement between those three and it became lethal.'

'You want to spell that out for me?'

'Remember what Lenora said of Gillespie the first time we called on her? "Personally, I thought he was a fink but Bernice liked him well enough".' Ashton broke off as the waitress returned with their orders and waited until she had finished serving them. 'Did you notice how vehemently she felt about Gillespie,' he continued presently, 'and how critical she was of Bernice for liking him? It was all there in her tone of voice.'

'So?'

'You've seen Gillespie's photograph, he was pretty good-looking back in 1970. I imagine a lot of women would find him attractive.'

Treptow picked up a fork and broke the yolks on both eggs. 'Are you saying Lenora fell for him and is uptight because he dumped her for Bernice Kwang?'

'No. If it had been that simple, she would have put the affair behind her long ago. I think for operational reasons she told Bernice to get close to him and it all went horribly wrong.'

Before he even started, Ashton knew Warren Treptow would find it hard to believe that even now British Intelligence wasn't a hundred per cent sure their Head of Station in Hong Kong had in fact recruited Gillespie. But extreme secrecy had been a fetish with Reeves and he had insisted on concealing the identities of his agents.

'When he dropped dead on Fanling golf course, the whole Intelligence network in that part of the world died with him. His successor had to start again from scratch. Not even the Chief Archivist knew who had been on the payroll.'

'My God, what were you guys playing at?'

'Yes, it was a nonsense, and recruiting Gillespie was the worst mistake Reeves ever made. Forget double agents, moles and Communist sympathisers, Gillespie was in it for the money, and probably still is. If he's offered enough, he'll cut his own grandmother's throat without batting an eyelid. We were using the Black Dragon Triad to carry out cross-border operations against Communist China. In return for their help, the Hong Kong police were told to go easy on the Triad. Gillespie wanted a piece of the action; when the Triad failed to come across, he sold a number of their people to the Communists.'

'You think Lenora knew this?'

'Well, let's say she'd heard whispers and decided to do something about it.'

'And she gave the job to Bernice who wasn't up to it.' Treptow pursed his lips. 'I guess Lenora would feel bad about that,' he said thoughtfully.

'She was gagged in Hong Kong, Warren, because the CIA didn't want British Intelligence to know what they'd been up to. Now she has been gagged again because, make no mistake, Lenora has been told what she can and can not say. That's what really angers her. It's also why we need to interview her again.'

'We've got to find her first,' Treptow said, chasing the last piece of egg around his plate.

'So how do you propose to go about it?'

'We start at 841 Lawn Green Drive. Maybe that neighbour who called the cops saw her leave the house.'

'Can I come along?'

'Only if you stay in the car,' Treptow told him. 'The moment you open your mouth, the neighbours are going to know where you come from, and I don't want to have to dream up some cockamamie story to explain why an Englishman should be interested to know where she's gone.' Treptow swallowed the last remaining dregs of his coffee, then wiped his lips on the napkin. 'I'm ready when you are,' he added.

The Central Police Station on State Street and East 11th was nine blocks south of the hotel. Warren Treptow figured it was worth going out of their way to avoid a repetition of yesterday evening's fiasco. He also thought there was a chance the Chicago Police Department might offer to assist them with their house-to-house enquiries, which indeed proved to be the case. By the time they reached Lawn Green Drive, a blue and white from the local station was already there waiting for them.

The neighbours either side of Lenora Vassman weren't able to help but the one across the street from her place was a regular crime prevention officer. Confined to a wheelchair because she had been paralysed from the waist down in a traffic accident, she spent most of the day watching the street, a self-appointed guardian of law and order. It was she who had reported them to the police.

'The lady also saw Lenora Vassman leave her house about an hour after we had departed for the second time.' Treptow clipped the seat belt into the housing and started up. 'She had packed a bag and drove off in her car, a red-coloured BMW.'

'Give you the licence number, did she?'

'Most of it.'

'Oh well, nobody's perfect,' Ashton said drily.

'The cops are on to it now, filling in the blanks. Our problems start after we've got the full number. Like, what the hell we are going to do with it?'

Treptow shifted into gear, released the handbrake and pulled away. At the top of Lawn Green Drive, he made a right turn into Addison

Street to follow what was becoming a familiar route back to their hotel.

'We can't ask the police to put out an APB for Lenora Vassman because she hasn't committed a crime. She's mobile, she can go anywhere and I can't think how we are going to trace her.'

'Credit cards?' Ashton suggested diffidently.

'American Express, Diners Club, Carte Blanche, Discover Cards, MasterCard and Visa – she's probably got a walletful. I guess the Agency could ask for a credit rating; that would give us a list of the cards she's got together with the account numbers.' Treptow filtered into Lake Shore Drive. 'But anything she purchases could take two, maybe three, days to show up on her account.'

It seemed to Ashton that he was looking for difficulties. If somebody at Langley had ordered Lenora Vassman to keep her mouth shut, he could understand why Treptow would be reluctant to ask the Agency to obtain her credit rating.

'There may be another way we could trace her movements, Warren.'

'For instance?'

'Couldn't we check the parking lots near the major airports?'

Ashton didn't get any farther. Taking one hand off the wheel, Treptow pointed to the glove compartment and suggested he might care to take a look at the Rand McNally map of Chicago and Vicinity and count the number of airports listed in the margin. A quick check showed there was a total of twenty-three.

'Now look on the back sheet and see how many there are in Gary and Michigan City just across the State Line.'

'You've made your point,' Ashton told him.

'You know something? I still find it hard to believe Lenora Vassman was running the show out there in Hong Kong. I mean, she was only twenty-five years old for Christ's sake and the feminists had barely got a foot in the door in those days.'

'It was only a post, not a full-blown station, Warren.'

'Yeah, but even so . . .'

'Our Head of Station in Hong Kong was answerable to the Far East Bureau in Singapore. Perhaps Lenora was controlled by your people down in Saigon?'

'It's possible,' Treptow conceded.

They were into the Gold Coast now between North Avenue and Oak Street where many of Chicago's most prominent citizens lived on the west side of the boulevard looking out to Lake Michigan. The vista however failed to inspire Ashton; try as he might, he couldn't think what other avenues they could explore.

'The phone company,' Treptow suddenly announced.

'I'm not with you.'

'If you are right and Lenora had been warned not to say too much, I think she would have called whoever it was after we left that second time because you really had her on the rack. The phone company can give me the area code, subscriber's number and listing.'

'You reckon?'

'I know it,' Treptow said confidently.

It was almost a quarter of a century since Lenora Vassman had been in the nation's capital. In 1970, she had spent one night in a motel at Dulles International Airport before being processed at Langley following her resignation from the Agency. Unless it was absolutely unavoidable, she didn't plan on staying any longer this time around. She had flown into Washington National yesterday evening as dusk was falling and had taken a cab from the airport to the Hotel L'Enfant Plaza. Without a reservation, finding a hotel room in the metropolis was often difficult but fortunately, there were no conventions in town and she hadn't had to go chasing all over Washington looking for somewhere to stay.

Brad hadn't been hugely delighted to hear she was in Washington when she had finally managed to contact him at home last night after he and his wife returned from the theatre. 'Funny place to spend a vacation,' he'd said, calmly dismissing the fact that Washington DC was a major tourist attraction. Lenora wasn't sure whether she had imagined it or not, but she thought Brad had sounded relieved to learn that it was her intention to fly on out to the west coast after seeing him. 'Okay, your hotel, coffee in the lobby eight o'clock,' he'd told her in his cryptic manner.

Brad was Bradley Davidson, a third-generation American whose great grandparents, Andrei and Yekatorina Davidov, had come from Minsk in Belorussia. He was five years her junior, was married, had three sons aged sixteen, fourteen and twelve and a daughter of nine. And that was really all she knew about him, which perhaps wasn't so very surprising since they had met only the once. Brad had flown to Chicago the day after the CIA had informed her that the British had approached the Station Chief in London to ask if the Agency knew her present whereabouts. In confirmation of what the Administrative Directorate at

Langley had already intimated, Bradley Davidson had assured her that she would not have to face British Intelligence on her own. Somebody from Langley would be present at all times. That somebody had been the very youthful-looking Warren Treptow.

Observing Brad as he entered the lobby, she thought no two men could be less alike. Where Treptow gave the impression of not being too sure of himself, Davidson radiated confidence and inspired it in others. Even dressed for the office in a dark suit, buttoned-down shirt and knitted tie, he had the rugged look of a man who spent the greater part of his time outdoors in all weathers. She felt that nothing could faze him and there was no problem he couldn't handle.

'Hi there,' he said with an easy smile, and pulled out a chair. 'I see you ordered coffee,' he added and sat down at the table.

'Black or white?' she asked.

'Black.' The smile faded and was replaced by a concerned expression. 'From what you said on the phone yesterday, I guess Warren Treptow failed to do his job?'

'You could say that.'

'You want to tell me exactly what happened when he and this guy Ashton came back to the house?'

'Ashton did all the talking and he was really aggressive. Treptow just sat there and let him walk all over me.' Lenora stopped. Davidson wasn't interested in hearing what a rough time she'd had. He was only interested in the facts and they were simple enough. 'He said I was responsible for what had happened to Bernice because I had given her a task way beyond her capability and she had fouled up. Then the insulting son of a bitch went on to say it must have been a case of the blind leading the blind and whoever had put me in charge of the Hong Kong post must have taken leave of his senses. Who told him I was in the CIA, Brad?'

'Nobody. Ashton was guessing, he tried to bounce you into admitting it.'

'And he succeeded.'

'Don't worry about it, no harm's been done.'

Only to me, she thought. After years of suppressing it, Ashton had reawakened a feeling of inadequacy which had overwhelmed her when Bernice Kwang had been murdered.

'Ashton's got a fixation about Gillespie, kept on and on at me as though he knew there was a whole lot more I could have told him about the man if I hadn't been gagged.'

'Nobody did that to you, Lenora,' Davidson said, but she appeared not to hear him.

'He kept asking me if Gillespie was now working for the US Government, hinting all the while that maybe I'd been ordered not to say too much about his background.'

'Ashton is a trouble-maker. Warren Treptow should have told him he was out of line.'

'He did, but it was pretty half-hearted.' Lenora checked to make sure smoking was permitted where they were sitting, then took out a packet of Marlboro and offered one to Davidson.

'Thanks, but I don't smoke,' he told her.

'Lucky you.' Lenora shook one loose from the pack and lit it with a Zippo. 'Are you with Administration, Brad?' she asked and got a firm headshake. 'Funny, I though they were responsible for conducting background checks. They're certainly the people who have been keeping tabs on me all these years.'

'I'm in Operations,' Davidson said and left it at that.

Operations, sometimes referred to as the clandestine service, was the largest directorate with some two thousand case officers. In her day, apart from the Central Eurasian, Near East, Europe, East Asia, Africa and Latin America branches, the directorate was also responsible for Military Affairs, Counterintelligence and the Defector Resettlement Centre. She wondered if Davidson belonged to Counter-Intelligence.

'Have you read my file, Brad?'

'Of course I have,' he said. 'I got it out of Administration as soon as I learned the Brits were looking for you.'

'What about Treptow?'

'He would have needed to see it.'

'I guess he would.' Lenora flicked her cigarette over an ashtray. 'What I don't understand is why I've got two case officers.'

'That's my fault. I should have explained the setup when I saw you in Chicago. Warren Treptow is with the East Asia Department; his brief is confined to what had happened in Hong Kong all those years ago. It's my job to discover what Ashton is really up to and take whatever action is deemed appropriate. That's why I gave you my unlisted home number so that you could alert me if things started to get out of hand. And let me say I'm very glad you did.'

'What are you going to do about Ashton?'

'We'll let him run around in circles for a few more days, then the Secretary of State will have a quiet word with Her Majesty's Ambassador and let it be known that he had outstayed his welcome. And that will be that – I guarantee it.' Davidson spread his hands. 'What more can I say?' he asked, smiling.

'Nothing. I feel a lot happier.'

'Good.' Davidson pushed his chair back and stood up. 'Now you be sure to let me know where you're staying so that I can inform you the moment Ashton is on his way home. Okay?'

Lenora nodded. 'Just one more question, Brad,' she said quietly. 'We're not protecting Gillespie, are we?'

'Absolutely not,' he assured her.

It had been a long empty afternoon. With little to do other than kill time until Treptow returned from seeing the phone company, Ashton had lunched in the French Quarter Restaurant, then walked through Grant Park as far as Soldier Field before retracing his steps. On the way back to the hotel, he'd called the embassy in Washington from a pay phone, but Head of Station had nothing more on the cargo of Stinger missiles which the *Tristan da Cuhna* had been offloading at Istanbul. In the absence of any further information, he'd assumed the Security, Vetting and Technical Services Division at Benbow House were still looking for Gillespie's birth certificate. Back at the hotel, he'd tried, without much success, to get into a paperback he'd bought in the arcade. He was still on page six when Treptow knocked on the door.

'Success,' he announced when Ashton let him into the room. 'One hour after we left her house, Lenora Vassman made a long-distance call to Alexandria. The number was unlisted.'

'You mean it wasn't in the telephone directory?'

'Damned right,' Treptow said cheerfully. 'I had to do some fast talking to get the listing. The phone bills on the Alexandria number go to a Mr Bradley Davidson. That's when I decided to call my boss.'

'Why?' Ashton said, knowing Warren expected him to ask.

'Because I know that part of the world. Alexandria is pretty handy for Langley. You take the Glebe Road out of town all the way to the Old Georgetown Pike and—'

'You can't miss it,' Ashton said, cutting him short.

'Miss what?'

'Nothing, it's what every Englishman says when he's giving directions. It practically guarantees you'll lose your way.'

'Who's telling this story?'

'You are,' Ashton said.

'Okay. Bradley Davidson is a good ole Company boy, and don't you dare ask me why I didn't already know that because we are a pretty big organisation.' Treptow grinned. 'Not some itty-bitty two men and a dog outfit.'

'You want to watch the dog,' Ashton told him. 'It still has teeth.'

'So I've discovered. Anyway, I didn't know two of us were looking after Lenora Vassman which is one reason why I'm flying back to Washington in the morning.'

'Is there another?'

'I went out to O'Hare, talked to the security of all the airlines operating out of there, and guess what?'

'Lenora Vassman has flown to Washington DC,' Ashton said in a flat voice.

'Courtesy of American Airlines yesterday afternoon.'

'I hope you booked me on to your flight.'

'You owe me four hundred and seventy-eight dollars,' Treptow told him.

CHAPTER 26

I n his capacity as Head of the Administrative Wing, it wasn't often
that Roy Kelso attended morning prayers at Vauxhall Cross. Today
however was one of those rare occasions when his presence had
been required. Hazelwood thought he looked very pleased with himself
and clearly relished the prospect of holding forth in front of his peers.
Disappointment set in when it dawned on him that his captive audience
consisted only of Jill Sheridan and Roger Benton whom Hazelwood asked
to remain behind after dismissing the other Assistant Directors.

'It's all yours, Roy,' he said when the others had departed.

Kelso cleared his throat. 'We have found a Charles Thomas Gillespie
who was born on 14 April 1939 in Southampton. The birth certificate
was signed by the registrar for the subdistrict of Shirley.'

The Registrar General at St Catherine's House had then produced the
marriage certificate of the parents. Ronald Gillespie had described himself
as a motor mechanic while his wife, Vera, who at nineteen was his junior
by four years, had been a shop assistant.

'Is that it, Roy?' Hazelwood asked, knowing from the smirk on his
lips that there was more to come.

'Not quite,' Kelso said. 'In view of his age, I knew Ronald Gillespie
would have had to register for National Service during the war and might
well have been called up if he wasn't in a reserved occupation.'

'Well, don't keep us in suspense,' Hazelwood growled.

Kelso stretched his lips in what was intended to be a smile. 'He was
called up in March 1940 and went into the RAF. He was ground staff up
until November 1944 when he became a Flight Engineer.'

'We are sure of this, are we?'

'Absolutely. Our Armed Forces Desk obtained his personal documents
from RAF Records.'

'Ashton told Head of Station in Washington that the parents had
emigrated to Canada when Gillespie junior was only a few months old.

Either we've got the wrong Gillespie or Lenora Vassman gave Peter a bum steer.'

'I don't think so,' Kelso said briskly. 'Ronald Gillespie was demobilised in February 1946 with Age and Service Group 28. At his resettlement interview, he stated he was planning to emigrate to Canada.'

'It's got to be the right family,' Benton said. 'Be a hell of a coincidence if it wasn't.'

'I'll go further,' Kelso announced triumphantly. 'Charles Thomas Gillespie is definitely our man. I gave his date and place of birth to the Department of Social Security and asked if they would check their records. You won't be surprised to hear that he had never had a National Insurance number.'

'Your people have done a good job, Roy. Please tell them so from me.'

'Thank you, Victor, I will. What I'd like to know now is whether we take our enquiries any farther.'

Hazelwood ignored the question, turned instead to Benton. 'I don't suppose we've got anything from Maurice Yule on Gillespie?'

'Afraid not.'

Hazelwood nodded. It was silly of him to have asked. Roger would have sought him out if he had heard from Hong Kong. The truth was they would find no tax records for Gillespie in the colony or anything else which might fill in the blank periods of his life. With his almost manic obsession for secrecy, Reeves would have made sure Gillespie was virtually untraceable. There was only one way forward.

'I want you to send a signal to our High Commission in Ottawa, Roy,' he said, then spelled out what was required.

Ronald Gillespie might have told the resettlement officer that he intended to emigrate but that wasn't quite the same thing as knowing for a fact that he had taken his wife and seven-year-old son to Canada some time after he had been demobilised in February 1946. If it transpired he had done so, Hazelwood wanted everything the Canadian authorities had on Charles Thomas Gillespie concerning his education, employment record and present whereabouts or last confirmed address. He was particularly keen to know if Charles Thomas Gillespie had applied for US citizenship. Throughout the discourse, Jill Sheridan beat a slow cadence on the table with her gold propelling pencil. There was also the visual signals which he found hard to ignore, the furrowed eyebrows and the slight, negative movement of her head.

'Why don't you share your thoughts with us, Jill?' Hazelwood said tetchily. 'Something is obviously troubling you.'

Nothing ever ruffled Jill Sheridan who seemed totally impervious to the sharpest of barbs. Her peers reckoned God had given her a hide tougher than that of a rhinoceros. Had the Almighty also bestowed on her a face and body like a wrinkled prune, they might not have felt quite so threatened, but He had been in a slightly mischievous mood the night Jill Sheridan had been conceived. Although not in Harriet Egan's class for looks, she was undeniably attractive and unlike the former MI5 officer, she made full use of her charms.

'Something is troubling me,' Jill said coolly, 'but it's really none of my business.'

'That's never stopped you before,' Hazelwood said and drew a snigger from Kelso.

'Well, since you insist, Victor, I just don't see what we are hoping to achieve. Our friends are sensitive enough as it is over the missiles – we give them the lot and batch numbers and they coolly tell us where and when they were manufactured. Now it seems we are determined to embarrass them to an even greater extent by demonstrating that in the matter of arms trafficking we're snow-white because we are going to prove that Gillespie is an American citizen.'

The Foreign Office wouldn't give them a thank you for that. The Government had got off on the wrong foot with the Clinton administration and they had been working overtime to put the old special relationship back on its feet again. In Jill's opinion, what Hazelwood was proposing would go a long way towards undoing everything they had achieved to date.

'I keep asking myself the same question over and over again, Victor. Where is the threat to our country in all this? And as for Gillespie, has he actually been seen in England?'

Hazelwood shook his head. The really irritating thing about Jill Sheridan was her uncanny instinct for getting to the crux of the matter. And the fact was Special Branch had drawn a blank with Gillespie. They had shown his photograph to all the budding entrepreneurs from Russia who had come to London to make their fortunes and not a single one would admit to even knowing him by sight.

'In that case, I think we should leave well alone.'

'All right, Jill,' Hazelwood said wearily, 'your objections are noted.'

'Actually, I was offering an opinion.'

'Well, okay. For the record, your opinion is noted.'

'Will there be any minutes of this meeting?' Jill asked in a sweetly innocent voice.

'Only if you write them up,' Hazelwood told her. 'But the first thing you do is go back to the CIA and ask them politely to find out what the Pentagon did with those bloody missiles that fetched up in Istanbul.'

'I already have, Victor.'

'And Gillespie?' Kelso enquired.

'You get a signal off to Ottawa on the lines we've already discussed. Then we will think what to do next after we get some answers to both questions.'

In another twenty-two and a half years, Warren Treptow would be the proud owner of a neat two-bedroom clapboard and shingle house in Falls Church, Fairfax County, which he'd purchased with a hefty mortgage, courtesy of Wells Fargo, on his return from Bonn thirty months ago. If what he'd said was anything to go by, Ashton thought this was extremely unlikely. Treptow was single and disillusioned with the CIA; should he marry, he would eventually need a larger house, should he change jobs he would probably have to sell the property anyway.

The interior lacked a woman's touch and showed little imagination. The furniture was good quality but looked as if it had been arranged with mathematical precision. The same observation applied to the prints positioned at the mid point of every bare wall. Even the den, as Warren liked to call it, was equally impersonal and reminded Ashton of a window display in a furniture store.

They had caught United Airlines UA 0600 out of Chicago O'Hare which had arrived on schedule at 08.49 hours. From Washington National they had taken a cab out to the house where the American had told Ashton to make himself at home while he got the customised Beetle out of the car port and went on over to Langley. Ostensibly, he'd wanted to have a quick word with his chief but three hours later Ashton was still waiting to hear from him. He had read *USA Today* from cover to cover including the sports pages which had left him completely baffled. As he browsed through a much thumbed cop of *The Lawless Decade*, a picture collation of the twenties, a series of toots on a horn disturbed the quiet neighbourhood. Leaving the den, Ashton walked through the hall and opened the front door to find Treptow beckoning to him from inside the Volks.

'Caspar would like to meet you,' he said when Ashton got into the car.

'Who's Caspar?' he asked.

'My chief,' Warren said and left him to wonder whether Caspar was his first or family name.

'Where are we off to? Langley?'

'You've got to be joking. We're going to take a run out to Mount Vernon, have ourselves a cup of coffee.' Treptow checked to make sure the road behind was clear, then made a U-turn and headed east on US 29 to pick up the Leesburg Pike. 'We traced Lenora Vassman to Loews L'Enfant Plaza Hotel.'

'Is she still there?'

Treptow shook his head. 'She checked out yesterday morning around 9.30. This was after she'd had coffee in the lobby with some guy.'

'Bradley Davidson.'

'You're just guessing.'

'I'd call it a reasonable assumption,' Ashton said. 'Lenora Vassman rings his unlisted number in Alexandria, then packs a bag and leaves for Washington DC. Who else do you suppose she could have met?'

'Look, the waiter could only give us a vague description of her companion. She ordered a pot of coffee for two, the waiter brought it to her and the man arrived some time later. He never got a real good look at the guy.'

'So show him a photograph of Bradley Davidson – maybe that will jog his memory.'

'I wish it was that simple.'

There were a number of very good reasons why Caspar was reluctant to go public. First and foremost was the fact that Bradley Davidson was the Assistant Director, Operations. He had been the world's greatest living Kremlinologist and what he didn't know about the newly constituted Confederation of Independent States could be written on a pinhead.

In the time it took Warren Treptow to spell out Davidson's curriculum vitae, they had passed through Seven Corners, Baileys Crossroads and were heading south on the George Washington Memorial Parkway. The road ran straight and true through gentle undulating countryside. Every now and then, Ashton caught a glimpse of the Potomac beyond the belt of trees bordering the parkway.

'The general opinion around Langley is that Brad could have been the Director of the CIA if he'd sent out the right signals. But he liked his job so much, he even declined the opportunity to head up the Operations Directorate, and a lot of people are grateful that he did. If you want to know which way the Russians are going to jump, Brad is the man you look to for advice. Ford, Carter, Reagan and Bush; they all valued his opinion.'

'If he's that big a number,' Ashton said, 'how is it you'd never heard of him before?'

273

'What?'

'After the phone company gave you the name of the subscriber Lenora Vassman had telephoned, you had to call your boss to find out who he was.' Ashton smiled fleetingly. 'At least, that's what you told me.'

Treptow didn't say anything, just tightened his grip on the steering wheel until the knuckles on both hands looked as if they were about to burst through the skin. Ashton was pretty sure he had called Langley more than once; the first time to seek advice after learning that Lenora Vassman had the unlisted home number of one of the top men in the CIA and then again after he'd discovered that she had flown to Washington.

'Don't worry about Lenora,' Treptow said, breaking an awkward silence. 'If she's still using a credit card, we'll pick up her trail again soon enough. Chances are she's gone to California; that's where her mother is living, and her younger brother too.'

'With whom she has had no contact since 1973,' Ashton reminded him.

'Yeah, as far as we know.' Treptow cruised past a parking area for tour buses only and turned into the next lot and went to the far end of the sixth row to start a new line behind a Pontiac convertible. 'This is it,' he announced. 'From here on we walk. You can load and unload outside the gates to Mount Vernon but you can't park there.'

'Makes sense.'

'It surely does,' Treptow said, then cast an appraising eye over Ashton. 'I guess what you're wearing could pass for a sports jacket but maybe you should remove your tie. Make yourself look more like a tourist.'

'You should have warned me, I'd have brought a camera.'

Treptow frowned briefly, then grinned. 'You Brits,' he said, 'I can never tell when you're joking,' and then got out of the Volks.

The North Gate Entrance to Mount Vernon was about six hundred yards away and out of sight from the parking area because of a convex bend in the road. Caspar was sitting on a stone bench roughly midway between the gift and coffee shops to the right of the entrance gates. The script they had presumably agreed beforehand called for Treptow to appear surprised to see him. Compared with some amateurs Ashton had seen on stage, his performance was both natural and convincing.

'This is Pete,' Treptow said when he finally got around to introducing him.

'Hi,' Caspar said and shook hands.

The American was a good three inches over six feet and was skinny with it. What little hair remained was of the pepper-and-salt variety and was carefully trained across the crown from left to right to hide as much of the pink scalp as possible. His face resembled an inverted triangle with the cheekbones spaced well apart and the jawline narrowing to a relatively small chin. The horn-rimmed spectacles together with a mouth that seemed permanently on the brink of a smile made him appear kindly and benign. No one observing the loafers, Daks, and plain openneck shirt he was wearing could possibly suspect he was a high-ranking Intelligence officer.

'And this is Meg,' he said, introducing Ashton to a diminutive middle-aged brunette whose head didn't quite reach Caspar's shoulder.

Ashton was left to guess what she did. At first, he assumed Meg was a senior officer in the same department as Warren Treptow. However, as the small talk between the four of them went on, he changed his mind and came to the conclusion that she was married to Caspar and had been roped in to make the encounter look more natural.

'Shall we take a walk?' Caspar suggested.

Coffee, it seemed, was not on the agenda after all. 'Let's do that,' Ashton said.

They moved off down the road past the entrance to Mount Vernon, Caspar still making small talk and using his hands a lot to give added expression to what he was saying. Warren Treptow and the lady called Meg did not accompany them; instead, they went in the opposite direction towards the parking lots.

It wasn't until Caspar was satisfied that nobody was within hearing distance of the pair of them that he raised the subject of Gillespie. 'Why are you so interested in him?' he asked.

'Hasn't Warren told you?'

'Yeah, but I'd like to hear the story from you.'

With the practice he'd had, Ashton was able to lay out the whole case history in a few lucid sentences. As always, he began with the death of Bernice Kwang and the treatment Lenora Vassman had received from the coroner at the subsequent inquest. He told the American about Reeves, Jackson, Cosgrove, Oakham and the two men from the Chechnya Republic, Stefan Afansiev and Ruslan Ovakimyan who had come to London hoping to buy upwards of two thousand air defence missiles.

'You've got a number of loose ends,' Caspar observed when he'd finished.

'You're right. I don't know why Warrant Officer Jackson believed Gillespie had had Bernice Kwang murdered. I've no proof he was the man who shoved Jackson head first into a snowdrift. We're only guessing that Cosgrove ran into Gillespie again in London and tried to put the bite on him, and I certainly can't explain how the Chechens knew where to find Louise Oakham. But the picture hangs together and looks right; that's what counts in our business.'

'Maybe.'

'Well, look at it this way,' Ashton said, 'we can always ask Gillespie to fill in the blank spaces if ever we catch up with him.' He paused, wondering how he could say what was really on his mind without giving offence. 'I don't know how to put this,' he began.

'Try being completely frank,' Caspar suggested with a smile.

'Okay. Why is Bradley Davidson keeping such a fatherly eye on Lenora Vassman? I mean, Warren himself seemed a little surprised that he should be in touch with her.'

'Brad's not only the best man on Russian affairs we have, he also runs the Operations Directorate to all intents and purposes.' Caspar turned about and started walking back towards the gift shop. 'Anything with a Russian involvement, no matter how remote, is his concern. He began to take an interest the moment Walter Maryck, the Station Chief in London, told us that you people had established a link between Gillespie, Lenora Vassman and the two gunmen from Chechnya.'

'When was this? Before or after Warren was sent to Chicago to warn Lenora that she could expect a visitor from London?'

Caspar didn't answer the question, told Ashton instead that Brad had been very open with him. He was aware that Davidson had asked Lenora Vassman to keep him fully informed of developments. Furthermore, Davidson had told him that he had met her again yesterday in Washington.

'So you've no qualms then?' Ashton said.

'I didn't say that.' What bothered Caspar was the fact that Davidson had given her his unlisted home number instead of his extension at Langley. 'That's why I propose to run a limited surveillance operation.'

'How limited?' Ashton asked.

'Within the resources of my own department. That means I've given Warren a bundle of money and told him to go hire somebody outside the Agency. The success of this operation will depend on maximum secrecy coupled with minimum risk. If anything goes wrong and the Director hears I've mounted an unauthorised operation against one of his top men, my head will be on the block and so will Warren's.'

Ashton was about to ask Caspar why he didn't go to the FBI with the problem and ask for their assistance, then thought better of it. If he didn't have enough evidence to persuade the Director that the CIA should use its own security organisation, there was no way he could take the matter to another agency.

'Is there anything I can do to help?' he asked tentatively.

'I didn't hear that.'

'Yes, it was wrong of me, I've no right to poke my nose into your business.'

'You're on borrowed time, Mr Ashton.'

'What?'

'Lenora Vassman has made an official complaint alleging that you are harassing her. Brad has already taken it up with our Director; if it goes the way I think it will, you'll get the old heave-ho tomorrow or the day after at the latest.'

An answer to one question was received by Hazelwood at ten minutes to six, courtesy of Jill Sheridan who delivered the cable from Langley in person instead of routing it through the Chief Archivist. Had it been anyone else, he would have suspected the personal touch was the opening move in an attempt to mend a few fences. He did not however expect Jill to apologise for the altercation they'd had that morning or to withdraw the minutes of the meeting she had subsequently drafted and wasn't disappointed when she did neither. Before Hazelwood had time to read the cable Jill had put on his desk, she informed him that the CIA now claimed that the Stinger missiles were part of a consignment transferred to the Saudi Arabian armed forces after Desert Storm.

'They're lying of course. The *Tristan da Cuhna* never went anywhere near a Saudi port.'

Hazelwood eyed her thoughtfully. Here it was, the end of the day and Jill Sheridan still looked fresh, unruffled and immaculate in a severely cut dark grey pinstripe jacket and a skirt which stopped a good inch from her knees. 'What do you suggest we do? Ask the Saudis for an explanation?'

'Absolutely not. They are fiercely proud and quick to take offence. They would regard such an enquiry as a slur on their integrity and defence contracts worth several hundred millions to British companies would be cancelled. It's happened before with much less reason. Remember the TV documentary called *Death of a Princess*? The one where the boyfriend gets his head chopped off and she's shot to death for having sex out of wedlock with a commoner?' Jill paused, then said, 'You want my advice? I think we should let sleeping dogs lie.'

'Well, thank you,' Hazelwood said, his voice dry as dust. 'I have always valued your opinion.'

'It's nice of you to say so, Victor. Indeed, I'm encouraged to suggest we recall Ashton as soon as possible. Head of Station would certainly be glad to see the back of him.'

'Are you telling me he's in Washington DC?'

'Yes, he's with Treptow, the CIA man. Seems they followed Lenora Vassman in the hope she would lead them to Gillespie. It's all pretty vague and sounds fraught with risk.'

'What does Roger Benton think?'

'He agrees with me. We decided that in view of the Mid East connection, I should handle all incoming signals from the US.'

Hazelwood wondered why he was surprised that Roger had allowed her to walk all over him. When you came right down to it, Benton was essentially a grey man lacking all ambition. Content in the knowledge that he had reached his ceiling, his one aim now was to keep his nose clean until he was eligible for a pension. From his point of view, the Lenora Vassman affair was a potential minefield and he wanted no part of it. However, Jill Sheridan was made of stronger stuff and was as tough as tungsten carbide which was an essential ingredient if you were ambitious. That had been the whole object of the minutes she had drafted.

'I hope you are happy with this arrangement, Victor?'

Hazelwood wasn't. Unfortunately, he couldn't think of a valid objection. In the field of office politics, Jill Sheridan was a master tactician. It was one of the reasons why there was not the slightest doubt in his mind that the day would surely come when she would be running The Firm.

It had been a long, tiring day. Washington DC to San Diego by American Airlines, then a cab from the airport to the Le Meridien Hotel in Coronado and a room with a breathtaking view of the harbour front and the downtown area of the city across the bay. But it had also been a very depressing day. Shortly after checking into the hotel, Lenora Vassman had rented a Cadillac de Ville from Avis and had made a painful journey to the clinic in Roseville.

Although she hadn't seen her mother since October '92, she had phoned the clinic religiously once a month to ask after her. Nobody on the staff had ever attempted to minimise the distressing nature of Karen Vassman's medical condition and this had led Lenora to believe that she knew what to expect. Years of alcohol abuse had been the principal cause of her mother's physical and mental deterioration and while she had shown unmistakable signs of senile dementia eighteen months ago, it was now far more advanced than Lenora had imagined from the reports she had received.

Karen hadn't recognised her, that had been the really distressing thing. She was frail, incontinent and dribbled like a baby. Looking at the ravaged face with its blank expression, Lenora had had to remind herself that her mother was only seventy-two. She thought a psychiatrist would have a great time analysing her motives for making this trip to Southern California. A sense of failing in her filial duty had something to do with it. Although she paid all the bills from the clinic, she rarely visited her mother and there were times when she felt guilty about that. But it was really that damned Englishman, Ashton, who was responsible for her sudden decision. Without knowing it, he had reopened old self-inflicted wounds and coming to San Diego to spend a few hours with her mother was, in a curious way, an act of atonement for what she had done to Bernice Kwang.

'Stop that,' Lenora chided herself. 'Get a hold of yourself.' She walked to the writing table, picked up the phone and called Davidson. 'Have you got any news for me, Brad?' she asked when he came on the line.

'About Ashton? Things are moving along. I told the Director he'd been harassing you and the Agency's lodged an official protest with the State Department.'

'Good.'

'Where are you calling from?'

'San Diego.'

'You got a number where I can reach you when I have some more news?'

'I'm staying at the Meridien, but I'm moving on tomorrow.'

'Where to?'

'I'm not sure,' Lenora told him. 'Palm Springs, Pasadena, Santa Monica – who knows?'

'Only you,' Davidson said with a hollow laugh. 'Just be sure to let me know once you have made up your mind.'

'Oh, I'll certainly do that,' Lenora said in a dull voice and then put the phone down.

CHAPTER 27

Lenora released the central locking system, then waited for the bellboy to put her bag into the trunk of the Cadillac de Ville and open the car door for her before tipping him five dollars. Leaving the forecourt of the Meridien Hotel, she turned on to 4th Street, picked up the State Highway and drove across the Coronado Bridge to downtown San Diego. From there she headed north-west on Interstate 5, then switched to the Cabrillo Freeway. Palm Springs, Pasadena or Santa Monica? No need to make up her mind where she was going just yet. Could be she might surprise Brad and pick some other place.

It was a clear bright morning. According to the forecast on the local TV station, the temperature was set for a high of eighty-one with the promise of a gentle offshore breeze towards mid-afternoon which she would not be around to enjoy. On such a day, she did not want to think about Bernice Kwang but the memory of the Chinese American girl kept intruding. So did Gillespie which was almost inevitable given the special relationship that had existed between the three of them. Ashton had hinted that she had been eaten up with jealousy because Tad Gillespie had dumped her and taken up with Bernice Kwang. In her own mind, Lenora was sure it had been a wild guess on his part but unhappily the allegation was not without some foundation. She had met Gillespie at a cocktail party hosted by the chairman of the import/export house of Butterfield and Swire's and he had taken her on to dinner at Gripps.

That first meeting had led to other dates and she couldn't deny that at the time she had been infatuated with him. She would have done anything he had asked of her, but the curious thing was that they had never been intimate. There had been no inhibitions on her part and she had sent out enough signals to indicate she was more than willing. Gillespie, however, had ignored them and his phone calls had become fewer and farther between until eventually he had stopped calling her altogether.

To this day, she had no idea when he had started doing a number with Bernice Kwang or how he'd met her.

It had been Bernice who'd discovered that Gillespie was in British Intelligence and had identified Reeves as the SIS Head of Station. Had the Viet Cong suddenly laid down their arms, she could not have been more surprised and at first she had not believed her. Bernice had proved a reliable courier but that had been about the extent of her talents. Neither of them had been in the business of Intelligence gathering. In accordance with their brief from Saigon, they were responsible for gauging the morale of US servicemen in Hong Kong who were on R and R from Vietnam. Bernice had started producing high-grade material on the internal security situation in the British crown colony shortly after she had taken up with Gillespie. 'Pillow Talk,' Bernice had said with a wink when she had asked about her sources.

Poor Bernice. There was no doubting which of her parents had had the strongest genes. Instead of the typically demure, obedient and self-effacing Chinese girl, they had bred a liberated American woman, a free spirit from California. Almost wilfully naïve, she had refused to see that Gillespie was using her. He had first hooked Bernice by feeding her with classified information gleaned from the cables the SIS regularly dispatched to London, then he had set her up as the double agent who was working for Chairman Mao. It had been done very cleverly. On two occasions to Lenora's knowledge, he had arranged to meet Bernice at Sha Tau Kok up in the New Territories and had either failed to show or had arrived late. Sha Tau Kok was a small border village, half in Hong Kong, half in Communist China; some buildings were virtually split down the middle, like the restaurant where Bernice had waited for him. It was, in fact, the kind of place an agent might use for a meeting with their case officer. Although unable to prove it, Lenora was positive Gillespie had made sure members of the Black Dragon Triad had seen Bernice there when he had not been present.

She should have insisted that the Agency recalled Bernice while there had still been time to do so. Had she done this, the Chinese American girl would still be alive today. But her superiors in Saigon and the East Asia Department had made it clear they thought Bernice was doing a magnificent job and she had therefore refrained from taking remedial action. It was only after she had been killed that the CIA had rewritten their appraisal of Bernice Kwang and had decided she had not been up to speed.

The Cabrillo Freeway merged with Interstate 15. Lenora stayed with it, cruising along at a steady fifty-five, not caring where the highway was taking her. Decision time came after she had joined Interstate 215 and was approaching Edgemont. Palm Springs or Lake Arrowhead? Heads or tails? Taking one hand off the wheel, Lenora opened her purse, dug out a quarter and flipped it. When she caught it in the palm of her hand, the Eagle on the reverse side of the coin was uppermost in favour of Lake Arrowhead.

The view from the office of the CIA's Deputy Chief of Operations was one of the very few at Langley which did not encompass a vast parking lot and could therefore be described as truly rural. From this room located on the top floor of the main building, Davidson could see the muddy waters of the Potomac beyond the dense belt of trees if ever he chose to leave his desk and walk over to the window. It was the first time Warren Treptow had set foot inside the place and he sincerely hoped it would be the last. The atmosphere which greeted him was full of menace and even though Caspar was present, he felt he had been summoned to appear before a latter-day Star Chamber.

'We have a problem,' Davidson announced in a grating voice. 'Lenora Vassman has made an official complaint alleging that this Mr Ashton is deliberately harassing her. She also told me that you just sat there and allowed him to get away with it.'

'Neither allegation is true,' Treptow told him. 'I'm not denying that Ashton didn't come down on her pretty hard, but there was no harassment.'

'Ashton drove Ms Vassman out of her own house, made her run.' Davidson picked up the paperknife on his desk and pointed the blade at him. 'If you don't consider that harassment, Mr Treptow, I'd like to hear your definition of it.'

'I don't understand why she took off.'

'You don't, huh?' The blade waggled up and down as if it had a life of its own. 'He tells Vassman it's her fault Bernice Kwang was killed and you don't think she has a right to be upset?'

'All he did was point out the inconsistencies in her story when she tried to justify herself.'

'You're wrong,' Davidson snapped. 'Ashton was hellbent on hounding Vassman and you fell down on the job. One session wasn't enough for him, was it? Hell no, he persuades you there's more to Lenora than meets the eye and back you go to put her through the mincer. But it doesn't end there. You take him back to the house in the late afternoon and then finally, for the fourth time, the following morning.'

Treptow swallowed nervously. How did Davidson know that? Had Caspar told him? He pushed the thought from his mind, reluctant to open that particular can of worms. Lenora Vassman must have rung one of her neighbours from Washington. Maybe she had talked to the one across the street from her place, the lady in the wheelchair who'd reported them to the police?

'A wonder you didn't pull a gun on her.'

'What?'

'You were carrying a Ruger .357. Beats the hell out of me why you were.'

'Security advised me to. They said it was better to be safe than sorry when you were dealing with someone like Ashton.'

'That's got to be a joke . . .'

Ashton had thought so too and had fallen about laughing when Treptow had told him the reason.

'Where is Ashton now?' Davidson asked in a quieter voice.

'I've no idea,' Treptow said instinctively. 'I mean, why should I know where to find him?'

'Well, he sat next to you on the United Airlines flight out of Chicago yesterday morning. Matter of fact, you paid his air fare.'

Treptow thought he was going to throw up. It was no use looking to Caspar to throw him a lifeline; he was in one of his contemplative moods and scarcely on the same planet. He drew some comfort from the fact that he had never discussed the matter of the air fares with Caspar. That meant Davidson must have obtained his information from some other source. The Deputy Chief of Operations must have put the Security Department on to it. Davidson knew when he had returned to Washington; all Security had to do was check with the airlines. And bingo, they would have the complete answer – flight number, seat number, who had been sitting next to him and how he had paid for the tickets.

'You want to give me an explanation, Warren?'

'About the plane tickets? Well, it's a little complicated . . .'

'I bet it is,' Davidson said.

'My orders were to keep a watching brief on Ashton and speed him on his way at the earliest opportunity,' Treptow said, ignoring the Deputy Chief's sarcasm. 'I couldn't have asked for a better stroke of luck than Ms Vassman gave me by flying to Washington. My reading of Ashton was that he would want to go after her and we decided it was to our advantage to make sure he did. If Ashton was here in town, we figured the British Embassy would find it difficult to pretend they had no idea of his present whereabouts.'

'You keep saying "we",' Davidson complained.

'I took advice.'

'From me,' Caspar added.

At last, Treptow thought, at last Caspar has come down off the fence. Late yesterday evening, on Caspar's instructions, he had contacted Elcon Electronics, a slightly shady outfit specialising in high-tech surveillance. He had put down two thousand dollars in cash to hire an Ultimate Infinity Receiver and the part-time services of an operative for one week. He had also given Elcon Electronics Davidson's unlisted number in Alexandria which he wanted them to cover. This morning, the operative had called Davidson's telephone and passed a coded signal down the line instructing the instrument to act as a bug. As of now, every incoming and outgoing call was being recorded. So was every conversation which took place in the room when the phone was not in use.

Treptow was only too aware that what he had set in motion directly contravened the US Privacy Law. Furthermore, the manufacture of the equipment Elcon Electronics was using was prohibited in America. Worse still, the Ultimate Infinity Receiver had been made in Britain and had, in all probability, been illegally imported. 'The Japanese make a cheaper version,' the Elcon specialist had told him, 'but it's not a patch on the UK model.' There had, however, been moments since then when Treptow wished he had rented the Japanese equivalent because if Caspar should leave him holding the shitty end of the stick, it would look as though he and Ashton were a team.

'It didn't work, did it?'

Treptow suddenly realised that the Deputy Chief of Operations was waiting for him to answer a question he hadn't been following. 'You mean Ashton has disappeared?' he said, making a stab at it.

'That's more or less what the British Embassy would have the State Department believe. They don't deny that they've heard from Ashton since he arrived in Washington but claim he refused to say where he was staying.'

'Is he being deported?' Treptow asked.

'It may yet come to that. What State has done so far is advise the British Embassy that Ashton has been abusing his position as a guest in this country and has outstayed his welcome.' Davidson laid the paperknife aside. 'We have to find him because the Brits certainly won't. That means checking every hotel, guest house and motel in town.' He stared at Treptow, his eyes unblinking. 'However, before we go to all that trouble, I'd like to be assured that you don't know where he is, Warren.'

'We parted company at Washington National Airport; I haven't seen or heard from him since then.'

'I'd like to believe that.'

'Are there any other questions you want to ask Warren?' Caspar growled.

It was the second time Caspar had intervened and although it was no more than he had a right to expect, Treptow was grateful to him for that. He was even more relieved when Davidson dismissed him.

Back in his office again, reaction set in and he felt breathless. How far would Davidson go? Would he tell the Security Department to search his house? He eyed the telephone on his desk, wondered if he should call the house, then decided it was unnecessary. He had foreseen that possibility and had warned Ashton to make himself scarce during daylight hours. But the most persuasive factor was the almost paranoic fear that the Agency had already bugged his home number.

His name was David Sibbick. He was forty-one and described himself as a private enquiry agent, a profession for which he had received no formal training whatever before setting up in business. His work included debt collecting, tracing missing persons, and the acquisition of industrial information, a job description which covered a multitude of sins. Two nights ago, he had broken into Canary Wharf with the intention of bugging the boardroom of the Morgan Humbolt Trust and had been caught red-handed by a couple of security guards. Attempting to escape, he had punched one man in the stomach and had then wrenched a heavy fire extinguisher from the wall and thrown it into the path of the second man who was pursuing him. The fire extinguisher had hit the security guard below the knee and sent him flying, with the result that he had fractured the right leg and broken his nose on the floor.

The whole incident had been witnessed on the closed-circuit TV by a third security guard in the lobby so that the police had been waiting for Sibbick by the time he had made his way down to the ground floor by the fire escape. Apart from burglary, he had also been charged under the Offences Against the Person Act of 1861 with an Assault Occasioning Actual Bodily Harm and one of Causing Grievous Bodily Harm. Yesterday, he had appeared before the magistrates' court and had been remanded in custody for seven days after the police indicated that they wished to question him about a number of other offences. Acting on the advice of his solicitor, Sibbick had decided to help the police with their enquiries.

In the course of a full and frank disclosure, word of what he had told the officers of H District had reached Special Branch who in turn had alerted Clifford Peachey. That morning, he had come to the Limehouse Divisional Station at 29 West India Dock Road to hear what Sibbick had to say for himself.

'I'm Clifford,' Peachey said, introducing himself before he sat down facing Sibbick and his solicitor across the table.

The Special Branch officer set the tape running, formally identified those present, giving Peachey's Christian name as his surname, and then stated the interview had started at 10.38 hours.

'Now, what's all this about Louise Oakham?' he asked after the formalities had been completed.

'I was hired to find out where she was living,' Sibbick told him.

'When was this?'

'Nearly four months ago.'

'In other words, before she was murdered?'

Sibbick glanced at his lawyer as if hoping he would object to the question and was visibly disappointed when he didn't. 'Yes, that's what bothered me,' he mumbled. 'Then I saw the photographs of those two Russians on the telly who were supposed to have shot her and I stopped worrying. I mean, neither of them had hired me.'

Although it was a thin excuse for doing nothing, Peachey let him get away with it. If the police wanted to do something about it, that was up to them. He had other fish to fry. 'Tell me about the man who hired you, David.'

'It's Dave,' Sibbick told him. 'Mind if I smoke?'

'I don't,' Peachey said.

'Trouble is, I haven't got any cigarettes. The duty sergeant took them off me along with my other things before they banged me up.'

The Special Branch officer produced a packet of Embassy with a loud sigh and passed it across the table, only to be asked if he'd got a light. 'Sure you wouldn't like me to smoke it for you?' he said and dug out a box of Swan Vestas.

'Oh, I think I can manage that, Squire.' Sibbick lit a cigarette, then leaned back in his chair. 'Now, where were we?' he asked.

'You were on the point of telling me about the man who hired you.'

'So I was. Well, he came into my office in Archway one afternoon in early January.'

Sibbick couldn't remember the exact date but was pretty sure it had been a Monday because his part-time secretary only came in on four afternoons a week. On that basis, he thought it could have been either the 3rd or 10th of the month.

'He was an amiable sort of guy in his mid-fifties, about five feet eleven, and looked very fit for his age. No gut to speak of – know what I mean? He had darkish hair flecked with grey, pock-marked cheeks like he'd had a bad dose of chicken pox when he was a kid.'

Either of the dates fitted. Oakham had been interviewed by Brigadier Baring in connection with his enhanced positive vetting clearance on Monday, 14 February and had gone absent on 18th. Peachey also thought the age and height of the client was about right. However, the colour of his hair was all wrong. In the colour snapshot which Ashton had given him, the man tentatively identified as Charles Thomas Gillespie had had flaxen hair.

'His accent made me think he was a Yank,' Sibbick continued. 'But when I asked him, he said no, he was a Cannuck and hailed from Nova Scotia.'

'Did he have a name, Dave?'

'Thomas. He told me his name was Chad Thomas, said his family originally came from Cardiff.'

An alias was always easier to adopt when it consisted of the same initials. Gillespie had simply used his Christian names, calling himself Chad instead of Charles to substantiate the claim that he was of Welsh extraction.

'What about means of identification?' Peachey asked.

There was a significant pause before Sibbick told him that Chad Thomas had shown him his Canadian passport. It was enough to convince Peachey that the private enquiry agent was lying in his teeth. The police had told him that Sibbick represented the less reputable side of the business and wasn't too fussy who he worked for as long as the client had money.

'Thomas said he was in London on business and was anxious to get in touch with a lady his daughter had worked for as an au pair when she was over here eleven years ago.' Sibbick stubbed out his cigarette and helped himself to another. 'Seems they'd lost touch in 1987. The woman was married to an army officer called Simon Oakham who was serving in the Pay Corps in those days. He had tried to get their home address out of the Ministry of Defence but they had refused to disclose it on security grounds. Something to do with the IRA.'

Peachey nodded; that was standard procedure. Oakham's rank would also have been omitted on all official mail sent to his home address. But Gillespie wouldn't have approached the military authorities, he had more sense than that. However, the story he had given Sibbick indicated he was familiar with current anti-terrorist measures.

'So what arrangements did you come to, Dave?' he asked.

'Thomas gave me two hundred up front for expenses with a promise of a further two hundred if I got a result. I tell you, it was money for old rope.'

Sibbick had gone to the main library in Camden Town and looked up Oakham in a copy of the Army List to satisfy himself that he was still a serving officer and to check if he had more than one Christian name. Satisfied that the information he had been given was correct, Sibbick had then visited a number of branch libraries, compiling a list of Oakhams from the telephone directories in the reference section.

'I started with the South of England because that's where most of the army is stationed. Fortunately, Oakham is a fairly uncommon name and there weren't too many of them with just the letter S as an initial. I then went back to my office, rang them up one by one and gave them the old sales patter about the advantages of double-glazing. I started by pretending I was conducting a survey on behalf of some well-known company. Doesn't matter how sales resistant they are, that gambit always hooks them. And if you can just keep the subscriber talking for a couple of minutes, it's amazing how much you can learn about the person on the other end of the line.'

It had taken Sibbick nineteen phone calls to establish that the address of the Mrs Oakham he'd been hired to locate was 104 Greenham Avenue, Guildford. After asking her when it might be convenient to have a word with her husband, she had inadvertently told him that he was in the army.

'Can you beat it? All those security measures which were meant to protect went down the toilet because she couldn't wait to get me off the phone.'

It took a lot of provocation to make Peachey lose his temper but Sibbick came close to succeeding. The private detective bore a considerable responsibility for what had happened to Louise Oakham and his complete lack of remorse sickened him.

'So how did you pass on her address to Thomas?' he asked in a voice tight with anger.

'I didn't, he came to me.' Sibbick crushed his cigarette in the ashtray and was about to reach for a third when the Special Branch officer removed the packet of Embassy from his grasp.

'What do you mean, he came to you?' Peachey demanded.

'He phoned my office every day to see how I was getting on. That was the arrangement. See, he was going up to the Midlands on business and wasn't too sure where he would be staying from day to day.'

'And you were happy with that explanation?'

'Why not? I'd no reason to doubt him.'

Peachey thought he was a fool to have asked. Put enough money in his hot little hand and Sibbick would swallow any tale you cared to pitch him.

'Would this man be your client?' he asked and passed the colour snapshot of Gillespie across the table.

'That's Chad Thomas,' Sibbick told him without a second glance. 'Must have been taken twenty years ago and he's dyed his hair since then, but it's him all right. I'd swear to it.'

Peachey believed him if only because Sibbick had nothing to gain and everything to lose by lying. Gillespie had been in London between 3 and 10 of January. That fact alone was something Special Branch could get their teeth into when they made house calls on the Russian community again.

CHAPTER 28

The Blue Marlin was a colourful name for a run-down bar in South San Francisco, two miles from the International Airport between the Bayshore Freeway and State Highway 82 to Monterey. The bar was off the beaten track, dimly lit and noted for the high-decibel level of the Country and Western tapes, three good reasons why Gillespie had chosen to meet the client there.

The client was an Armenian, born and bred in Erevan near the Turkish border. It was his first trip abroad and he had arrived in California after an epic journey via Tbilisi, Kiev, Warsaw, Berlin, Frankfurt and New York. He was wearing a loud sports shirt under a tan-coloured jacket and a faded pair of jeans, an outfit which was intended to make him instantly recognisable to Gillespie. Four years ago he had been a tour guide in Moscow, now he was a Deputy Minister of Defence with special responsibility for Arms Procurement. He was travelling on a diplomatic passport and had in his possession letters of credit for six point three million US dollars. He was also carrying a letter of introduction from Ernst Roeder in East Berlin, a former major in the People's Army of the German Democratic Republic with whom Gillespie had done business in the recent past.

'You are good friends, yes?' the client asked when he'd finished reading the letter.

'We know one another pretty well,' Gillespie told him.

'Herr Roeder said that you were the man to consult about providing an effective air defence system for my country. You see, we are surrounded by enemies – Turks, Shiite Muslims from Azerbaijan, and Kurds. Always we are being massacred . . .'

Gillespie drank from the can of beer the Armenian had bought for him and wiped the froth from his lips using the back of his wrist. 'What are you in the market for?' he asked, interrupting the potted history of Armenia. 'Guns or missiles?'

'Missiles, but they have to be man-portable.'

'Would I be right in assuming you've already tried the Russians and they've refused to sell you their SAM-7?'

'We didn't even bother to approach them.'

'Well, you're not exactly spoiled for choice. I'm pretty sure the British wouldn't let you have either the Blowpipe or the more advanced Javelin. On the other hand, the French might be prepared to do a deal with you and their Mistral system is highly regarded.'

'No, it would have to be the Stinger.'

'I'm afraid that's out of the question,' Gillespie told the Armenian politely. 'I'd never get an export licence for them.'

'Oh? We heard the Kuwaitis had managed to obtain a large number of those missiles.'

'You've been misinformed. They belong to the US Army, part of the stockpile of weapons the Pentagon has positioned in Kuwait in case Saddam Hussein decides to try his luck a second time.'

'What about the two thousand missiles which were found on board the *Tristan da Cuhna*?' The Armenian smiled. 'Were they part of another stockpile for the US Army?'

Gillespie affected to be amused. Behind the mask, he wondered how the hell the Armenian knew about the shipment when word of the mishap in Istanbul had only reached him yesterday. 'Your guess is as good as mine,' he said with studied nonchalance.

'We understand they were destined for Grozny. We also heard the Chechens were planning to sell half the consignment to their fellow Muslims in Azerbaijan. At a profit, of course.'

Gillespie tried to keep a smile on his face but the effort was beyond him and it slipped away. The son of a bitch was too well informed and he was losing control of the situation. Those two clowns Afansiev and Ovakimyan must have shot their mouths off in London and somebody in the Armenian community had got wind of it. Although this was the most likely explanation for the leak, it was of no use to him now.

'Listen,' he said earnestly, 'I'm just an arms broker, a middle man between the client and the manufacturer or whoever is in a position to supply the desired munition. And if the weapon is manufactured in this country, I have to go to the State Department and ask for their permission to export it. Now, I don't know who arranged the shipment of missiles to the Chechens, but it wasn't me.'

'The thought never entered my mind,' the Armenian told him blandly.

'What I can do for you is go to my friends and say that you are interested in acquiring X number of Stinger missiles for Armenia and how do they feel about that? I'm not guaranteeing anything but I will do the best I can for you, and who knows, maybe they will give me a green light to go ahead.'

'Well, if they don't, you won't lose out, Mr Gillespie.'

'I won't?'

'No. We'll give you half a million dollars to ensure no further missiles are dispatched to the Chechnya Republic.'

'I'd like to accept your offer,' Gillespie told him, 'but I have to say you're over-estimating my influence in Washington.'

'You're too modest.'

'You're wrong. I just don't want to take on something I can't deliver.' Gillespie drained the can of beer and crushed it in his fist. 'But let me think about it and I'll get back to you.'

'It's best if I call you.'

'Fine.'

'Shall we say tomorrow?'

'Better make it the day after. There are people I need to talk to in Washington and they may not be readily available.'

The Armenian was all sweetness and light. 'I'm sure you will come to the right decision,' he said.

Gillespie stood up, said it had been a pleasure meeting him, and edged out of the corner booth. As he walked out of the Blue Marlin into the late afternoon sunlight, Kenny Rogers was complaining at full blast that some woman called Lucille had picked a fine time to leave him.

He got into the Lincoln Mark VIII which he'd left on what passed for a parking lot outside the bar and headed back to town. No way would the man in Washington allow him to do business with the Armenian. Nothing that happened in the south-west of Transcaucasia would hurt the Russians because Moscow had written that region off long ago. How would it hurt Yeltsin and help to dismember Russia? That was the litmus test for his partners. The old Russian Soviet Federal Socialist Republic had consisted of fifteen Autonomous Republics plus six regions, and it was these potentially independent states which needed all the encouragement and practical assistance they could get if they were to break away. That was why his partner in Washington had approved the dispatch of two thousand Stinger missiles to Chechnya.

All the same, they ought to do something for the Armenian. 'I'm sure you will come to the right decision.' The more he thought about that parting remark, the more it sounded like a veiled threat. As if he didn't have enough problems already with Lenora Vassman. The way the situation was developing, they would have to do something about that bitch before she caved in and brought them all crashing down.

Treptow ran the Volks under the car port and cut the ignition, then got out and locked the doors. He'd stayed late at the office principally to give Davidson the impression that he was unconcerned, and it had gone 7.45 and was pitch dark when he had collected the Volks from the parking lot. All the way home he had been worried by what might be waiting for him in Falls Church, Fairfax County, but now it seemed his fears had been groundless. There were no unmarked cars in the immediate neighbourhood and as far as he could tell, no one was watching the house which happened to be in darkness, the curtains in both front rooms still undrawn.

He walked up the steps leading to the stoop, dug out his set of keys and let himself into the house. He groped for the switch, put the light on in the hall and walked through to the back where he did the same in the kitchen-diner. As he let down the Venetian blind and closed it up, he saw a reflection in the window and nearly jumped out of his skin.

'Jesus H. Christ,' he gasped, 'where the fuck did you spring from?'

'Down in the cellar,' Ashton told him. 'I've been there all day, keeping company with your oil-fired central heating boiler.'

Treptow stared at him, eyebrows almost knitting together; then the penny dropped and the frown disappeared. 'You mean the furnace?'

'That's what I like about travelling,' Ashton said drily. 'It broadens the mind and you learn something new every day.'

'Has anybody called at the house?'

'Not a soul.'

'How about the telephone?'

'It rang twice and on both occasions the caller was nothing if not persistent. I was ready for him the second time and it was two and a half minutes before he hung up.'

'It must have been somebody from the Agency,' Treptow said. 'He was hoping that if he held on long enough, you would eventually answer the phone. Davidson's working overtime to get you thrown out of the country.' Treptow opened the fridge-freezer and looked inside. 'Have you had anything to eat today?' he asked.

'An apple at lunchtime.'

'I've got a pizza with ham, cheese and tomato topping and some French fries.'

'Sounds good to me.'

'I meant to pick up a selection of TV dinners on the way home but it's been a hell of a day.'

'I like pizzas,' Ashton assured him, but Treptow had other things on his mind and wasn't listening.

'Davidson suspects that you are staying with me. I was summoned to his office this morning and interrogated for upwards of two hours. I've never experienced such hostility; you'd have thought I'd been caught passing Top Secret information to a foreign power. Caspar sat on the fence so damned long, I thought he'd pulled the plug on me.'

All afternoon he had been on tenterhooks expecting to be informed at any moment that Ashton had been picked up. When he had stopped worrying about that possibility, he recalled what the specialist at Elcon had told him about the Ultimate Infinity Receiver. If the Agency had supplied Davidson with a Radio Transmission Detector, he would know his telephone had been tampered with.

'A hell of a day,' he repeated.

'Sooner you than me,' Ashton murmured sympathetically.

'Jesus, I forgot . . .' Treptow left the pizza on the kitchen table, moved to the sink and turned the faucet on. 'They could be listening to us right this minute.'

'The phone's not here,' Ashton pointed out, 'it's in the study.'

'Right.'

'And it's ringing, Warren,' he added, and turned off the water.

Treptow went into the study, lifted the receiver and heard the operative from Elcon say that he had something for him. Although warned it meant listening to a lot of dross, he opted to hear the whole tape, then rapidly wished he hadn't because it seemed to him that Jackie Davidson was never off the phone. She spoke to her dentist and then had a long conversation with some lady called Ginny who was a leading light of the PTA concerning the problems her youngest son was having with one of his teachers. There followed several equally long conversations with various committee members about a fund-raising event in aid of the local Baptist church, so that he was almost caught off guard when he heard Davidson answer an incoming call to the house. Reacting swiftly, he hooked the receiver into the amplifier in time for Ashton to hear Lenora Vassman say hello.

'So where are you calling from?' Davidson said.

Treptow hit the two-way record button on his answer machine in order to catch her reply.

'Lake Arrowhead,' she told him.

'Lake Arrowhead? Well, that's a surprise. Last time we talked you were thinking about Palm Springs, Pasadena or even Santa Monica.'

'I changed my mind,' she said tartly. 'Anything wrong with that?'

'Hey, it's your vacation, Lenora. You can go where you like. I'm the guy who told you to pack a bag and go. Remember?'

'I'm not likely to forget. What's the score on Ashton?'

'State has told the British Embassy he's no longer welcome.'

'Is he on his way?'

'He will be, soon as we find him.'

'Are you telling me you don't know where he is?' Lenora asked in a brittle voice.

'The Brits are being obtuse, but don't worry about it; they will produce his body because they've got a lot of fences to mend with this Administration. At least, that's what we keep hearing from the President.'

'Well, that fills me with confidence.'

'I thought it would,' Davidson said in an even more laconic tone. 'How long are you planning to stay in Lake Arrowhead?'

'I haven't given it much thought, Brad.'

'Think you could stay put for a day or two? I doubt if you want to continue this nomadic existence a moment longer than you have to and it would help me if I knew where to find you in a hurry. Okay?'

'I'll stay over until Monday. I don't imagine that will be a problem for the Hilton.'

'Terrific. You want to give me your room number?'

'Ask for 371.'

'Good. You hang in there, Lenora, it won't be long now.'

'Thanks, Brad,' she said and put the phone down.

Davidson followed suit. Moments later they heard him drumming his fingers on a wooden surface as if he wasn't sure what to do. Presently, he called to Jackie and told her he was going to pick up a bottle of champagne from the liquor store and was there anything she wanted while he was in town? Jackie's reply was unintelligible but her tone of voice suggested she was not best pleased with her husband.

'The last telephone conversation took place approximately eight minutes ago,' the man from Elcon announced. 'I'm now going off watch but the surveillance of the target will continue throughout the night. I'll call you tomorrow morning at seven if we've picked up some material. Okay?'

Treptow said that was usually the time he left for the office but no problem. The answer machine would be on and would record anything the Ultimate Infinity Receiver had picked up. He then replaced the phone and turned to Ashton.

'What do you make of that?' he asked.

'What are the Davidsons celebrating? A birthday? Wedding anniversary?'

'You're referring to the bottle of champagne?'

'Yes. If you want my opinion, I think it was just an excuse to leave the house, something he dreamed up in a hurry. Remember how he was drumming his fingers before he called out to Jackie?'

'I'll go along with that,' Treptow said. 'The question is, why did he want to leave the house? I doubt it was to see another woman. Seems to me Davidson would have come up with a better excuse if that was the case. Besides, if you go out to buy a bottle of champagne and you're away for any length of time, your wife is liable to get a mite suspicious.'

'He needed to use a pay phone,' Ashton said. 'There were things he had to say which his wife couldn't be allowed to overhear.'

'That's a novel theory, Peter. Would you care to flesh it out a bit?'

'It has to do with Lenora Vassman. He really pushed hard to discover her whereabouts. "Where are you calling from?" he asks Lenora and she tells him Lake Arrowhead, which is evidently a bit of a surprise because he thought she might be going to Palm Springs, Pasadena or Santa Monica. Anyway, knowing where she is now isn't enough for Davidson. He's anxious to find out how long she is staying there. When she hedges, he tells her it would make life much easier for him if she would stay put for a while. And in persuading her to agree he learns she has checked into the Hilton. Next thing you know, he's got her room number.'

'And you believe Davidson left the house to pass this information on to a third party?'

'Don't you?'

'Let me think about it.' Treptow wandered out into the kitchen, put the French fries and pizza into the microwave, set the timer and switched it on. 'I sure as hell don't like the implications,' he said presently.

'Then I'll spell it out for you,' Ashton said. 'Right now he's on the phone to Gillespie.'

'Boy, that's a leap in the dark.'

'Okay, maybe Davidson's got somebody else lined up for the job.'

'Job?'

'He sees Lenora as a threat, Warren, which is why he wants her silenced.'

'You're guessing again.'

'Why did he go to Chicago ahead of you? Have you any idea what he said to Lenora?'

'No.'

'Neither have I, but I'm betting he let something slip about a relationship with Gillespie which she hasn't cottoned on to yet.'

'There's no reason for Davidson to sign a death warrant on Lenora Vassman. He's getting rid of you, State is seeing to it.'

'He's bluffing,' Ashton said tersely. 'Oh, he might have spoken to the SIS Head of Station in Washington and told him I was one big pain in the arse and would he please put me on the next plane to London, but that's as far as it went. The rest is bullshit.'

Ashton was right, Davidson was bluffing. He knew that to be true as surely as there would be a tomorrow. All that talk about the Agency having to find Ashton because the Brits were pretending they didn't know his whereabouts was a load of crap. He might get Security to ring all the hotels in town but he would never launch a full-scale manhunt because people would begin to wonder why he was so fired up over one British Intelligence officer. To all intents and purposes, Davidson had accused him of sheltering Ashton yet nobody had followed him from Langley, nobody was watching the house and the place wasn't under electronic surveillance. If it had been, Security would have come knocking on the door as soon as they heard Ashton's voice.

'Where is Lake Arrowhead, Warren?'

'California, about ninety-five miles from Los Angeles. We used to go there when my folks were living in Redondo Beach.'

'I think someone should get out there in a hurry.'

'Someone will, but not you.'

'You may not be dealing with a one-on-one situation. What are you going to do, call the local chief of police and tell him you have reason to believe someone will try to murder Lenora Vassman? Think he will take much notice if you can't offer him any proof?'

'Okay, that's enough.' Treptow pointed to the microwave. 'Soon as it pings, take the pizza and French fries out and divide them in two. I'm going to phone Caspar.'

Gillespie headed south on Interstate 5 in preference to US 101 which, though it was a more attractive route, included a thirty-mile stretch full of hair pin bends between Carmel and Big Sur. When you were faced with a five-hundred-mile drive from San Francisco to Lake Arrowhead the scenery wasn't important. What counted was a good straight highway where you could set the cruise control, then sit back and relax a little. It might have been quicker to fly down to LA and rent a car at the airport but this was a maximum hostility assignment and he didn't want his name on a computer. The trick was to go in, do the job, and get out without leaving a trace.

There had been no message waiting for him on the answer machine when he had arrived home after meeting the Armenian and he'd thought the man in Washington was still ducking the issue. Then the phone had rung just as he'd sat down to dinner and he'd been given the green light and told where to find the target.

It had been shortly after 6 p.m. Pacific Time when he'd taken the call from Washington and he'd been on his way less than twenty minutes later. Glancing at the odometer, Gillespie saw that he had covered a hundred and twelve miles in a little over two hours. At the present rate of progress and barring any mishap, he calculated he would reach Lake Arrowhead around four o'clock in the morning. Then, with any luck, the situation would finally be resolved and he would be safe.

Luck. Gillespie scowled; he hadn't had much of that lately. He wished to God he had never heard of Stefan Afansiev and Ruslan Ovakimyan, wished even more fervently he'd never set foot inside their town house at Lancaster Gate that fateful evening back in January. Although he'd known Ovakimyan's younger half-brother consorted with prostitutes, he'd no idea that Afansiev swung both ways, and it had come as something of a shock when the Chechens had introduced him to some old queen Afansiev had been screwing while he and Ovakimyan were talking in the next room.

He'd never met Cosgrove before and hadn't expected to see him again after Afansiev had shown him to the door. However, the following day, Cosgrove had phoned him at his hotel and had acted as though they had known one another for years. Then Cosgrove had mentioned the nursery slopes at Winterberg and suddenly he had been standing on the brink of a dark abyss. Twenty-four hours later he had learned that the homosexual ex-army major had an accomplice called Oakham. He had, in fact, already decided to kill Cosgrove; the discovery of an accomplice had simply meant that he'd had to deal with both men at the same time, a condition which had demanded careful planning. He did not believe Lenora Vassman would pose anything like the same problem.

CHAPTER 29

He had watched for the English warrant officer from the shelter of the tree line at the top of the nursery slope. The man had already had too much to drink when he'd accosted him in the men's room at the *Gasthof*. 'Sheen you somewhere before,' he'd said in a slurred voice. 'Don't deny it, never forget a face, part of the job. Singapore, was it? No, don't tell me.' Then he'd snapped his fingers and his face had lit up. 'Hong Kong, five years ago. Name's Jackson but everybody calls me Jacko.'

He had walked out of the men's room and left the *Gasthof* by the back door, hoping to shake off the man, but Jackson had followed him outside into the snow. He had grabbed the sleeve of his anorak and told him not to walk away while he was talking. 'You were running around with that Chinese American piece,' Jackson had continued aggressively. 'Bet you were screwing her brains out.' He had backed away towards the ski rack but the English warrant officer had refused to let go.

In the course of a long, sometimes incoherent monologue, Jackson had told him that in 1970 he had been in charge of the Hong Kong detachment of the army's Special Investigation Branch. 'Seen you up at Sha Tau Kok with that Bernice Kwang one afternoon,' he'd leered. 'A tea room called The Green Jade. Don't suppose you noticed me, you were too busy touching her up. Never could understand why you weren't called as a witness at the inquest. You were working for Mr Reeves in those days, weren't you? Maybe he had something to do with it?'

Although Jackson hadn't demanded anything from him, he had represented a long-term threat which it had been essential to neutralise while there was still time. Fortunately, no one had seen them together outside the *Gasthof* which had simplified things. He had given Jackson twenty Deutschmarks to have a drink on him and had then parted company after promising they would meet again outside the *Konditorei* on the Sunday morning at eleven o'clock.

The warrant officer had been staying at a ski hut run by the army at the bottom end of the village. The shortest way to get there from the *Gasthof* was to follow the path of a gentle downhill run across the face of the nursery slope. It had been a long, bitterly cold vigil and there had been moments, especially after the last of the inebriated revellers had left the *Gasthof*, when he'd thought he'd somehow missed him.

Jackson had eventually appeared a few minutes after three, very much the worse for wear. It had taken him the best part of fifteen minutes to fasten the bindings on his skis, having fallen over a couple of times in the process. Intent on keeping upright, Jackson had neither seen him nor heard the swish of his skis as he had swooped down the hill. The warrant officer had been a small man. In his intoxicated state, he had also been incapable of defending himself and it had required little effort on his part to up-end and bury him head first up to his waist in a snowdrift.

A crick in the neck finally got to Gillespie and roused him from a fitful slumber. He sat up, stretched both arms above his head and gave a loud yawn, then stared blankly at the windshield in front of him. Fir and pines trees; until he caught a glimpse of the lake in the distance, he thought for a split second that he was back in Winterberg. He had driven all the way to Lake Arrowhead to kill Lenora Vassman because of that ill-fated encounter in the *Gasthof* nineteen years ago. Davidson had been running the Warsaw Pact Department at Langley in those days and had flown over to mastermind the poaching of an East German double agent from British Intelligence. He'd wanted a bagman to make the down payment and his name had been pulled out of the hat. It was an ironic fact that, if Davidson hadn't sent him to Winterberg, six people would still be alive today.

Gillespie sighed. He had done some pretty fancy footwork in Hong Kong, first convincing Reeves that Bernice Kwang was a Communist spy, then fingering the lady to the Black Dragon Triad in the certain knowledge that they would take her out. After the inquest, the CIA down in Saigon had sent one of their top-notch investigators to Hong Kong to discover what the hell had been going on. He had sought out the American and had succeeded in persuading him that Reeves had sanctioned her execution. From that moment on, his star had been in the ascendant with the CIA. His cause had been furthered in no small way by Reeves who had blamed himself for what had happened and had then had the grace to drop dead on Fanling golf course.

Although the Agency had never taken him on as an 'insider', he hadn't done too badly out of their long association. After some domestic work among the students of Ohio State where he had been employed as an *agent provocateur*, the CIA had sent him to the Federal Republic. There they had set him up with a travel agency in Bayreuth as cover while he ran a series of black operations against the Czechs.

A year on from Winterberg, Davidson had taken him under his wing and he'd left Germany to become an Overseas Aid official. The aid had consisted of arms and ammunition and he had travelled the world supplying material to any guerilla movement which was in open conflict with a Soviet-backed régime. His best work had been done in Afghanistan where he had also earned himself a considerable fortune together with US citizenship, courtesy of Bradley Davidson. Now he stood to lose everything. If running into Jackson five years after leaving Hong Kong had been an unbelievable coincidence, he wondered what the odds were against Cosgrove twice being in the wrong place at the wrong time? About the same as winning the Florida State Lottery, but nobody would be greasing his palm with fifty-five million dollars.

Gillespie got out of the car, opened the rear offside door and unzipped the bag he had dumped on the back seat. He took out a battery-powered shaver and ran it over the stubble on his face, then he stripped off, looked out a clean shirt and put it on. In place of his jacket, Gillespie chose a loose-fitting cotton sweater which concealed the 6.35mm Walther PPK semiautomatic pistol in the hip holster on his right side. He combed his hair, checked the parting in the wing mirror, then satisfied with his appearance, got back into the Lincoln.

The clock on the instrument panel was showing 6.18. On the assumption that not too many people were up and about just now, he decided to ride around for an hour or so before driving into the village. Cranking the engine into life, he reversed into a clearing, then came out on a right lock and made off towards Hook Green Road.

Lenora Vassman walked through the lobby of the Lake Arrowhead Hilton conscious that high heels and a figure-hugging silk dress looked a little out of place at 7.30 in the morning, but what the hell, she didn't have to explain anything to anybody. Turning right beyond the desk, she walked down the corridor towards the bank of elevators and went on up to her room on the third floor. Surprise, surprise, the bed hadn't been slept in. She wondered what the maid would make of that and grinned at her reflection in the dressing table mirror.

Yesterday afternoon, she had gone down to the village and walked around. She would never know just what had prompted her to walk into Loman's Sports and Leisure Wear store. She hadn't intended to take up jogging but the owner had sold her all the necessary gear and himself as well. She had taken to Art Loman on sight. He was forty-two, a widower with two sons, one ten, the other eight and he had been equally attracted to her. Before she knew what was happening, she had accepted his invitation to have dinner at his place. She had walked back to the hotel in a daze and had nearly forgotten her promise to call Brad.

It was crazy. She had told Art things about herself that she hadn't told another soul, not even the psychiatrist who had tried to straighten her head out after she had lost her child. They had established such a bond that staying the night at Art's place had seemed the most natural thing in the world.

Lenora kicked off the high heels, removed the make-up on her face with a tissue, then unzipped the silk dress and stepped out of it. She stripped off the pantyhose and opening the chest of drawers, took out a pair of briefs and the sportswear she had purchased yesterday afternoon. It was only after she had finished dressing that she had noticed the light on the telephone and flashed the hotel switchboard.

'Hi,' she said. 'My name is Lenora Vassman, room 371. I understand you have a message for me.'

The fact that a Mr Caspar was anxious to get in touch made little impression, and indeed, had Brad rung to say that Ashton was on a plane to England, she would have accepted the news with equanimity rather than the intense relief she would have felt only twenty-four hours ago. But she dutifully made a note of Caspar's phone number on the memo pad before she thanked the operator and hung up. He would have to wait, she decided. Right now, she had better things to do than waste time on a phone call to Georgetown.

Gillespie turned off the highway and ran down the hill into Lake Arrowhead Village and Resort. Two hundred yards ahead of him on the left side of the road, a woman in trainers, white ankle socks, silk running shorts and the top half of a blue tracksuit was out jogging. 'Nice piece of ass,' he said aloud, then angled the rear-view mirror to see what she looked like from the front as he overtook her. Even though he hadn't seen her in years, there was no mistaking Lenora Vassman. Reacting instinctively, he stood on the brakes and got an angry blast from the driver of a pick-up behind him. Unnerved by the near collision, he continued on down the hill and eventually found a space for the Lincoln in the lower level parking lot.

He got out, locked the car and walked back up the road. Gillespie had no idea what he was going to do; he had never been to Lake Arrowhead before and he had intended spending some time familiarising himself with the place before he made a move. But this chance encounter called for a swift change of plan. As yet, there weren't all that many people about and if he could just catch up with Lenora in some isolated spot, he could use the thin leather belt around his waist to strangle her.

There was no sign of Lenora and he guessed she must have turned into the side road by the Arriba Mexican Restaurant. He followed suit and caught a glimpse of her at the far end of the street near the village festival area by the lake. There was a man with her whom she was extremely fond of judging by the way they were hugging and kissing. Then they ran off together along the promenade fronting the lake and suddenly things began to look very complicated for him.

It was the first time Ashton had been to Los Angeles, but even though he was a native of the city, Treptow had been too preoccupied to point out the sights to him. He had in fact hardly said a word from the moment they had driven off in the Ford Thunderbird he'd rented from Hertz at the airport. North on San Diego, east on Santa Monica to pick up Pomona, then looping round to join San Bernardino; the writhing snake-pits of the freeways made Birmingham's 'Spaghetti Junction' seem childishly simple and Ashton could understand why Warren needed to concentrate on what he was doing. But the San Bernardino Freeway had now become Interstate 10 and he was still giving a fair impression of a deaf mute.

'All right,' Ashton said, 'let's have it. What's on your mind, Warren?'

'Several things.'

'So share them.'

'Okay. First of all, you shouldn't be here. This isn't your problem and the shit will really hit the fan if there's a total foul-up.'

'Well, we shall just have to hope your luck changes for the better.'

Nothing had gone right for Treptow. When he had phoned Caspar yesterday evening, the last flight from Washington to Los Angeles had been about to depart, which had meant catching the first one in the morning and that wasn't scheduled to arrive in LA until 11.06 hours. It was possible Gillespie had been faced with a similar problem; unfortunately, he'd been given a head start of something like eleven hours and they had been unable to contact Lenora Vassman. Between 22.00 and 05.00 hours Eastern Time, Caspar and Treptow had rung the Lake Arrowhead Hilton at least a dozen times between them but

Lenora hadn't answered the phone in her room and the hotel staff had had no idea where she was.

Caspar had found himself in an impossible position. Both the Director of the Agency and the Chief of Operations were attending a NATO seminar on Bosnia in Brussels, which meant that Davidson was effectively in charge of the CIA. The only thing Caspar could do in the circumstances was call the Sheriff's Office in Lake Arrowhead and ask the local police to keep an eye on Lenora Vassman without saying precisely why. The same constriction had applied when approaching other departments of the CIA for assistance. It would have been nice if he could have prevailed upon Security to provide a few good men but the back door approach still hadn't yielded anything when check-in time for the US Air flight had come around.

'Maybe I should have caught a later flight,' Treptow mused. 'At least it would have given Caspar more time to put things together.'

'He had almost ten hours to persuade your Chief of Security that Davidson had sanctioned the murder of an American citizen. What makes you think another two would have made any difference?' Ashton shook his head. 'Hell, the only thing we've got on him is the tape recording of his conversation with Lenora Vassman and that can be interpreted in any number of ways.'

'Maybe,' Treptow said doubtfully.

'Listen, you and I know the recording has sinister implications but it doesn't to people who haven't been involved. Before they can accept it, they have to recognise that Davidson is a dangerous lunatic.'

'That's too much.'

'Is it? You told me yourself that Davidson has devoted the whole of his life to destroying the Soviet Union. It isn't enough for him that the Communist Party has been swept from power and the whole monolithic apparatus has come tumbling down. He wants to grind Russia into the dust. He means to achieve this by fermenting civil war between Moscow and the sixteen autonomous republics. That's why he was ready to supply Stinger missiles to the Chechens. Davidson's a lunatic because he knows damned well there are Frog and Scud missile launchers within the boundaries of some of those republics and he could be starting the first nuclear civil war in history.'

'You won't get Lenora to believe that,' Treptow said.

'Persuade her to listen to the recording of her conversation with him and at the very least, she may feel threatened.'

If she did, securing her agreement to protective custody would be so much easier. There would still be the problem of ensuring she was delivered to Washington in one piece, but there was nothing like the same urgency about that. With Lenora Vassman safely behind bars, Caspar would have all the time he needed to square things with the Director on his return from Brussels.

'I don't think you should be present when I see Lenora Vassman. No offence, Peter, but you're not her favourite man.'

'You're calling the play,' Ashton told him.

'And Gillespie is our business too, not yours.'

'I'm not going to argue with you, Warren.'

Last night he had made two international calls on Treptow's phone. A brief one to Hazelwood who'd told him they were still waiting to hear from the British High Commission in Ottawa about Gillespie's current nationality, and a much longer one to Harriet. 'You don't know how much I miss you,' she had told him, then asked when he was coming home. 'Soon,' he'd said, 'very soon' and had meant it. Whatever happened at Lake Arrowhead when they caught up with Lenora Vassman, he intended to head back to Los Angeles no later than the crack of dawn tomorrow. Then he would get himself on the first available flight to London.

'Suppose Gillespie has already got to Lenora?' Treptow said.

'Look on the bright side, Warren. Caspar's probably got in touch with her by now. Maybe he's even got desperate enough to ask the Sheriff to pick her up on some pretext.' Ashton glanced at the instrument panel: 12.19 on the clock, forty-six miles on the odometer, another fifty to push. 'Better give it the hammer,' he said.

'What?'

'Sod the speed limit,' Ashton said, 'put your foot down.'

Seventeen minutes after one o'clock and still no sign of Lenora Vassman. Where the bloody hell had she got to? Gillespie clenched his right hand, digging the fingernails into the palm in sheer frustration. What was she doing for Chrissakes? Taking part in a marathon? How much longer could he sit over a drink in the Arriba Mexican Restaurant without ordering lunch? He'd told the waitress that he was expecting a friend to join him, but the restaurant was beginning to fill up and the time was coming when she would ask him if he minded sharing his table or would he prefer to wait at the bar.

It was better he shared his table with strangers than vacate the one position where he could be sure of spotting Lenora as she walked back to the hotel. She had to pass the restaurant; the only other way to reach the Lake Arrowhead Hilton was through the grounds of the private yacht club and that was barred to the public by a wire-mesh fence some ten feet high. Somehow, he couldn't see Lenora scaling that obstacle even with lover boy there to give her a helping hand.

Lover boy. What if the bastard owned a yacht and they had gone sailing? It could explain why she had been gone for over five hours, and if they were out there on the lake, there was no telling when they might return. Gillespie felt his stomach knot. Dipping into the pocket of his slacks, he took out a packet of Chesterfields, shook one loose and lit up. He drew the smoke down on to his lungs and slowly exhaled. He took another drag and felt better for it; then a waitress tapped his shoulder and reminded him that he was sitting in a No Smoking area and would he kindly put his cigarette out.

Gillespie was not the only man who was cooling his heels waiting for Lenora Vassman to put in an appearance. The twenty-four-year-old officer from the Sheriff's Department who had been instructed to bring her in for questioning about a credit card fraud had already spent two hours in the lobby of the Lake Arrowhead Hilton. However, unlike Gillespie, he was quite happy to wait all day and all night for her provided no one relieved Arlene, the Julia Roberts lookalike on the reception desk. Right now, she was busy tucking room keys into envelopes for the forty-four guests expected on the tour bus shortly after two o'clock, but prior to that he'd had her almost undivided attention.

He had already discovered that Arlene lived in nearby Crestline with her elder married sister, was unattached, and was taking a year off from her UCLA Bachelor of Arts course. He hoped to discover a great deal more about her once she had finished doing the room keys. Meantime, he was more than content to ogle her from the comfort of an armchair.

Lenora kissed Art Loman goodbye, gave him an extra hug to last until they saw each other again later that afternoon, then set off back to the hotel. When Art had asked her to go jogging with him, she had thought in terms of three to four miles and had been surprised when after a mile, they'd come to an inlet and he had left the path through the woods to lead her down to the cabin cruiser moored to a jetty.

'Borrowed it from friends of mine,' he'd explained. 'The boys are in the galley cooking brunch for us.'

Life, it seemed, was never dull with Art Loman around, maybe a little hare-brained but never dull. And his happy-go-lucky attitude was infectious, certainly where she was concerned. In a few days' time it was possible she would come down to earth with a bump and start being boringly responsible again, but right now she was enjoying life too much and didn't want to think about tomorrow. Turning the corner by the Mexican restaurant, she started up the hill.

Gillespie saw her pass by the window, left a ten-dollar bill to cover the bar check and went after her. By the time he'd edged his way through the now crowded restaurant and stepped out on to the sidewalk, she was a good twenty yards ahead of him. The distance between them was, however, immaterial. You couldn't effect a quick, silent kill in broad daylight on a busy street. No, the place to take Lenora was in the privacy of her hotel room.

Alerted by the directional sign, Treptow signalled he was turning left and swept into the driveway leading to the Lake Arrowhead Hilton. As he circled the parking area in front of the hotel looking for a vacant space, Ashton noticed a prowl car from the Sheriff's Department in the end space of the front row.

'Looks as if Caspar has the situation under control,' he observed.

'I surely hope so.'

Treptow completed one circuit of the parking area and started round again, then, losing patience, he stopped, shifted into reverse and backed up to tuck the Ford Thunderbird at the other end of the front row. The fact that the vehicle was outside the proscribed parking area and causing an obstruction was the least of his worries.

'I'll leave the keys in the ignition,' he said. 'If it happens we're blocking somebody, you can move the car out of the way.'

'Right.'

'And I don't want you following me inside the hotel.'

'You've already made that very clear,' Ashton told him.

'Just so long as we understand one another.'

Treptow opened the door, got out of the Ford and walked across the forecourt, leaving Ashton to take his place behind the wheel.

There was a concrete staircase to the right of the hotel which Ashton assumed led to the road below. As Treptow disappeared into the lobby, Lenora Vassman came into view at the top of the steps where she paused briefly as if to catch her breath before moving on. She was just a few paces from the entrance when an old lady with a walking stick stopped her. They were still talking when he saw Gillespie.

Ashton did the only thing he could and hit the horn to blast out the international distress call. If there was one transmission in the morse code that was known to practically every man, woman and child it was the dot, dot, dot, dash, dash, dash, dot, dot, dot of the SOS. Unfortunately, the loud discordant signal did not have the effect he had hoped for.

Lenora simply turned about and stared in his direction looking both perplexed and angry. Gillespie also zeroed in on the Ford Thunderbird, but he had read the message and was a lot quicker at putting two and two together. Ashton saw him glance around the forecourt as if sizing up his chances, his right hand stealthily reaching for something under his loose-fitting sweater. It could be wasting precious time as well as unproductive to stick his head out of the car and shout a warning; drawing the seat belt across his chest, Ashton clipped it into the housing, then switched on the ignition and started the engine. Before he could shift the selector into drive, the first round came through the windshield and struck his left shoulder immediately below the collarbone.

The impact knocked Ashton back in the seat, then he toppled forward and would have folded over the wheel had not the seat belt locked to arrest the motion. He heard more gunshots and somehow found the strength to punch a large hole in the shattered windshield.

Gillespie was sideways on to him and firing at a police officer who had already been hit and was lying face down on the ground. There was no sign of Lenora Vassman or the old lady with the walking stick, but somewhere out of his line of vision a woman who sounded pretty much like Lenora was screaming abuse at the top of her voice. It occurred to him that maybe she was trying to distract Gillespie while Treptow crawled towards the revolver the police officer had dropped.

Half crazy with pain, his hand slippery with blood, Ashton forced the selector into drive and released the handbrake. He floored the accelerator and steering one-handed, aimed the car at Gillespie. There was a sickening thud as the vehicle smashed into Gillespie with the force of a pile-driver and then he saw him fly over the roof, arms and legs flapping like a scarecrow in a gale force wind. A split second later, the offside wing of the Ford clipped the guardrail by the concrete staircase so that the car flipped over and began to roll down the steep hillside towards the road below.

There was a limit to the amount of punishment the Ford Thunderbird could absorb and still retain its aerodynamic configuration. Already distorted by the initial impact, the roof subsequently caved in when the vehicle completed a second cartwheel. Both door pillars then buckled under the strain causing the windows to implode with a ferocious crump that sounded like a mortar bomb. Under the impression that the motor was still running, Ashton tried to cut the engine with his right hand but was too disorientated to locate the ignition key. Earth and sky continued to revolve at a frightening speed until the car hit the road and finally came to rest upside down.

'I've had it,' Ashton told himself calmly before falling into a bottomless black hole.

The odour was pungent and strong enough to bring tears to his eyes. Ashton didn't want to seem ungrateful but he wished the medic who was endeavouring to revive him would go easy with the smelling salts. Then suddenly he realised the noxious smell was emanating from the carburettor and he began to panic because the fuel was obviously vaporising on the exhaust manifold and could blow at any moment. Hearing voices outside, he called out to his would-be rescuers to douse the bloody petrol, but nobody took any notice of him. Petrol? Jesus Christ, no wonder they didn't understand what he was talking about; these people on the other side of the pond spoke a different version of the English language.

'Gasoline,' he screamed, 'for Christ's sake do something about the gas, it's pissing out of the tank.'

A man said, 'No sweat,' and began to hose the engine compartment with something that smelled suspiciously like cleaning fluid. It was, in fact, the start of a deluge which threatened to asphyxiate him as more and more people equipped with fire extinguishers arrived on the scene and blanketed the upturned vehicle in foam. He knew others were dumping sand and earth on the overspill from the tank but it was hard to shake the horrible feeling that they were burying him alive in a steel coffin.

And the Thunderbird was a coffin. The roof had been compressed until it was bearing down on the steering wheel and somehow he had ended up under the dashboard lying on his injured side, his right hand clutching the seat belt which had been ripped from the door pillar. But he could see daylight and suddenly a face appeared in the small aperture that had once been the nearside window. Then the face disappeared and a hand reached inside the car, grabbed hold of his right arm and dragged it towards the light. A wave of pain shot through his body; moments later, some lunatic began to hack away at the sleeve of his jacket, baring his forearm. A needle went in and in the blink of an eye he was wrapped in cottonwool.

'Morphine,' Ashton told himself, 'lovely stuff.'

He slipped effortlessly in and out of consciousness. At one time he heard Warren Treptow telling him that Lenora Vassman was okay even though he couldn't recall asking after her. She had, Warren said, been extremely brave, first dragging the old lady to safety behind one of the cars on the forecourt, then creating a diversion at great risk to herself while he tried to recover the patrolman's revolver. But the really important thing was that she would be able to help put Davidson away until he was a very old man because even if Yeltsin crushed the Chechens, a fanatic like the Deputy Chief of Operations would find another ally in some other dissident republic with whom he could continue his crusade against Moscow.

The discordant wail from an orchestra of sirens kept Ashton awake while all he wanted to do was close his eyes and go to sleep. 'The Fire Department,' Warren informed him before he could ask who was making the racket. 'Maybe the paramedics too. They will have you out of there in no time.'

Treptow was being optimistic. In the event, it took the firemen twenty minutes to cut Ashton out of the wreckage and lift him into the waiting ambulance. Everyone who spoke to him repeated over and over again that he was going to be okay. He sincerely hoped they were right because he was a long way from home. And Harriet.